CW01619430

Sixty Degre[illegible] n

Beyond the Ice Wall

Andy Ross & John Hamer

First Published January 2025

Sixty Degrees South: Beyond the Ice Wall©
First Edition (second amendment late February 2025)

This work is protected under copyright law and is the intellectual property of Andy Ross & John Hamer©

Copyright © Andy Ross & John Hamer 2025
All Rights Reserved

Cover Design: Nathan Lucius©
Publisher: NATHAN LUCIUS PHP©
Courtesy of Nathan Lucius & Charlotte Woodhead

No part of this book may be reproduced or transmitted in any form or by any means, electronic, mechanical, photocopying, recording, or otherwise, without permission from the author(s), except for the quotation of brief passages in criticism.

All reasonable efforts have been made to contact the copyright holders and that anyone who believes their copyright to be infringed is welcome to contact the author(s).

The views and opinions expressed in this book are entirely those of the author(s) and are not intended to cause harm or offence.

Publisher Contact Details: nathanluciusphp@gmail.com

ISBN: 978-1-0685059-1-1

Reviews

"Andy Ross and John Hamer's truly unique book, Sixty Degrees South; Beyond the Ice Wall, has it all—action, adventure, intrigue, mystery, fantasy, history, romance... but better still, it is chockfull of shocking, eye-opening, truth bombs! While technically classified as a fiction, it is littered with historical facts, rendering it at turns highly educational and wonderfully entertaining. This riveting page-turner will take you on a fantastical, magical ride, stimulating your imagination, and keeping you up late into the night wondering what really is beyond the ice wall and will any of we plebes ever be able to travel there to find out for ourselves? Ross and Hamer's rendition of the "other side" may also leave the reader (as it did me) sighing, "if only...." Shannon Rowan, author.

"I really enjoyed reading your book. There was not one dull chapter, full of action and very fast paced. Extremely clever how you added real history and characters from the recent past of the last 100 years, into the story and explained what had happened or why they were murdered. I hope that people will see the real from the fantasy. Saying that, may be a future reality still waiting for us all to find one day. I hope to read the continuation of the story when you have finished writing it. Absolutely Brilliant both of you. Thank you, let's hope we ALL win." Helen Moon.

"Could not put Sixty Degrees South down and loved it. Such exciting info about Amelia Earhart and further info on Richard Byrd who I have researched. Found it a little difficult to get into the generations covered but once there I stayed up all night to finish it!" Noeline Clayfield.

"Totally engaging read from the off! Can't wait to devour the next instalment. Thank you for producing a book that both entertains and enlightens. It was also such a lovely touch to receive a personalised copy. Much appreciated, come on guys, get 'authoring' on part two please." Debs Pearce, Hampshire.

"Having read other books by John Hamer, we bought this new novel written by John and Andy Ross. A compelling read, excellent storyline with a fusion of fact and fiction. It's a film worthy book. Highly recommended." Pauline Price.

Acknowledgments

Karen Ross and Karen-Louise Hamer – for being absolute rocks and for 'singing from the same hymn sheet' as we authors – as well as their ongoing love and support!

Lawrence Stoker – for helping greatly with all the original ideas.

Paul Hargreaves and Nathan Lucius – for being some of the best mates anyone could wish for and being there for him through the most difficult period of John's life (2021-2022).

Nathan Lucius – for his publishing and cover design skills.

Andy Lovatt – for the med-beds idea.

Lucy Cherrington – for sending Andy the link to *The Lost Histories Of Flat Earth* by Ewaranon back in 2021 along with the message *'My God, we live in The Truman Show!'* But for that and the journey of discovery Andy then embarked upon, this book would never have been written.

Trevor John – for his sterling work in composing (and singing) Dobbo's song.

https://trevorjohnmusic.com/wp-content/uploads/2025/01/Beyond-The-Ice-Wall.mp3

https://trevorjohnmusic.com/about/

Five Times August – for all his wonderful music since the world imploded in 2020.

Fiona Mann – for her beta-reading expertise and invaluable input.

Shannon Rowan – for her formatting skills and suggestions as to how to improve the 'look and feel' of the book.

"...But strangely enough, there is left in the world today an area as big as The United States that's never been seen by human beings. And that's beyond the pole on the other side of the South Pole."

U.S. Admiral Richard E. Byrd in a TV interview in 1954

"We accept the reality of the world with which we're presented. It's as simple as that."

Christof (Ed Harris), *'The Truman Show'* 1998

"And God made the firmament and divided the waters which were under the firmament from the waters which were above the firmament."

Genesis Chapter 1, Verse 7

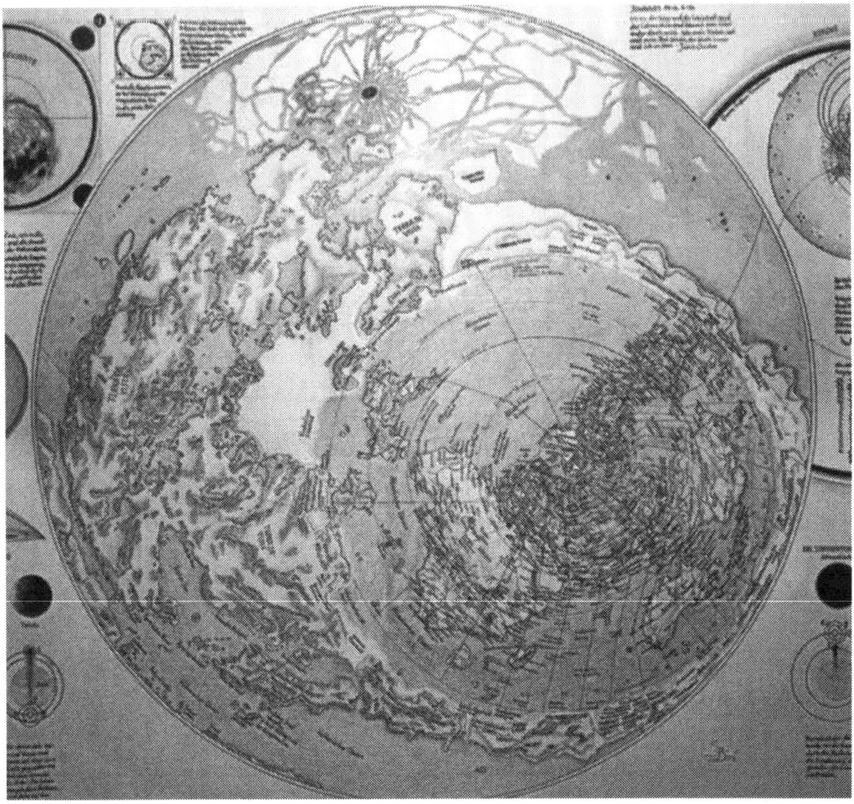

What is wrong with this picture…?

This map of the world hangs in the lobby of the U.N. building in New York City.

Introduction

This novel is the result of a collaboration between the two authors, Andy Ross and John Hamer.

Whilst this is Andy's first venture into professional writing, it is in fact John's ninth book spread across thirteen years of being a professional author and his second novel. Now good friends, they first got together in early 2024 when Andy contacted John for advice and invited him to be co-author on what was Andy's original idea for an extremely compelling storyline—and John was more than happy to accept once the idea and concept had been proposed to him.

Based on all the intrigue and rumour surrounding Antarctica and the copious evidence that suggests that something extremely secretive and sinister is happening beyond that two-hundred foot ice wall, this book takes the reader on a journey like no other.

Partly based on fact and interspersed with plenty of circumstantial evidence coupled with copious amounts of 'truth' as well as 'real' history, this story is a fascinating glimpse into the real-life mysteries of the Antarctic region.

It has therefore been constructed around all the information Andy and John unearthed through their many years of research and, although overall the story is fictional, including all the main characters, some of the events are based on actual incidents.

There has been a certain degree of legitimate inference based on little-known facts and apocryphal events. For example, minor characters such as James, Peter, Katherine and Francesca Forrestal did and do actually exist.

Having said that, it is however important to reiterate that all the four main characters, Adam Haylock, Sam Dobson (Dobbo), Mike Prendergast and Mateo Forestello are entirely fictional, as are the intertwined stories in which they all play their parts.

Also, we hope it goes without saying that the portrayed outcome of Captain Scott's Antarctic expedition is also the product of the authors' very vivid imagination but which is nevertheless a fascinating possibility given the evil machinations that we know take place in this world on a regular basis.

In summary, this story may be regarded as just one possible scenario, reflecting what really goes on beyond the **Sixty Degrees South** parallel and we, the authors, trust that you, the reader will both appreciate and enjoy the alternative approach to what is truly a real, modern day mystery.

Andy Ross and John Hamer, January 2025

Chapter 1

Sunday 8th January 2023 – The Southern Ocean

A powerful, streamlined boat ploughed its way southward through heavy, grey seas. The vessel, a New Zealand-registered sportfishing boat, *The Antarctic Truth,* was heading due south, current position approximately three hundred and fifty miles off Campbell Island, New Zealand, latitude 59°, just 7° shy of the Antarctic circle. Aboard were its three crew members, fifty-seven-year-old skipper Jerry Taylor, his nephew Brett Taware and Brett's girlfriend, Janine Morrison. All three, residents of the South Island town of Invercargill, had sailed out twenty-four hours earlier on a clear, calm, January summer morning from Bluff Harbour, the most southerly port in mainland New Zealand.

Jerry Taylor's normal day aboard *The Antarctic Truth* at this time of year involved taking big game anglers marlin and bluefin tuna fishing in the turbulent waters off Stuart Island. But this time, as well as a good selection of fishing tackle, the sixty foot Bertram 61 was heavily laden with ten days' food supplies, sufficient diesel to travel over three thousand nautical miles and plenty of winter clothing.

Though capable of much higher speeds, Jerry was keeping the *'Truth'* at a steady eighteen knots to conserve fuel and enable a smooth, level passage through the heavy swell. *'We Didn't Start the Fire'* by Billy Joel was blaring out from the Bluetooth speaker strapped to the bulkhead. Taylor absolutely loved Billy Joel, much to the consternation of his two younger companions and, as skipper, felt he was entitled to dictate the playlist for the voyage. Janine, completely oblivious to Joel's warbling was scouring the horizon through her binoculars whilst Brett was down in the galley cooking breakfast. The smell of eggs and bacon wafted-up from below, nectar to Jerry's nostrils after a long night at the wheel. He inhaled deeply—boy was he looking forward to this—when he was rudely awakened from his fry-up euphoria by Janine shouting from the stern.

"We're being followed Jerry... and they're closing," she exclaimed, trying her very best to sound calm.

"What a fucking surprise eh Jan? Not!" replied Jerry, outwardly unconcerned but inwardly feeling anything but.

The pursuing boat was moving fast, very fast, quickly catching up with *The Antarctic Truth* and eventually pulling alongside. Its markings and livery revealed it to be the U.N. gunboat, *Shackleton*, an intimidating, state-of-the-art fighting machine that would not have been out of place on the front line of any naval conflict.

Antarctic Truth's radio crackled briefly and then burst into life. *"Antarctic Truth, this is the U.N. gunboat Shackleton. Turn around and head back north immediately. Over"*

"This is Antarctic Truth, Shackleton. Why? We're only heading out for some whale watching and fishing. Over." Janine, in control of the radio, tried to sound as nonchalant as she could but failed to disguise the slight tremble in her voice.

"Antarctic Truth, you are about to enter restricted and forbidden waters, contrary to the 1959 Antarctic Treaty. Over," came the unequivocal response.

"And…? Over."

"You are posing a serious risk to international security," snarled the Shackleton's Captain sternly. *"And if you do not return immediately we cannot guarantee your safety. Over."*

"Which means? Over."

There was no mistaking the menacing tone—or the intent behind it. However, Janine was still, despite her trepidation, trying to bluff her way out of what was rapidly becoming a thoroughly sticky situation. Meanwhile Brett, picking up this exchange from down below, abandoned his cooking duties temporarily and climbed up on deck looking deeply concerned, an expression which was shortly to turn into blind panic.

"…We shall be forced to destroy your vessel and attempt to rescue any survivors. Over," came the stern declaration from the gunboat.

"But what harm are we doing? Over," Janine pleaded.

The Shackleton's skipper was evidently in no mood to discuss anything. *"I am not interested in a debate about this,"* he barked. *"Turn around now or we* ***will*** *use reasonable force. Over."*

"We know all this Antarctic Treaty stuff is just bullshit so why don't they?" Janine asked her two companions.

"Well, if it were my job to blow innocent people out of the water," replied Brett, *"I'd certainly have looked into the reasons and the history behind it but psychos like that don't care. They just blindly follow orders."*

"Yeah mate, most people just do as they're told and don't ask questions so why should these bastards be any different?" Jerry added, increasing the '*Truth's*' speed slightly.

"Well, I don't reckon they mean it." Janine's defiance was becoming ever more apparent. *"Ignore 'em I say."*

"Antarctic Truth, this is your final warning. Turn around now. Over," announced the Shackleton, menacingly.

"OK Guys, hold on tight," shouted Jerry, increasing speed rapidly, the '*Truth's*' bow rising sharply from the water. Brett and Janine grabbed hold of the rail firmly, worry and anxiety etched on their faces.

The *Shackleton* responded by speeding-up, effortlessly gaining on them. *"That is a serious piece of kit,"* thought Jerry, realising very quickly that their chances of outrunning the gunboat were slim to non-existent. The sound of gunfire then filled the air as the U.N. vessel fired a salvo of warning shots across the stern of the 'Truth,' ripping the flag to shreds and splintering the gunwale.

"Shit!" exclaimed Brett. *"They mean it Jerry. Turn around—now!"*

"Nah, Brett, they won't do it," countered Jerry somewhat unconvincingly. *"They're bluffing."*

"They fucking **will** *do it Jerry, I'm telling you"*, screamed Brett. *"For Christ's sake man, turn around now. I reckon….!"*

"Look don't panic Brett, it's a bluff," said Jerry cutting him short. *"I'm telling you they're bullshitters. What do you reckon Jan?"*

"I reckon they're bluffing too, Jerry," replied Janine. *"Let's try and outrun them!"*

Jerry increased throttle to the *'Truth's'* maximum thirty-six knots, resulting in the *Shackleton* increasing its speed accordingly. On the bridge of The *Shackleton*, Captain Ed McMaster and first mate Colin Williams stared at each other in disbelief.

"The stupid bloody idiots—they don't believe us Williams. Full throttle guys, they mean business this lot."

Within a minute, the gunboat had reeled-in the distance between it and the Antarctic Truth, and was soon speeding alongside her, a hundred metres to starboard, its torpedo fully-armed and ready for action.

"Prepare to fire," ordered McMaster to the crew manning the torpedo tubes. *"We've wasted enough time on these fools."*

Chapter 2

Friday 9th September 2022 – Adam's Posting

RAF Squadron Leader Adam Haylock, from Cambridge and based at RAF Coningsby in Lincolnshire, glanced nervously at his expensive *Omega Seamaster Coaxial* watch, a wedding gift from his ex-father-in-law, and with more than a hint of irritation stared at the second-hand in its customary sweep around the dial for almost thirty seconds. The time was now 10.38am on this sunny but breezy early September morning in 2022 and he should have been out on a training mission but instead had been summoned to Group Captain Iain Moffat's office for a 'very important briefing' at 10.30am. Yet here he was in Moffat's office, no sign of the captain as yet and not an inkling of what the briefing could be about. After nineteen years in the RAF, fifteen as a fully operational fighter pilot, with the last seven flying the Eurofighter Typhoon, he fully expected his senior officer to keep him waiting like this. He always did. They all did. A bunch of upper and middle-class manchildren with superiority complexes and a huge sense of entitlement who just loved to make a subordinate squirm and fidget.

Iain Moffat was the descendant of a long line of Moffat clan chieftains based around the Scottish border region of Dumfriesshire. He could trace his ancestry all the way back to Robert the Bruce, King of Scotland in the late 13th century—and way beyond. His wealthy parents, Sir Francis and Lady Isabelle had of course made sure that he received the best private education possible, culminating in a scholarship to St. Andrew's University following which he maintained recent family tradition by joining the RAF, as was expected of him.

A further five whole and immensely frustrating minutes passed before Group Captain Moffat blustered through the door, powerfully slamming it shut behind him. A tall and stocky Scotsman, six-three, early fifties with a developing beer belly, he had been Adam's Group Captain at Coningsby for just over three months. Adam knew very little about him, nor cared in the slightest about finding out. However, Moffat was his commanding officer and as such worthy of some respect, however superficial or begrudging that may be, so he slowly began to lift himself from his seat.

"Don't stand, Haylock for heaven's sake," he snapped in his distinctive, mild Scottish lilt, *"... no time for that bloody nonsense—but thanks for waiting. I've been reading the report I've been sent about you and your most recent escapades. Very enlightening I must say."*

"Enlightening sir?" Adam asked, looking puzzled.

"Yes, well... but before we go into any of that, I'd first like to say well done on your promotion to Squadron Leader. It says here you've got an exemplary, if rather unorthodox record and you're certainly one of the very best Typhoon pilots we have. You fully deserve it, I think."

"Thank you, sir," replied Adam, somewhat unconvinced and sensing that he was being 'damned with faint praise,' as the old saying goes.

"...and it's caught someone's attention," Moffat added. *"Somebody very, VERY high up and as a result, you're being assigned to Special Operations in the South Atlantic."*

"The South Atlantic? What the hell is going on down there, sir? Falklands kicking-off again?"

"No, nothing to do with the Falklands or the Argies, thank God. Actually, it's more Southern Ocean than South Atlantic," he explained. *"In fact, to be precise, it's a Chilean installation called..."* Moffat stared down at the report. *"Teniente Rodolfo Marsh Martin Airbase on King George Island—latitude 62° south, over five hundred miles off Tierra Del Fuego. Ever heard of it, Squadron Leader?"*

"No, I haven't sir," replied the by now rather puzzled airman. *"I didn't even know there were any military bases that far south."*

The senior of the two officers peered at his notes once more. *"Well, technically, it's not a military base Haylock but the Chilean Air Force have 'loaned' a couple of fighters to the U.N. who have deployed them there for the purposes of this operation."*

"But may I ask sir—why me precisely?" Adam enquired.

Moffat continued, *"Well, apart from your top-notch flying ability and outstanding, though as I said earlier, unorthodox service history, you're single. OK, divorced but with no children or living parents and very few close relatives. You're far less likely than most to get lonely down there and start missing people, which is vitally important given it's going to be at least a twelve-month posting."* He glanced down at the report again. *"And according to our records you are romantically unattached at the moment. Is that correct?"*

"Err... yes sir, that is correct—unfortunately." Adam admitted, slightly embarrassed. *"So, these Chilean fighters, they won't be Typhoons, will they? I mean, the Chilean Air Force don't have them as far as I know."* He had quickly changed the subject to a topic more comfortable to him.

Moffat paused for a second, thinking. *"Well, no, you're right. They don't. They're actually two ex-US Air Force F-5 Freedom Fighters from the 1960s they tell me—ancient as hell but, and I have no reason to doubt this, both aircraft are fully airworthy and well maintained—there's a small crew down there looking after them—and combat-ready. It's a U.N. thing so they're in their livery and you're going to be flying one of them. You will receive full training when you get there but a man of your calibre will find them a piece of cake, I'm sure."*

"So, what's the brief, sir?" asked Adam, looking and feeling rather perplexed. *"Can you give me any more details, as it all sounds rather odd to me?"*

Moffatt waved his hand dismissively. *"Oh, you'll find out exactly why soon enough Haylock but all I'll say for now is it's something to do with protecting and defending Antarctic airspace. Can't really tell you any more than that but don't worry—although it's bloody cold down there, most of the time below freezing I believe, the sun does still shine. Well, occasionally anyway."*

Adam paused for a while, wondering what on Earth would be expected of him so far south in such a godforsaken part of the world. Then with a sly grin on his face asked, *"And my exemplary yet unorthodox service history you mentioned earlier sir?"*

"Oh, I can't be bothered with any of that malarkey right now Haylock," answered the now preoccupied Group Captain, *"...and I'm sure you can't either. Look, I'm expected at another meeting in around ten minutes, so I need to get a bloody move on. Here are your transfer papers. All the very best young man and I'm sure it will be a very interesting posting. Dismissed, Squadron Leader."*

"Thank you very much indeed sir." breathed Adam sarcastically to himself, standing and saluting as Moffat turned on his heels and strode manfully out of the office, slamming the door heavily again behind him, leaving Adam alone once more, puzzling at this sudden and very unexpected posting and intrigued by what the next few months would bring.

Chapter 3

Thursday 6th October 2022 – Adam's Arrival at Teniente

On a bitterly cold, grey afternoon with light sleet falling, the lumbering RAF C130 Hercules transport touched down on runway two-niner at Base Teniente Rodolfo Marsh Martin Airbase, 62° south, five hundred and twenty miles off the tip of Tierra del Fuego in South America. The transport plane pulled on to the small, concreted apron area and shut down its four Allison T56 turboprops. The crew and its single passenger unbuckled their seatbelts and gathered their belongings together.

Just a few minutes later, Adam disembarked down the aircraft's rear cargo ramp and surveyed the scene around him. The base, which also served as a civilian airport for Antarctic sightseeing tourists, comprised a couple of white-painted hangars, a cluster of grey outbuildings which, he surmised, could be accommodation blocks, the odd freight container here and there and away to one side, the main control tower and terminal building.

"Not a lot here," thought Adam, *"How the hell will I last a year in this bloody dump?"*

The landscape surrounding the airbase, flat and greyish-brown with no trees or vegetation to be seen, stretched away from the coast to the north, south and east before giving way to snow covered mountains, their summits shrouded by the low-lying cloud. It felt very chilly indeed, -2°C according to his newly-acquired smartwatch, so he zipped up his parka, pulled the fur-lined hood over his head, braced himself against the icy blast and walked briskly across the tarmac toward the terminal building.

He entered by the door marked 'Arrivals,' finding himself in a room no larger than twenty feet square with a desk along the right-hand side under a sign stating, 'Baggage Reclaim' and a couple of Perspex-fronted booths on the left declaring themselves as 'Passport Control.' He paused momentarily, and as nobody was manning either the desk or the booths, decided to take the exit door at the far end. This led into what was obviously some sort of lounge area containing a small bar on the left, four low tables each with a set of well-worn armchairs around them, a pool table to the right and in the far corner, on the wall, an ancient, battered dart board that looked more like a pincushion than anything else.

Behind the bar, polishing glasses with a checked tea towel, stood a tall, stocky, bespectacled man in his early fifties with greying blond hair, bald at the crown and interspersed by the odd wispy combover. Adam recognised him instantly. Wing Commander Prendergast from his time in Cyprus.

The familiar figure suddenly broke the silence.

"*Good afternoon Haylock and welcome to the arse-end of nowhere. Good to have you back in my life again,*" he declared cheerily but with more than a hint of sarcasm. "*As I'm sure you remember, my name is Prendergast and I'm still Wing Commander Prendergast officially but everyone here calls me Mike—or worse! I'll be your superior officer throughout your time at Teniente Rodolfo but to be honest, my main job these days is manning the mess bar—and do you know, I'm bloody good at it too!*" He put down the glass and tea towel and offered his hand across the bar. Adam stared at it and paused for a second before shaking it rather awkwardly. He normally greeted his superiors with a salute.

"*Good afternoon, sir—sorry, Mike,*" he replied. "*Good to see you again after all these years,*" he lied—reasonably convincingly, he hoped!

"*Pint?*" chirped Prendergast, "*I can't remember what your favourite tipple was back in Akrotiri? It's a straight choice between Budweiser and Guinness here I'm afraid but they're both on draught, which is good.*"

"*God, I could kill for a pint sir—err sorry, Mike. I'll have a Bud please, if I may?*"

"*I'm sure you could old man, coming right up.*" Prendergast poured a pint of the golden liquid into one of the recently and very meticulously polished glasses, poured himself a Guinness and then walked around the bar, setting the glasses down on one of the tables and beckoning Adam to take a seat.

"*Cheers,*" he declared, holding his pint aloft. "*Here's to... well, whatever.*"

"*Cheers... Mike,*" Adam responded, clinking glasses with his commanding officer.

Both men took a large quaff from their respective glasses and Prendergast wiped the froth from his lips with his sleeve. "*So, my friend, welcome to the arse-end of nowhere!*" he repeated. "*I'm sure you're going to find it rather interesting down here with all that's going on at the moment. It's not for everyone I can tell you, which is why you've been specially selected.*"

"We sure are a long way south here sir, so what exactly is the mission?" quizzed Adam.

"Well basically, we're protecting the sixtieth parallel and the restricted Antarctic air space south of it," Prendergast explained. *"Been doing it since the late fifties actually and for most of that time it's been pretty quiet down here. Just the odd incursion now and again. For some reason though, since 2020, there's been a massive increase in people trying to get south of it and overfly the continent. Boats are pretty easy to deal with, the maritime patrol guys sort them out with little trouble but private executive jets have become a lot faster and have a greater range than they used to—so we're finding ourselves a little busier than usual."*

"So it's our job to scare them off then?" asked Adam, his curiosity growing.

"Yes, and most of the time we're successful," Prendergast answered, slightly uneasily.

Adam didn't like where this was going. Not one bit. *"Most of the time sir... sorry, Mike?"* he added, not really wanting to hear the obvious answer to that implied question.

Prendergast looked down awkwardly, pointedly ignoring the question and shuffled uneasily in his chair. *"It says here you're good at following tough orders so you'll do just fine. Your F-5 training starts in two days so go settle in, your billet is room three in accommodation block A. Unpack, maybe take a shower, and meet back here at 17.00 hours. And guess what, there's another reprobate in this Godforsaken hole who you'll remember from those halcyon Akrotiri days—and he's very much looking forward to meeting-up again."*

Chapter 4

Thursday 6th October 2022 – The Mess Room

In the air base's modest, but cosy mess room—cum guest lounge—cum waiting area, the only two 'customers,' Squadron Leader Adam Haylock and Flight Lieutenant Sam 'Dobbo' Dobson hugged warmly, exchanging backslaps by the score. Dobson, a gruff and forthright thirty-six-year-old Yorkshireman from Scarborough had been an old squadron colleague of Adam during missions over Libya and Syria in the twenty-teens but their paths had not crossed for the last four years or so. Single like Adam, Dobson had been posted to Teniente Rodolfo in the spring of 2022 and after a half-year at the base was, in his words, *"chuffed to buggery"* to be reunited with an old cohort.

"My God, Dobbo!" exclaimed Adam. *"Brilliant to see you again. What the hell are you doing down here?"*

Dobbo stepped back, beaming. *"Great to see you again too, Adders. Same as you I suppose. They told me you were joining us this month and it's gonna be great having you around. Anyway, me old mate, welcome to the back of beyond!"*

"So how long have you been stationed here then?" Adam asked, still not quite believing what was happening.

"Six months, eighteen days and ooh... about five hours and twenty minutes, which means I've got five months and thirteen days to go," replied Dobbo. *"Honest mate, you're gonna hate it here—there's no women, it's freezing cold all the sodding time and there's very little entertainment—unless you count pool, darts, cards and the penguins that is. Mind you, we do have a well-stocked bar which never seems to run out—oh yes, and a permanent landlord,"* he added with a grimace, looking pointedly over at Prendergast, once more positioned behind the bar, polishing what looked like the same glass as earlier in the day. *"But it ain't all bad I don't suppose. Two pints of Bud please, Mike!"*

"I must say, it is seriously cold here, isn't it?" declared Adam. *"I've just looked it up and we're at 62° south, which is more or less the same as the Faroe Islands is north. Have you ever been to the Faroes?"*

"I haven't mate, no," Dobbo responded, rather disinterestedly. *"What's your point?"*

Prendergast delivered the two full pint glasses to the airmen, clanking them down clumsily on the table beside them and spilling about two millimetres' worth on the Formica in the process. *"Cheers, gentlemen!"* the genial mine host chirped as he turned and meandered his way back to his favoured habitat behind the bar.

"Well, I've been there a couple of times on reconnaissance missions and it's very green and in summer, it is pretty warm. There are lakes and rivers all over the place and a shitload of people live there," Adam responded. *"So why isn't it the same here? You'd think it would be more or less the same climate, flora and fauna, yet barely anything survives here from what I can see. And right now, we're in the middle of summer and it's still below freezing."*

"Ah, but if it were the same as the Faroes there'd be no sodding penguins would there?" Dobbo explained sarcastically. *"Actually, I've never even considered that one Adders because, unlike you, I don't overthink stuff—or give a toss for that matter. Anyway, enough of that nonsense—as I said, we have our very own pool table and it's almost flat! Fancy a game old chum?"*

Adam noted that his friend was still the typical, blunt Yorkshireman that he knew so well.

"Why not," he sighed, reluctantly abandoning the point he was trying to raise.

"So, when did you last play?" Dobbo asked, placing the balls neatly into the plastic triangle—all in their correct positions.

Adam removed a cue from the rack and peered down its length, checking it for straightness. *"Can't remember Dobbo, ages ago—probably in Cyprus during the whole Libya thing. And most likely against you I bet."*

"Right then, let's play for money!" Dobbo suggested. *"Bugger all to spend your hard-earned cash on down here so we may as well make it interesting. Twenty quid?"*

The two old squadron pals played three extremely competitive frames of pool, downing two pints of Bud each in the process. Much to Dobbo's annoyance, Adam triumphed by two frames to one to claim the twenty pounds prize which, totally in line with the cliché regarding the stinginess of Yorkshiremen the world over, was begrudgingly handed over as they made their way back to their armchairs. After having no contact with each other for a few years, they spent the next hour or so catching up on their respective adventures but once that was over and done with, Adam ordered two more pints and then quizzed Dobbo on the rationale for them both being posted so far south.

"So, why us two RAF bods—flying obsolete Chilean aircraft? Can't the Chileans spare any pilots of their own?" he enquired.

"They do supply pilots, as do most of the other countries signed up to the Antarctic Treaty," Dobbo replied, sipping his pint and licking the froth from his top lip. *"Each nation sends two pilots every so many years, staggered six months apart. Before you came, my fellow aviator was an Argentinian called Mateo. Great pilot, but what an utter bellend he was! Totally crap at pool, didn't drink and boy did he hate the British? In fact, he'd gone off his head a bit by the end of his stint so I was glad to see the back of him, I can tell you."*

"But why is no-one allowed beyond the Antarctic Circle?" Adam continued with his questioning. *"I don't get it."*

"Never mind the Antarctic circle," Dobbo exclaimed. *"They can't even venture further than sixty degrees south. Can you believe that?"*

"That's bloody ridiculous Dobbo," declared Adam in disbelief. *"It effectively means a third of the Southern Hemisphere is out of bounds to over ninety nine percent of the world's population. Why the hell should that be? What possible reasons could they have to justify it?"*

"Dunno exactly Adders, but it's all to do with the bloody Antarctic Treaty I think," Dobbo replied. *"They don't want us humans interfering with the penguins down here for some bizarre reason,"* he quipped. *"Whoever drafted that treaty must have been a massive fan of the little buggers. I fucking hate them actually; they stink to high-heaven and they're everywhere. I tell you, if they were rats, we'd be putting poison down for them."*

"It just seems totally weird to me," Adam continued. *"All those nations together in total lockstep going to so much trouble over a few cranks wanting to fly over the South Pole. How many incursions have you had to deal with since you've been here?"*

Dobbo took a long swig of beer, swallowed and then belched slowly and loudly. *"Pardon me—well, it's currently running at two to three a week and has been since 2020. Before that apparently, it was just seven or eight a year—at most."*

"What—two or three a week?" Adam was shocked. *"That's just totally off the scale. What on Earth do you reckon could have caused that then?"*

Dobbo leaned back in his armchair, crossing his legs, pint in hand. *"Well, all I can tell you is what some of the folks on the planes have said over the radio. That's one thing you will have to get used to actually, the spiel they give you when you make radio contact. Fascinating stuff. Anyway—loads of 'em have said that since Covid, which, by the way, they nearly all say was a complete load of bollocks, they've started to question a lot of things—some even think the whole Antarctic Treaty thing is one huge deception and that 'they'—whoever 'they' may be, are hiding something down there. It would appear that the mystery and secrecy of the Antarctic seems to be a 'conspiracy theory' that has sparked a lot of interest."*

"Hmm—so, all of this has ramped up massively since Covid? Very interesting." Adam interjected.

"Ah, they're all a bunch of fucking nut-jobs Adders!" Dobbo sneered dismissively. *"As if Covid was a load of bollocks…?"*

Adam continued, *"Well, as they nearly all seem to be saying it, maybe there IS something in it? I mean, look at all the nonsense rules we were bombarded with! They had us doing all that social distancing stuff; standing five foot eleven apart was bad, but six foot was ok; everyone had to walk in the same direction down the pavement; you could take your mask off in a restaurant when you sat down but not if you were stood up."*

"I must admit, you do have a point there, mate," agreed Dobbo. *"A lot of the rules did seem bonkers when you really think about it."*

Adam continued his tirade, *"All absolute garbage if you ask me, Dobbo and despite the huge existential threat the government said it posed, they paid virtually no heed to those rules at all, did they? Having parties all over the place, taking their masks off when they thought the cameras had stopped rolling and basically laughing at us while they did it. Also, did you know that for two consecutive winters they told us there were no flu deaths in the UK whatsoever? Yet the number of people they said had died of Covid was about the same as the total who succumb every year to colds and flu."*

"Is that right?" Dobbo asked. *"Because I'd never heard that before. And has it come back again? I suppose it must have done given the fact they're still handing out flu jabs in the winter."*

Adam nodded. *"Yep—it has come back. Once the pharmaceutical industry decided that they needed to sell more flu vaccines—hey-presto, as if by magic, the flu makes a miraculous comeback."*

Dobbo sipped at his beer, thoughtfully considering Adam's words. *"So how did you feel through all the lockdowns, Adders? Because I loved the whole thing, the weather was great, I got paid yet did bugger-all for months. It was brilliant."*

Adam's expression tensed, betraying a combination of sadness and anger. *"The whole Covid escapade took a huge toll on me to be honest, buddy. Physically and psychologically. I don't think I'll ever be the same person again. The stress and anxiety of lockdown was almost unbearable at times and since the end of 2021 I just haven't felt right. My heart rate became erratic, my blood pressure soared and mood-wise, I just haven't felt truly happy ever since. I've had tests and am now on blood thinners and beta-blockers. At my age! It just isn't right and I'm pissed off about it."*

Dobbo paused, and looked at Adam as earnestly as Samuel Dobson possibly ever could. *"Fucking hell man, I'm really sorry about that. But it's not just Covid that the incursives bang on about,"* he went on, reverting back to the original topic. *"These people think almost all of what we've been told over the years is total bollocks. They mention all kinds of events; the moon landings, nine-eleven, JFK, the London 7/7 bombings, Princess Diana's death, Lee Rigby's murder, Westminster Bridge—and plenty of other shit too. But I just follow orders— I do precisely what I have to do and then put it all out of my very tiny mind. You should do the same! Another game pal?"*

"No thanks—happy with my winnings for one day," Adam replied wearily. *"I need to hit the sack soon."* Then a sudden thought occurred to him. *"By the way, do they all turn around when you intercept them?"*

Dobbo paused and sighed. *"Yeah, most of 'em."*

"But not all?" quizzed Adam, shocked.

Dobbo started to squirm, looking extremely uncomfortable in his chair. *"No, not all of them turn back and when that happens… "*

"Yes?" Adam asked, already knowing but dreading the answer anyway.

Dobbo took another sip before continuing, *"…and when that happens it's bloody horrible Adders but we have to stop 'em don't we? It's orders."*

"How?" Adam asked the question, knowing the answer full well. *"How do we stop them?"*

"Well, how do you think my friend?"

"Look Dobbo, we're talking about civilians here for God's sake!" retorted Adam emphatically. *"Sightseers is basically all they are. So how many have you 'stopped' then?"*

Dobbo shifted in his chair and looked down at his feet, fidgeting. *"Two or three, but I'd rather not go there mate if you don't mind,"* he mumbled.

"Fucking Hell Dobbo!" Adam exclaimed, shaking his head, incredulous and extremely apprehensive at what potentially lay ahead of him.

Chapter 5

Saturday 23rd December 1911 - Antarctica

Even by Antarctic standards the weather, this summer of all summers, was truly appalling. As the five weary explorers shuffled their way through several feet of snow, dragging behind them their heavy sledges carrying their meagre supplies and survival equipment, extreme exhaustion was already beginning to tighten its insidious grip upon their seriously undernourished bodies.

Too tired and weary to indulge in anything other than essential conversation, the leader of the expedition could not help but begin to worry. His already niggling doubts about the accuracy of his compass had now given way to extreme concern, mingled with a growing sense of dread. 'Where the hell are we?' and 'what on earth is going on here?' were merely two of the questions buzzing around in his mind at this point.

He had prudently decided not to worry his four companions with his justifiable concerns—not yet at any rate, he reasoned. Then suddenly, whilst lost in deep thought, he felt a sharp tug on his sleeve and turned to his right to face his accoster. The two weary men stared at each other's ice-coated features and his companion, shouting in order to overcome the incessant wailing and howling of the blizzard which raged around them and whilst gesturing to his own compass said, *"I think my compass is malfunctioning, skipper."*

Struggling with his own thick mittens and the almost frozen pockets of his outer protective yet barely adequate coat, he eventually managed to extract his own seemingly malfunctioning compass and without a word showed it to his concerned companion. The two readings were identical—as were the expressions on their frost-gnarled faces. They merely looked at each other with puzzled grimaces for a few seconds before the leader spoke for the first time in several hours.

"Let's make camp here for the night," he shouted above the cacophony to his four subordinates, who all briefly managed to nod their assent as they slowly, and without a word to each other, began to unpack their equipment whilst simultaneously battling the elements.

An hour or two later and with the five weary explorers all fed and firmly ensconced in their small tent, which at least offered a modicum of protection against the raging elements outside, one of the party broke the uneasy, prevailing silence at last.

"What's the story skip?" he enigmatically asked the leader. *"We're about two miles shy of our intended stopover point—according to my calculations."*

"I know Teddy, I know," came the reply and, turning to the group with a serious look on his craggy, frost-ravaged face, told them the grim news about the two malfunctioning compasses.

"I didn't want to mention it before, skipper, but mine is exactly the same," Oates interjected. *"We should have arrived at the Pole two days ago by my reckoning but we are still heading due south according to my readings! What exactly is going on?"*

In the tent there was a communal shaking of heads and the tension in the group was clearly palpable. The deep concern engraved on the faces of the quintet told a very sombre story indeed. They knew they were totally lost—with potentially catastrophic consequences. But the blindingly obvious question remained unanswered. How could it be possible that all five of their compasses were malfunctioning at the same time?

Determined to reach their ultimate goal, the South Pole, a quick vote was taken as to whether to continue on in hope or to prudently abandon their mission, which had been in the planning for well over two years. But under the circumstances it was unanimously agreed to continue onward for a maximum of three more days in their quest for glory and the honour of becoming the first humans to set foot at the elusive Pole. If their objective had not been achieved by then, the expedition would reluctantly head back to base camp—almost one thousand miles to the north, it was decided—the apparently malfunctioning compasses notwithstanding.

The next morning the blizzard conditions had eased greatly and although the mind-numbingly cold temperatures persisted, at least the mood in the camp was elevated slightly by the prospect of continuing their perilous journey in far more hospitable conditions—relatively speaking, of course!

The party was supplied with rations of pemmican,[1] sledging biscuits, sugar, butter, tea and cocoa powder that provided about 4,500 calories per man per day on the way to the Pole and about 3,800 calories on the return journey. But in fact, and unbeknown to them, in the debilitating weather conditions

[1] A pressed cake of dried meat, dried berries, and rendered fat.

that prevailed, they were expending in the region of 7,000 calories per day, greater than elite athletes in training—and for months on end. This actually amounted to a slow starvation diet whereby they were losing body mass, initially as fat and then later, muscle. Fat is used by the body as an energy store and also as insulation against the cold but with reduced insulation in a very cold climate, the body has to work even harder and burn more fuel in the form of food and then body fat and muscle simply to stay warm.

After a substantial, almost tasteless yet nourishing breakfast of pemmican, the tent and equipment were stowed away on the sledges and the quintet mentally prepared themselves for the ordeal ahead. Very soon they were on their way again through the deep snow but thankfully, which surprised them all, they could feel some slight warmth from the sun that morning. It was invisible through the high altitude heavy cloud cover yet despite this, they all agreed the temperature had risen somewhat and was a vast improvement on the weather they had previously endured—especially during the previous ten days or more.

Averaging only around seven miles per day, the bedraggled explorers were now way behind schedule but the sudden, unexpected break in the weather saw them depart on their journey in a brighter mood than at any time in the past few weeks, despite their concerns about the compass issues.

For the next six hours and four miles no-one spoke. Their only communication being through glances at each other's compasses and the worry etched on their faces which told a story of growing desperation as they realised that they were still no nearer their intended goal. Visibility was good which was a minor blessing of course and then slowly, almost imperceptibly over the course of the next two hours, an apparent miracle occurred. The snow was actually melting under their sodden feet as an ever-increasing warmth seemed to be emanating from the sun. Then, the landscape ahead eventually changed from a total 'white-out' into something more akin to the northern Russian tundra and they could clearly make-out several snow-free areas ahead and to the right of them.

Eventually, the expedition leader broke the long silence at last.

"I have absolutely no idea where we are chaps, but my compass is showing that we are STILL heading south! By my reckoning we are 1.5° south of the pole, if that were actually possible and it's getting warmer and warmer, not to mention the improvement in light. It's as if we're heading north again but we're not. This is a bloody nightmare. Someone please wake me, will you!?"

The wind had now long since ceased its howling and wailing and as they progressed, the snow was melting at an ever-increasing rate and they were now encountering patches of bare soil and even sparse grassy areas. The air around them was undoubtedly becoming warmer too, so much so that unbelievably, they had to actually remove some of their outer protective layers.

"Sir, we can't carry on much longer in these conditions, we will have to abandon the sledges soon," observed Oates, incredulously.

"Yes, I know Larry. There's a large patch of grass about two hundred yards ahead. Let's stop there and have a good old think about how to proceed." The puzzlement in the skipper's voice and imprinted on his now ice-free face was plain enough for everyone to see and hear.

The sledge ground to a halt about fifty yards short of the said grassy patch. There was simply no longer enough snow for the sledge's runners to glide smoothly!

"Right, gather round everyone..." He waited patiently without a word for them to lay down their backpacks and form a tight little group in front of him. *"... If any of you have any ideas or suggestions, I'm all ears! None of this makes any sense whatsoever to me!"*

"Could we have done a U-turn in the dreadful weather without realising it and ended up travelling back northwards?" Wilson suggested in the hope rather than expectation of a positive response.

Their compasses however, told a different story, so that particularly weak explanation was soon dismissed. But they all realised that by now the errant compass needles should ALL have swung around 180°. It was all too puzzling, not to mention extremely worrying.

"Even if that was the case Teddy, it would be too soon to encounter these mild conditions. It would be barely possible even on the Antarctic coast—and that's well over nine hundred miles north of us. No, we have to face facts, men; this is an unprecedented situation but the question still remains... what the hell do we do about it?"

As he stared absent-mindedly around, taking in the strange scene, Oates' eyes came to rest on a familiar sight. *"Oh my God!"* he cried suddenly, startling the others—whose nerves were of course already frayed. *"Look. Over there! It can't be, can it?"* he blurted out, striding purposefully over to the object of his attention. Sure enough, it certainly was! But how could it possibly be? How could a series of human footprints and naked ones at that be right here in this godforsaken hellhole? After a long pause during which none of them spoke a single word—partly through sheer exhaustion and partly in shock—the leader made a decision.

"In the circumstances I think we have no option but to continue heading south, at least for two more days as we agreed last night. The weather ahead looks much more benign and have you noticed; it's getting warmer by the minute here…?"

"I don't like it skip," interjected Bowers. *"Surely, we'd be better off admitting defeat and turning back whilst we can? To go on now seems like suicide to me!"*

"I'm not sure we have a choice," reiterated the skipper. *"To turn back into those treacherous conditions… now THAT would be suicide in my book. If this warmer weather is not just a one-day wonder then maybe the further south we go, the milder it will become and the footprints suggest that there may be another civilisation—and another civilisation means animals and food crops… you name it! We could replenish our supplies, recover our physical condition and generally rest up for a few weeks before tackling the thousand mile walk home."*

"But, the Pole, skip!?" Wilson persisted. *"What about the Pole? Where the hell is it and have we given up on it now after everything we've all been through!!?"*

"That's enough now Teddy. I understand your feelings but I'm responsible for us all and that is my final decision. Now, let's rest here a while and eat and then we'll plough onwards and see what fate has in store for us." The leader was calm and adamant, his mind now definitely made up—and there was to be no changing it now.

Chapter 6

Tuesday 15th November 2022 – Training

Adam's flight training on the F-5 Freedom Fighter commenced 15th November 2022 and was scheduled to last two months. Built by the American aerospace giant Northrop, the F-5 is a supersonic light fighter jet which first entered military service with the US Air Force way back in the mid-sixties. Capable of 1050 mph, one and a half times the speed of sound, it has a range of just over fifteen-hundred miles on a full tank of fuel. Its chief weaponry comprises two M39A2 20mm cannons and a pair of AIM-9 Sidewinder air-to-air missiles. The two aircraft stationed at Teniente Rodolfo since 2021, one a single seater and the other in two-seat trainer configuration, were officially 'on-loan' to the U.N. by the Chilean Air Force, although nobody at the base had any idea when they might be wanted back, if ever. Dobbo told Adam they were brilliant aircraft, easy to fly, very fast and for their vintage, incredibly agile. He emphasised also how safe and reliable they were, both jets being scrupulously and religiously maintained by the two Chilean maintenance guys, Jorge and Eduardo, who also lived onsite at the base.

On the very first morning of his training programme, Adam met Dobbo outside the base's only hangar at 9.30am on a bitterly cold but cloudless and windless morning, perfect conditions for a first training flight. Adam was surprised to find that, just like him, Dobbo was also dressed in a flight suit, his helmet under his arm and a broad, beaming smile on his face.

"Welcome to your first F-5 Freedom Fighter training mission, Squadron Leader Haylock," he announced. *"I'm your instructor, Flight Lieutenant Samuel Dobson. You'll be flying with me up to the point when I consider you sufficiently competent to go solo, which knowing you Haylock, should take about what? Three days max I reckon!"*

Adam stared at him in utter disbelief. *"This assignment just gets weirder and bloody weirder, Dobbo. How the hell are you qualified to be my instructor? Is this some sort of joke?"* he asked.

Dobbo shook his head and put an arm around his new student's broad shoulders. *"No joke whatsoever my friend. The training you will undertake with me will qualify you—if you pass of course—not only to fly these ancient old rocket-powered tin cans, but also to train others to do the same. 'Ow's about that then?"* he added in an exaggerated Yorkshire accent, worryingly reminiscent of the late and not so great Jimmy Saville.

Adam just stood there in disbelief, trying to take it all in. Truly lost for words.

"So what happens if we're up there training and someone makes an incursion?" he enquired, fully aware that for the time being, the only trained F-5 interceptor at the base was Dobbo.

"Oh don't worry about that, mate," Dobbo replied dismissively. *"I'll be able to deal with that little problem when it happens, which it will for sure. None of the training flights will take place any further than two hundred miles from base so it'll be a doddle to get back here and take Esmerelda up on my own. And Jorge and Eduardo never take long to get her ready for combat. Honest man, they're bloody brilliant, those two."*

"And the very first thing is to introduce you to our two lovely kites," Dobbo added. *"Mine's called Celeste and yours is Esmerelda. We'll be training in Celeste as she's got two seats, so let's go meet her, eh?"*

The two airmen entered the hangar through the slightly ajar main sliding door, stepping into the brightly lit, spotless interior. They were met by the sight of two gleaming, silver-grey F-5 Freedom Fighters in U.N. livery. The one with *'Celeste'* immaculately inscribed on to the fuselage just behind the gleaming black nose cone had its canopy fully open, stepladders at the fuselage, ready for boarding. The two middle-aged Chilean engineers, Jorge and Eduardo, sporting matching, immaculately pressed blue boiler suits bearing the crest of the Chilean Air Force, were tending to the aircraft, both seemingly oblivious to the two younger men who had just entered the building. Adam was rather taken aback by how tall both men were—around the six-six mark, he estimated—very tall for Chileans—in fact, neither of them actually looked particularly Hispanic, but then again, many different nationalities had settled in that country, particularly after World War II. Dobbo halted a few feet from the waiting aircraft and introduced her, theatrically sweeping his arm left to right, from tail to nose.

"There you are Squadron Leader... Celeste," he declared. *"What do you think?"*

"Wow, I've never seen such a polished aircraft. She's absolutely gleaming," Adam exclaimed. *"Pretty damned impressive if you ask me. To look at, anyway."*

"I know," Dobbo added. *"These two guys are like steam railway enthusiasts, I tell you—a right couple of lanky nerds they are. I reckon these dazzling kites*

must be the most pampered military jets in the whole sodding world. Honest, they get fully valeted after every flight—and every day in-between too, I bet. I mean, look at the bloody tyres, jet black, not a speck of dust and you can see your face in them. You never see Jorge and Eduardo anywhere around the base cos they're always in here. I get on with them okay but they're boring bastards."

Their conversation was suddenly interrupted by Jorge, the more communicative of the two apparently, who strode across to the two airmen, declaring proudly, *"Señor Dobson, Esmerelda está lista para ti. Podéis subir a bordo."*[2]

"Muchas gracias, Jorge," replied Dobbo, winking at Adam mischievously. *"OK pal, let's get going, shall we?"*

Just as Dobbo predicted, Adam was pretty much ready to go solo after only a few days flying Celeste, though to be safe, and more importantly, to satisfy Prendergast, they gave it two weeks before allowing him out on his own. His solo training in Esmerelda proceeded for another four weeks, following which the extra tuition to qualify him as an instructor took place. During this time, he managed to find out more from Dobbo about Mateo, his Argentine predecessor.

"Like I said," Dobbo pointed out. *"The wackos on those planes make some extremely good points—it can get you thinking—if you let it that is. So, I just put it out of my mind, just can't be doing with it—but Mateo? Well, the poor sod asked way too many questions, and it got to him, man—big style. In fact, it resulted in an order from Prenders not to engage in any more conversations with them, but it's hard not to. By the end of his assignment here, he was a fucking basket-case. I heard that he resigned from the force as soon as he got back to Argentina."*

On 15th January 2023, two months to the day after his training commenced, Adam touched down expertly at Teniente Rodolfo with barely a hint of tyre rubber-smoke following his final training flight. Now fully qualified as a solo F-5 pilot and instructor but more importantly, fully mission-ready, he disembarked from Esmerelda to be greeted on the apron by Prendergast and Dobbo.

---

2 "Esmerelda is ready for you. You can get on board."

"Well Haylock, that's you up to speed then," declared Prendergast. *"How have you found the F-5?"*

"Pretty damn good actually Mike," Adam replied enthusiastically. *"Fast as hell, really agile and a doddle to fly. And it's really great for you to be in control rather than a computer. The seat's horrible though but I can cope. Just hope my arse can too!"*

"Yeah, those seats are pretty crap but I love flying the F-5," Dobbo said. *"She feels like a proper plane and not just some sort of simulator like the Typhoon. Plus, she deals with the cold conditions really well, unlike a lot of modern fighter jets which to me seem to have been set up more for warm, dusty conditions."*

Adam nodded in agreement. *"Well, I'm absolutely knackered after these last two months even though it's been an absolute blast learning to fly this kite. Never thought I could switch to another fighter as quickly as that. Glad it's over and done with though."*

Prendergast reached into the brown leather satchel slung over his shoulder and handed Adam a rolled-up sheet of paper held in place with an elastic band. *"Yes, that certainly was two months of pretty intense stuff eh Haylock, but that's why you were chosen. Here's your F-5 training diploma—for want of a better description. Feel free to pin it on your bedroom wall if you like. You'll see it says you've passed with distinction and that you're now a fully-fledged F-5 pilot and instructor. Anyway, take a couple of weeks R&R—if you want to that is. There's a C-130 returning to Santiago later this afternoon so why not take advantage of that and treat yourself to a Chilean sun holiday?"*

Adam's eyes lit up at the prospect of some time off in sunnier, warmer climes. *"Thanks, Mike, I think I'll do just that. See you both in a fortnight."*

Chapter 7

Wednesday 25th January 2023 – Rest and Recuperation

Adam sipped on a long cold cerveza, sighed and leaned back in his chair. From his position on the sun-drenched terrace of Bar Pared de Hielo he could see the whole way along the oceanfront promenade of the beautiful Chilean coastal city of Vina del Mar as it stretched towards the mountains on the southern side of the bay. After ten glorious days in this truly wonderful place, he was feeling relaxed, refreshed and most importantly warmed to the core. It was scorching hot, mid-thirties Celsius and Adam was loving every single minute. This particular lunchtime, after a morning's snorkelling on the spectacular coral reef next to the hotel, he'd decided to lunch at Bar Pared on the recommendation of Agustin, one of the hotel waiters who had served him at breakfast time. Agustin told him not only did they serve fabulous calamari but more importantly, that it was his brother's bar, who had pumped his life's savings into it so now desperately needed the custom.

A song he had never heard before was playing from the speaker mounted on a pole beside him. He didn't recognise the artiste either but the music had a stirring rhythm and the words of the chorus really grabbed his attention...

'Oh God, help us all. Look what we've become. Oh God help us all. And fix what we have done,' it went.

Over the hubbub of the busy terrace, Adam couldn't make out many of the words in the verses but managed to pick out one or two interesting lines such as *'Anti this and anti that, cancel this and cancel that,'* along with *'worship actors, food and drugs'* and *'truth is whatever they say.'*

He was curious to discover the name of the performer, so he intercepted the next waiter to pass his table and decided to give his basic and rather dodgy Spanish a run-out. *"Disculpe, señor. Qui es cantante por favor?"* he enquired, hoping not to show himself up too badly.

"Is okay señor," replied the waiter very politely, yet obviously unimpressed with Adam's attempt at Spanish. *"I speak good English so no worries. The singer is an Americano called 'Five Times August.' We listen to him all the time since the Covid in 2020. He is a man who tells the truth and gives us all hope here at Bar Pared de Hielo. Do you like what he sings about, my friend?"*

Adam shrugged his shoulders. *"Well, the lyrics seem interesting, those few I could pick up anyway, but I love his voice and the guitar playing. I'll check him out on Spotify™ later. Gracias señor."*

As he awaited his food, ordered quite some time earlier, he began to snooze, relaxing deep into his chair. Thoughts of Esmerelda and Teniente Rodolfo began to drift into his mind. He could see the runway from the cockpit as he made his approach, along with the outbuildings and the barren wastes surrounding them. But before the dream could develop any further, he was wrested from his slumber by four new customers squeezing past to get to the table and chairs next to his, the last ones still available on the terrace.

Adam lurched forward in his chair, checked that his wallet and phone were still beside him on his table and panic over, relaxed again, taking another long drink of his beer. The new arrivals rearranged the chairs, settled themselves down and called the waiter over.

As the waiter took their order, Adam checked them out. He loved to people-watch and had worked out that whilst wearing sunglasses you could do this quite sneakily, without being noticed. Three guys, one woman. The men were all in their forties he reckoned, each one deeply tanned and most likely Chilean, two of whom sported goatee beards flecked with grey. The woman, slightly younger he felt, very slim and attractive, appeared English or American with long mousey hair gathered at the back in a ponytail. 'Surfer dudes,' surmised Adam, given how fit they all looked and the way they dressed.

After a few minutes the waiter arrived with their drinks, placing each one with considerable precision on a small paper coaster, before depositing the bill on the spike in the centre of the table and returning briskly to the interior of the bar. He reappeared just a few seconds later with Adam's food, grilled calamari on a bed of peppers and herbs and, with great aplomb, positioned the plate, cutlery and napkin on the table before him.

"Wow, fabulosa!" Adam enthused. *"Gracias señor."*

"Buen apetito," the waiter replied as he turned away, leaving Adam to enjoy his feast.

As he tucked enthusiastically into his lunch, Adam couldn't help but overhear the chattering of the new customers to his left, which surprisingly was in English. It soon became apparent that the woman was a New Zealander called Robyn who, as it turned out, hailed from Dunedin in South Island.

After a few minutes of pleasantries and small talk and as the alcohol began to take effect, their conversation became more animated and passionate, all the talk of sun, sand and surf eventually giving way to a topic which really made Adam's ears prick up. Robyn began to tell the others about a boat called the *Antarctic Truth* which had allegedly 'gone missing' on a deep-sea fishing trip in the Southern Ocean, south of New Zealand. According to news reports, it had 'run out of fuel, drifting unpowered for three days before eventually being dashed upon rocks off Campbell Island with no survivors.' One of her friends back in New Zealand—Adam didn't catch her name—whose younger sister had been on board the boat—had told her that the crew were all members of an organisation who were convinced that the powers that be, or 'the powers that shouldn't be' as she put it, were keeping secret something very significant about Antarctica. The boat's mission, her friend told her, was to sail beyond sixty degrees south to test how far they could get in an attempt to discover what was actually going on down there—if anything. Apparently, the crew had been streaming a video of the voyage on YouTube which her friend had been watching and said she'd seen a naval gunboat come alongside the *Antarctic Truth* telling them to turn around, at which point the streaming abruptly stopped. She reckoned the transmission had most probably been scrambled by the gunboat shortly before it blew the *Antarctic Truth* out of the water.

It was clear to Adam that neither Robyn nor her three male companions had even the minutest of trust in the official news story, 'total bullshit' being their shared, common opinion. Indeed, it transpired that they also held little to no respect for government, corporations, the law, the health 'industry,' the military or indeed anyone in a position of power or authority and pretty much disbelieved and mistrusted anything put out by the mainstream media. 'Twats' or 'bastards' were the group's favourite epithets for anyone associated with these groups and one of the goatee-bearded guys, Jens, who it turned out was German, was particularly vociferous and scathing, seemingly unable to control his rage and utter contempt for them. His outbursts actually made Adam laugh to himself. It was almost as if Jens had anti-establishment Tourette's or something.

What particularly sparked his interest in all of this was the name of the boat and the fact that its crew were all part of an organisation which was clearly passionate and determined to get to the real truth. He sat there fascinated by the conversation and made a commitment to himself that, once back at Teniente Rodolfo and to help stave off the boredom, as well as listening to more *Five Times August*, he would research the *Antarctic Truth* incident to see what he could find out for himself. For the time being though, he would put both to the back of his mind and simply enjoy the remainder of his holiday, which he did—in no uncertain manner.

On the morning of Sunday 29th January 2023, he reluctantly boarded the C-130 transport for the return flight to base, wondering with trepidation what the next days, weeks and months of this crazy assignment would bring. As it turned out, he would not have to wait very long to find out.

Chapter 8

Adam Ryan Haylock – b. 1986, Cambridge, England

Adam was orphaned at the tender age of two, his parents Helen and Mike Bridges having been tragically killed in a car accident in the Cambridgeshire fens involving a teenage uninsured driver well over the drink-drive limit. The collision had sent their VW Golf careering off the road into a deep drain, their cause of death being officially documented as drowning.

As an only child and with no surviving grandparents, uncles or aunts, he was taken into care by social services and adopted just a few months later by Robert (Rob) and Jane (née Bryant) Haylock. Rob was a GP with a practice in the nearby village of Fulbourn and also a prominent member of The Cambridgeshire Meridian freemasonic lodge, having been the youngest Worshipful Master ever elected in the county. He and his wife of fifteen years Jane, a local magistrate and youngest daughter of former Lord Chief Justice Sir Edmund Bryant, had been unable to have children of their own. The couple were well above the average age for adoptive parents at forty-six and forty-three respectively but had been accepted on to the register of prospective adopters due to their backgrounds and status in the local community, plus the connections they had built during their professional lives.

Sadly, Rob passed away in the late spring of 2021 at the age of seventy-eight, due to a stroke and yet oddly, despite no autopsy taking place, his death certificate gave the cause as 'Covid-19,' a fact which had preyed on Adam's already questioning mind ever since. Poor Jane never really got over the death of her life-partner and loving husband and passed away herself around eighteen months later at the age of seventy-six from what Adam believed to be grief-related causes but which was officially categorised as 'old age' in the absence of any obvious physical ailment.

Adam was an exceptionally bright child who took school and education in his stride, always being in the upper five percentile of achievers in his class, throughout the entirety of his school days.

He had a seemingly unquenchable thirst for knowledge coupled with a natural aversion to authority and, despite his academic achievements, was regarded by most of his teachers as an irritation, someone who would never take received knowledge or 'wisdom' at face value. He would constantly question and even argue with his tutors whenever he felt he was being fobbed-off about this or that piece of knowledge or alleged 'fact.' This trait remained with Adam throughout his time at Cranwell and into the RAF itself, where he was viewed by his superiors in a similar vein. Indeed, Adam was seen as a bit of a rebel, not a bad lad as such but one who would never be cowed by any form of authority and as a result was often in conflict with those who would seek to control or influence him in any way.

After leaving sixth form college with four A* passes at 'A' level in 2005, the world was metaphorically Adam's oyster. He could have taken his pick of virtually any university, including Oxford and Cambridge, but with absolutely no interest in education for education's sake and having had a childhood obsession with aircraft, his burning ambition was to fly them one day—and fly them fast! Therefore, as far as he was concerned, only one option was available to him—RAF Cranwell, the very same elite RAF officer training academy attended by his one-day-to-be colleague and friend Samuel 'Dobbo' Dobson.

However, being a year older than Dobbo meant that they were also one year apart in their Cranwell training and as such never really came into contact with each other at the college. Indeed, when their paths eventually crossed during active service in Cyprus four or five years later, they had no real memory of each other from those years.

Both airmen had been posted to Cyprus just two months apart in 2011. At that time a civil war had broken out in Syria, a short eastward hop across the Mediterranean from the island and the U.N.'s, as well as several individual countries' (including the UK's) military forces were closely monitoring and policing the activities—unofficially of course. Nevertheless, there was constant apprehension in the air regarding any possible escalation of the conflict and of it spreading throughout the Middle East like a wildfire, hence the presence of British as well as other international forces in the region.

Then later there were new calls for international military action in Syria after suspected chemical weapons attacks in the suburbs of Damascus killed hundreds on 21st August 2013. The Syrian opposition accused pro-Assad forces of carrying out the attacks but Syrian officials denied having used chemical weapons and asserted that if they had been deployed, then rebel forces were to blame. While U.N. weapons inspectors collected evidence at the sites of the alleged attacks, U.S., British, and French leaders denounced the use of chemical weapons and made it known that they were considering retaliatory strikes against the Assad regime. Russia, China and Iran spoke-out against military action and Assad vowed to fight what he described as 'Western aggression.'

However, the prospect of international military intervention in Syria began to fade by the end of August 2013, in part because it became evident that the majority in the United States and the United Kingdom were opposed to military action. A motion in the British Parliament to authorise strikes in Syria failed on 29th August and a similar vote in the U.S. Congress was postponed on 10th September. Meanwhile, diplomacy took centre stage, resulting in an agreement between Russia, Syria and the United States on 14th September to place all of Syria's chemical weapons under international control. The agreement was implemented with all parties declaring that the weapons had been removed from the country by the deadline of 30th June 2014.

Then in the spring of 2015, Adam was posted back to England and the squadron's home base of Coningsby. During his summer break he returned to Cambridge to spend time with Rob and Jane and during that period was introduced to Sophie, the eldest daughter of Rob's best golfing and lodge buddy Gordon Milner-Partington, a prominent barrister and former UK Olympic rower. Two years Adam's junior, Sophie was already a fully-qualified chartered accountant and a very talented golfer. They had been paired together during a mixed team tournament at her father's golf club and hit it off immediately, if you will pardon the pun and, thanks largely to her prowess, took home the Stableford trophy with her winning the individual handicap score by a country mile.

Their romance blossomed very quickly and they announced their engagement in the spring of 2016, shortly after which the couple purchased a small cottage together in the village of Ruskington, a short drive from the base. Their wedding on 24th April 2017, was a lavish affair at an exclusive golf village in the Caribbean islands of St. Kitts and Nevis to which over one hundred and fifty guests made the transatlantic trip and attended. Adam had been steamrollered into agreeing to such a major event by Sophie and her father, fully endorsed by Rob and Jane. He would have much preferred a nice low-key event in the local village hall followed by a disco but, as a leading Cambridgeshire personality, Gordon wanted to make a splash and was always going to get his way—and his daughter was more than happy to go along with that. He had even managed to use his influence to persuade the RAF to allow Adam to take eight weeks fully-paid leave for the honeymoon of all honeymoons; an ultra-high-end, luxury cruise from the Caribbean through the Panama Canal and down the Pacific coast of South America, visiting eight different countries in the process. And true to form, 'Squire' Milner-Partington had organised and financed the whole trip for them.

Adam didn't have to wait long for it to be made crystal-clear to him what Sophie wanted above all else from their union. *"Children, children and more children,"* she told him on only the ninth day of their honeymoon. Her career and her golf meant almost nothing to her, she insisted and all she really wanted from Haylock-wedlock was to continue the Milner-Partington bloodline, chiefly for the benefit and pleasure of her parents—to whom she felt an unusually strong bond, loyalty and obligation.

Though rather taken aback by this surprising revelation so early in his married life, Adam was happy to oblige. He was fairly ambivalent towards children but loved Sophie dearly and anyway, the production of a child was going to be lots of fun so he threw himself at the challenge with his utmost commitment, gusto and enthusiasm. However, the weeks soon turned into months and almost before they knew it, the summer of 2018 had come and gone with still no sign of the 'patter of tiny feet' on the horizon. Sophie was by this time becoming desperate and Gordon, an opinionated, tetchy and belligerent individual at the very best of times, began to exert his own unique brand of pressure. He paid for them both to visit his friend's Harley Street fertility clinic and from the tests that ensued, Sophie was proven to be as fecund as a prize Hereford, whereas Adam was devastated to find that his sperm count was virtually zero. Unlike the aircraft he flew into combat, he was firing blanks. He didn't even simply suffer from slow swimmers; they had all drowned long before the starting gun had sounded—and that was all simply too much for Sophie and Gordon.

The decree absolute came through in early August 2019, ten months after they had eventually separated. Adam kept the cottage and Gordon agreed to settle the mortgage to keep everybody sweet and resolve things quickly, with as little acrimony as possible. Adam never again laid eyes on Sophie from the day they separated. However he did hear on the grapevine that she had emigrated to Croatia for the golf and the climate and had fallen in love again there too. Good riddance to her was his overriding emotion, pitying any poor sod who in future would have to deal with the whims, not to mention the pressures and unreasonable expectations of the damned Milner-Partington clan.

Since his split with Sophie however, he had been nowhere near a woman in any amorous way whatsoever, choosing instead to throw himself into fishing, learning to play harmonica and the challenge of reading a classic novel every month. He even began playing rugby again in the autumn and by the end of the season had established himself as first-choice fly half in the RAF's fourth team. Then in March 2020 the world literally went stark-raving mad! No fishing, no rugby and no missions either, as it transpired that even terrorists and rogue nations were assiduously obeying the onerous Covid restrictions. Imprisoned and isolated by the imposition of the seemingly interminable lockdowns, he quickly became a half-decent harmonica player and managed to get through thirteen classic novels before the year was out. For him though, the world never really returned to anything like sanity again after 2020 and 2021, a fact borne out by his being posted to Teniente Rodolfo with a mandate to shoot down innocent civilians simply for venturing too far south.

Chapter 9

Monday 6th February 2023 – Mission One

A Bombardier Global 8000 headed due south from Presidente Carlos Ibáñez del Campo International, the most southerly civilian airport in Chile. Eight passengers and two crew were on board the sleek, executive jet as it traversed the sixtieth parallel cruising at around 40,000 feet and a touch shy of six hundred mph. These incredible machines were built for speed, comfort and range, a perfect choice for such a risky, experimental foray over unknown, forbidden territories.

After a pursuit lasting an hour or so, Adam eventually caught-up with the intruder and reduced Esmerelda's speed to match that of the Bombardier, positioning the fighter about five hundred feet from its port wing and reported the current situation to Prendergast, who was manning the communications room back at Teniente Rodolfo.

"Just made contact with the incursive Mike," he announced. *"Bombardier executive jet, registration PP-ANT. Brazilian—no livery. Am alongside her now. Altitude 40,000 feet, speed five hundred and twenty knots. Over."*

"Copy that Esmerelda," came the reply from Prendergast. *"Make contact with the incursives and ensure they turn around. Use standard warning protocols only and do not—I repeat—do not engage in conversation. Over."*

"Roger that," chirped Adam and attempted radio contact with the Bombardier.

"Global PP-ANT, this is U.N. Freedom Fighter 807," he announced. *"Turn around immediately and return to your departure airport. Over."*

No response was forthcoming from the Bombardier.

"I Repeat—Global PP-ANT—turn around immediately and return to your departure airport. Over," insisted Adam sternly.

Once more, nothing from the Bombardier.

Adam turned up the heat, impatience now clearly evident in his tone. *"PP-ANT, if you do not turn around and return to your departure airport, I have orders to shoot you down. Over."*

After a few further seconds of silence, there was a click, a crackle on the radio and a crew member responded. *"Freedom Fighter 807, what are your reasons for intercepting us? Over,"* came the response in English, albeit with a distinct American or possibly Canadian accent, Adam thought.

"Global PP-ANT, you are violating airspace protected by the 1959 Antarctic Treaty. Over," he informed them, maintaining a stern, formal tone in strict adherence to the standard protocol.

There was a brief delay before the same crew member responded with, *"Fighter 807, this is Captain Darrell Kowalski speaking on behalf of everyone aboard this airplane. My question to you my friend is, why is this airspace so fucking precious? Over."*

Adam hadn't expected such a defiant response but stuck firmly to the protocol. *"Global, that is not for me to question or to explain to you I'm afraid. My orders are simply to shoot you down if you do not end this illegal incursion. Over."*

"Fighter 807, is it not your duty as a serving officer to question the rationale behind all orders and to ignore them if they are immoral and/or unjustified? Kowalski suggested. *"Over."*

By now Adam's stress levels were rising rapidly but, as per Prendergast's order he composed himself and continued with the standard spiel. *"Global PP-ANT, this is my final warning. If you do not alter course and return to Carlos Ibáñez, then I will have no choice but to shoot you down. Over."*

The only response from Global PP-ANT to this final, crystal-clear threat was silence once more, a stalemate broken very abruptly and forcibly by Prendergast. *"Fire warning shots Esmerelda. Over,"* he barked sternly.

Adam pointed the F-5's nose toward the Bombardier and fired salvos of 20mm cannon fire above and below the aircraft. Then as per the protocol, he awaited their response.

Fortunately for him however, he did not have to wait very long at all before the gleaming, executive jet turned steeply to starboard to then execute a 180° turn and commence its reluctant return back north.

After completing the manoeuvre, a clearly deflated Kowalski resumed the radio dialogue. *"OK Fighter 807—as you can see—we have made our turn and are now returning to Carlos Ibáñez. You win this time, buddy. Over,"* he replied, an angry resignation plainly apparent in his tone.

"Global PP-ANT, thank you for seeing sense. Over," one very satisfied and relieved F-5 pilot responded.

Then, to Adam's astonishment, Kowalski piped up, with considerable vitriol. *"Sense—yeah, right! Some psycho in authority was giving you orders to murder innocent fucking civilians for something YOU know nothing about. And you were more than willing to comply? Sure, let's call that sense my friend. Over."*

Adam really hadn't expected that broadside. He took a few seconds to ponder Kowalski's rant which, if he was being honest, had rattled him somewhat. *"Global PP-ANT, I have my orders for good reasons. Over,"* he blurted, straying slightly from protocol.

Kowalski was evidently unimpressed by Adam's response. *"Well 807,"* he barked, *"We suggest you check out those reasons, but let me warn you buddy, you're in for a wild ride once you open your eyes and start to look below the surface. Over."*

Though still rather agitated and annoyed by Kowalski's tirade, Adam tried his utmost to remain calm, professional and polite. He was reluctant to poke the bear again—all he desired at this point was to rid himself of these idiots and return to base. *"Global PP-ANT, I might just do that, but for now—thank you for your advice, and have a great flight back. Over and out,"* he said, shutting down the radio conversation.

He followed the Bombardier until it had crossed the fifty-eighth parallel at which point he turned Esmerelda's nose to the southeast and returned to base deep in thought, scarcely able to believe the pantomime that had just taken place.

Chapter 10

Monday Evening, 6th February 2023 – The 'Inquest'

Alone in his billet that evening, showered and now sprawled out on the bed in his dressing gown, Adam mulled over the extraordinary events of the day, astonished and decidedly troubled by what had actually taken place and the things he'd heard over the radio. *"I need to chat with someone about this,"* he finally said to himself, so he texted Dobbo suggesting they meet in the lounge bar for another game of pool. Dobbo, desperate to win back his twenty pounds, happily agreed. As always.

'See you down there in ten, mate—twenty quid again?' came his texted reply and just over ten minutes later both airmen were in position at the table, ready for the revenge match—cues in hand, full pints on the shelf next to them and the pool balls set up in triangular formation on the perfectly flat slate and blue baize, ready for the break-off.

"So, Adam, how did it go today?" Dobbo enquired. *"First mission is proper weird I tell you. I suppose that's why you texted me eh? To chat about it? Anyway, Prenders told me the incursives saw sense and turned round."*

"Well," Adam replied, breaking off powerfully, noisily scattering the striped and spotted balls all over the table. *"I'm not sure they considered it as seeing sense exactly. I don't think they were quite ready to die for the cause just yet. Reckon they were just testing things out to see what happened."*

Dobbo leaned on the table and took aim. *"Honest, Adders, they're a bunch of crazy conspiracy theorist nut-jobs if you ask me,"* he sneered, his annoyance clearly apparent.

Adam waited while Dobbo took his shot. *"You say that Dobbo, but the guy I spoke to over the radio was pretty calm, articulate and seemed very sincere. He asked why they weren't allowed to overfly Antarctica and to be totally honest mate, I couldn't really answer that because I don't actually know the real reasons. He also said I'd be carrying out immoral orders and to be fair, he did have a point. I have no bloody idea why we're intercepting them and if I don't know the reason why I'm potentially going to blast innocent civilians out of the sky, then maybe I shouldn't be blasting them out of the sky,"* he conceded.

"Bloody hell Ads, you're not going all soft on us, are you?" Dobbo scoffed sarcastically.

"No, no, not at all," insisted Adam. *"They just made me think a little, that's all."*

"Look man, you're military. You are not paid to think, PERIOD!" Dobbo barked. *"So don't give them any airtime. They're all total losers if you ask me. I bet they also think we never went to the moon either."*

As Adam prepared to take his next shot, Dobbo reached for his glass and took a long, slow drink.

"Well, are you convinced we went to the moon Dobbo?" Adam enquired, steadily drawing the cue back, ready to strike the ball. *"Cos I'm not."*

"Oh my God!" Dobbo spluttered, spraying beer all over the table. *"I suppose you think 9/11 was an inside job as well, do you?"*

Adam jumped up, staring aghast at the beer-spattered surface in front of him. *"Well, that's another one I've pondered about over the years. I mean, ignore what may or may not have caused the twin towers to collapse, how do you account for WTC7?"*

"What the hell is WTC7?" snorted Dobbo, his irritation apparent.

"What the hell WAS WTC7 more like. Look it up mate and then let me know what you think, and while you're doing that, check out WTC6 as well—that is if you can even find a single mention of it on the internet anymore," Adam suggested. *"It doesn't take much research to cast a whole lot of doubt on that particular event, I tell you. Honest man, it's a total crock of shit—the whole thing."*

Dobbo wiped his mouth with his sleeve. *"Nar—don't think I'll bother with that one. Look Adam, don't mention any of this to Prendergast or I kid you not, you'll be transferred to somewhere like Yemen to train rebel pilots—or worse. And I'm sure you wouldn't want that, would you, pal?"*

Adam paused to chew over this advice for a while, considering the potential consequences of his actions, whilst meticulously chalking his cue. Dobbo took the opportunity to gulp down another good slake of beer followed by his customary exaggerated belch. Adam tutted, shaking his head in mock disgust as he replaced the chalk on the edge of the table and took a long drink of his own beer prior to his next shot. No belch from him though.

"Absolutely not, mate," he agreed, deciding that discretion was probably becoming the better option. *"Look, forget what I just said. I'm not going to let a bunch of bloody lunatics get to me."* He returned to his cueing position and was just about to take the next shot when Dobbo stopped him.

"Ooh, hang on mate, there's some dust or something on that ball. I'll give it a wipe."

"Thanks," Adam replied. *"I couldn't see it from this position as it was over the curve."*

Dobbo plucked the ball from the table, scratched at it with his thumbnail and cleaned it on his shirt before placing it carefully back on the table. Adam, still in the cueing position, took aim once more, drew back the cue slowly and slammed the newly cleaned object ball expertly into the far corner pocket, the loud crack of the ball against the pocket wall reverberating around the room.

"Top quality shot my friend," applauded Dobbo. *"I think my twenty quid is in mortal danger again by the look of it."*

Chapter 11

Samuel James Dobson – b. 1988, Scarborough, England

Sam was an only child, the son of Elizabeth (Liz) and James (Jim) Dobson, a car mechanic, of Scarborough, England. He was, in his early childhood, a 'loner,' a shy, reclusive child who found it difficult to make friends and establish any kind of meaningful peer relationship and even worse than this, his speech ability was not developing normally for a child of his age. His parents eventually became so concerned that they arranged for him to see a child psychiatrist at the tender age of six, in order to allay their fears of mild autism or ADHD and also to gain a better understanding of young Sam's 'problem,'—whatever it may or may not turn out to be.

The result of the psychiatric appointment was a surprise, if not a complete shock to both Liz and Jim. It turned out that Sam had no psychiatric issues whatsoever—it was simply a matter of his hearing. From an early age he had developed a fairly common, but outwardly invisible condition colloquially known as 'glue ear,' an ailment whereby the child's middle ear contains a build-up of sticky fluid (or glue).

This can affect hearing because the middle ear cannot move freely, but the level of hearing loss is usually quite moderate. And of course, because of the hearing problems that come with glue ear, this can cause speech and language development issues as well as impeding a child's ability to interact successfully with his peers.

However, the condition is easily treatable and so it wasn't too long before young Sam began to blossom and develop at a rapid rate. By the age of eight, as if making up for lost time, he had become a normal, outgoing, ebullient child, one of the most popular in his class at Gladstone Road Primary School, a mere three-minute walk from their modest family home in Candler Street.

As a point of historical interest, it was this small area of the town that had been amongst the worst hit by the 1914 bombardment of Scarborough at the hands of the Imperial German Navy at the beginning of World War I. Both Candler Street and Gladstone Road suffered several casualties and the school itself was badly damaged. Fortunately however, the attack took place at around 8.00am when no children had yet arrived for their day's lessons, otherwise the carnage would most likely have been appalling.

On that fateful morning of 16th December 1914, two huge German battlecruisers and a light cruiser, the *SMS Derfflinger*, the *SMS Von Der Tann* and the *Kolberg* arrived just off the South Bay area and without warning began shelling the town and its utterly defenceless civilian population. In the space of twenty-five minutes, more than five hundred, six and twelve-inch diameter shells had rained down on the town, causing widespread mayhem and devastation, killing or seriously injuring almost one hundred people including women, children and babies.

At around 7.30am, on what had begun as just a normal winter's morning, Scarborians were getting up and going about their daily routines. Mothers woke their children, maids prepared breakfasts and made beds and postmen and delivery drivers were already out and about on the streets. And as the shops began opening for business, a young boy scout, Dobbo's great, great uncle, fifteen-year-old George Taylor excitedly ran to buy that morning's edition of *The Scarborough Mercury* to check if there was a report on Lord Baden-Powell's recent visit to the town—and most importantly to him, whether or not his photograph taken alongside the famous scout leader had been included.

Anchored in the bay below was the steam trawler *St. Cloud*. Her captain had sailed into the South Bay earlier that morning but had experienced difficulty in finding the harbour entrance because of the heavy sea-fret that had settled on the seaside resort—a common enough occurrence at that time of year. The lighthouse had not been in use since the war began some four months earlier, not that it would have made much difference to the visibility in the prevailing conditions at that time, anyway.

The captain of the *St. Cloud* was among the first to see the three imposing warships as they rounded Castle Hill into the bay, heading swiftly and surely towards Scarborough. He was surprised to see what he at first took to be British warships far closer to the shore than any he had seen before but his surprise soon turned to horror when he saw one of them hoist the German war flag and open fire on the undefended town.

When the town had slowly began to reveal itself through the gradually dissipating morning mist, Kapitan von Reuter of the *SMS Derfflinger* raised his field glasses and took-in the beauty of the area; the twin bays (north and south) separated by the stunning headland topped by the twelfth century castle and the beautiful harbour area dotted with dozens of small trawlers and fishing boats—and carefully picked his targets.

As soon as the *St. Cloud*'s captain realised that the ships were German, he fled into the harbour as the early morning mist began to clear and, although fired upon, somehow managed to reach safety. The Germans however, had their sights on other prey—with the castle being one of their main targets before they moved northwards up the coast, seeking other victims, namely the towns of Whitby and Hartlepool.

In total, seventeen people were killed in Scarborough that morning, with two others dying later of their injuries. More than eighty were seriously wounded and overall, in Scarborough, Whitby and Hartlepool, one hundred and thirty seven people died during the space of a few short hours. Although Hartlepool suffered more casualties and the greatest destruction, it was the civilian deaths in Scarborough that caused the greatest outrage. News soon spread of those who had been killed going about their everyday lives. The victims included Dobbo's great, great grandparents' postman Mr Beal, as he delivered letters on his daily round and sadly, the very last casualty of all was Dobbo's fifteen-year-old great, great uncle George, killed outright by a twelve-inch shell on the way to buy his much-anticipated newspaper and obviously never made it back home. He was the first and only British boy scout to be killed in the First World War.

The attack was notable for its lack of any kind of warning and this begged the question as to why British Naval Intelligence had not been aware of any enemy presence and indeed had made no attempt to defend the town, despite its extensive intelligence network, meaning that they would almost certainly have known the precise movements of the three German battlecruisers. However, Winston Churchill, First Lord of the Admiralty at the time and famous for, in his own words, 'never letting a good crisis go to waste,' made excellent political capital and propaganda from the raid with many soon-to-be popular slogans including ones such as *'Remember Scarborough, Enlist Now!'* and *'Men of Britain, Will You Stand for This? Enlist Now!'*

It was a mark of the outrage felt at the attack on defenceless civilians that *'Remember Scarborough!'* became a rallying cry for recruiting officers across the nation. The slogan featured on a range of recruitment posters, which prompted men to enlist in large numbers.

And Churchill's response in a 'rousing' speech to Parliament that very day was to accuse the Germans of being, *"The baby-killers of Scarborough!"*

All of which was rather suspicious, not to mention convenient—for the powers-that-be, of course. And it was even reported, several months later that *'This is for Scarborough'* had been the battle-cry of British troops storming the German trenches during the second battle of Ypres in April 1915.

Was defenceless Scarborough deliberately left to its fate by those in high places in order to generate a powerful tool of propaganda, facilitate an intensive military recruitment campaign before conscription was introduced and to inject a sense of outrage into the British public—or was this just a coincidence? It would not be a unique occurrence as exactly the same thing happened in World War II when undefended Coventry was subjected to a huge and deadly air raid, while British Intelligence knew all along what was coming but did not wish to raise the alarm for fear of alerting Germany to the fact that their security codes had been decrypted. We will never know for sure but it is at very least a strong possibility. The power and value of propaganda to those in authority is immense.

But back to Dobbo's story... At the age of eleven in September 1999, Sam progressed from primary to secondary education when he duly took his place at Scarborough College as a result of gaining a scholarship. The College is a private school at South Cliff on Filey Road, a far more affluent area of Scarborough than he had been previously used-to but by this time Sam had become a confident, highly intelligent child with outstanding academic abilities and so took the change entirely in his stride.

As expected, young Dobbo (as he had now come to be known amongst his many friends) was an A* level student throughout all of his secondary education and duly passed all his GCSEs and 'A' levels with flying colours and unsurprisingly, easily gained a place at RAF Cranwell in Lincolnshire, the elite training school for would-be RAF officers. In the process he committed himself to a minimum of twelve years' service, commencing from his graduation from pilot training. And as it turned-out he actually signed-on for another twelve-year term at the culmination of the first one at the age of thirty-three.

During his time in officer training, Dobbo had bought a cheap second-hand acoustic guitar and taught himself to play with the help of one of those ubiquitous 'teach yourself the guitar' books. And eventually, after torturing a veritable procession of disgruntled roommates with his caterwauling, actually became quite proficient and even used to perform publicly occasionally, singing folk rock songs in a kind of Arlo Guthrie / 'Alice's Restaurant' style in the local hostelries around and about Cranwell itself.

It was about this time that he embarked upon a couple of romances, both short-lived, much to his disappointment. Firstly, at a pub in a nearby village, during one of his gigs, he met a local girl called Chloe Martindale, the daughter of the local butcher who supplied meat to the college. She was a petite redhead, talkative, funny and enjoyed the same music as he did. And she fancied him too—very much but after a tumultuous and very physical two months, she unceremoniously dumped him, telling Dobbo and most of her friends, that he was a total control-freak as well as being too boisterous in the bedroom!

Then six months later he decided to chance his arm again, this time dating the prettiest female trainee in his year, Jessica Armstrong. She was an incredibly bright student, too smart for him really and although not as attractive as Chloe in Dobbo's eyes, had the ability to captivate an audience and folks simply gravitated to her. Many of the other male trainees, plus a few of the female ones too come to that, fancied her and when she agreed to go out with him he felt like he'd won the lottery—twice over. His elation was short-lived however as less than a month later she also unceremoniously dumped him, stating that he was too serious in wanting a long-term relationship, something for which she was in no way ready just yet.

These two failures, monumental ones in his young and inexperienced mind, engendered within him a profound fear of rejection and so to prevent further painful and embarrassing disappointments, he simply stopped asking girls out, preferring instead to play the fool, the joker in the pack, the 'jack-the-lad.' Although making him one of the most well-liked and popular students amongst his peers, it unfortunately resulted in malicious whispers questioning his sexual proclivities during his final year at Cranwell, which continued throughout his first few years of active service. He eventually managed, in a seafront bar in Aya Napa, Cyprus, to dispel those adverse rumours in no uncertain manner; not something that looking back on he was particularly proud of but which put an end to the whispers once and for all. It had not unfortunately, freed him from his profound fear of rejection and as a result he remained single and unattached, a fact that played a significant part in his deployment to Teniente Rodolfo in 2022.

During his second year at Cranwell, his domestic life was devastated by the death of his parents in a house fire. The story he was given by the police and fire brigade was that they had been suffering severe financial difficulties due to his father's gambling addiction. As a result, Jim, a keen though gung-ho DIY enthusiast, had made some illegal modifications to their gas and electricity meters to rid themselves of the burden and inconvenience of utility bills. However, one of his fixes had gone dramatically wrong. He had bypassed parts of the fuse box which three days later resulted in a major electrical fire whilst they slept in their beds, killing them both without either of them knowing anything about it. Dobbo received no inheritance whatsoever, the sale of what was left of the house and their few remaining meagre possessions just about covering the repayment of Jim's gambling debts. The funeral costs were very generously, and much to the young trainee pilot's relief, provided by the RAF benevolent fund.

As his flying career progressed and blossomed, not only did he become one of the more popular members of his group but he also soon gained a well-deserved reputation for being the 'class clown,' a larger than life character who often found himself at odds with authority and was frequently in trouble for various minor infractions due mainly to his over-exuberance rather than any wilful disobedience. Despite these small blemishes on his service record, he nevertheless was very well-respected for his flying and leadership abilities by his superiors who rewarded him with several promotions and 'bonuses' as a result.

After postings in various parts of the world where he saw active service in several minor theatres of war and progressing through the ranks to Flight Lieutenant, he eventually and much to his surprise, found himself at Base Teniente Rodolfo Marsh Martin Airbase in the godforsaken Southern Ocean.

The reasons he had been given for that posting were that he was a highly talented flyer, could follow orders to the letter and, because he was unattached with no children or surviving parents, would be more than capable of enduring the twelve-month stint than a pilot with family and dependants.

Dobbo's wing commander at RAF Coningsby, Martin Haines, had informed him he would be taking over from an Argentinian pilot and that his fellow pilot for the first six months would also be Argentinian. After that period he would be joined by someone from the RAF so did he have any recommendations? Apparently, there was a shortlist but if Dobbo had any personal favourite, it would be taken into consideration. Without hesitation the Antarctica-bound airman volunteered the name of his long-time colleague and friend, fellow Flight Lieutenant Adam Haylock, now part of a different Typhoon squadron but as it turned out, Adam was already number one on the shortlist, in part due to his equally unattached status.

However, his reunion with Adam was bound to be somewhat of a double-edged sword as their relationship had not always been cordial. When the two first met whilst stationed in Cyprus, Dobbo had thought Adam a 'posh upstart,' who looked down on anyone from a lower station in life than himself. In effect the worst kind of snob and as a result made every effort to avoid the man if he possibly could. Until one day, 1st July 2011 in fact, this all changed.

Adam, Dobbo and two other Typhoon pilots had been engaged in a routine reconnaissance mission in the eastern Mediterranean, when they were suddenly confronted by two Russian-built Syrian air force MiG29S twin-jet engine fighters. The MiG pilots circled the four British planes menacingly, pointing and gesturing westward and in effect warning them not to enter Syrian airspace, at which point the two other British pilots, Flying Officers Dave Spencer and Jeremy Knight, took the broad hints seriously and prudently decided to withdraw, immediately turning-tail and heading back to RAF Akrotiri in Cyprus.

However, Dobbo was having none of it. He waved cheerily, sarcastically even, at his adversaries in his usual devil-may-care manner and accelerated eastward towards the Syrian coast, now about seventy kilometres away. Adam immediately intervened.

"Fucking hell Dobbo. What are you doing man? Over!" Adam crackled excitedly over the radio as the Syrians gave chase. *"Tally Ho, Haylock old man!"* was the only response from the utterly reckless Dobbo, who had by now left Adam trailing way behind in his slipstream.

Adam was at once both shocked and terrified but recovered in seconds and set-off in pursuit instantly, very rapidly catching up with the Syrians but was nevertheless still some way behind Dobbo's Typhoon, which was still just about visible through the haze in the far distance. He had the Syrians between his Typhoon and Dobbo's and as he pursued them, Adam could clearly see the unmistakable sight of tracer bullets arcing towards the tiny speck that Dobbo and his ride had become.

Nevertheless, Dobbo sped onwards, seemingly oblivious to the extreme peril and then suddenly realising the clear and present danger he faced, banked steeply downwards and to the left in a defensive manoeuvre born of sheer desperation. The Syrians followed instantly, undeterred and determined to teach this British upstart a salutary lesson and Dobbo, now weaving and bobbing in every conceivable direction to avoid sudden, bloody death at the hands of his would-be assassins, knew he was in serious trouble and the realisation hit him hard as hot sweat oozed from his every pore in response to his deadly predicament.

By now, Adam was hot on the tail of the Syrians and let loose a volley of cannon-fire from his wing-mounted Mauser 27mm cannons, narrowly missing the rearmost MiG29S but catching the tailplane of the leading one but yet without inflicting any serious damage. In an instant, the two Syrian MiG pilots, now only too aware of the presence of yet another far more agile and manoeuvrable adversary, suddenly decided to call it a day, peeled away and rapidly fled at full throttle toward the perceived safety offered by the Syrian coastal defences.

Dobbo's sheer relief was palpable and after a minute or so, during which time both British pilots had had a chance to draw breath and compose themselves, without a word they turned westward, back towards their base.

After several minutes Adam's radio burst into life suddenly. Dobbo was now much calmer.

"Cheers man—you saved my life for sure. You risked your own to save me and I feel such a fucking idiot—I don't honestly know what came over me or how I can even begin to thank you... " he began.

*"You **are** a stupid fucking idiot!!"* Adam blurted out, now almost incandescent with rage. *"I must be mad. I should have left you out there to die. Over."*

"So, so sorry. It was a totally irresponsible thing to do. I not only endangered my own life but I put yours in jeopardy too and that's unforgivable," lamented the now extremely contrite Yorkshireman. *"I just didn't think they would attack me. It was just a bit of a lark 'cos things have been a bit tame around here lately. Over."*

"A bit of a bloody lark...?" Adam sighed heavily but his anger soon subsided at Dobbo's obvious distress and contrition, and his attitude mellowed considerably when the realisation hit home that his fellow airman would now be in serious trouble and most likely face a court martial and a possible dishonourable discharge from the service.

'Yes, it was sheer stupidity,' he thought to himself. *'But in the end, there was no real harm done I suppose, and I would hate to see a comrade in arms suffer that fate.'*

Almost reading his thoughts, Dobbo said in suitably cowed tones, *"What are you going to do Adam? You know what will happen to me now don't you—if this gets out? Over."*

"What you did was certainly stupid Dobson, but you don't deserve being kicked out of the service for that childish stunt, even though it nearly got one or both

of us killed, never mind creating a serious diplomatic incident! But no, I don't suppose I will report you. Over."

"Seriously Adam, you'd really cover it up for me?" Dobbo was stunned. *"I don't deserve it, I know. Over."*

"No, you bloody-well don't deserve it. Not one bit. But as I said, at the end of the day there was no real harm done—apart from a few frayed nerves—fortunately! And Spencer and Knight buggered-off pretty damned sharpish, so I highly doubt they saw what happened. So, here's what we'll say… We tried to contact the Syrians but they were having none of it and suddenly turned on us without warning. There was a bit of a skirmish with shots fired on either side but we managed to scare them off and they chickened out and overall, it was just a bit of a storm in a teacup. Over." Adam seemingly had it all worked out, much to Dobbo's relief.

"Bloody hell mate, I don't know what to say—except I owe you big time. Thanks aren't really enough but it's all I have! Over," Dobbo said, realising how badly he had misjudged Adam previously.

"I reckon you owe me several dozen pints of that disgusting Cypriot piss they laughingly call lager in the mess—that's for sure! Over." Adam laughed, partly in sympathy and partly in relief that he (and Dobbo) had not just become yet another sad statistic of war.

Dobbo laughed too, in his own great relief! *"Several dozen pints, mate? Wanna make that several dozen gallons? You deserve it! Seriously though Adam, I owe you big time and one day I hope I can repay the favour in kind. Over."*

"Thanks for the sentiment, Dobbo but I really mean it when I say I sincerely hope we never find ourselves in a situation where you need to do that! Over." They both laughed again and prepared for landing as the Akrotiri runway appeared in the distance. Their friendship had begun but little did either of them realise that some eleven eventful years later, Dobbo would have the opportunity to make full amends and return the huge favour.

Chapter 12

Tuesday 7th February 2023 – The Calm Before the Storm

Later that evening back in his billet, Adam undressed, picked up his laptop, settled in under the duvet and began googling. He first searched for news on the *Antarctic Truth's* fatal last voyage and was presented with numerous hits. New Zealand newspapers such as the *Southland Times, The Otago Daily Times* and the *New Zealand Herald* were the most prominent and as Adam scrolled down, there were other entries from Australia's major broadcaster, ABC, a couple from Sky News Australia and one from Reuters. Absolutely nothing whatsoever from the BBC, Channel 4, The Guardian, Times or any other mainstream UK news organisation. 'Probably not surprising though,' he deduced, 'given where it took place.' Every single organisation purveyed the precise same story; that the Antarctic Truth, on a big-game fishing trip, had ventured beyond the range of rescue vessels and helicopters, run out of fuel and was then dashed against rocks off Campbell Island with the loss of the three lives on board. Identical gushing tributes appeared in each report, amongst them a couple of lame and insincere eulogies from minor New Zealand politicians.

Searches on YouTube produced a significant number of hits, not only from the same New Zealand and Australian media outlets but also by a whole host of independent video makers from all over the world. He searched in vain for the video stream from the voyage itself, causing him to doubt the authenticity of Robyn's claim back in Chile that her friend had watched it and witnessed the gunboat pulling alongside. Then he remembered something her companion Jens had mentioned which had sparked his interest at the time. Jens had told Robyn that the video stream would most likely be removed from YouTube for breaking, as he put it, *"All that community guidelines shit!"* and hoped that the group would publish it on... *"Now what were those other channels he mentioned?"* he pondered aloud, resting his head back on the pillow, closing his eyes and delving into his memory banks. *"Yes! That's it—Bitchute—can't remember the other one though."*

He initially searched Wikipedia for Bitchute who labelled it *'an alt-tech video service describing itself as offering freedom of speech but known for hosting far-right individuals, conspiracy theorists and hate speech.'* With some trepidation Adam typed 'Bitchute' into his browser search bar and was presented with a home screen rather like YouTube with its own search bar. Into this he typed 'Antarctic Truth' and was then offered twenty or more videos satisfying that criterion, several of which also mentioned Admiral Richard E. Byrd in their title. He needed only to scroll down halfway before spotting 'Antarctic Truth Final Voyage–Banned Video Stream.' So Jens had been right all along and his prediction had come true—the video had indeed been taken down from YouTube—so, with excitement and anticipation rising, he clicked on it and after what seemed like an eternity for the video to load, an image of a very impressive, modern game-fishing boat was displayed with a large play button over the top of it. Adam peered at the image, noticing the boat's name on the bow and eagerly clicked the play button.

The video stream commenced with the title *'Antarctic Truth – Beyond Sixty Degrees South,'* the initial footage showing the vessel leaving a very scenic harbour. There then followed a section where the three crew members introduced themselves, each one setting out what they hoped to achieve from the expedition. Adam noticed that the video was two hours and forty eight minutes in length so decided to quickly skim through it, stopping occasionally to play short sections, the majority of which comprised footage shot from a camera mounted at the front of the cabin pointing to stern, with the captain at the wheel and a young woman scanning the ocean through binoculars. There was very little if any dialogue and it certainly did not make for interesting viewing, so after playing a few short snippets, all pretty much showing the same thing, he fast-forwarded to ten minutes short of the end and pressed play again.

The self-same scene played out once more but Adam stuck with it this time, not wanting to miss anything. After around seven minutes, the woman at the stern began pointing excitedly and very animatedly to starboard.

"We're being followed Jerry. And they're closing," Adam heard her shout.

"What a fucking surprise eh Jan? Not!" the skipper, obviously Jerry, responded tersely.

The next thing he heard was the boat's radio bursting into life. *"Antarctic Truth, this is the U.N. Gunboat Shackleton. Turn around and head back north immediately. Over."*

The young woman took control of the radio whilst the skipper continued to propel the boat steadily southward. *"This is Antarctic Truth, Shackleton,"* she responded. *Why must we turn around, we're only heading out for some whale watching and fishing. Over."*

A third crew member, a rugged, bearded man, late twenties Adam reckoned, then appeared on deck from below, clearly alarmed at what was taking place, concern etched on his face.

Shackleton's answer was unambiguous. *"Antarctic Truth, you are about to enter restricted and forbidden waters, contrary to the 1959 Antarctic Treaty. Over."*

"So...? Over," queried the woman insolently.

"You are posing a serious risk to international security and if you do not return immediately, we cannot guarantee your safety. Over," the gunboat's radio operator explained.

There was another response from the *Antarctic Truth* which Adam could not make out as it tailed off after just a few words, rudely interrupted by a fuzzy scrambling of the picture, following which the streaming abruptly stopped. That was it, just as Robyn's friend had described.

"Holy shit!" Adam breathed incredulously, closing his laptop.

Chapter 13

Monday 8th January 1912 – Antarctica

A little over one week after arriving in the area that they believed should have been the South Pole, the expedition commanded by Captain Robert F. Scott and consisting of four other members; Lawrence Oates, Edward Wilson, Henry Bowers and Edgar Evans, were preparing for their long, long walk back to 'civilisation.'

All five men, although they did not know it—and indeed were never to know it, were dying a slow but sure, lingering death from starvation and an extended period of exposure to unusually cold temperatures—even by Antarctica's extreme standards. As previously related, Scott and his men were supplied with rations of pemmican, sledging biscuits, sugar, butter, tea and cocoa powder that provided about 4,500 calories per man per day on the way to the Pole and about 3,800 calories on the return journey. But they were expending in the region of 7,000 calories per day, equivalent to that of modern-day athletes in training and had been doing so for months on end.

For the previous week they had vainly trudged onwards hoping for some kind of miracle to happen in the form of their finding their holy grail—the elusive yet unbeknown to them, non-existent South Pole. Yet all that had happened was that they had simply travelled further and further south in totally snowless and increasingly warmer weather conditions. 90.0° south (the ostensible location of the South Pole) had long since come and gone, followed rapidly by 90.1°, 90.2° and now here they were at 90.3° south and seemingly still no nearer to their objective. Their five compasses all STILL defiantly refused to swing around to the 'new' north.

However during the course of their surprising journey into warmer climes they had come across various signs of life in the form of human footprints, both naked and with shoes and even the remains of old campfires, animal bones of unknown species and discarded artefacts from what they deduced to be hunting parties, despite never having encountered another living being during this entire period.

"It's utterly pointless to continue onwards now chaps. I have no idea what the hell is going on but I do know that if we don't turn back soon, then we won't have enough supplies to get us home safely—and there's no guarantee that we will be able to re-stock our provisions by simply continuing southwards," Scott

reluctantly announced to the by now thoroughly disheartened and demoralised group.

"Either the Earth is much, much bigger than we have been told for centuries or it's just simply a flat, endless plain as was believed until around four hundred years ago," opined Oates. *"... Unless anyone has any other ideas, of course?"*

The group were all too exhausted and totally downhearted to argue or even contribute to the discussion but at least all agreed that the only sensible course of action open to them now was to reluctantly turn around 180° and head for home.

So the long journey homeward began, with a trek of almost eleven hundred miles ahead of them until they could reach the relative safety of 'One Ton Depot' at 79° south and replenish their ever-dwindling supplies.

For the next several weeks the dismal, bedraggled group ploughed on northward towards safety, eventually hitting the snow-bound areas again at around 90.3° south and encountering even worse weather than the appalling conditions they had experienced on their utterly miserable outbound journey. Then, on 16th February, on or around the eighty-seventh parallel, Edgar Evans collapsed from extreme exhaustion, malnutrition and exposure and was unable to continue for several hours, so it was decided to make camp there for the night and resume the next day, in order to allow him a short period of recovery. Then after having rested for twelve hours, with Evans having now somewhat recovered, it was thought prudent to continue their travels.

However, a little over four hours into the resumption of the journey, on 17th February 1912, poor Evans collapsed again—but this time there was to be no recuperation. He passed away and was buried by his disconsolate companions deep in the snow. With heavy hearts, the four remaining members of the party continued onwards in silence and grief at the passing of their comrade.

Then, exactly one month later, on 17th March with morale at an all-time low and yet with One Ton Depot teasingly only eleven miles distant, Captain Lawrence Oates also began suffering from extreme mental and physical exhaustion. Fearing he had become detrimental to the survival of the other three remaining members of the party, he decided he had had enough and uttered the now famous and immortal words, *"I am going out now and I may be gone some time."* He then stoically walked out into the blizzard raging all around their flimsy tent, never to be seen again.

For three more days, the apocalyptic blizzard kept them trapped in their tent until at last, the fourth day dawned clear, bright and reasonably free of wind and falling snow. And so the three remaining members of the expedition, now sufficiently rested, albeit on the verge of starvation, decided it was now or never—they simply had no choice but to strike out for their goal of One Ton Depot where there would be plenty of supplies of all essentials lying there in wait for them. Here it was hoped that they would be able to spend several days building up their strength and recuperating sufficiently to carry on to base camp.

After a monumental effort and against all odds, they eventually arrived at the depot, suffering from severe frostbite and exposure, each of them dangerously malnourished, demoralised and weak. Two full days had now elapsed after leaving their last camp, a mere eleven miles to the south of them.

With a tremendous amount of willpower, Scott managed to use every last ounce of the remaining strength in his body to prise open the door of the depot stores, wedged as it was behind two feet of tightly-packed snow. And there to his absolute shock and amazement he suddenly came face to face with his worst possible nightmare.

Chapter 14

Saturday 11th February 2023 – Mission Two

It was mid-morning and high above the turbulent waters of the Southern Ocean, a state-of-the-art Boeing Dreamliner Business Jet, registration 9H-AMU was cruising southwards towards Elephant Island having departed some ninety minutes earlier from Port Stanley Airport in the Falkland Islands. With just over one hundred passengers and crew onboard, it was to-date the largest aircraft to venture into restricted Antarctic airspace on any kind of illicit, truth-seeking mission. The luxury, long-range aircraft had been hired from a Maltese executive charter company by the name of *ValettaJet* by a UK-based group calling themselves *The Deceptionists*. Although the majority of their escapades were largely self-funded, for this particular flight they had received considerable financial support from a like-minded and extremely wealthy benefactor, who himself was also onboard the flight. Their intention was to fly in pretty much a straight line across the South Pole, continuing more or less on that direct course right through to Perth in Western Australia; a route, surprising though it may seem, never taken by any scheduled civilian airliners on their intercontinental southern hemisphere routes.

Adam needed only a short flight in *Esmerelda* from Teniente Rodolfo to intercept the luxury jet, powering her away from base and heading northeast for just fifteen minutes before making visual contact with the giant Boeing.

"Just made contact with the incursive Mike," he announced. *"Boeing Dreamliner Executive would you believe, registration* 9H-AMU. *Maltese—VallettaJet livery. Am alongside her now. Altitude 44,000 feet, speed five-thirty knots. Over."*

"Copy that Esmerelda," came the familiar reply from Prendergast. *"Make contact with the incursives and ensure they turn around. Use standard warning protocols only and do not—I repeat—do not engage in conversation. Over."*

"Roger that," Adam replied and attempted radio contact with the airliner.

"Dreamliner AMU—this is U.N. Freedom Fighter 807," he declared. *Turn around immediately and return to Stanley. Over."*

Just as with the previous mission—silence was the only reply, the Boeing seemingly oblivious to his announcement.

"Dreamliner AMU, I repeat, turn around immediately and return to Stanley. Over," he reiterated, this time with much greater authority.

Further silence ensued.

Adam sighed and then increased his tone in both volume and sternness. *"Dreamliner AMU, I repeat once more, turn around immediately and return to Stanley. Over."*

This time, the Dreamliner replied to the warning. *"U.N. Freedom Fighter 807, this is Dreamliner AMU, chartered by the truth-seeking group, The Deceptionists. And if we don't turn around? Over."*

Adam sighed and exhaled long and hard. *"Then, Dreamliner AMU—I will have to use force against you. Over,"* he replied unequivocally.

"What does 'use force' mean, Fighter 807? That you will shoot us down? Over," the Dreamliner requested.

"Affirmative, Dreamliner AMU," Adam confirmed. *"Over."*

There was a delay of about ten seconds before the Dreamliner came back with, *"807, This is First Officer Ash Pardoe speaking. We have over one hundred people on board this aircraft. Do you know why your superiors would want to turn you into a mass murderer? Over."*

Adam shook his head in bemusement, took in a deep breath and replied, *"Dreamliner AMU, negative and irrelevant. Over."*

"Well, 807–we believe there are secrets beyond the ice wall that 'they' do not want we plebs to unearth and publicise," Pardoe explained. *"We may well be wrong but at least it'll be fun flying to Perth this way rather than the ridiculous routes we normally have to take on southern hemisphere passenger flights. Over."*

Adam, totally bemused, began straying somewhat from the standard protocol. *"Dreamliner AMU, what grounds do you have for those beliefs?"* he asked, immediately regretting the question. *"Over."*

"807, have you heard of Admiral Richard E. Byrd and Operation Highjump by any chance? Over," Pardoe quizzed.

Caught completely off-balance by this question, Adam paused for thought and then answered. *"Dreamliner AMU—er—I've heard of Admiral Byrd but know nothing specific about any of his missions. Over."*

The Dreamliner's first officer had him securely by the throat now. *"Well 807, we suggest you research it very closely when you get back to base. In particular, his suspicious death shortly after his famous TV interview plus the alleged suicide of his closest confidante James Forrestal, the then US Secretary of Defense. Over."*

"AMU, I may just do that..." Adam glibly replied. He really wasn't sure where this was going so decided to turn the heat up just a little. *"...but for now—I repeat, turn around and return to Stanley or I shall be forced to shoot you down. Over."*

The radio fell silent for what seemed an eternity to Adam. He assumed Pardoe was discussing the threat with the other crew members and hoped to God they were going to respond in his favour. Their defiant response, when it finally came through, could not have been any further removed from that.

Pardoe was not letting Adam off the hook. *"807, before you do that, did you know that a year after Byrd's death, NASA was created and then the following year the Antarctic Treaty was signed—by all the world's superpowers, despite them supposedly being engaged in the Cold War at the time and completely at loggerheads with each other! Over."*

Adam pondered this last comment, not really knowing where to take things next. Totally nonplussed, he simply held his position alongside the mighty jet, scanning the flat horizon ahead of him for some kind of inspiration.

He was very abruptly aroused from his ponderings by Prendergast, who had thus far remained silent during the radio conversation. *"Fire warning shots Esmerelda,"* he barked, impatience and irritation patently clear in his tone.

Adam returned to script and obediently pointed the F-5's nose toward the Dreamliner, firing several rounds of cannon shot above and below the aircraft. He awaited their response, but nothing was forthcoming from the Boeing so, after a pause of a few seconds, he reluctantly continued the dialogue.

"Dreamliner AMU, I do not want to shoot you down but I must follow orders," he growled menacingly. *"Return to Stanley immediately or you will be shot down. Over."*

"We don't believe you will shoot us down 807," Pardoe responded with increased defiance. *"Over."*

Adam simply could not believe his ears, baffled as to why these people were willing to lay down their lives for a cause such as this. He repeated his threat very earnestly. *"AMU, I will shoot you down—those are my orders. Over."*

Pardoe was both unconvinced and unimpressed and continued unabashed. *"The same excuse as always, 807. Throughout history—whenever anyone is accused of crimes against humanity and having to explain why they slaughtered innocent people, what do they plead? 'Just following orders,' every time. Not a valid excuse though—sorry. Over."*

"Dreamliner AMU. About to fire missile. Please—I repeat, please turn around. Over," Adam pleaded desperately.

"No 807, we will not turn around because you will not do it! Over," came Pardoe's unwavering response.

"For Christ's sake, Dreamliner AMU. I beg you—turn back," Adam shrieked back. *This is your absolute final warning. Over."*

He was almost in tears by now, the blood pulsing through his veins, and was about to position his thumb over the firing button and take aim when he was suddenly interrupted again, this time by an even more frantic interjection from Prendergast.

"Esmerelda—abort mission immediately and return to base. Over," yelled the Wing Commander desperately.

Adam was totally and utterly flabbergasted. Could this really be happening? *"Control, this is Esmerelda. Please repeat and confirm. You no longer wish me to intercept? Is that correct? Over."*

"Affirmative 807," replied Prendergast adamantly. *"Do not discharge your weapon and return to base immediately. Allow Dreamliner AMU to continue her flight in peace. Over."*

Adam shook his head in disbelief, breathing one almighty sigh of relief. *"Copy that, Mike—but I'd sure like to know why I almost lit up over a hundred people? Over."*

"Just carry out your orders, 807," instructed a once again calm and composed Prendergast. *"And get your arse back here—PDQ and you will receive a full debriefing on your return. Over."*

"Roger that Mike. See you in half an hour or so—in the bar. Pint of Bud and a packet of cheese and onion crisps please. Over and out," chirped Adam.

He bade a genuinely heartfelt adieu to the Dreamliner. *"Have a great flight AMU and I hope you have a great time in Perth. Really nice talking with you. Over."*

"We certainly will have a great flight, 807—now!" Pardoe exclaimed, barely able to conceal his joy and relief. *"And we all hope you enjoy the rest of your day too—but please take time out to do some research my friend—in fact, why not check out our website, thedeceptionists.org? Over and out."*

Adam steered Esmerelda away from the Boeing, putting on the power and returning very rapidly to Teniente Rodolfo, one very relieved but utterly perplexed Squadron Leader.

Chapter 15

Saturday 11th February 2023 – Mission Two Debriefing

In Teniente Rodolfo's 'compact and bijou' locker room, Adam removed his helmet, placing it carefully on the shelf unsurprisingly marked 'Flying Helmets.' He then stepped out of his flight suit and placed it on one of the heavy-duty coat-hangers in the locker equally unsurprisingly marked 'Flight Suits.' He washed his face, combed his helmet-flattened locks, stepped into his trainers and headed for the bar.

As he closed the locker room door behind him, he felt a tap on his shoulder, making him jump. He turned round quickly to be confronted by a rather stern looking Prendergast in his officer's uniform.

"Sorry to startle you Haylock," he apologised. *"I assume you're heading for the mess, right?"*

"Err… yes Mike, I was. Is there a problem?" quizzed Adam.

"Well no, not exactly—but I'd rather hold the debriefing in my office if you don't mind old chap. Away from any twitching ears."

"As you wish, Mike," he replied, confused and somewhat concerned.

He followed his commanding officer the full three metres along the dimly-lit corridor to a flimsy, plywood door on the right marked '*Wing Commander*' and a wooden sign in a slider below it with 'Prendergast' scrawled in black marker pen. Both men entered the tiny, sparsely furnished room and took seats at either side of a ramshackle, Formica-topped table.

"You said on the radio that you wanted to debrief me, Mike," Adam stated.

"Too right Haylock," Prendergast confirmed. *"I think it's only fair that you are told exactly why you were asked to abort the mission."*

Adam nodded thoughtfully. *"I'd certainly appreciate that, Mike."*

"Well, as you were heading off to intercept the incursive," Prendergast added, *"I was down here doing what I always do during these incidents—and that is trying to identify exactly who is on board the aircraft. Anyway, this time, just at the last minute, a very surprising name came up."*

"Who was it sir?" enquired Adam.

Prendergast paused and cleared his throat, conscious of the order he had received to keep this under wraps. *"Unfortunately, I can't tell you that, Haylock, but let me say it was a very influential player in world affairs who jumped ship a couple of years ago and joined the 'dark side.' He's the one who chartered the Dreamliner apparently. We immediately contacted U.N. Headquarters and were told that in no way should this individual be harmed and that the aircraft be allowed to continue on its way."*

"The dark side?" queried Adam. This thing was just getting weirder.

Prendergast leaned back in his seat, folding his arms. *"Oh, you know old man—the Q people, the anti-vaxxers, the climate-change deniers. But this guy ain't for messing around with—he means business by all accounts."*

Adam shook his head in disbelief. *"So, will the aircraft be met by a reception committee when it reaches Perth, sir?"*

Prendergast cleared his throat once more, stood up, slid his chair under the table and turned for the door. *"No sodding idea Haylock but I very much doubt it. In fact, I'm fairly certain they won't reach Perth by that particular route!"*

Adam desperately wanted to know what Prendergast was alluding-to by that statement. *"Sir?"* he implored.

Without affording Adam the courtesy of a reply, Prendergast opened the door and held it ajar, beckoning his subordinate to vacate the office. *"End of briefing Squadron Leader. Dismissed."*

On his way to the mess room, Adam stopped off at his billet to collect his laptop. *"This is just getting silly,"* he muttered to himself as he grabbed the device from the bedside table.

He needed to get to the bottom of this once and for all—to find out what was driving these people and maybe discover the name of the mystery benefactor. He thought about messaging Dobbo to see if he wanted to join him in his investigations but decided against it. Dobbo would not be interested, for sure. He'd probably scoff and disparage like he always did whenever anyone raised anything contentious or against the edicts of the establishment. So for once he'd settle down in the mess room by himself, grab a pint and some food and head-off down the rabbit hole!

Chapter 16

Friday 1st July 2011 – The Aftermath of Dobbo's Indiscretion

In the immediate wake of Dobbo's 'indiscretion' and his contretemps with the Syrian MiGs—and Adam's agreement to keep quiet about the entire episode, the two new friends arrived back at RAF Akrotiri in Cyprus. Their colleagues, Flying Officer Dave Spencer and Pilot Officer Jeremy Knight, had returned around twenty minutes earlier and immediately reported to their commanding officer, Squadron Leader Mike Prendergast, as they were under instructions so to do in the event of any untoward incidents.

The two young officers knocked on Prendergast's office door with slight trepidation.

"Enter," came the gruff command from within.

"Sir!" the two said in unison upon entry to the tiny office. *"Reporting an incident during the latest reconnaissance mission!"*

"Go on... " prompted the superior officer.

"Well sir, we were confronted by two Syrian MiGs. They made it plain that we shouldn't enter Syrian airspace and gestured to us to turn around. They were really quite menacing and so, rather than risk any kind of conflict or diplomatic incident, we decided discretion was the better part of valour and returned to base—so here we are!" related Knight.

"Right, yes well—that was the best thing to do under the circumstances... So, where are Dobson and Haylock then?" Prendergast asked them.

"Dunno sir, we thought they were immediately behind us but as far as we know, they've not landed yet," said Spencer, who by now was becoming quite worried about the other two squadron members.

"Well, check with comms and see if they've been in touch, would you—and let me know immediately?" ordered the now similarly concerned squadron leader. *"Dismissed."*

The two young officers saluted smartly, turned on their heels and set out for the communications room, a short walk from the squadron leader's office but they had only got halfway along the corridor when the smiling faces of Dobbo and Adam appeared around the corner.

"Are we glad to see you two," Knight sighed rhetorically with more than a touch of relief. *"We were just wondering where the hell you were—and so was Prenders. Is everything OK?"*

"We're fine thanks, but that was one hell of a moment for sure," laughed Adam.

"Fill us in on the details later—we are in dire need of a pint! In the meantime though, you'd best go see Prenders and let him know you're back safe!" said Spencer cheerily.

"Yes, that's the intention. And by the way if you hadn't chickened-out and buggered-off so quickly you would have seen what went on!" Adam replied with a cheeky wink whilst nevertheless secretly pleased for Dobbo's sake that they had decided not to hang around!

At this, Spencer and Knight scowled and sloped-off down the corridor, muttering between themselves.

"Get the beers in lads, we'll be there in ten mins," shouted Adam, teasing them further.

They knocked on Prendergast's door, briskly. *"Let me do the talking, Dobbo,"* whispered Adam. *"Diplomacy's not your strong suit!"*

"Enter!" came the response from Prendergast, fully expecting to see Spencer or Knight returning with news of the errant flyers. As Adam and Dobbo entered he glanced up, did a double take, then recovered quickly and asked... *"Where have you two reprobates been and what the hell happened out there?"*

"Yes, sorry sir. We had to deal with a little err... incident," Adam replied, his heart beating a little faster now as he realised he had to think on his feet.

Pendergast said nothing but gave them an expectant look and raised his eyebrows, conveying the unspoken message 'go on...'

"Well sir...," he began hesitantly. *"...What exactly did Spencer and Knight have to say?"* he ventured, in the hope of gaining some clue as to how best to address the issue.

"Nothing, except that they thought you were immediately behind them. But why they didn't bother to check is another question I'll be asking next time I see them." Prendergast was patently not amused.

"OK, well anyway—just as we were about to follow, the Syrians attacked us. Dobson took off with two MiGs hot on his tail and I followed and let loose a couple of cannon rounds, one of which clipped the tail of one of 'em without doing any real damage. This seemed to scare them off and they hot-footed it out of there—and that was it! A storm in a teacup really sir!" Adam related breathlessly, fervently hoping that his slight bending of the truth would satisfy his superior.

"Hmm. Very well then, not too much harm done I suppose. Let's keep this to ourselves chaps. No point stirring up a diplomatic hornet's nest, eh? Who knows where all that nonsense may lead! ... Dismissed."

To their relief, Prendergast seemed satisfied and so the two now very relieved airmen saluted and left the office, heading in the direction of the officers' mess where they hoped a couple of ice-cold beers would be there waiting for them.

They were not disappointed.

Chapter 17

Monday 25th March 1912 – The Ross Ice Shelf, Antarctica

As Captain Scott flung open the door of the One Ton Depot stores with a dramatic flourish, his brief euphoria at arriving safely was suddenly and dramatically extinguished by the sight that lay before him. Every single shelf, every barrel, every box, every container of any kind, in fact everything, had been completely removed by person or persons unknown, leaving a completely empty storehouse.

The realisation that he and his comrades' fate was now sealed beyond any question, hit him hard and he sank to his knees in utter despair and anguish. His grim-faced companions Wilson and Bowers, who had now appeared in the doorway behind him, simply stood in abject horror and stunned silence as they too realised the fate that now inevitably awaited them.

They knew that they were ninety miles now from base camp and safety and although not that far in the grand scheme of things—after all they had just completed a two thousand plus mile round trip on foot in the most dreadful of conditions—base camp may as well be on the moon, for all the chance they would have of completing that trip with no food or supplies. And especially so, considering the terrible physical and mental shape in which they found themselves at this time.

"Oh my God skipper!" cried Wilson in sheer despair. *"This is ridiculous, it was full when we left it all those weeks ago. Who the hell could have done this to us? Just look, there's nothing in there—we're finished."*

"It would appear so, yes Teddy," replied Scott dejectedly. *"I have been in many a scrape in the course of all my previous expeditions but this one definitely trumps them all, I'm sad to say..."* his voice tailing-off to a whisper as the enormity of the problem they faced was becoming a desperate reality. Then, in typical British 'stiff upper lip' fashion he managed somehow to gather his composure.

"I'd just like to say though to both of you—and I include Lawrence and Edgar in this, too—that it has been an absolute honour and a privilege to share this adventure with you all. We knew from the outset that there was more than a possibility that some or all of us may not make it back but it's so damned disappointing that it should end like this."

"So near and yet so far, eh skipper?" Bowers forced a weak, ironic smile at the thought. *"How fate likes to play tricks on us all!"*

"So we have two choices now I believe. Either we sit here and wait for a slow lingering death through starvation or exposure..." At this he pulled out his Webley Mk. V revolver and stroked it gently as if anticipating the blessed relief it would bring them all, *"...or we take the easier way out,"* he said pointedly whilst staring transfixed at the gun, seemingly the only obvious solution to all their problems.

But then, as if by some miracle, the slowly throbbing engine of one of the expedition's motor-sledges was suddenly heard in the far distance. At once, all the hopes of the three weary travellers were suddenly revived.

"Thank the good lord," Bowers uttered under his breath. All their unspoken hopes and dreams had suddenly been answered and they immediately dragged their weary bodies outside at this incredible piece of good news—and to welcome the new arrival.

Chapter 18

Saturday Afternoon, 11th February 2023 - Mission Three

Adam sat himself down in one of the mess-room's not too uncomfortable armchairs, laptop on his knee with a pint of Bud and a plate of cheese and pickle sandwiches on the low table beside him. He nibbled disinterestedly at the sandwich in his left hand as he studiously worked the mouse pad with his right. After several relatively fruitless searches, he found a Bitchute video of Richard E. Byrd's famous 1954 TV interview describing exactly what he had discovered during Operation Highjump, a large military expedition to Antarctica in 1946/7. He watched the whole interview intently, followed by a perusal of Byrd's diary which was published in full shortly after his sudden death.

"Jaw-dropping stuff, wow!" he acknowledged. Further investigation confirmed that less than three years after that TV interview, Byrd died of a heart attack aged just sixty-eight. The following two years saw the formation of NASA and the signing of the Antarctic Treaty, which pretty much closed off the land, sea and airspace beyond sixty degrees south to anyone other than authorised government, scientific or military personnel. *"Coincidence?"* he pondered quietly to himself. *"Could the three be linked in some way? Hmmmm... looks slightly dodgy to me."*

The next name Adam searched for was that of James Forrestal, the former U.S. Secretary of Defense and close confidante of Admiral Byrd, the results of which made for some incredibly interesting viewing. Having been briefed by Byrd about what had taken place during Operation Highjump, notably the resource-rich, ice-free land discovered beyond the South Pole and the manner of the abrupt curtailment of the operation, Forrestal planned to go public and tell the American people about the mission and its findings. However, in the March of 1949, he was forced to resign by the newly-elected president, Harry S. Truman, after which he was reported to have suffered a severe mental breakdown and immediately admitted to Bethesda naval hospital in Maryland. Then, in the early hours of 22nd May, the very day he was due to be released from hospital, he was found dead on the third-floor roof, thirteen storeys below his sixteenth-floor room. He was clad only in the bottom half of a pair of pyjamas with the cord of his dressing gown knotted around his neck. It turned out that Forrestal was anti-communist, opposed to the formation of an Israeli state in Palestine and very much against the destruction of the German nation and its people in the aftermath of World

War II. A particularly notable fact and one which Adam found extremely fascinating, was that Forrestal was a close friend and political ally of a certain John F. Kennedy, sharing a common hatred of the deep state, organised crime and totalitarian regimes.

He paused for a short while, trying desperately to make sense of the information with which he had just been presented. It certainly confirmed everything that the incursives had told him over the radio and with those earlier conversations still fresh in his mind, he typed '*thedeceptionists.org*' into the laptop's browser bar.

As he navigated meticulously through their site, deep in concentration, each page dropping its own unique Antarctic bombshell, it became more and more apparent that there really could be far more to this whole thing after all. There was just so much secrecy and deception regarding the region, too many coincidences and a whole host of draconian restrictions. *"Why was this? Maybe these people really are on to something after all?"* he considered out loud inadvertently, suddenly realising what he had said and glancing around furtively to check that he had not been overheard. *"And maybe somewhere on here I can find out who the wealthy...."* His investigation into the identity of the benefactor was rudely brought to a halt by a loud and high-pitched bleeping from his phone, jerking him abruptly back into the here and now. A message box flashed up on the laptop screen and the airbase's siren began blaring.

"Shit," he cursed. *"Not another one!"* Today was his mission standby shift—Dobbo was on a rest day—so it was down to him—yet again.

He swiftly downed the remainder of his by now tepid beer, fortunately he'd only had the one, wolfed-down the last morsels of the cheese and pickle sandwich and with laptop under his arm, sped to the locker room to change back into his flight gear. Esmerelda was already waiting for him on the apron, sparkling clean as always, canopy open and stepladder at the ready. Jorge and Eduardo had worked their magic once again to have her fully mission-ready in the time it took Adam to prepare himself for the flight. How the hell the dedicated engineers did that every single time never ceased to amaze him.

An Argentine-registered Gulfstream G550 executive jet was gracefully and effortlessly cruising due south—like all those before it—but this time from Ushuaia Airport on the island of Tierra del Fuego. On board were seven passengers and two crew, all from an Argentine truth seekers group calling themselves the Alianza Universal de Verdad y Libertad or AUVL.[3] On both sides of the plane, just below the cockpit windows, were emblazoned the movement's initials along with their logo, a map very much akin to that used by both the United Nations and The World Health Organisation in their respective insignias. The aircraft, the ultimate in long range, luxury executive transport, with a range of 6,750 miles and a maximum cruising speed of almost six hundred mph, had been fully fuelled at Ushuaia in preparation for this long, most out of the ordinary flight.

The aim of those aboard was to cross the Antarctic ice wall, attempt to locate and overfly the unfrozen, lake-covered area described by Admiral Byrd following Operation Highjump and to test whether or not, once the South Pole had been traversed, the southerly trajectory would switch instantaneously to a northerly one, with the compasses they had all brought along with them swinging round a full 180° the second they passed it.

As *Esmerelda* darted skywards through the low grey cloud enveloping the base, Adam wondered what this particular intervention would bring. He headed west-south-west from King George Island and intercepted the Gulfstream at 61° south, a full eighty miles inside the exclusion zone, immediately informing Prendergast.

"Just made contact with the incursive Mike," he announced. *"Gulfstream G550, registration* LV-FLA*. Argentinian*—no *livery as such, but it does have some initials on the side which I can't quite make out from here —oh yes and a logo too—some kind of world map I think. Am alongside now with the G550 to starboard. Altitude 43,000 feet, speed five-hundred knots. Over."*

"Copy that Esmerelda," replied Prendergast rather wearily—maybe two incursions in a day was one too many for him too. *"This one departed Ushuaia about ninety minutes ago Adam,"* he added. *"Make contact with the idiots and turn them around. Use standard warning protocols only and do not engage in conversation—unlike you did last time. Over."*

"Roger that Mike. Over," Adam responded and made radio contact with the Gulfstream.

"Gulfstream LV-FLA*, this is U.N. Freedom Fighter 807,"* he announced with as much authority as he could muster. *"Turn around immediately and return to your departure airport—which I believe is Ushuaia. Over"*

---

[3] Universal Alliance for Truth and Freedom

Silence. Adam gave them ten seconds to respond.

"Gulfstream LV-FLA, I repeat—turn around immediately and return to Ushuaia. Over," he reiterated.

Silence. This time he waited half that time before repeating the command again.

"Gulfstream LV-FLA, I repeat once more, turn around immediately and return to Ushuaia. Over."

His radio crackled. *"Freedom Fighter 807—you're joking right? Over,"* came the response from the Gulfstream—in English but with a Spanish or Portuguese accent, Adam reckoned.

"God, not again!" he exclaimed under his breath and then continued. *"I am deadly serious LV-FLA. Over."*

The next communication from the executive jet was completely unexpected. *"U.N. Freedom Fighter 807, this is Captain Mateo Forestello. Am I speaking with Squadron Leader Adam Haylock by any chance? Over."*

Adam was so taken aback by this question that, had he been at the wheel of a car rather than the joystick of an F-5, he would probably have lost control and ended up in a ditch.

"How do you know that? Over," he spluttered, utterly gobsmacked.

"Ah, we have our sources, Squadron Leader," Forestello replied. *"Plus, we also do a lot of research. That is why we are down here, because when you dig below the surface to find out the facts about anything, you will nearly always find lies and deception. And Antarctica has SO many mysteries surrounding it —as well as a gigantic ice wall. So, we are here now to find out for ourselves. Over."*

"LV-FLA, you must turn around immediately and return to Ushuaia. Over," Adam reiterated sternly.

"We shall not be doing that 807. Over," came Forestello's defiant retort.

"Come on LV-FLA—please see sense," Adam pleaded. *"It just isn't worth it. Over."*

"It is worth it to us, Adam. We need to discover the truth and tell the whole world," Forestello very calmly explained. *"We have been lied to by Governments and rulers for too long now and this is one of their biggest lies ever—along with the size of the planet of course. Over."*

"So, LV-FLA, you're Flat-Earthers as well, are you? Over," Adam replied disparagingly.

Forestello paused for a second or two then replied, *"Not necessarily Squadron Leader but we don't believe our earth is the size and shape we are told it is. Over."*

Adam shook his head in bewilderment. *"Now you're really talking nonsense LV-FLA,"* he scoffed. *"Over."*

"You say that mi amigo but look around you," countered Forestello. *Your F-5 is flying at over 40,000 feet—so use your eyes and your senses—look around you. Can you see any curve on the far horizon? Over."*

Adam swiftly scanned the horizon, as near to 180° as the F-5's canopy would allow. He was surprised to notice that the low cloud through which he had initially ascended earlier in the flight, had by now all but disappeared and the ocean's horizon was clearly visible.

"Er... well, no but..."

"And to maintain level flight on our 40,000-kilometre circumference spinning ball, do we constantly have to keep dropping our aircraft's nose to stop us flying into outer space? Over," quizzed the Argentine, closing in for the kill, metaphorically speaking.

Adam was starting to flounder somewhat. *"Well, no LV-FLA—of course we don't, but again..."*

"So those facts alone should make you suspect that maybe we live on a much, much larger globe than the one NASA, the United Nations and the scientific community tell us we do," Forestello continued, turning up the heat even more. *"Who knows Squadron Leader; we may even live on an eternal flat plane or perhaps a..."*

"Look LV-FLA, I've had enough of this crap," Adam shrieked, unable to hide his irritation and frustration. *"You are violating Antarctic air space contrary to the*

1959 treaty. Simple as that—and if you refuse to turn around and return to Ushuaia, you will be shot down. Over."

There was a short pause. *'He's probably checking with the others,'* Adam surmised, correctly as it turned out. Then came Forestello's chilling response.

"We don't think you will do that Adam. Over."

By now Adam's stress levels were running on overdrive. *"LV-FLA, I implore you—do not make me do this. Over."*

The silence of the Gulfstream's response was deafening as it unerringly maintained its southerly course.

Right on cue, Prendergast once again interrupted the dialogue. *"Fire warning shots Esmerelda,"* he commanded.

For the second time that day, Adam pointed Esmerelda's nose toward an incursive target, firing two rounds of cannon shots, one above and one below the aircraft. Having returned well and truly to script, he awaited their response.

More deafening silence from the executive jet so it fell to Prendergast to issue the ultimate, fatal command.

"807, fire Sidewinder 1 at the incursive. Over," came the grim order.

Adam, with tears welling in his eyes, scarcely able to believe what was happening, fixed his eyes on the Gulfstream, his right thumb trembling, reluctant to press the fire button. His heart raced, beads of sweat rolled down his forehead as the horror of this moment unfolded and began to tear his soul to shreds. What would happen if he disobeyed the order? Could he possibly get away with a deliberate miss? Would he ever be able to forgive himself if he went through with it? Why was he being ordered to kill innocent civilians? At some point in the future, could he be held to account for what he was about to do?

The seconds ticked inexorably by as the young airman simply sat there, paralysed and alone in the cockpit, not wanting to fire and yet reluctant to disobey orders. A whole minute passed and still he could do nothing. He tried several times to move his thumb on to the button and fire, but each time it recoiled, as if in horror at what it was being asked to do.

An impatient, decisive and terse intervention from Prendergast wrenched him unceremoniously from his paralysis. *"Prendergast to 807,"* he bellowed. *"As your commanding officer, I order you to fire Sidewinder 1 at the target—now! Over."*

Adam gulped, steeled himself and prepared to fire, but suddenly the Gulfstream disappeared behind a thick cloud. A few seconds later it reappeared so he took aim once more and plunged his thumb down on the firing button, sending the Sidewinder hurtling towards the totally unarmed Gulfstream, scoring a direct hit on the fuselage just above the port wing.

He winced in horror and disbelief as the missile exploded, splitting the fuselage apart in one huge, dreadful fireball and ripping-off both wings. Time seemed to stand still as he waited for the smoke and flames to disperse and then watched with revulsion as thousands of fragments of debris, the body parts of peaceful, innocent human beings amongst them, began their silent downward journey toward the dark ocean, over forty-thousand feet below. As he made his way back to Teniente Rodolfo, banging his fists against the canopy window, he sobbed relentlessly, yelling and screaming, *"Fuck you Prendergast, fuck you United Nations, fuck you Antarctica!"* at the top of his voice over and over and over again, traumatised and broken by the heinous crime against humanity he had just committed.

Chapter 19

Late Afternoon Saturday 11th February 2023 – Back at Base

Adam stepped down from *Esmerelda*, totally ignoring a very sombre-faced Jorge who had just placed the chocks under the wheels. He walked disconsolately across the apron traumatised with guilt, anger and disbelief over what he had just done. He then entered the locker room, slammed the door shut behind him and hurled his flying helmet against the wall, putting a huge dent in the grey plasterboard and most likely ruining the helmet completely. Collapsing on to the bench and with head in hands he began to sob uncontrollably. Barely able to breathe, he wailed in anguish, gasping for air, his body shaking and juddering like a building being hit by an earthquake.

He remained in that position for well over an hour until sheer exhaustion caused the sobbing, wailing and shuddering to subside. He lay back on the hard plywood bench staring at the bare ceiling above him and soon fell into an uneasy and disturbing sleep.

He was woken up by a very worried and concerned-looking Dobbo, perched on the edge of the bench gently tapping his shoulder. *"Come on old chum, let's get you back to your quarters, eh?"* he whispered.

Adam nodded obediently and tried to lift himself up but his legs, completely drained of strength, would not obey any of the commands arriving from his brain.

"Don't worry, I'll help you up, mate," assured Dobbo, putting his strong, broad arms under Adam's armpits and raising him on to his feet. Adam slumped forward but Dobbo held him tight, pulling the distraught airman tight to his body and walking him very slowly and gingerly out of the locker room and across the concrete to the accommodation block.

It took the two men almost five minutes to reach Adam's room whereas normally, the locker room to quarters journey took around thirty to forty-five seconds. Dobbo kicked at Adam's door which thankfully was unlocked, helped his colleague across to the bed and rolled him carefully on to it. Adam curled up into the foetal position, his legs almost touching his chin, hands tightly clasped together. His eyes stared vacantly toward the bedside table, the air entering and leaving his lungs in rapid and very shallow gasps.

"Poor Bastard!" Dobbo exclaimed under his breath, removing Adam's flight suit and boots and hanging them on the hook on the door. *"Much worse than I was."* He lifted Adam slightly so he could release the duvet from underneath the body of the listless airman and then lay it gently over him. He made sure Adam's head was resting on the pillow and then crossed to the kitchen area to pour a glass of water from the purifier, which he placed on the bedside table. He looked at Adam, shook his head in resignation, turned-off the glaring, fluorescent light and sat beside him on the bed, stroking his brow and making shushing sounds. After about ten minutes, Adam's eyes flickered, then closed so Dobbo lifted himself from the chair and very stealthily left the room, quietly latching the door closed behind him.

He made his way to the mess room, deeply disturbed for the welfare of his fellow airman. His first kill hadn't been great but he'd not reacted anywhere near as badly as Adam had—the poor sod! He reckoned that he and Prendergast might have a job on their hands pulling Adam around, but at least the distraught airman was sleeping now, which was something he supposed. He resolved to check on his friend in four or five hours to see how he was doing—it was now 7pm so he'd pop in on his way to bed. He entered the mess room, deserted as usual but for the omnipresent Prendergast who, true to form, was polishing a glass behind the bar and having finished, he held it up to the light for a clearer inspection and to check for unnoticed smears.

"How is he?" enquired Prendergast, filling the newly polished glass with a pint of the amber nectar and passing it across the counter.

Dobbo took the glass and in one gulp downed half of it. No crude, comedic belch this time though. *"Fucking 'ell Mike, he's totally distraught. I went over to meet him in the locker room but I could hear him sobbing and wailing so left him to it until he'd calmed down. Honest man, he was lying there on the bench just staring at the ceiling and he couldn't even lift himself up, never mind walk."*

Prendergast shook his head, biting his lip. *"It's bad for everyone, although you weren't too upset were you Dobbo—well you didn't seem to take it too badly."*

Dobbo pulled a barstool towards him and perched himself on top, resting against the coppertop. *"I just bottled it up for an easy life, Mike. Felt like shit for quite some time but somehow managed to hold myself together. I'm reasonably OK about it all now but certainly don't want a second or a third kill. Please God they all see sense from now on,"* he pleaded to the heavens. He raised the half-full glass to his mouth, emptying the remaining contents in one go. This time he performed his customary drawn-out belch, slammed the empty glass down on the bar and winked mischievously at Prendergast. *"Another one Prenders old bean if you would be so kind?"* he snorted.

Prendergast called time on Dobbo after pouring his third pint. *"There's no way Adam will be flying tomorrow, Dobson so you need to keep yourself relatively sober this evening,"* he declared, pulling rank on his very disappointed customer. Dobbo took his time over the third, ordered a Prendergast-special; Hawaiian burger and chips with a side salad and settled-down in one of the armchairs. After fifteen minutes his burger arrived and he ate it slowly while reading the latest copy of *The Dalesman*, the most recent monthly edition of which had just arrived that day on a C-130 supply plane. He loved that magazine—his absolute favourite read which, although far more suited to older readers, kept him in touch with his much-beloved Yorkshire.

One burger, the aforementioned third pint, two pisses and all one-hundred and ten pages of *The Dalesman* later, Dobbo, now completely alone in the bar, Prendergast having left an hour or so earlier, finally decided to call it a night. He placed his empties on the counter and left the room, turning off all the lights as he exited. Adam's room was between the mess-hall and his own quarters, so he quietly entered using the torch on his phone to save him turning on the main light. Adam, lying in a much more relaxed position than when Dobbo had left him, was sleeping like a baby, his breathing slow, even and rhythmic. The glass of water on the bedside table was now half empty, meaning he had taken a drink at some point, which was a good sign. But, most importantly, he looked at peace, Dobbo reckoned, and with a bit of luck would sleep through until morning.

"Goodnight, buddy," he whispered, leaving Adam to his slumbers. *"Sleep tight."*

Chapter 20

Michael Joseph Prendergast – b. 1973, Wilmslow, Cheshire, England

Mike Prendergast, Adam and Dobbo's commanding officer was of fairly humble origins having been born and raised on the Colshaw Farm overspill council estate a mile or so from the town centre of Wilmslow, a somewhat upmarket and desirable country town some four miles from Manchester Airport. Indeed Wilmslow was becoming quite famous at the time as it still is to this day, for the host of TV stars and top-tier footballers who call it their home. He was the youngest of four children, all boys, and in reality an 'afterthought,' being ten years younger than the next youngest of the three other brothers.

At the time of his birth, his father Joseph (Joe) was a lathe operator in a small, local engineering firm on the nearby Handforth Dean Industrial Estate and his mother Daphne, a checkout assistant at the local *Fine Fare* supermarket. In the late 1960s they were rehoused in the leafy north Cheshire suburbs from their previous home in Gorton, a seedy, crime-infested slum located east of the centre of Manchester. This was part of a huge population redistribution and slum clearance plan proposed and implemented by the City Council. Joe and Daphne had married in 1956, moving into a rundown Victorian terraced house in Gorton before of course being forcibly relocated out of the city and into a far more rural setting.

They had 'produced' Michael at a fairly advanced age, Joe being 44 and Daphne 42 at the time. It had been quite a shock when they learned that Daphne was pregnant once again as they had assumed, not unreasonably, that after a gap of ten years, and at their advancing years, their child-bearing days were now well and truly behind them!

Young Michael was from the very beginning, an intelligent and precocious child. He attended Springfield School, a brisk ten minute walk from his modest three-bedroomed council home in Colshaw Farm. There he excelled in all subjects, being regarded by his peers as what they referred to as a 'swot,' an intense, studious child who took great pride in being top of his class and almost always being first to raise his hand whenever the teacher asked a question of said class.

Following his primary education, Michael attended Wilmslow Grammar School, achieving excellent grades in both his GCSEs and 'A' level exams before being accepted at the very same, prestigious RAF Cranwell as his two subordinates, Adam and Dobbo, albeit around a decade and a half earlier.

Cranwell however, was not a happy experience overall for young Mike. He quickly gained a reputation for being a loner, a stand-offish individual, who would take no part in all the high-jinks and escapades that were the usual preoccupation of young students of all disciplines everywhere. As a result, he tended to lock himself away in his room for weeks on end and bury his head in all the theoretical aspects of his RAF officer training, rather than mix socially with the young men and women of his peer group. Having said that however, he quickly became very adept at the practicalities of the role too and was regarded by all the staff of the college as well as, albeit begrudgingly, his classmates as one of the best prospects in his year.

And unsurprisingly to everyone who knew him, Mike graduated from Cranwell as indisputably number one in his year—with one of the most exemplary records ever recorded and this had not gone unnoticed from 'the outside,' either!

On the day of his graduation and as he was preparing to leave for a short holiday before joining his new squadron, Mike was approached by one of the college's senior staff, Air Commodore Tony Stables and was invited to join him in his study in one hour's time. Wondering and worrying what on Earth he had done wrong to warrant such a summons, at the appropriate time he duly knocked tentatively on the door of his superior officer and was immediately invited in.

"Do come in and close the door behind you, Mike," said Tony, kindly.

"Thank you sir. May I ask what this is all about?" queried Prendergast with a perturbed tone in his slightly quavering voice, as well as wearing a worried look on his face.

"Firstly Mike, just relax. You've done nothing wrong. Well, not really, and this is not a reprimand of any sort," he was reassured. *"On the contrary, old boy,"* he continued, "There *are some quite influential people who have taken an active interest in you and your almost exemplary Cranwell record to date."*

"Almost exemplary, sir?"

Tony cleared his throat. *"Uhm, yes, well. We know all about your little, shall we say, tendencies and proclivities, old chap. But that's all perfectly healthy and exactly the kind of thing we look for when selecting the very best candidates."*

At this, Mike blushed a little but nevertheless visibly relaxed, his body language instantly and dramatically reflecting his enormous relief.

Stables continued... *"Yes, it seems you've made quite an impression in some quarters, shall we say. And I am tasked in my position as recruiter for the said organisation, with asking if you would be at all interested in joining the foreign office, but not the foreign office, if you know what I mean?"* he queried with a knowing wink.

Prendergast was shocked by the sudden realisation that he was in the process of being recruited by the security services, 'the foreign office but not the foreign office' being a well-known code name for MI6 no less, at least among the senior ranks of the armed forces.

After quickly recovering his composure and without missing a beat, he responded. *"Sir, I don't know what to say really. I have my heart set on a flying career and had never considered anything of this sort..."* He was immediately cut-off right there.

"Oh, don't worry about that Mike. It will not affect your career in the slightest, other than the fact that you will have an additional, different boss to the rest of your colleagues, of all ranks. Your normal RAF duties will sit side by side with your surreptitious 'foreign office' ones and rather complement each other. And of course no-one will ever know, not even your superiors and especially not your subordinates, about your 'other' duties and loyalties. There will be no conflicts whatsoever," he was reassured once again.

"Well, again I'm not sure what to think sir. Are you able to give me any more details at this stage about what may be involved...?" He was once more cut-off in mid-sentence by the senior officer.

"Look Mike, this is just a preliminary, casual discussion and not the forum for anything more formal. There is quite a protracted process to come—if that is, you are interested in continuing? No pressure at all old boy. If it's a 'no' at this stage then that will be that, no pressure at all as I say, and you will never be contacted by us again. It will not in any way be held against you either or be a hinderance to your future career. At this point we just need to establish whether or not there is a desire to continue the process to the next stage. A simple yes or no will suffice."

"Well in that case, sir, it has to be a yes," Mike confirmed after a short pause to collect his thoughts.

"Excellent, excellent! That's settled then and we'll be in touch in due course," Stables announced emphatically whilst unceremoniously ushering him towards the door. *"Good luck young man and all the very best to you in the future, wherever this may lead,"* he enthused, closing the door abruptly and without waiting for a response.

Somewhat shell-shocked, Michael J. Prendergast, security services operative elect, wandered back to his quarters in quite a daze. 'The next few weeks and months are going to be VERY interesting,' he thought to himself as he packed his bags, whilst simultaneously musing on what the future would hold for him now.

Chapter 21

Monday 13th February 2023 – Two Days After The First Kill

Dobbo's alarm clock woke him at 7.00am after one hell of a fitful, anxiety-filled night's sleep. The previous day he'd twice visited Adam's room, finding the door locked on both occasions and with no response to his knockings. He had informed Prendergast who told him to leave it a day and if there was still no response, they would force their way in. *"He most likely needs to be alone,"* he explained. *"Perfectly normal. I've seen this type of thing countless times. I'm sure he'll still be with us in the morning though."*

"I hope so, Mike!" Dobbo exclaimed, unable to conceal his anxiety. *"But what if he fucking well tops himself?"*

"If he tops himself, he tops himself and there's nothing we can do about that," Prendergast replied calmly and very matter of fact. *"But to be on the safe side,"* he went on, *"I'll get Jorge to pop round and check on him later this morning. When Mateo was going off the rails he offered to speak with him and somehow managed to pull him around. I think he might have been some sort of shrink or something in an earlier life. I didn't need to involve him with you though, hard-nosed bugger that you are."*

Well, that was yesterday and today they would find out for real. Although still incredibly tired, Dobbo jumped out of bed, took his quickest shower ever, threw-on some clothes and hurried along the corridor to Adam's room, a gigantic knot in his stomach, his heart beating fast and erratically. He was amazed to find Adam's door ajar; the room empty but eerily tidy with the bed made. *"What the..."* he muttered to himself and raced to the mess room as fast as his legs could carry him.

As he entered the mess-room, there was Prendergast, as always busying himself behind the bar and at one of the low tables, a full English breakfast beside him, laptop on knee, sat a very relaxed, fresh-looking Adam. He was clean-shaven and bright-eyed, his clothes recently ironed—completely back to normal by the look of it. Dobbo could not believe what his eyes were telling him and just stood there for a while saying nothing, mouth wide-open, blinking in amazement. He looked across at Prendergast who beamed back at him, surreptitiously giving him a thumbs up.

"Full English for me too Mike please—oh, and an espresso with three shots too if you don't mind," he whispered, then made his way tentatively over to Adam, not really knowing how to greet his pal. True to the Samuel Dobson form book, he carefully chose jovial and flippant as the best approach.

"Morning, mate. You're looking bright-eyed and bushy-tailed this morning," he announced cheerily, tousling Adam's hair and taking the armchair next to him. *"How're you doing?"*

Adam closed his laptop, placed it under the chair, took a drink from the steaming coffee cup beside him and began cutting one of the slightly-charred sausages on his plate.

"I'm doing OK thanks Dobbo—surprisingly enough," he replied.

Dobbo sat back in the armchair, placing his size twelve feet on the corner of the table. *"Well I can't believe how good you seem today. I've never seen anyone react like that before, even old Mateo. Prenders said it was pretty normal though and to leave you alone for a day or two. Isn't that right, Mike?"*

Prendergast who had just arrived with the triple-shot espresso, handed the tiny cup to Dobbo, nodded in affirmation and returned to the kitchen to check on the progress of the full English.

"Talking of Mateo, what was his surname? Can you remember?" enquired Adam.

Dobbo took a sip of the steaming dark liquid, wincing at the strength and bitterness of the triple-shots. *"I can remember yes, it was Forestello. I used to call him 'Gumpy' for short, after Forrest Gump—although 'Gumptard' might have been a better name for him, the way he was at the end."*

Adam dropped his knife and fork and stared in disbelief at Dobbo. *"What? Never? The pilot of the plane I just shot down was called Mateo Forestello,"* he spluttered.

"So—you've just shot down your predecessor Adders? Holy shit!" Dobbo exclaimed, as Prendergast re-appeared with the breakfast plate. *"Mike, Mike, guess what—Mateo was the pilot of the plane that Adam destroyed. Did you know that?"*

Prendergast positioned the plate in front of Dobbo and handed him a knife and fork, wrapped in a red paper napkin. *"Yes, I did know that but was going to keep it to myself..."* he explained and then continued, *"...but it didn't take you two sleuths very long to suss that one out, did it?"*

As Prendergast returned to his station once more, the two airmen fell silent, taking in the enormity of all this, the only sound being the clicking and clanking of cutlery on porcelain as they worked their way through the cooked breakfasts.

Adam wiped the last trace of egg yolk and brown sauce from his empty plate with a slice of thin, unappealing white bread and looked earnestly at Dobbo. *"These last two days have been like nothing I've ever experienced, Dobbo,"* he confided. *"I've never ever felt like that in my entire career and God knows I've dished out some shit to many a poor soul over the years. You know—Iraq, Afghanistan, Libya, Syria—but this? Well, this is off the charts."*

"Yep, but it has to be done my friend," Dobbo replied.

"But does it?" pleaded Adam. *"I mean, what harm would it have caused to simply allow them to continue? We could have followed them on radar, maybe even sent up a long-range escort from one of the research bases to shadow their flight—make sure they weren't up to no good."*

Dobbo placed his knife and fork on the plate, wiped his mouth on the napkin and pushed the plate away from him. *"Well, whatever the reasons, the U.N. simply won't do that, so you just have to follow orders—like I do. If the stupid buggers on the planes won't heed our warnings and turn back, I'm sorry mate, but it's their own bleedin' fault."*

"Maybe you're right," declared Adam. *"But at this precise moment it feels mighty raw, I tell you. I've come round from how I felt on Saturday evening, but what we're being asked to do here just doesn't feel right—I mean, these people are civilians for God's sake—they have no weapons and mean nobody any harm. I just feel..."*

"I know mate," Dobbo interjected, *"but it'll pass—I can assure you. And like I said to you before, keep how you're feeling between the two of us eh? No mention of it to Prendergast whatsoever—just keep your head down, use me as your therapist when you need to, and I reckon you'll be ok."*

Adam considered this offer as he finished the last of the coffee in his cup. *"I'm not sure I'll be needing any therapy, actually. The really weird thing is that yesterday I woke-up feeling almost suicidal but as the day progressed, particularly after I had spoken with Jorge, a peace, a calmness and a strange kind of acceptance slowly and gradually came over me. By lunchtime I felt I could get up, shower and shave and by late afternoon I was ironing my clothes, tidying the room and starting to feel like I could face the world again. It was very, very strange. I slept brilliantly last night, woke up absolutely ravenous this morning and felt totally normal—no, better than normal actually, I haven't felt like this in years. Bizarre! And all this 'just following orders' crap—now I sympathise with how many of the Nazis must have felt at Nuremburg!"*

Dobbo drained his coffee cup and jumped up from his chair, slapping Adam on the back as he did so. *"Come on then pal, let's resume our little pool challenge,"* he suggested. *"I must be due a win sooner or later."*

Chapter 22

Friday 17th February 2023 – Adam Continues his Research

The next few days saw no further incursions. Apparently, this always happened 'whenever there'd been a 'kill,' Prendergast had explained and, more often than not, the hiatus lasted a week or two before the flights started again. Adam had been relieved of his duties anyway, with Dobbo standing-in for him but with no action whatsoever, the long, cold, tedious Antarctic days were largely filled with highly competitive games of pool, darts, cards and Scrabble. Late each evening alone in his room Adam spent his time deep in research, meticulously working his way through the plethora of articles, podcasts and videos on the mysteries and controversies of Antarctica.

As his fervour and hunger to shed light on this murky conspiracy grew and grew, he could not believe how increasingly energised he felt as the week progressed. He had decided that he would not disclose to either Dobbo or Prendergast exactly what it was that had turned him around from his near suicidal despair. Even if they could have been bothered to ask him—which was highly unlikely, he would keep it himself. And he was sincerely glad of that, he just wanted to be left to his own thoughts to try to make some sense of what was happening to him right now.

Each night he scoured the web for as much information about the mysteries of Antarctica as he could find, avoiding as best he could the major mainstream sources such as Wikipedia and YouTube, relying instead on sites like Bitchute, Rumble, Twitter and Spotify podcasts to provide the enlightenment for which he hungered. His research had introduced him to the brave, new alternative-media world, where no subject was taboo, censorship was unheard of and free speech positively encouraged, a far cry from the likes of the BBC, The Guardian, The Economist, The History Channel etcetera. And Adam was loving it!

He revisited the Admiral Richard E. Byrd story, for whom there was a huge amount of content on his life, career and controversies. For example, Operation Highjump, his premature death, the alleged 'suicide' of his confidante and political ally, James Forrestal plus an intriguing narrative of an encounter beyond the pole with a race of people resembling humans whose intellect, ethical values and technology we could only possibly dream of—even today.

His next port of call was the website of *Alianza Universal de Verdad y Libertad*, from where, with considerable help from Google Translate, he managed to glean plenty of detail on the organisation's raison d'être, along with information on its founder members, including a brief biography and glowing tribute to the late Mateo Forestello. Then, as he perused Mateo's story, a realisation dawned on him—Mateo Forestello, James Forrestal—incredibly similar names in connection with Antarctica, albeit more than seven decades apart. Coincidence? Or was there possibly some kind of connection? He returned to Mateo's story.

Born in 1982 in Cork, Ireland, he emigrated to Argentina with his mother Shannon shortly after his birth. He subsequently served as a fighter pilot with the Argentinian Air Force from 2008 until his premature retirement in the autumn of 2022. He had joined the AUVL whilst still in the military during a posting to Antarctica and had been at the controls of the Gulfstream which U.N. forces had shot down. So, he was definitely Adam's predecessor at Teniente Rodolfo but was he also somehow connected with James Forrestal, the former US Secretary of Defense? Most likely not Adam concluded but the name similarity was definitely somewhat strange.

Another perusal of *thedeceptionists.org* website, which he'd been browsing at the time he was hurriedly summoned for the Gulfstream mission, shed further light on the mysterious benefactor. Though not providing a name, the site confirmed he was male, single and a key member of a renowned international banking family with influential connections to the U.N. and World Economic Forum. Apparently, he had stumped-up all the cash for the Dreamliner charter and used his influence and contacts to find a charter company and flight crew sympathetic to the cause. There was no information on the result of the mission nor indeed the whereabouts of the Dreamliner, so Adam attempted several general news searches on Google to see if the mainstream agencies had anything on it. To his surprise there was absolutely no mention of it whatsoever; it was as if the plane and those aboard had simply never existed.

On numerous occasions during his studies, references popped up regarding the disappearance of the legendary US aviator Amelia Earhart on her final flight attempting to circumnavigate the Earth, so Adam decided to spend some time researching that particular topic too. Of particular significance was the fact that she was photographed several times with Richard Byrd indicating a likely close friendship with the Admiral. Earhart had stated many times during her celebrated career that at some point she would write a book about 'the true topography of the Earth' and what particularly intrigued Adam was the fact that she completely ditched the traditional Mercator map for her intercontinental flights in favour of what was effectively a flat Earth map, declaring the traditional chart completely useless for plotting accurate and realistic routes. During World War II, just a decade after her infamous last flight, both the Allies and the Germans used almost identical maps to hers for planning and navigation on their naval and overseas campaigns.

The possibility of a flat, non-globe Earth was constantly being raised in almost every single piece of Antarctic research, so Adam put some time aside to research that particular theory also. There was so much content on the subject, it was difficult to decide which people or groups to follow and after wasting considerable time on the abundance of content put-out by The Flat Earth Society, which basically claims that we live on a huge 'compact disk' floating in space as per Terry Pratchett's *Discworld* novels, he came across far more credible theories by the likes of 'Flat Earth Dave' David Weiss, Eric DuBay and several others. Their view was that we potentially reside in one circular area on an eternal flat plane surrounded by a huge ice wall, with our own local sun, moon and stars mapped by the astrological clock. Beyond that barrier are other potential realms with their own local suns, moons and stars, quite possibly inhabited by beings similar, if not identical to us.

What particularly resonated with Adam was that they backed-up everything with facts and empirical evidence which were incredibly difficult, if not impossible to refute. Their willingness to question the standard historical narrative and dig below the surface enabled them to provide plausible answers to why the 1959 treaty had been signed and the subsequent ban on exploration and colonisation, which he himself had been enforcing.

Then, a few minutes before midnight on Friday 17th February, he was listening to a most fascinating Spotify™ podcast about the German colonisation of Antarctica in the late 1930s. They had allegedly annexed the Norwegian territory of Queen Maud Land, renaming it *Neu Schwabenland* and established several military bases and settlements there. Then suddenly, he received a text from Prendergast requesting his attendance at a nine o'clock briefing the following morning. The Wing Commander had something very interesting to put to him, it said. Curious, Adam replied with a thumbs-up emoji, then considered settling down for the night. However, captivated by what he had just been listening to, he decided to continue his research—deep into the wee, small hours of the morning.

Chapter 23

Amelia Mary Earhart – b. 1897, Atchison, Kansas, USA

On 1st June 1937, just prior to her fortieth birthday, Amelia Earhart, the most famous female aviator of her day, began her epic attempt to circumnavigate the world alongside her long-time companion and navigator, Fred Noonan. The intrepid pair embarked upon their proposed twenty-nine thousand mile flight, departing from Miami, Florida in their twin-engine Lockheed Electra.

Over the course of the following weeks they made various refuelling stops before reaching Lae in New Guinea on 29th June. At that point in time they had travelled just over twenty-two thousand miles. Then three days later after refuelling once more and fully refreshed, they were ready to tackle the next stage of their hazardous voyage and duly departed 2nd July 1937 heading for Howland Island in the mid-Pacific, approximately two-thousand six-hundred miles distant.

The flight was expected to be arduous, especially since the tiny coral atoll was difficult to locate. In those pre-war days, in order to help with navigation two brightly lit American ships were stationed to mark the route. Earhart was also in intermittent radio contact with the *Itasca,* a U.S. Coastguard cutter near Howland. Late in the journey, Earhart radioed that the plane was running out of fuel and about an hour later she announced, *"We are running north and south,"* which was rather strange for an east-west journey.

That was the last transmission received by the *Itasca*. Her plane was believed to have gone down some one hundred miles from the island and an extensive search was undertaken in an attempt to locate Earhart and Noonan. However, on 19th July 1937, the search operation was eventually abandoned and the pair declared dead—lost at sea.

Earhart's mysterious disappearance captured the public's imagination and generated numerous theories and claims. Notably, some believed that she and Noonan had crashed on a different island after failing to locate Howland, whereas others posited that they were captured by the Japanese. However, no definitive evidence was ever found for these claims and most 'experts' at the time believed that Earhart's plane had crashed somewhere in the Pacific near Howland after running out of fuel.

...Or so the 'official' story goes. However, the truth is often somewhat different to reality. The plain fact is that, by the time Earhart and Noonan arrived in Lae, and after much heart-felt deliberation during the expedition, they had already decided that the proposed leg of the journey to Howland was to be purely a cover story. Their real objective was to head to Antarctica, cross the ice wall and investigate what really lay beyond. Amelia had been secretly encouraged by her close friend and confidante Richard E. Byrd, or *'Dickie'* as she preferred to call him, to undertake this particularly hazardous journey. During Byrd's second Antarctic expedition of 1933-34 where he spent five months alone, falling sick and almost dying in the process, he made several discoveries which had the potential to completely invalidate all previously published narratives regarding the ice-bound continent. Over the subsequent two years he and Amelia held several lengthy and impassioned discussions, in secret it must be said, regarding an alleged 'land of plenty' beyond 90° south, inhabited by people not of our realm. He for one was convinced it really existed and, unable to return there himself due to his Naval commitments, they decided between them that Amelia would take up the mantle of Antarctic explorer. She had the perfect opportunity to attempt the impossible and discover this rumoured paradise and after she departed with Noonan on the first leg of her epic flight, Byrd prayed regularly and earnestly for their safe return, confident that they would bring back confirmation of its existence.

For Noonan, a former Pan Am navigator and long-term friend of Earhart, 1937 had already turned out to be an eventful and tumultuous year. As well as being involved in a serious automobile accident, his marriage to first wife Josephine ended in divorce after he fell in love with a woman called Mary Beatrice Martinelli, reported to be a divorcee with no children who ran a beauty salon in Oakland, California. It was rumoured that Noonan was an alcoholic, fired by the airline for being drunk on duty and that that was the cause of the divorce. However, there is little or no real evidence to support this assertion.

He was well aware of the meetings between Amelia and Byrd and suspected that she had been given information that 'the powers that be' would not be happy with yet had no idea that their planned circumnavigation attempt was to be altered so dramatically. Earhart had to use all her powers of persuasion as they progressed eastward but once she had him on her side, he was as excited and determined as she, to head south and discover the truth.

Earhart and Byrd had planned the clandestine operation in the minutest of detail. The Electra was to depart Lae on 2nd July, but not for Howland. Instead, the route it would take was southeast to Ouvéa, an atoll in the remote Loyalty Islands archipelago, one hundred miles or so off the coast of New Caledonia. They were to land at a small private airstrip where Byrd had arranged for the plane to be fitted with seaplane floats, additional fuel tanks and an improved heating system. His team there would also disguise the Electra so it wouldn't be so easily recognised during its onward journey, painting it in a fake airline livery, *'Air Ouvéa'* with the registration *ZK-EANO*. Byrd's main contact on Ouvéa, Vivian Walsh, a former New Zealand Flying Corps pilot and engineer, had estimated the refit to take at least three weeks but the plan was for the renegade adventurers to rest there until the end of August before continuing their journey.

From Ouvéa they would fly to Bora Bora in French Polynesia and from there to a secluded bay near Hanga Roa on Easter Island where they would be picked-up by a German Navy cruiser and taken to Santiago, Chile. There they would remain under false identities until mid-October before setting out once more, this time for Antarctica itself. Byrd had told Earhart that he had been invited by the German armed forces to assist them with Operation Neu Schwabenland, a huge initiative to establish bases and colonies in the Queen Maud Land Antarctic territory and, although he was later to decline the offer, he was on sufficiently good terms with his German counterparts to persuade them to transport Earhart and Noonan to one of their stations on the Antarctic peninsula and for them to fly south from there.

As the Electra lifted away from the runway at Lae on that historic morning, Fred Noonan looked across at the lady in the pilot's seat beside him. *"Well here goes, Mary,"* he grinned, using the pet name he had for her. *"With you one hundred percent—and whatever happens to us from now on—never, ever forget, I've always loved you and always will."*

Chapter 24

Saturday 18th February 2023 - Mission Four, Reconnaissance

Prendergast and Adam faced each other across the tiny, rickety table masquerading as the Wing Commander's office desk.

Prendergast cleared his throat in his customary manner and began. *"Squadron Leader, I have 'volunteered' you…"* he announced, signalling quotation marks with his fingers, *"…for a reconnaissance mission—well more of a rehabilitation exercise actually—to get you back into the swing of things. Esmerelda has been fitted with two auxiliary fuel tanks to extend her range to over four-thousand miles and is armed with nothing more than a couple of cameras and a few cannon rounds, just in case. Your job is to fly south to the edge of the ice shelf and then to follow it one thousand miles to the east, at low altitude, to photograph its density and any signs of retreat or spread. You must report and photograph any evidence of incursion by non-military persons, be it a settlement, vessel or wreckage. Once you have covered those one thousand miles, you must turn around and return to base. How do you feel about that?"*

Adam pondered this for a few seconds before replying. *"Er… well, I wasn't expecting that so soon, Mike but yes, why not? I have to get back into the saddle sometime, so it may as well be now I suppose. When do you want me to go?"*

His superior grinned. *"This afternoon actually if you feel you can handle it that is. The weather is really good today and the skies are clearer than they've been for some time. Perfect conditions. So, what do you say Haylock? Yes, or no?"*

Adam rubbed his stubbled chin as he considered the proposal while Prendergast shuffled his papers nonchalantly, awaiting the Squadron Leader's response.

"OK, count me in Mike," Adam replied enthusiastically, grinning back at his commanding officer with a mischievous glint in his eye. *"What time do I depart?"*

Prendergast glanced down at his watch. *"Well now let me see…… 13.00 hours?"*

Adam nodded, rising from his chair. *"That's perfect for me. I'll get myself prepared for it and make sure I'm ready in plenty of time."*

"Thank you, Squadron Leader. Dismissed," said Prendergast, gathering his notes as he stood to leave.

By 12.45pm Adam was on the apron, fully flight-suited with a brand-new replacement helmet in his right hand and a bag containing provisions across his left shoulder. Esmerelda, shimmering impressively in the pale, watery light and looking as immaculate as ever, was fully prepared for the mission, canopy open and steps ready with a six-hundred gallon 'drop tank' under each wing.[4] Closer inspection of the underside of the jet revealed two high-definition cameras hanging from the fuselage, similar to those used on the latest drones, both capable of taking still shots and high-definition video.

He clambered aboard the fighter jet, stowed his provisions sack behind the seat and pulled out a walking compass from his top pocket. He had found it in the storeroom earlier when gathering together all the items he felt he needed for the trip and had adapted it, using some double-sided tape, so that he could attach it to Esmerelda's instrument panel. Once secured he inspected it closely. Esmerelda was currently facing almost due east on the apron, the red, north-facing half of the needle pointing to just past nine o'clock.

The F-5 pulled away from Jorge and Eduardo, both Chileans standing side by side sporting matching ear protectors, proudly admiring their pride and joy in all her pristine magnificence as she trundled towards the runway. Adam was feeling pretty nervous but nevertheless knew precisely what he had to do on this flight—he had been thinking about nothing else all morning. But did he really have the balls to do it just one week after the event that had led to the lowest point in his life?

Initially he guided Esmerelda south-east in crystal clear blue skies, the forbidding, though on this day, unusually calm waters of the Southern Ocean a full thirty-eight thousand feet below him. He kept Esmerelda at a steady cruising speed of six-hundred and twenty mph to conserve fuel.

At 71° south, just over an hour into the flight, he reached the ice wall, or 'ice shelf' as Prendergast had referred to it, a two-hundred-foot-high barrier rising formidably from the frigid Antarctic waters. Adam gasped in sheer amazement; he had seen photographs of it online but nothing had prepared him for the panorama with which he was now presented. It stretched east and west as far as the eye could see; a vertical wall of blue-tinted ice, with no

---

[4] Auxiliary fuel tanks

sign whatsoever, from his current position anyway, of any inlets or sea passages either into or through it.

Adam's research during the previous week had also revealed the many expeditions of Sir James Clark Ross, the nineteenth century polar explorer who was among the first to venture to Antarctica in an attempt to determine the position of the South Magnetic Pole.

When confronting the massive vertical face, he had famously remarked, *"It was an obstruction of such character as to leave no doubt in my mind as to our future proceedings, for we might as well sail through the cliffs of Dover as to penetrate such a mass. It would be impossible to conceive a more solid-looking mass of ice; not the smallest appearance of any rent or fissure could we discover throughout its whole extent, and the intensely bright sky beyond it plainly indicated the great distance to which it reached southward."*

For several years, on and off, Ross and his expeditionary fleet attempted unsuccessfully to fully circumnavigate the ice wall but were consistently thwarted in their attempts to locate any kind of sea passage to the interior.

His lengthy investigations had been his first tentative steps in challenging the Antarctic paradigm, an attempt to identify any gaps, limitations or downright falsehoods in the current knowledge and understanding. Was this frozen, near-vertical precipice, as per the accepted mainstream narrative, simply the northern edge of a floating, oceanic ice shelf beyond which lay an inhospitable, barren, ice-covered landmass at the underside of our twenty-four thousand mile-circumference globe earth? Or could it perhaps be an actual true wall, holding the oceans in place and separating our world from others beyond it? How far does the ice extend; how and where does it terminate and what if anything, exists beyond it, were questions to which neither he nor the vast majority of mankind could possibly answer, an ignorance successfully perpetuated by the restrictions imposed by the Antarctic Treaty.

All we currently know is what we have been told; that snow and hail, howling winds, indescribable storms and hurricanes prevail and that in every direction human ingress is barred by unscalable escarpments of perpetual ice, extending farther than eye or telescope can penetrate, and becoming lost in gloom and darkness. Some alternative theories hold that the tundra of ice and snow stretches forever eternally, others that the frozen wastes contain oases of ice-free areas, teeming with life and resources. Some even suggest that the Antarctic landmass stretches southward way beyond 90° south giving way to other oceans and continents, quite possibly inhabited by intelligent beings similar to us. Those to which Admiral Richard E. Byrd had quite possibly alluded.

The flight plan presented to Adam had been to head due east along the perimeter of the wall for a thousand miles and then make a 135° turn to port (northwest), but instead of making that manoeuvre he pointed Esmerelda 90° to starboard (south), all the while watching the needle on the compass he had attached to the instrument panel. Now heading due south, the black half of the needle pointed straight ahead of him with the red half indicating that north was on a straight line directly behind the aircraft.

He slowed and reduced altitude to get a better look at the terrain below him. As the deep azure blue of the Southern Ocean began to diminish into the horizon behind him, he scanned left and right, completely awestruck by what he was witnessing. From this vantage point, the icy, frozen plain appeared almost dead flat for as far as his eye could see. Not one single fissure, indentation or exposed area of ground was visible across its entirety, which stretched away like an infinite, white and very smooth, pool table. At this his thoughts drifted back to his old friend back at base and he chuckled to himself. Dobbo still hadn't won his twenty quid back, had he? Maybe now he never would.

Chapter 25

Saturday 18th February 2023 – The Interception

Some fifteen minutes after crossing the ice wall, a distance of around one hundred miles, with the F-5's latitude indicator now showing 72.5° south, Adam's solitude was abruptly terminated when, completely out of the blue, his radio suddenly burst into life. *"Freedom Fighter 807, Adam—it's Dobbo here,"* came the dulcet yet unmistakably Yorkshire tones of his buddy from the base. *"What the fuck are you doing man?"*

Adam almost jumped out of his skin. *"Never mind me Freedom Fighter 808,"* he blurted angrily. *"What on earth are you doing here? Have you been following me all this time?"*

"Affirmative my friend," Dobbo replied. *"And I'm amazed you haven't spotted me actually—but I have to inform you that you are now flying off-course, contrary to your mission's flight plan, so I am ordering you to return to base immediately. Over."*

Adam ignored him and increased Esmerelda's speed to six-hundred and fifty mph.

Dobbo increased his speed accordingly and intensified the warning, annoyance very apparent in his tone. *"I repeat, 807—Adam, you are flying off-course, contrary to your mission's flight plan. Return to base immediately. Over."*

Adam paused for a few seconds, deep in thought before replying, *"808, this is 807. Look Dobbo, I just want to keep flying south to see what is...."*

Dobbo cut him short in no uncertain terms. *"Adam, if you continue, I have orders to shoot you down and seeing as you're carrying barely any weapons and therefore cannot defend yourself, I suggest you do as I say—now! Over."*

"Please let me carry on Dobbo," Adam pleaded. *"What harm is there in finding out the truth? Over."*

"I honestly don't know the answer to that Adam—and actually, I don't care," replied Dobbo dismissively. *"All I know is that you're acting like a sodding idiot. Turn around right now and return to base—for God's sake. Over."*

Their conversation was rudely interrupted by an angry and exasperated interjection by none other than Prendergast, who had been listening-in the whole time from the control centre back at Teniente Rodolfo, his voice ringing loud and clear across the radios of both pilots.

"808, engage in no further conversation with 807. Fire Sidewinder 1 immediately and destroy the incursive. Over."

Adam stiffened in his cockpit seat, startled by Prendergast's eagerness to blast him out of the skies so readily. He maintained his course, altitude and speed, with no desire to head back north, yet at the same time in no hurry to be blown to smithereens by his best buddy over the frozen Antarctic wastes. Meanwhile Dobbo, also taken aback by Prendergast's aggression, muted communications with Adam and responded to his commanding officer. *"Sir... Mike, I think Adam will turn around if you just leave things to me a while longer,"* he optimistically suggested. *"I think I might be able to get through to him. Over."*

Prendergast was not impressed in the slightest and was becoming more and more agitated—irrational even. *"Look Dobson, I ordered you to shoot the bastard down, so shoot the bastard down..."* he shrieked, swiftly adding, *"...If you allow him to continue to fly south across the mountains to Extrema then... SHIT!"*

Dobbo paused for a few seconds, puzzled by Prendergast's last sentence. He cleared his throat and spoke calmly and composedly, *"What or where is Extrema, Mike? Over,"* he enquired.

"Forget that last sentence Dobson—I was talking bollocks. Over," Pendergast replied dismissively.

"But you said 'shit' after the word 'Extrema,' Mike," said Dobbo adamantly. *"Have you let something slip here? Do you know something we don't? Over."*

"Look, 808, forget all that. Simply obey my command and shoot down the incursive—NOW!" yelled his by-now apoplectic commanding officer.

Dobbo ignored this latest tirade and muted Prendergast before re-opening communications with Adam. *"Come on Adders, see sense for Christ's sake and follow me back to base. You know it makes sense. Over."*

Adam tried another tactic. *"Look mate, my career's finished now whether I return or continue, so I may as well continue. Anyway, what does it matter to you and Prendergast if I carry on? Over."*

The Yorkshireman was having none of this. *"Quite right on the first point; your RAF career will certainly be well and truly shagged but continue with this escapade and you're a dead man! Return to base or you will be shot down. I don't want to do it, mate but if I have to I will. Over."*

"Come on Dobbo, it's me—your old chum—Adders. You wouldn't shoot down your best pal surely, would you? Remember your promise to me over the Med back in 2011? You owe me that at least, surely? And after everything else we've been through together over the years. All those missions, watching each other's back time and time again—brothers in arms! Over," Adam declared, hoping to play on Dobbo's former gratitude, loyalty and camaraderie.

There was a brief interlude while Dobbo considered Adam's plea. If he were to yield and give in to this kind of emotional blackmail, he would be dead meat. But then again, Adam had history on his side by covering for him back in 2011.

"Shit mate you're right, I do owe you—big style," he conceded. *"Plus, and I wasn't going to tell you this, but it was actually me who recommended you for this tour in the first place. I wouldn't have wanted anyone else down here with me—that's the honest truth, yet now I'm ready to send you on to kingdom come just 'cos that pathetic fat git says so. What the hell am I playing at?"*

Both pilots fell silent at this point, Adam shocked and angry that Dobbo had been instrumental in him being posted to Antarctica in the first place; Dobbo hoping his pal would offer some kind of rational explanation to ease his conscience and maybe even conjure up some brilliant scheme to save both their necks. When he realised nothing was forthcoming, he broke the deadlock.

"Look, I'm not going to shoot you down in a million years, Adders. Prenders can go stick his order up his fat arse but as you can probably tell, I'm not quite ready just yet to give up either my career or my life, not that I have much of a life outside of the cockpit. So, have you any suggestions for getting us both out of this mess, cos I'm going to have to turn back soon as I only have a normal fuel load?"

"Yes, I'd sussed that one straight away, Dobbo," Adam announced. In fact, the moment the two pilots had made visual contact, Adam had spotted that

Celeste was not carrying any drop tanks and, unbeknown to Dobbo, a plan had been formulating in his mind throughout their radio dialogue. *"I already have something up my sleeve, buddy that will hopefully save both our necks,"* he said.

"Brilliant, mate. What is it?" Dobbo enquired enthusiastically.

But Adam was playing his cards close to his chest. *"If I tell you, you'll spill the beans for sure with your big mouth so I'm saying nothing. Just get Prenders back on the line so everything from now on will be heard back at base and placed on record. Then just stick to the standard spiel—don't ask any dumb questions and leave the rest to me."*

"Copy that 807. Over," replied Dobbo, quickly getting into character before reopening comms with Prendergast who, frustrated and angry at the radio silence, wasted no time in making his presence felt once more.

"So, you're back, 808?" he boomed, *"Now shoot down 807 before the bastard either talks you out of it or you are forced to return due to lack of fuel. Fire Sidewinder 1 immediately. Over."*

Dobbo swallowed hard, hoping he could carry this off. *"I'm sorry 807,"* he said as gravely as his meagre acting ability would allow. *"You've had your last chance. I'm almost at the limit of my range now so turn around immediately or I will shoot you down in twenty seconds. I repeat, twenty seconds. Over."*

Ten of those twenty seconds passed in silence whilst Adam pretended to ponder what Dobbo had just said. He glanced at his latitude display which indicated their current position—74.5° south. *"OK mate, you win. Turning back now. Over,"* he said in mock resignation, slowly pointing the F-5 to starboard and beginning a 180° turn.

Dobbo audibly breathed a mock sigh of relief at his chum's U-turn. *"Thank God for that, you crazy sod. Look—let's chat about it when we get back to base eh? If they don't send you straight off to MCTC[5] that is—and me as well, come to that. Over."* He performed the same manoeuvre and followed closely behind Esmerelda as she made her way back toward Teniente Rodolfo Airbase. After about ten minutes of northerly flight, he contacted Prendergast.

"Control, this is 808. Do you read me? Over," he asked.

---

[5] Military Corrective Training Centre

Prendergast almost jumped down his throat, his response was so immediate. *"Of course I fucking read you—idiot,"* he blurted. *"I ordered you to shoot the bugger down, not give him another twenty seconds! You're in major trouble flight lieutenant but for now, just get yourself and that retard Haylock back here pronto. His career is definitely over and if I have anything to do with it, yours will be too! Over."*

Though delighted he had not shot Adam down and hopeful that his pal still had an ace up his sleeve, Dobbo was confused and anxious at Prendergast's rage. Surely, he had done what he was supposed to do which was to bring Adam back if he had decided to go rogue on them. Not only was he in the process of repaying the twelve-year-old debt he owed his colleague, but a highly skilled airman was still alive and well and the U.N. had not lost a valuable F-5 from their Antarctic weaponry. He sat there in silence not knowing what to think or say, his eyes fixed on Adam and Esmerelda as he followed them back toward base, in fear and trepidation of the reception he would receive once he got there.

He escorted Esmerelda some three hundred miles back across the ice wall and on towards the Antarctic Circle. Deep in thought and unknown to Dobbo, Adam was closely monitoring the distance the two F-5s were from base, bearing in mind the range of Dobbo's aircraft compared to his. With the two drop tanks she was carrying, Esmerelda had over three times the range of Celeste and he calculated in his head that once they were north of the Antarctic Circle, Dobbo would have insufficient fuel for another pursuit or interception attempt. He watched the latitude indicator counting down and when it showed 65.5° south, he made a sharp, swift 180° turn and headed-off due south again, accelerating rapidly to Mach 1.2 and climbing to nigh on the F-5's ceiling of 51,800 feet. Dobbo looked on, at first in disbelief but then the penny dropped. Adam had played his trump-card which was to make it look like he had tricked his friend by heading south again, safe in the knowledge that Celeste's low fuel reserves would make further pursuit impossible. *"Brilliant, Adam, bloody brilliant,"* he said to himself and then continued the deception for the benefit of Prendergast. *"You absolute bastard, Haylock!"* he shrieked into the radio, faking the realisation that his old friend had completely outsmarted and outmanoeuvred him. *"What the absolute fuck? Return to base—now! Over."*

"Absolutely no way mate," Adam laughed, grinning from ear to ear like a Cheshire cat who had just heard the funniest joke in the world. *"I know you can't intercept me now and there are no other armed fighters in the area with*

the capability, so I'm heading south again. Maybe I'll see you again old chum—maybe I won't—but it's been nice knowing you. Over."

"You're an absolute bloody maniac Haylock," yelled Dobbo, also grinning like the aforementioned feline. *"And I'm a dead man now. Shit, shit, shit, shit, SHIT!"*

Chapter 26

Saturday 21st May 1949 – The Strange Death of James Forrestal

The U.S. Secretary of Defense, James Forrestal, as related previously, was a great friend of the aforementioned U.S. Admiral Richard E. Byrd and John F. Kennedy. In 1944 when, as Secretary of the Navy, he had proposed the racial integration of the US Navy, his fellow-pillars of American society suspected he had gone crazy and then later, as the nation's first 'Defense Secretary,' after the War Department was renamed, he confirmed everyone's worst fears by pressing for full racial integration of the armed forces, which must have made the Rockefellers, the Mellons, the Harrimans, the du Ponts, the Bushes and all the other cabal families very nervous indeed.

Forrestal was also in conflict with other members of the Truman regime over military budgets and was the most outspoken opponent of the creation of the state of Israel, a position which sharply conflicted with ruling cabal plans for domination of the oilfields of the Middle East using Israel as a military proxy in the region. After Operation Highjump, Forrestal debriefed Admiral Byrd in a series of meetings and subsequently became convinced that he was being followed and that his phone was tapped. As it turned out he was absolutely correct.

Then on 28th March 1949, Forrestal was forced out of office and flown to Florida where he was detained at Jupiter Island, a high-security enclave of the cabal families and where the fanatical terror-bombing advocate Robert Lovett and an army psychiatrist attended to him. He was then flown back to Washington D.C., locked in Bethesda Naval Hospital, Maryland and given insulin shock treatments for alleged 'mental exhaustion.' Forrestal told his wife that he did not expect to leave Bethesda alive and all requests to see his brother, one particular friend, Admiral Byrd and two priests were denied. Indeed, one priest attempted to visit him on seven separate occasions and was turned away each time. The naval authorities admitted only selected government officials, Forrestal's estranged wife and their son.

After threatening a lawsuit, Henry Forrestal was finally permitted to see his brother who had gained twelve pounds since his admission to Bethesda. He reported that James was *"acting and talking as sanely and intelligently as any man I've ever known"* and made arrangements to remove his brother from the hospital on 22nd May. However, a few hours before his brother was due to take him home, James Forrestal's body was found with his dressing gown cord tied tightly around his neck, after he had apparently 'jumped' from a sixteenth-story kitchen window.

Why a 'patient' who was said to be suicidal would be placed on the sixteenth floor of a hospital with unsecured windows and be allowed to retain so classic a suicide aid as the cord of his dressing gown are mysteries which will doubtless remain forever unsolved. A hint, however, came from Forrestal's doctor, who said that he was ordered by *"the people downtown"* to house Forrestal on the sixteenth floor, whereas he had wanted to place his patient on the ground floor of a nearby annex. Forrestal apparently left a 'suicide note' which was later discovered **not** to be in his own handwriting at all.

To add to the intrigue, Forrestal had an interesting new companion on the night of his death, a naval man named Robert Wayne Harrison, Jr. He had replaced Forrestal's usual guard, who had rather conveniently gone AWOL for the day. Harrison later claimed that Forrestal had sent him out on a 'brief errand' and that during this time he had killed himself.

The chief psychiatrist at Bethesda immediately labelled the death a suicide and the Montgomery County coroner rushed to concur before any proper investigation had been conducted. Since the death occurred on U.S. Navy premises, no police investigation was ever undertaken. An official Navy Review Board completed hearings on Forrestal's death on 31st May but waited until the 'dust had settled' and on 12th October released a heavily censored summary consisting of only a few lines. The version of events promulgated by the mass media was, in a nutshell, that he went insane and killed himself. All very convenient of course.

In 1966, '*The Death of James Forrestal*' by Cornell Simpson was published, raising serious questions about the alleged 'suicide.' Inevitably and true to form, the book was almost totally ignored by the mainstream media. But in 2004, after a long battle with the *National Naval Medical Center* under the Freedom of Information Act, a researcher finally obtained a copy of the long-suppressed report of the Navy Review Board. The report did not even conclude that Forrestal committed suicide, merely that he died from falling sixteen storeys, which again is unsurprising. Neither did it mention the much-reported suicide note.

What the report **did** say however, was that an eyewitness saw broken glass on the bedding in Forrestal's room. Since he allegedly jumped out of the kitchen window, that testimony flatly contradicts the suicide theory. The report also contained statements from Forrestal's doctors that, contrary to the rumours which were widespread at the time, he had never previously attempted suicide.

Earlier in his career, Forrestal had been a 'team-player,' explicitly following orders and by way of (very) small compensation, had an aircraft carrier named after him and an unusual inscription on his tombstone which reads in effect that he died, *"In the great cause of good government."* These people do like to have their little in-jokes.

Of course, it goes almost without saying that the media vilified Forrestal for opposing the creation of Israel and Truman's pro-Red, foreign policy and the venom continues to this day by characterising him, as is their custom, as a 'conspiracy theorist' and a 'nut.'

Chapter 27

Matthew Francis Forrestal (a.k.a. Mateo Francisco Forestello) – b. 1982, Cork, Ireland

Mateo was the illegitimate son of Peter Ogden Forrestal, one of the sons of James Forrestal, the assassinated, former U.S. Secretary of Defense. He was born as a result of a brief sexual liaison between his father and their feisty, teenage Irish housekeeper Shannon O'Driscoll who, in a fit of defiance and anger, insisted on giving baby Matthew his father's surname after Forrestal's categoric refusal to recognise him as his son—or indeed to admit any involvement whatsoever with Shannon.

Born in Manhattan in 1930, Peter had attended Princeton University and eventually emigrated to Ireland from the U.S. in the late 1960s. He had been employed firstly by *Dillon Read* and then moved on to *F. Ederstadt and Company* and later to *Train and Cabot*, an investment firm. His last job was with *Bankers Trust* in London but he nevertheless retained his home in Ireland where he bred horses. He died alone at his home in Cork in 1983 from what was officially recorded as a massive abdominal haemorrhage caused by years of heavy drinking. Peter was just fifty-two years old at the time of his death and is buried in 'Section 30' of Arlington National Cemetery along with his father, mother and brother Michael.

Twelve months before this and almost simultaneously with his brief affair with Shannon, he had married a young woman from New Jersey, Katherine 'Kit' Callahan, who was pregnant with their child when he died. She later gave birth to a daughter, Matthew's half-sister, and as a friend later noted with sadness, *"Kit was a bride, a widow and a mother, all within the space of a single year."*

However, as a result of Peter's one-off encounter with Shannon and his point-blank refusal to acknowledge what she regarded as his responsibilities, she had gone out of her way to make life as difficult as possible for him and his new bride. She had placed notices in the local newspaper announcing him as the father of her child, had sent numerous letters to his wife, describing in graphic detail all the intimate intricacies of their one sexual escapade, had thrown a half-brick through their window and even accosted them both in the street several times, whilst making threats of violence, including death to both he and the totally innocent Katherine.

It was as a result of these actions after Peter Forrestal's premature, sudden death, that suspicion fell upon Shannon and her new boyfriend in that small, tight-knit community in which even the wildest of rumours could suddenly transpose itself into solid facts in the minds of the local residents. Eventually, even though Shannon was totally innocent of any physical harm to Forrestal as the subsequent inquest had publicly confirmed, the pressure on her was becoming intolerable. One of her neighbours had even screamed 'murderer' right in her face and later had daubed the word in bright red paint on her front door and window.

Then a few weeks after the sudden death of Forrestal, when the witch hunt against her had reached its zenith and was becoming unbearable, she spotted an ad in a magazine whereby an Irish family living in Argentina, were seeking a nanny for their new-born, due to both parents wishing to continue their careers. She applied for the position and, after a two hour telephone interview, was offered the job. Within a week, she, young Matthew and her very forgiving boyfriend, Liam were on the plane from Dublin to Buenos Aires, via London Heathrow.

Matthew, soon to be known by the Spanish version of his name, Mateo, grew up in the city of Viedma, Argentina, around four hundred kilometres south of Buenos Aires and joined the Argentinian Airforce, *Fuerza Aerea Argentina*, as a trainee pilot at the age of eighteen, immediately following his graduation from high school.

Similarly to Dobbo and Adam he had been a precocious child but was also as full of life and as feisty and fiery as his mother. He knew what he wanted from life and wasn't afraid to pursue it wholeheartedly and grew-up with a sense of something not being 'right' with the world and would always question absolutely everything he was told. This earned him the unwelcome reputation of being a contrary, awkward character, simply for not accepting societal norms without question. He was also regarded by his contemporaries during his air force training days as being a 'crazy, tinfoil-hat-wearing conspiracy theorist,' after forcefully declaring to anyone who would listen, that '9/11 was an inside job' and that 'the moon landings were faked!'

In 1986 Shannon and Liam parted ways and Liam returned to his homeland shortly before Mateo's fourth birthday, leaving Shannon as Mateo's sole parent for the rest of his childhood and until Shannon contracted pancreatic cancer during Mateo's first year of training with the *Fuerza Aerea Argentina* and sadly passed-away within two months of her initial diagnosis. Mateo received the devastating news of her death as he was travelling home on compassionate leave from his base just outside Buenos Aires, in what turned out to be a futile attempt to be present at his mother's bedside before she died. She was just thirty-eight years old.

Growing-up without a father had proved a huge mystery to young Mateo. From the age of eight, he had insisted on knowing the background to the reasons why this was the case and for a long time Shannon had resisted telling him the full truth of his origins and spun him some fairytale about his father being stationed abroad in the armed forces. She believed that the child was not yet ready to hear that particular truth and so determined to put-off the fateful moment for as long as possible. But eventually she could not hide the facts from the increasingly insistent child and consequently, by the age of ten, he knew the full story behind his illegitimate birth. Totally unfazed by his unusual beginnings, he actually wore it as a badge of honour, such was his determination to be 'different' to his peers—even at that tender age.

Shannon had eventually told Mateo the whole truth—that his father had been a successful American businessman who had emigrated to Ireland and that his grandfather had been the U.S. Secretary of Defense for a period, shortly after the end of World War II. This fact piqued young Mateo's interest and excitement and by the age of fifteen he had become determined to discover as much about his famous grandfather as possible and it wasn't too long before he began to suspect that his grandfather and father's deaths may be linked in some as yet indeterminate way.

By the age of seventeen and whilst still at high school, he was spending every spare moment scouring the then fledgling internet, mostly on a very slow 'dial-up' connection, for all the information he could find about his grandfather. And this then led him down all kinds of other 'rabbit holes' to places that revealed the truth about world history, science and just about anything else he could name.

Eventually he began writing short articles himself and was thoroughly delighted when several 'truther' websites began accepting them for publication. Being fluent in both Spanish and English gave him two distinctly separate avenues to explore in that regard and it wasn't too long before he became something of a minor celebrity in the world of truth-seekers—particularly in the Spanish-speaking world where his research and writing services were very much in demand.

Here is one of his very early pieces written under his 'truther' pseudonym of Juan Gonzales and translated from the Spanish...

"I Used to Believe that...

We are all born equal
I was born FREE
My education gave me knowledge and wisdom
A college degree would bring life-long financial security
Our history books are accurate and true
We evolved from single-celled organisms
Fluoride would help stop my teeth from decaying
Vaccines would protect me from disease
Flowing electrons create electricity
The pyramids were tombs for Pharaohs
Ancient civilisations were primitive
Our tap water was safe to drink
All food on supermarket shelves is healthy
Science is the true source of all knowledge
Mathematical formulae can explain everything
Atoms are made of subatomic particles
Gravity is clearly defined and understood
Men landed on the moon
And they passed though the Van Allen Belts
Men returned to the moon several times
We landed a probe on Mars
The sun is a giant nuclear reactor
We have pictures of Earth from space
'Junk' DNA is just useless matter
Nothing can travel faster than the speed of light
Cancer cannot be cured
Drug companies develop cures for diseases
Mythology was just the imagination of people in ancient times
Alexander was 'Great' because he conquered the world
Adolf Hitler was evil because he wanted to conquer the world
Hitler started World War II and Churchill was a saint
We are the most scientifically advanced civilisation
We are at the pinnacle of knowledge
Humans are the most advanced species
Stonehenge was built by men in animal skins
Our calendar is accurate and we live in a year called 2004
Our governments are our servants
Our governments are doing the best they can for us
Armed forces are necessary for our protection
JFK was shot by Lee Harvey Oswald
William Shakespeare wrote all those great stories

Central banks are controlled and owned by governments
Economics is very complicated and only economists truly understand it
Our money supply is connected to our gold reserves
Two large jets flew into the twin towers
9/11 was planned by Osama bin Laden in a cave in Afghanistan
Saddam Hussein was hiding weapons of mass destruction
Hendrik Verwoerd was killed because of apartheid
Muammar Gaddafi was an evil, dangerous dictator
Royalty has some divine right to conquer and own the world
Nelson Mandela and the ANC freed the people of South Africa
Industrial development was the driving force behind our human progress
Rockets can travel in space
'Chemtrails' are just persistent vapour trails
The Earth is an oblate spheroid hanging in space and orbiting the sun
There is molten iron at the core of the Earth
This molten iron gives our Earth its magnetic properties
Magnetism is well understood
Banks are respectable, ethical institutions
People need jobs to survive
Human nature is to be greedy, violent and to wage war
All human misery is a consequence of our dark human nature
Columbus discovered America
The Big Bang 'theory' accurately describes the origins of the universe
Humanity evolved from pond slime
The Earth moves through space in several directions simultaneously
Every photo published by NASA is real
The Earth spins at fifteen hundred kilometres per hour at the equator
The Earth is a globe twenty-four thousand kilometres in circumference
Nuclear weapons are real and a great danger to us all
And dinosaurs roamed the Earth millions of years ago...

But today I am not so certain about any of this, anymore. What I do know though is that we have been manipulated and lied-to for so long that it has become almost impossible to separate the lies from the truth. I do however realise that the deeper I dig, the bigger the lies become and the deeper the rabbit holes are, within which the lies are concealed.

I also know now that our governments are not our friends or our servants and that they serve invisible masters unknown to most people and are covering-up certain secrets and knowledge that, if exposed, would cause them to lose control over the people of the world.

I suspect that it is this secret, which remains aggressively guarded by our draconian dictators, that holds the key to our infinite potential as humanity to create anything we choose to.

And also that we are the creators of our own reality and that this potential and ability has been hidden from us through lies, propaganda and manipulation for thousands of years.

We are undoubtedly ruled-over by billionaire psychopaths who use their puppet politicians as a front to cover their insidious actions and to create a false reality that most people believe is real.

Juan Gonzalez, 2004" (Mateo's pen name)

Then in 2006, he stumbled across an article on an English language website which was the result of an investigation by an American researcher who had uncovered the truth about his grandfather, James Forrestal's untimely death and which in equal measure shocked and fascinated him. Following this, he made several attempts over the course of many months to contact some of his distant relatives, Forrestal's descendants, without much success it has to be said. But then one morning in September 2009 when he had all but given up hope of ever hearing from his wider family, he received a very cryptic handwritten note in the mail.

Chapter 28

Saturday 18th February 2023 – To the Pole and Beyond

Adam, happy at last to be rid of his reluctant pursuer, relaxed back into his seat and continued his lonely venture southward. Intent on conserving his own fuel supply, he slowed Esmerelda down to subsonic speed and descended to twenty-thousand feet as he crossed the ice wall for the second time that day. Visibility was still excellent with barely any cloud cover and the sun, low in the sky behind him and slightly to the northwest, illuminated the ice below and to the far southerly horizon with a brilliant and dazzling purple-tinted, white light. Adam marvelled at the almost featureless and uniform frozen plain that stretched dead-level as far as he could see—in all directions. Surely, on such a uniformly flat surface, you would be able to see the curvature of the earth from this altitude, he pondered and would you not expect the land to fall away on all sides rather than rising to eye level? He thought back to that last, fateful intercept mission and his conversation with Forestello, notably the point that pilots never need to drop their aircraft's nose as they hurtle along at high speed. It was something he'd never had to consider throughout his entire flying career yet, when you considered the earth's curvature calculation formula, it would have made so much sense to do so.[6] He mulled this over intently as he cruised onward and southward above the barren, Antarctic wasteland, maintaining level flight throughout without having to make even one single altitude correction in order to maintain it.

As Esmerelda pressed her way on beyond 83° south, Adam noticed the appearance of the uniform, frosted terrain gradually changing. Hills and craggy areas began to appear though the ice, with the once dead-flat surface becoming increasingly dotted with undulations, ridges and isolated 'islands' of bare grey rock. Very soon the featureless, unbroken white plain had given-way completely to this new landscape.

The antique jet fighter and her intrepid pilot had just traversed the eighty-fourth parallel when, in and amongst this new landscape, Adam spotted a raised icy plateau, a few square miles in area upon which stood a trio of smooth, white, symmetrical four-sided peaks, one much larger than the others with the smaller pair appearing almost identical in size. He slowed the

---

[6] The simplest formula for calculating Earth's curvature is to square the number of miles and multiply the result by eight inches. Therefore, every one hundred miles, the earth should drop away by 6,666 feet!

F-5 and commenced a wide, spiralling descent over them. As they came closer and closer into view, he gasped in amazement at what lay beneath him. He levelled-off and slowly circled the three pinnacles. Completely covered in dazzlingly bright, marble-like ice, there was absolutely no question that they were man-made pyramids. Now at an altitude of just one thousand feet, he could clearly see that each corner was set at a precise right-angle, all four sides were the same length, the ridges plumb-line straight with the sharp pointed summit-peaks appearing almost diamond-cut.

"Don't tell me the bloody Egyptians or the Aztecs have ventured to these parts at some point?" he told some mysterious, invisible travelling companion and then, immediately realising the genuine possibility that nobody would ever be around again to tell him anything, he laughed out loud and, ridiculous though it seemed, took on the role of none other than Dobbo. *"Of course they've been down here Adam mate. In a few minutes you'll spot the Antarctic equivalent of the fucking Sphinx!"* he retorted in as rough-edged a Yorkshire accent as he could muster.

He stealthily circled the enormous icy pyramids for a full fifteen minutes, in wonderment, not only at the sheer enormity of the structures (the largest must have been four kilometres square at least) but also the precision with which they had been constructed and positioned. After making his lowest and slowest sweep of the site yet, to enable Esmerelda's cameras to capture as much detail as possible, he headed south once more, ascending to five thousand feet and accelerating to around five hundred mph.

At 85° south he was forced to increase altitude as the land rose-up rapidly beneath him, giving way to an enormous mountain range running east to west, with majestic peaks exceeding twenty thousand feet, mighty glaciers in almost every valley and the occasional smoking volcano thrown in for good measure. This seemingly impenetrable massif continued unbroken for over two hundred and fifty miles of latitude before dropping down again to another almost dead-flat ice-plain. This plain however, unlike the original one beyond the ice wall, lay at over ten thousand feet above sea level so Adam maintained an altitude some five thousand feet above it as, with heightening nervousness and trepidation, he reached the cusp of that mystical 90° south, the precise location of the legendary South Pole.

At 89.8° south, he slowed the F-5 right down to two hundred mph, as close as he dared to stall speed and fixed his gaze on the compass and his latitude location display, bracing himself for that magical moment when his compass would swing around 180° and the number on the latitude display start to decrease as he passed under the nadir of the globe to resume a northerly course. However, to his total bewilderment, the latitude display did not decrease—it continued to increase instead—to 90.1° with the compass needle staying exactly where it had been throughout the entire flight, the grey, southerly-pointing half continuing to point straight ahead and the red portion indicating that north was still behind him.

"Bloody hell!" exclaimed the bewildered yet now excited and energised airman. *"I'm still heading south. I should be travelling northwards now—surely."*

He was indeed still proceeding south; 91°, 92° and then 93° with no change whatsoever in the compass needle. He maintained the F-5's low speed, not only so he could easily monitor the compass and his latitude but also because he was becoming increasingly anxious about his fuel supply. He had just about enough to get back to civilisation if he turned around pretty soon but unwavering curiosity drove him onward and southward. Despite the grave risks involved, something deep within his soul urged him onwards and there was now no way in this godforsaken world that this intrepid explorer was ever going to turn back.

He had been paying very little attention to what had lain ahead or beneath him during the flight's last three or four degrees. He had been totally and utterly preoccupied with his location readings and had not noticed that the frozen wastes had begun to give way to ice-free oases of ground covered in sparse vegetation interspersed with lakes, rivers and streams. And by the time Adam had returned to scanning the view from the cockpit again, the ice had all but disappeared, replaced by a landscape more akin to Iceland or southern Alaska. He could even make-out what he thought were small trees and so decided to drop Esmerelda down to just a few hundred feet above the surface to take an even closer look.

As he reduced his altitude, the light faded considerably, the pale, weak sun behind him had dropped closer to the northern horizon without quite disappearing completely. He ascended a few hundred feet and in the improved light the extra altitude afforded him, scanned the terrain below him. *"Could this be the ice-free area that Byrd mentioned in his diary?"* he asked himself aloud. Well, it certainly looked very much like it and Adam felt privileged to be possibly following in that great adventurer's 'footsteps,' potentially one of the very first since Operation Highjump itself, he assumed.

He circled around, surveying the virtually ice-free area, overcome with wonder and the sheer enormity of what he was witnessing when something caught his eye, maybe twenty or thirty miles to the distant southwest. *"No,"* he yelled in utter disbelief. *"Never—it can't be—surely?!"* A straight line of bright red lights lit-up the ground, shining clear and bright against the dark terrain surrounding it. Adam steered Esmerelda towards the lights, reducing altitude as he approached and as he drew closer there was absolutely no mistaking what they were illuminating. On a narrow strip of land between two huge lakes lay a landing strip, fully-lit and long enough upon which to land a large airliner. He overflew it at one hundred feet inspecting the surface as best he could in the ever-encroaching twilight. The runway's surface looked perfectly serviceable, there were no obstructions that he could see and towards its far southeastern end stood a cluster of buildings around a small apron area, empty of aircraft. No lights radiated from the buildings, there were no vehicles parked nearby and it appeared very much as if the whole 'airport' although well-lit, was completely deserted.

After overflying a second time to check again for any possible obstructions, Adam turned Esmerelda around and brought her gently down on to the strip from its eastern end. The surface was excellent, better than excellent in fact, with no debris or hazards whatsoever. As he turned off the main runway, trundling along the slipway toward the apron, much to his surprise, the F-5's headlights illuminated what appeared to be two large fuel tanks at the opposite end of the apron to the buildings.

"Surely not!" he muttered in disbelief. *"Fuel—here? Bloody hell, whatever next?"*

As he reached the end of the slipway, the apron ahead of him automatically lit-up, displaying an illuminated message in blue across the surface of the concrete. 'A WARM WELCOME TO PORTA MUNDORUM III,' it read in both English and Spanish. *"Porta Mundorum?"* he breathed. *"What in God's name does that mean?"*[7]

He brought Esmerelda to a halt alongside the largest of the outbuildings, powered-down her engines, unbuckled his seat belt and raised the canopy. He then checked the compass before disembarking and gasped; the needle was now trembling, caught between an attempt to switch from its original north to a new one. Struggling to come-up with an explanation, he eventually decided that he must now be at or around the true South Pole, that the latitude indicator must have malfunctioned and any further onward progress would complete the process and swing the needle through the required, expected 180°. But for now, that would have to wait.

[7] Latin for 'Gateway to the World.'

He retrieved the provisions bag from behind his seat and clambered out of the cockpit, grateful for the reassurance of terra firma beneath his feet again and more than happy to give his backside and legs some relief from the cramped conditions to which he'd subjected them these last few hours. He placed the bag on the apron beside him, removed his helmet and then performed a slow, deliberate 360° turn to take in his surroundings, breathing-in the fresh, clean Antarctic air and stretching his legs as he did so. The first thing that struck him as he unzipped his flight suit was how much warmer it was here than back at base, he reckoned around 10°c as opposed to near freezing, something he really had not expected. Then, as he looked around him, a most bizarre phenomenon caught his eye. In addition to the familiar crepuscular glow to the northwest as the sun began to fall in the sky, there was also a very similar type of light emanating from the southwest—as if two twilights were taking place simultaneously. He focused his gaze towards the new light and realising it was in fact steadily increasing, stood transfixed for several minutes, perplexed by what could possibly be causing this 'false dawn' or whatever the hell it was. *"Could it perhaps be a city, or maybe the Aurora Australis, the southern equivalent of the Northern Lights?"* he pondered to himself.

Then, to his utter amazement, he spotted what looked exactly like our normal, standard sun rising from below the southwestern skyline, starting as a slender orange curved slither and steadily growing to a small dome as more of the orb became visible above the horizon. He turned around to the northwest where the northern sun, our sun, the sun he had been reliant upon all his life, was remarkably still visible, a shimmering quadrant steadily sinking below the horizon.

"Two bloody suns? No, it can't be, surely? This is so fucked-up," he muttered, grabbing his provisions sack from the concrete and marching toward the largest of the outbuildings, which by now were each casting two shadows, a weakening one to the southeast and another, gradually strengthening, to the northeast. *"So as our sun sets, another one rises, but the opposite way around!"* he added, shaking his head in utter bewilderment. He studied the structure as he strolled cautiously and with great curiosity across the immaculately concreted apron. Single-storey and built from smooth sandy-coloured stone with a leaded roof, it had a far larger than normal entranceway and its tall, arched windows reached several more feet above that. At each of the building's four corners stood a tall steeple at least double the height of the building, clad in what appeared to be copper, with intricately carved ball and point finials atop each one.[8] He arrived at the door of the

[8] A decorative element, employed to emphasize the apex of a spire, tower or dome.

building, which was six-panelled, manufactured from what looked like solid oak, sumptuously and flawlessly varnished and around nine feet in height. "*Now that is a big door,*" he mused as he grabbed the substantial, brass handle, fully expecting it to be locked.

Chapter 29

Sunday 12th February 2023 - Jorge's Intervention

Adam was woken from his fitful slumber at around 10.00am by a gentle tapping on the door. He blinked his eyes open and could make out a tall figure in the doorway, silhouetted by the light from the corridor behind. As he came to his senses, instantly recalling the events of the previous twenty-four hours, the weight of the world descended upon him in an instant. His heart began to pound again, once more missing beats in the process and the imaginary vice that held his head, tightened unbearably. He rolled over and groaned, clutching his knees to his chest once more and began to hyperventilate, unable to control his breathing. His life was over as far as he was concerned and he just wanted to die.

Jorge closed the door behind him, sat down on the bed beside Adam and took the younger man's hand in his. He stroked it gently and sang to him in a strange language unknown to Adam. The words were calming, the tune soothing and after a couple of verses, Adam's erratic breathing began to settle down, his body relaxed and his heart rate slowed to something approaching normal. Jorge continued the song for another two or three minutes then fell silent. He rolled Adam on to his back, laid a pillow under his head and turned on the bedside lamp.

"Señor Haylock, it is I, Jorge," he whispered. *"I have come to tell you what really happened on your last mission. It may come as a surprise but you did not commit the heinous crime that you think you did. You shot no plane out of the sky, well not a real one anyway, and you have killed no innocent civilians. Please believe me Adam, I am telling you the truth. You are neither a murderer nor a war criminal and everyone on board that plane is safe and well. They have continued their journey south and will come to no harm I am sure."*

Adam lay there, staring wide-eyed at the ceiling in an attempt to digest this revelation then lifted himself up, placed the pillows upright against the bedhead and leant back against them, switching his focus on to Jorge. *"But, but I watched the missile hit the target. I saw the explosion, the debris, everything,"* he insisted.

Jorge smiled reassuringly. *"What you hit with your missile, my friend was a drone, an unmanned holographic drone which you were convinced was the Gulfstream. My people try to launch one of these drones whenever we detect a truth-seeking flight about to cross the 60th southern parallel and most of the time we manage to fool the interceptors. But not on every occasion, unfortunately. If, for example, the incursive is out of drone range or we have insufficient time to reach them, then the outcome can be very distressing indeed. Unfortunately, at this current time, we have no such technology for those who venture in boats so there is nothing we can do to help them.*

Adam shook his head, wanting desperately to believe this version of events yet barely able to do so. *"So, does that mean everyone aboard The Antarctic Truth perished? I found out about that escapade from some folks in a bar when I was on my post-training R&R in Chile."*

Jorge nodded in grim affirmation but said nothing. Adam continued. *"Well, if what you're telling me is the truth, where was the real Gulfstream then?"* he pleaded. *"The one containing Forestello and his companions."*

"They were very close but the technology in our drone rendered them invisible to both the naked eye and radar," explained the flight engineer. *"Just like you, they had no knowledge of the decoy and will have been amazed and baffled by the explosion and your subsequent return to base."*

"So, where are they now?" asked Adam.

"That is for you to discover for yourself, señor," Jorge replied sternly. *"All you need to do for the moment is to rid yourself of all this guilt and self-loathing. You have nothing to hate yourself for, let me reassure you of that, so spend the rest of today coming to terms with what really happened and hopefully restore yourself to something like the man you were before all this happened."*

Adam's expression lightened, his shoulders relaxed and he felt, throughout his entire being, the first traces of release from his torment. He exhaled slowly, a long, satisfying, liberating breath, the vice-like grip on his temples loosened and then fell away completely and tears of joy and relief welled-up in his eyes. *"Thank you, Jorge,"* he said, his voice quivering with emotion. *"You have literally saved my life."*

"I am glad," said Jorge, standing and moving toward the door. *"But I am leaving now and wish you a full and speedy return to normal yet I must insist on one thing, you must say nothing of our conversation to anyone. Señor Prendergast knows I have been to visit you; in fact it was he who asked me to do so but he must not be told the truth of what happened. Just tell him and señor Dobson that you are feeling better after my intervention and that I have given you techniques to help you deal with the situation you have found yourself*

in. No talk of the drone whatsoever, that is vitally important. Can you give me your word on that, señor Haylock?"

"I swear I will reveal nothing of what you have just told me, Jorge," Adam assured him.

"Thank you, my friend," the Chilean replied as he left the room, closing the door behind him.

Chapter 30

Monday 23rd June 2008 – Mateo's Letter

Mateo Forestello received a letter that said simply…

'Mateo, please call me on 212-339-4001 anytime between 7 and 9pm EST. I am your uncle.

Regards,
David.'

Mateo was incredulous yet nevertheless elated and could not wait for the clock to tick around to 9.00pm that evening, Argentina being two hours ahead of the eastern seaboard of the U.S.

He let the clock run-on until 9.20pm so as not to appear too eager and then with slightly trembling hands he dialled the number in the message. It was a landline and after a few seconds due to the international delay, he heard the familiar, single, long flat note of the American ringtone signalling that a connection had been made. The ringtone sounded intermittently for around twenty seconds and then the sound of a breathless, American-accented voice was heard.

"Hello," it said, whilst immediately pausing to catch its breath. *"Is that Mateo?"*

"Yes, is that David?" he replied expectantly. Mateo's accent when speaking English was a pleasing-to-the-ear hybrid of Spanish tinged with a very slight Irish brogue.

"It certainly is. Thank you so much for contacting me so promptly." David seemed very friendly and equally delighted to hear from him, but then said...

"Please excuse me Mateo but I need to end this call right now—but if you give me your number, I will call you back within the next two minutes." Mateo complied and David enigmatically, immediately replaced the receiver in its cradle without a further word.

Mateo was puzzled and mildly irritated. *"What on Earth is going on here?"* he thought to himself. He did not have long to wait though before he heard his own phone ring and immediately answered it, concerned that he may miss the call.

"Mateo, it's David again. I am so sorry for all the intrigue but sadly I cannot be too careful. My calls are monitored I'm afraid," he informed him wearily.

"But won't they have my number now too? I just gave it to you on a monitored line." Mateo was concerned now.

"No, don't worry Mateo, it's just fine. The way the CIA's monitoring system works, is that it listens for pre-programmed keywords and phrases and the recording only starts when one of those trigger words are spoken. That way they don't waste hours of their time listening to me speaking to my kids about meeting-up for dinner next week!" He laughed loudly at the thought.

"James Forrestal, Michael Forrestal and Peter Forrestal are definitely trigger phrases, so it just isn't safe to speak on my landline, so here I am on my burner cell phone!" he said with undisguised satisfaction.

"So why didn't you just give me your cell phone number?" Mateo was becoming suspicious again now. However his growing fears were soon allayed.

"It's simple really Mateo, if my note had been intercepted, which it may well have been—they monitor my incoming and outgoing mail—then they would also now have my private cell phone number too." It made perfect sense of course, and Mateo involuntarily shook his head as he thought to himself, *'the hoops one has to jump through to escape the all-pervasive clutches of the security services!'*

David continued... *"As I said in my note, I am your uncle by blood and my full name is David Pearson. Like you I am illegitimate, the son of James, your grandfather and the half-brother of your father, Peter—and obviously Michael, but much younger than both. My father and my mother had a very brief but passionate affair shortly before his kidnapping and death, so of course I never knew him. Michael had no children but around ten years ago I finally managed to contact your half-sister Francesca and she eventually told me about you, having been told the story of your conception by her mother, Kit—and then of course Kit received your letter a few months ago and she finally got around to telling me about it. All I knew until then was that your mother Shannon was extremely angry with Peter for refusing to acknowledge you as his son, then gave you the surname Forrestal and ended up emigrating to Argentina with you as a very young child. Then—nothing at all! But of course I have spent the last several years looking for Matthew Forrestal and not Mateo Forestello!"* he chuckled.

A little shocked by this revelation, Mateo could only blurt out, *"I have a sister?!"*

"Yes Mateo, she is a year or so younger than you and was born shortly after Peter's wholly unexpected AND very suspicious death." David explained. *"Your father and Katherine—Kit, married literally a few weeks after your birth. She still lives in Ireland as you know, as does your sister Francesca."*

Mateo was still trying desperately to absorb all this new information and lots of questions were running around in his head—too many to articulate coherently but fortunately David came to his rescue.

"I am sure this is an awful lot for you to take in right now," he said sympathetically, *"but let me explain a little more..."* Mateo nodded dumbly to himself, deep in thought and not fully comprehending that David couldn't see the gesture. After briefly waiting for some kind of response that was never forthcoming, his uncle continued on...

"So, I'm sure you were wondering why my phone calls and mail are monitored by the security services? Well let me tell you, I am a total pain in their rear ends," he laughed. *"I have been campaigning for many years for the truth about my father's death to be acknowledged, but all I get is stonewalled at every turn,"* he lamented. *"But I am nothing if not persistent and I won't give up until I'm six feet under, I can promise you that!"* His determination was apparent.

"I am in touch occasionally with Katherine and Francesca Forrestal, but they are our only living family, apart from my children and grandchildren—as far as I can make out, anyway," he continued. *"Now, as you are aware, James was murdered by the cabal, the so-called 'deep state,' not only because of his views but also because of his extreme persistence in trying to bring the truth to the world, as he knew it. Because of his privileged position in society, he had become aware of many inconvenient truths—so much of what we believe to be real is so very far from it, as I'm sure you know. What you may not know though is that he was not alone. He had several other friends 'in high places' who held similar views—people such as the U.S. General Smedley Butler, who wrote extensively against the ruling cabal including a famous book called 'War is a Racket.' Well, General Butler was murdered by the deep state in 1940 for his pains but of course that has also been successfully covered-up—as the cabal always does.*

You may also be surprised to know that he was very good friends with no less a personage than John Fitzgerald Kennedy—JFK, but well before he ever became president of course. Again, they shared similar views and an obsession with bringing the truth out into the public domain. And sad to say, again, JFK was murdered because of his unacceptable views and because he naively perhaps, but nevertheless with good intentions, tried his best to 'clean-up' the corrupt cesspool that is American politics.

He also had a very close friend in Admiral Richard E. Byrd, who again was of a similar mindset and as a result met a similar fate to the others, after a perhaps unwise admission live on TV, back in 1954. In that interview he told of 'Operation Highjump,' his famous expedition to the Antarctic in the 1940s and foolishly, as it turned out, admitted to the entire world in his diary that Antarctica is not as it is portrayed to be and that far from being the 'underside of the globe' as we are constantly told, that there is in fact another realm beyond the ice wall and the thousand mile-wide ice zone, inhabited by other races—whom he actually met! It is for this very reason that the Antarctic Treaty of 1959 had to be formulated and now the sixty degrees south exclusion zone is stringently policed by United Nations forces and anyone who strays beyond that is firstly warned and if they don't turn around they are ruthlessly dealt with. I have heard several reliable stories of ships and planes that stray into the zone and ignore the warnings, being destroyed."

Mateo was surprised by David's revelations. But not shocked. He already knew that most of what we believe to be the truth, is in fact lies designed to distract us from the prevailing agenda. David continued...

"I have not so far been able to determine why the deep state doesn't want us to know about the other civilisations that exist beyond the ice zone but I suspect it has something more to do with the shape and size of the Earth. Some people believe that it's not a globe at all, but a kind of endless, slightly domed yet basically flat plane and there is a lot of evidence to suggest that this may well be true but as I say, I haven't been able to confirm or deny this just yet. And of course the enforced exclusion zone performs the useful role of preventing anyone from investigating properly. Consequently, if it is true that the Earth is not a globe, then this throws into doubt all the received knowledge about the existing model of the universe—at least in the form that 'they' tell us! And..." he added as an afterthought, *"...James Forrestal also had knowledge of the fact that the members of Scott's Antarctic expedition in 1912 were all assassinated on their return because of what they discovered down there."*

"That is all extremely interesting David, thank you for the information," Mateo replied. *"It's quite a lot for me to take-in in one bite and it may be a little while*

before it all sinks in, but let's keep in touch with each other and I will get back to you very soon when I have absorbed it all. Maybe we can work together to pursue this further—after all I believe that 'two heads are better than one,' as the saying goes, does it not?"

He then continued, thinking out loud as it were. *"I am not sure if you are aware, but I am with the Argentinian Air Force and maybe we can use this to our advantage? I am only a lowly pilot officer at the moment but I do have ambitions way beyond this and will try to make subtle enquiries to find out if any of my colleagues have any inside information on Antarctica. I do know that occasionally some of we pilots are seconded to the United Nations for secret duties of some kind—so as I say I will do some digging and get back to you very soon."* Mateo could barely contain his excitement at the thought of what secrets he may uncover.

"Yes Mateo, I would appreciate that. It has been a pleasure to talk to you—nephew, and I hope to hear from you again very soon."

And with that he clicked the 'off' button on his mobile phone to end the call.

Chapter 31

Saturday 18th February 2023 – Dobbo's Return to Teniente Rodolfo

Dobbo slowed Celeste down to under two hundred mph. He was in no hurry to get back to base and face the wrath of Prendergast—no hurry whatsoever. The initial euphoria over Adam's deception had dissipated as the prospect of the end of his flying career loomed large. What manner of punishment would be meted out on him for his insubordination? Would he be able to talk his way out of this mess as he had always managed to do previously during his time in the RAF? But at least the one person in his life who meant something to him and had once risked everything to cover his back when it was most important, was still alive. And not only alive but free too, heading to a new land, *Extrema,* and maybe a totally new life as well. As the distance between he and Prendergast narrowed, he wished to high heaven to be alongside his best-ever buddy, rather than having to face his superior and whatever may lay in store for him.

The knot which had already formed in his stomach tightened even more as the runway of Teniente Rodolfo came into view. He felt hot with anxiety and could feel the stickiness of his palms against the column as he guided Celeste down on to the runway and then on toward the apron where he could see the three members of his reception committee waiting in front of the hangar. Eduardo left the trio and waved the marshalling wands to guide him to the parking area whilst Jorge and Prendergast stood motionless, eyes fixed on the F-5 as Dobbo brought her to a halt beside them. As he raised the canopy, Dobbo glanced across at the Wing Commander who scowled murderously back at him, anger bordering on hatred etched on his pudgy face. 'This is not going to be pleasant,' Dobbo thought as he disembarked from Celeste, worried that this could well be his last ever fighter flight. When he finally reached Prendergast he removed his helmet, placed it on the ground and, now totally lost as to what to do, saluted awkwardly.

"Flight Lieutenant—my office—NOW," bellowed his irate superior. *"You retarded shit-brained moron," he* continued, cuffing Dobbo three times cross the back of the head as the disgraced pilot stooped to pick up the helmet, the ferocity of the blows causing him to stumble forward on to the tarmac.

"Mike, what the hell are you doing?" Dobbo shrieked in shock and pain as his knees banged into the hard ground.

Prendergast was unrelenting. *"Never mind what am I doing, what the bloody hell have you just done, Dobson? You disobeyed my clear and direct orders on several occasions and look what has happened. This is not going to reflect well on me you know but for you, young man, it's curtains! Now let's get to my office and start the ball rolling, shall we?"*

He grabbed the by-now crestfallen Dobbo by the scruff of his flight suit and virtually dragged him the one hundred yards or so to the office, kicking the door open with real venom and throwing his subordinate on to the chair furthest from the door. He slammed it shut behind him, locked it and placed the key into his breast pocket as he took his own seat at the opposite side of the desk.

For several minutes the two men sat there in stony silence, Dobbo hunched with head down and Prendergast leaning back with arms folded, eyeballing his young adversary. Eventually, the silence was broken by the wing commander who unfolded his arms, rolled up his sleeves and leaned forward, placing them on the table with a loud thump.

"So, flight lieutenant..." he began. *"You flagrantly disobeyed my orders and as a result have seriously jeopardised global security and international relations. By taking such action you are in direct contravention of section 34 of the 1955 Air Force Act which implicitly states..."*

He picked up the notes he had placed on the desk earlier, in readiness for the interview before continuing.

"'Any person subject to military law who, whether wilfully or through neglect, disobeys any command (by whatever means communicated to him) shall, on conviction by court-martial, be liable to imprisonment or any less punishment provided by this Act.' Therefore, I have no option but to put you before a court martial, pending which you shall be placed in isolation here under my supervision. I have already arranged for a colleague to be flown out from Port Stanley on the next available C-130 who will escort you back to Blighty, where you will face the full might of military law. I have also informed the U.N. of the urgent need to dispatch at least one replacement pilot to replace you two dick-brains before the whole world and his dog gets wind of this and flies out to discover the truth beyond the ice wall. That pilot, or pilots, depending on how many they decide to send, will be arriving the day after tomorrow so until then I shall be flying any intercept missions. I hadn't told you I could fly the F-5 as well, had I?"

He leant back once more, awaiting the response from the accused which, when it finally arrived, he had not anticipated.

"I think you will find that the wording says, 'lawful command' Mikey-boy," sneered Dobbo, summoning as much defiance as he could muster.

"Well, who's a clever little airman then?" Prendergast hissed, sarcastically. *"But pray, enlighten me, my most learned colleague, what does 'lawful' actually mean and who decides in this case which side of 'lawful' my orders actually fell? Tell me that, mister fucking know-it-all!"*

Dobbo raised himself in his chair, his confidence and authority increasing by the second. *"With all due respect, sir I would imagine that no right-minded court martial would ever view an order to kill a vastly experienced and highly valuable pilot purely for being curious as lawful, not to mention rule 154 of the Red Cross's humanitarian law database which implicitly states that 'every combatant has a duty to disobey a manifestly unlawful order' and 'that obeying a superior order is not a defence of a war crime.' Adam told me only last week to look this stuff up and do you know what, Mike, I did just that! Not like me that was it? I even surprised myself."*

The wing commander rose from his chair shaking his head, whether in resignation or pity was not clear to Dobbo.

"Because of what we're monitoring down here, EINSTEIN, normal definitions of 'LAWFUL' are pretty much null and void. All commanding officers on Antarctic operations are forced and sworn to comply with what is known as 'Code 33,' a sub-section of the U.N.'s 'Intra-terrestrial Protocols.' Only a very select few know anything of these protocols, in fact I have only been briefed on a small part but what that gives me pretty much, is immunity from any indemnity if I issue what you might deem 'an unlawful order.'"

He stood, turned and reached for the brown leather satchel which had been hanging on the back of the chair. He then returned to his seat, with the satchel in his lap and agitatedly rummaged inside.

"Lost something, sir?" Dobbo enquired, mirroring Prendergast's sarcasm.

"Don't think so, Dobson," Prendergast snarled. *"Ah, here it is,"* he said, removing his right hand slowly and deliberately from the bag.

Chapter 32

Monday 25th March 1912, Antarctica – The Motor Sledge

"Are we glad to see you?" Captain Scott enthused rhetorically as the sledge arrived at the otherwise deserted depot, several minutes later, after a tortuous eight and a half hour, ninety-mile journey from base camp through the ice and snow.

However his enthusiasm was short-lived, as puzzled, he failed to recognise the driver of the sledge and was rather disconcerted to say the least to suddenly notice that whoever this person was, in his right hand he was brandishing a standard military issue Webley Mk. V, identical to that of Scott's own, as he dismounted the now stationary and silent sledge.

But Scott was not kept in the dark too long though as the stranger abruptly and menacingly introduced himself to the trio. *"Brigadier Robert Arthur, His Majesty King George's Royal Marines,"* he announced whilst keeping the Webley firmly aimed at Scott. *"Do I have the pleasure of the company of Captain Scott and party?"* he asked formally.

"Yes you do," replied Scott. *"But may I ask why the need for the pistol aimed at me, sir?"* was Scott's not unreasonable retort in the circumstances.

Pointedly ignoring the question, Arthur steadfastly maintained his stance—pistol and all. *"I firstly need to ask if any of you are armed,"* he queried. *"And if so, I would like you to very slowly, reach into your pockets and place your weapons carefully on the ground in front of you... and by the way, no futile heroics please. This gun is loaded, the safety catch is off and if there are any false moves whatsoever, I WILL shoot Captain Scott between the eyes before any of you could react. I assure you I am a crack-shot and I will have no qualms whatsoever about doing exactly that. So please gentlemen, I would greatly appreciate your cooperation in this most serious matter."* Arthur was a cool customer for sure and the trio was not about to defy him.

Scott did venture to speak though, in his best diplomatic manner. *"I'm sorry sir, but we are a little puzzled by your actions. Would you kindly explain what this is all about, please?"*

"I'll ask all the questions Scott—if you don't mind? Please lay down your weapons NOW and then answer MY questions."

"Our solitary weapon is this Mark V Webley," Scott replied, slowly withdrawing his revolver, the barrel gripped precariously twixt thumb and index finger, in order not to incur the wrath of this very determined Marine Officer, whom Scott accurately calculated was very likely to blow his brains out at the slightest wrong move of any kind.

"Now throw it to the ground about six feet in front of you please," was Arthur's next demand which Scott reluctantly but sensibly, obeyed.

"Firstly, where are the other two members of the expedition?" he queried.

"Unfortunately they did not make it. Petty Officer Evans succumbed to the extreme weather conditions just over a month ago and Captain Oates sadly perished just last week."

"Very well," retorted Brigadier Arthur, wholly unsympathetically. *"Secondly, I need to know whether you actually made it to the 'the pole'—or not?"* He did not flinch and steadfastly maintained his pose, the gun at arm's length, aimed squarely at the forehead of Scott.

"Well, err yes and no, sir. You see, we believe we travelled beyond the pole and strangely continued travelling south, according to our compasses, to around 91° south in what had become a much more temperate climate." This time it was Bowers who answered the Brigadier's question.

"A much more temperate climate? Please elaborate," was the stark retort.

"Well, once we got beyond 89° south, the snow and ice began to disappear and the further south we travelled it actually began to get considerably warmer—we even saw evidence of human activity and although we never saw anyone else, there were plenty of human and other wildlife artefacts in the region. We would have continued onwards but feared running out of supplies and in fact we only just made it back to here—only to find the stores empty," related Bowers, breathlessly.

"And what may I ask, would you recommend we do about this situation?" queried Arthur as coolly as ever.

This time Scott answered. *"Sir, it's imperative that we get back to civilisation as soon as we can. This is a very important discovery and we need to organise another expedition to investigate this area as it could provide us with lots of information about this hitherto unknown region and what secrets it may hold.*

This discovery even casts doubt on the shape and size of the Earth as we know it and..."

"Stop right there Scott," bellowed the Marine, interrupting him in mid-sentence. *"I'm afraid I cannot allow you to return with this highly classified information and I'm equally sorry to say that neither can I allow any of you to live, having now discovered some of the truth about the true extent of the Earth. This information must be kept secret at all costs for the good of all humanity, so it is my unfortunate duty now to have to silence you all—forever. But before I carry out your death sentences I will allow you the great honour of briefly telling you the whole truth about what really lies beyond the Antarctic ice wall..."*

Chapter 33

Saturday 18th February 2023 – Porta Mundorum III

To Adam's great surprise, the door was unlocked, its handle turning effortlessly through 90° and with a reassuring click, it opened silently and frictionlessly. *"What a piece of engineering this thing is!"* he exclaimed, marvelling at the ease with which it had simply glided open on its hinges.

The moment he crossed the threshold the reception room's large central light switched on automatically, flooding the space in a warm, comforting glow and illuminating the entire area. Adam placed his belongings on the tiled floor and surveyed the space before him. He estimated the room's dimensions at around six hundred square feet. Above him was a high, timbered, vaulted ceiling stretching to the inner apex of the roof. There were six of the arched windows, each containing numerous diamond-shaped leaded panels in multi-coloured glass. At the room's centre stood a substantial, highly polished marble table with six sturdy legs around which were arranged sixteen cast iron chairs, each one manufactured to the highest standard with sumptuous purple velvet cushions on the seat and the back. In the middle of the table was a brass candelabra holding three unused and very chunky, ivory-coloured candles.

Two doors led from the room at the opposite end to the entrance. He first tried the one on the left which, just as the main door, opened effortlessly. The lights inside also illuminated the moment he entered to reveal a dormitory containing five rows of twelve steel bunk beds, each with its own tied-back purple velvet curtain plus a mattress, with two pillows and some bed linen in vacuum-sealed bags. Four additional doors led from the dorm into the toilet and washroom areas, two for men and the same for women, indicated on each door by pictorial engravings, inscribed in white on grey slate. *"I wonder where the loos for non-binary individuals are?"* he chuckled, by now comfortable in his solitude and more than happy to be speaking aloud to himself.

The second door from the reception room opened on to a well-equipped kitchen with a walk-in larder cupboard to one side. The units were constructed of stainless steel with substantial granite worktops out of which a double-bowled Belfast-style sink had been carved. The whole place was fabulously equipped with industrial-grade appliances; dishwasher, freezer, refrigerator, washing machine and dryer, plus a heavy-duty weighing scale at one end of the work surface alongside a thick-bodied, wooden chopping board. Sets of expensive-looking, premium quality pans and a myriad of utensils hung from hooks on the wall, above which were shelves containing crockery, glassware and labelled storage jars.

By now, Adam was absolutely ravenous—he had not eaten in over seven hours. In the provisions sack he had brought along with him were a few meagre rations gathered from Teniente's stores; nuts, chocolate, dried fruit and some canned drinks, but with a bit of luck he thought, he may be able to rustle-up something more nourishing. He exclaimed with delight when he opened the freezer which contained six voluminous sliding trays, packed to the brim; one each for fish, veg, meat, poultry, fruit and another containing sundry items such as bread and dairy products. The steel shelves of the walk-in larder carried tins, dried food, condiments, and what looked to Adam like breakfast cereals. He closely studied the packets and although most were in English, the others being Spanish, not a single one of the brands did he recognise.

"Boy, am I spoilt for choice here or what?" He felt like a kid in a sweetshop. *"Now what do I fancy?"*

For the moment anyway, he resolved to put aside all the questions to which he needed answers and set about selecting something for dinner. He settled on a rump steak, potatoes, green beans and a tin of sweet corn to be followed by a fruit salad and selected the ingredients from the freezer along with an uncut, brown bread loaf, placing them on a tray on the granite worktop to defrost. As they would take quite a few hours to thaw, he helped himself to some dried fruit, nuts and what looked very much like muesli from the larder and was then delighted to find a large container of long-life milk plus a selection of fruit juices in the fridge. He made himself a coffee—as far as he could see there was no 'proper' tea anywhere, just the usual exotic varieties and returned to the reception area to devour his mini-feast. He consoled himself with the thought that nowhere in the world apart from good old Britain, with the possible exception of Ireland, can you get 'proper' tea anywhere!

As he perched at the table devouring his food, he spotted a large wooden bureau beneath one of the windows, upon which sat two large, leather-bound books. There was a chair beside the bureau, so he ambled across to it and placed his bowl, plate and cup to the right of the two volumes which he then arranged side by side. The more slender of the two was bound in black leather with '*Welcome Friends*' in six languages stamped in gold italics on the cover. He recognised five of the languages; English, German, Spanish, French and Portuguese but not the sixth which appeared completely alien to him.

The other book, a much thicker tome in extremely worn soft brown leather, had the word *'Visitors'* in silver, in the same six languages. Adam settled himself down, slowly and carefully opened the heavy front cover of the welcome book and, with his curiosity running wild, launched into the text within the section marked 'English.'

'Welcome, dear friends to Porta Mundorum III (PM3) in the land known as Extrema,'[9] it warmly commenced. *'This landing strip and base was constructed in your year 1936 by the German military during their occupation of Antarctica prior to the outbreak of World War II. They constructed four bases in total around the outer rim of your world, and this one is the third of those four. The first is due south of Tasmania, the second directly below Tahiti in French Polynesia, PM3 serves anyone venturing from South America and the fourth is for travellers from Southern Africa. Since the German's abandonment of the area in the late 1940s we, the good men and women of Thoth and Extrema, have maintained and supplied this particular base in order to assist all intrepid and brave souls on their southerly truth-seeking odysseys.*

Around the apron of the base you will see five buildings. The one you are in currently is the main guest area, to the left is the stores building in which you will find tools and equipment for servicing your aircraft and also many recreational items (for example, fishing equipment) which you are free to use to make your stay as enjoyable as possible. The building beyond the stores is our wellness centre housing the spa and the infirmary. The spa, which is fully natural and fed by a geothermal spring beneath the base, contains pools of various temperatures, hot-beds, showers and a small but well-equipped gymnasium. Our infirmary, should anyone be taken ill or find themselves injured, contains the very best equipment and technology to enable a full and swift recovery. At the opposite side of the apron, close to the fuel tanks, is a much less glamorous building—the waste disposal unit. It is an intelligent system that processes all the waste from Porta Mundorum in such a way that no pollution of any kind is inflicted on our natural environment other than hot air and steam.

In the bottom drawer of this bureau we have provided information booklets and packs covering everything you will need for your stay here. There are many maps of both the base and the surrounding region, instructions and manuals for all the appliances and for the spa and leaflets and guides showing the flora and fauna you can expect to encounter as you explore the area. You will also find a medical manual should you need to use the infirmary explaining the workings of

[9] Latin for extremities.

the equipment therein along with a list of the ailments and/or injuries each one is designed to address.

There is fuel here for your aircraft, whether you wish to continue south or return to your own realm and sufficient supplies and accommodation for a maximum of one hundred and twenty people for up to one of your months. There are also chocks for the aircraft's wheels in the stores building next door. We strongly recommend that you put these in place immediately to ensure the safety of your aircraft should the winds build-up, which can happen very quickly and spectacularly in this region. Please make yourselves at home, enjoy the accommodation, eat and drink whatever you like and take walks around the area surrounding the base (there are several trails which we also maintain). You may well come into contact with certain indigenous wild creatures during your visit, none of which you need to fear and whilst out there, why not take time to enjoy the nearby river and the two lakes, Falco Lacus[10], a mile to the north and Porta Lacus[11], just a couple of hundred metres to the south. All are excellent for swimming; the lake temperature is a constant twenty-two degrees and the fishing is tremendous—you will find rods and tackle in the aforementioned stores building if you would like to give it a try.

The heating, lighting and appliances at Porta Mundorum III run on free electrical energy extracted from both the ether, through the spires on each building and from subterranean geothermal sources. The electricity supply is unlimited and flows constantly and cannot be exhausted. The warmer temperatures here in Extrema, compared to those further north in Antarctica, are due in part to those same geothermal influences, which stretch east and west around the entire circumference of your realm from just beyond the ninetieth parallel all the way down to the shores of the Ahtian Ocean, approximately five hundred miles south of here. Also, depending on the time of day you arrived here, you may already have noticed an additional sun in the sky to the south even when your sun, what the locals here call 'Machu Inti' or 'old sun' is still slightly visible above the northern horizon. Well, that is the light from one of the suns local to Extrema as it waxes and wanes in an anti-clockwise direction around this land. In total there are four almost identical suns revolving around these latitudes, much smaller than Machu Inti and a great deal lower in the sky. All four are spaced equally apart and rise from the west and set in the east. The days they bring to Extrema increase and decrease in length throughout their year, giving them four very distinct seasons but there is no synchronisation with the periods of daylight provided by Machu Inti. In the 'Northern Hemisphere' summer, for example, Machu Inti is never visible here but in their winter it can occasionally

---

[10] 'Falcon Lake' in Latin.
[11] 'Gateway Lake' in Latin.

be seen, albeit very low in the sky, between November and February. The local suns here however, can be seen anywhere south of the eighty-eighth parallel, which is another reason why the normal inhabitants of your world are prevented from venturing anywhere close to that latitude.

We would suggest that you spend a minimum of two days at PM3 before continuing your adventure to enable you to fully refresh yourselves for the next stage of your journey and to contemplate which direction that may take. All living men and women who believe in love, truth, freedom and a creator-force are welcome in our realm. If you do not subscribe to and live by those principles, or you are a member of what we call 'The Cabal,' then not only are you unwelcome here but you will most likely not survive very long as your negative energy would be so conflicted with the frequencies that surround us that you will almost certainly fall sick and die. Some of you may already be feeling unwell following your arrival here as the frequencies of your world are much reduced in Extrema. If that is the case, we recommend you return home while you still can as incapacity will arrive quickly if you linger too long. Fortunately, the vast majority of those sufficiently brave to venture to these latitudes are totally committed to such ethics and so historically, very few have felt the need to return north.

Should you wish to continue your pilgrimage southward to lands previously unknown to you, their existence denied and concealed for centuries by those of the Cabal, you must first ensure your aircraft has sufficient fuel to fly four thousand kilometres. There is no need for you to stock-up with provisions other than those you may need for the flight itself, because wherever we direct you to land, an abundance of everything you need will be made available. The course you need to take from here is simply to head due south down the entire length of Porta Lacus and continue due south from there.

Regardless of whether or not your aircraft is fitted with an autopilot, at some point in the flight, we will take command remotely in order for us to guide you safely to your final destination. You may well be alarmed when this happens and feel tempted to wrest control back; this is perfectly normal—and understandable, therefore you will be given three opportunities to allow us to administer the flight. If after three attempts you refuse to yield, denying us the faith and trust necessary for leading you to our realm, then unfortunately you will have no option but to return north, as it will be impossible for you to negotiate the route under your own jurisdiction, regardless of your flying abilities.

Please take time to read through the list of previous visitors; it makes for some very interesting reading and we earnestly request that you add your details too, to ensure our log is maintained as a treasured historical record for future generations—of both realms.

With love, respect and the utmost admiration for your free-thinking, open minded curiosity and bravery.

Sincerely, the good men and women of Thoth.'

Adam closed the cover, leaned back in his chair and closed his eyes in an attempt to fully comprehend all that he had just read. He shook his head slowly from side to side, pondering on just how he had managed to get himself into this predicament. Should he return north or press on southward? Who were these *'good men and women of Thoth'* and where on Earth was Thoth? Were they indeed *'good people'* or could they in fact be bad guys? What if this whole thing was just one huge deception—or a dream even? And who the hell could have travelled here before from our world?

He paused, looking around the room and pinched the skin on his left arm with the thumb and index fingernails of his right hand, very firmly. *'Well, that hurt,'* he thought, *'which it wouldn't have done in a dream.'* The food and drink before him looked and tasted real so he turned his attention back to it, hungrily devouring the nuts and muesli before washing it down with the remaining coffee and then wiping his hands and mouth on the paper napkin which he had found in one of the kitchen drawers.

He took the thicker of the two tomes, the visitors book, placed it in the centre of the bureau's desktop and opened the cover, inside of which was an end-sheet, once again in six languages, explaining the origins of the book.

'This end-sheet was inserted in Earth-year 1953 by the 'good men and women of Thoth' following the abandonment of Porta Mundorum III by the German occupiers who had installed the visitors book here at the base seventeen Earth years previously. Although they had occupied the territory, naming it Neu Schwabenland, and established bases here, they welcomed intrepid adventurers and explorers of all nationalities from all realms, allowing them to land here to refuel, feed and rest before deciding on their next move. The only demand they made was that everyone complete the visitors book before departing, regardless of which onward direction they choose. Although we do not DEMAND the same from you, we earnestly request that you kindly add your details to it as a token of your gratitude for what we have provided here for your benefit.'

He turned the page to find the beginning of the visitor's entries. The first few were from 1935 and 1936, in German; the names on which he did not recognise. Then below them, dated 1937, appeared an entry with a name he knew only too well—that of none other than Amelia Earhart. The entry read...

'Amelia Earhart and Fred Noonan, Lockheed Electra NR16020. Arrived December 30th, 1937, departed January 2nd, 1938. Onward direction due south along Gateway Lake, our destination believed to be The Isle of Thoth—but who knows? Many thanks to our friends in the Japanese and German navies for transporting us and our aircraft to Antarctica and directing us to Porta Mundorum III where we were warmly welcomed by our hosts, Hans and Wilhelm. Their most generous hospitality over the New Year period was much needed and greatly appreciated, as was their help in preparing the Electra for our onward journey. Many thanks to you both for everything. We will never forget your kindness and friendship.'

Adam was dumbstruck. *"Bloody hell fire!"* he gasped. *"So, she didn't die in the South Pacific on her final flight after all—she came here!"*

Several more entries followed, in German, for names that again meant nothing to him. The next name he recognised and one which virtually leaped from the page was from 1947...

'Admiral Richard E. Byrd, pilot Bernt Balchan and the crew of Douglas R4D-8 CZ50826, Operation Highjump. Arrived February 4th, 1947, departed February 6th, 1947. Onward direction confidential. May we express our utmost gratitude to all at Porta Mundorum III, where we were made most welcome and then cared for superbly by our hosts, Gunther and Reinhart, not forgetting to mention the fabulous technical expertise of the ground crew who refuelled and serviced our aircraft before we departed. We hope to return sometime very soon in the near future.'

"So, Byrd's been here as well, has he?" he mused, continuing to scour the list. *"Boy, have we been fed some bollocks in our history books—this is absolute dynamite!"*

There were around twenty further entries during the 1950s, the two most notable being...

'Wernher von Braun, L. Ron Hubbard and Jack Whiteside Parsons, USAF Boeing RB50 80114. Arrived January 6th, 1956, departed January 8th, 1956. Onward direction due west, destination Porta Mundorum II as part of our Antarctic

circumnavigation expedition, the information from which is proving invaluable in our preparations for the creation of an American Space Agency. Porta Mundorum III has proven to be the perfect stopover for us to refuel and relax. The facilities here are first rate.'

'Walt Disney, senior board members of the Disney Corporation and several of our young, up and coming starlets. Lockheed Constellation N6024C leased from TWA. Arrived February 9th, 1957, departed February 14th, 1957. Here on a sightseeing trip to Extrema as a reward to our most loyal associates for all their recent hard work and commitment; to bond as a team, rest and relax and, for me to experience the fabulous salmon fishing that the local rivers, lakes and streams provide.'

The few remaining contributions, those he could understand anyway, contained no recognisable names. The majority were members of U.S. and U.K. government agencies with a smattering from investment banks and oil companies. Every single one however, gave a glowing review of the facilities, comfort and hospitality at the base.

"Boy, this place would be the top-rated joint ever on Tripadvisor—by a country mile," he chortled.

There were around forty entries from the 1960s, the first of interest being...

'President John Fitzgerald Kennedy, Vice President Lyndon B. Johnson and security personnel. Boeing 707 SAM2600 aka Air Force One. Arrived February 2nd, 1963, departed February 6th, 1963. No onward destination. Following our summit meeting here at PM III we shall be returning to the U.S. via Buenos Aires, Argentina where Lyndon will be examined at the military hospital, as he has been unwell since our arrival here.'

He looked up from the book and stared blankly to one side, shaking his head in total bewilderment. *"Who the hell were they holding a summit meeting with for them to have to come all the way down here, I wonder?"* he muttered, returning to the log.

'HRH Queen Elizabeth II and HRH Prince Philip, Duke of Edinburgh. Royal Air Force Vickers VC-10, 'Sir Guy Gibson VC,' ZA148. Arrived 4th December 1966, departed 5th December 1966. This stopover is part of an unofficial and unpublicised state visit to Antarctica and Extrema. However we are cutting-short our stay and returning to Port Stanley, Falkland Islands as we are both suffering severe nausea.'

"And now the bloody Royals are tied-up in all this as well, are they?" he exclaimed in surprise.

The next entry, though significant, did not come as a huge surprise...

'Neil Armstrong and Michael Collins on board NASA Convair 990 711. Arrived January 22nd, 1969, departing January 23rd, 1969. This overnight stay has enabled us to refuel and spend valuable time observing the night skies over Extrema in all directions, but most particularly the south. The sky overnight was crystal-clear, enabling us to capture all the information we required. Heading back to the U.S. tomorrow via Santiago, Chile. Not sure why but we are both suffering high temperatures and severe headaches. Maybe it's something we ate?'

During the 1970s and 1980s many famous names stood out, notably...

'Henry Kissinger, Roman Polanski, Andre Previn, Frank Sinatra, Woody Allen and Mia Farrow along with a few friends aboard Air Force One. Arrived November 15th, 1972, departed November 16th, 1972. Just stayed one night as Henry started with uncontrollable diarrhea and vomiting just minutes after arriving.'

"What a weird combination!" he mused. *What was all that about I wonder? And strange that so many in this decade seem to be falling ill and going back early."*

He continued.....

'L. Ron Hubbard and my dear wife Mary Sue from the Church of Scientology with our young disciple David Miscavige. Boeing 707-138 N108BN *kindly loaned by our friends at Tracinda Investment Corp. Arrived December 14th, 1976, departed December 16th, 1976. My second visit to PM III but unfortunately I have developed a fever with a really high temperature so sadly we are cutting short our visit.'*

On and on the entries went, some of which he felt were not only intriguing but also highly significant...

1980 – Stephen Spielberg

1982 – Margaret Thatcher

1988 – Boutros-Boutros Gali

1992 – Bono and The Edge

1998 – Tony and Cherie Blair

1998 – Jeffrey Epstein, Ghislaine Maxwell, HRH Prince Andrew

1998 - John Travolta and Tom Cruise arriving in the very same Boeing 707 as L. Ron Hubbard's party in 1976.

1999 –Bill and Hillary Clinton plus security personnel

Between the year 2000 and the first quarter of 2020, the number of visitors dropped-off markedly, taking up just two pages of the log, with only a handful of items capturing his attention...

2000 – George W. Bush and his father George H. W. Bush, plus senior advisers

2008 – Barack and Michele Obama

2011 – Elon Musk and Donald Trump

2015 – Jeff Bezos and Mark Zuckerberg

2017 – Bill and Melinda Gates

2019 – Klaus Schwab from the World Economic Forum with Emanuel Macron, Keir Starmer, Angela Merkel and Justin Trudeau.

All of whom gave varying reasons for their visits, such as summits, fishing, rest and recuperation and sightseeing yet with most but not all returning home following some manner of illness or malady.

However, from May 2020 onwards, there was a plethora of entries—affirming completely the rationale behind his posting to Teniente Rodolfo. Each month contained at least five items, which confused him somewhat. *'So they must have all escaped interception,'* he surmised to himself. *'Drones to the rescue for them, too, eh?!'* He decided to concentrate on the most recent additions and turned several pages to the last non-blank page which contained just two entries. Both were thankfully written in English and he began with the penultimate item which read...

'First Officer Ash Pardoe, the crew and our guests from thedeceptionists.org. ValettaJet Dreamliner 9H-AMU. Arrived 11th February 2023, departed 12th February 2023. Our onward destination should have been the Isle of Thoth but

unfortunately, several of our party became seriously ill immediately after arrival, therefore sadly we have no alternative but to return north to Ushuaia.'

"So, the deceptionists had a few baddies on board," he muttered out loud. *"Spoilt it for all the others then? What a bloody shame."*

The very last journal entry however was simply on another level...

'Captain Mateo Forestello and all on board Gulfstream LV-FLA. Arrived early hours of 12th February 2023, departed 15th February 2023. Amazed to meet up with the group calling themselves the deceptionists, who had arrived the previous evening in their Dreamliner. Such a shame they had to return home due to illness but we wish them Godspeed. Our group of explorers owe everything to the good people of Thoth for ensuring our safe transit to Porta Mundorum III and the opportunity to rest here before continuing our amazing journey. Next destination, if the guidebook is to be believed, is the Isle of Thoth, but who knows what adventures may lie ahead for us.'

Slowly and carefully, Adam read the entry once more, sending a wave of sheer relief through him. *"So Jorge definitely was telling the truth!"* he exclaimed loudly and rushed outside in sheer delight. He ran over to Esmerelda, slapped her on the nose cone and shouted, *"Hear that Esmy? Mateo made it here safely. Absolutely brilliant, eh?"*

He bent over to get his breath back and a rather sobering thought came to him. *"What the hell has happened to me these past few weeks? I've stopped believing just about everything I've ever been told, I've gone AWOL, stolen a plane and I've travelled beyond the pole and am still heading south. I've landed at an airstrip in an ice-free land beyond Antarctica and, just to put the icing on the bloody cake, I'm now talking to fighter jets!"*

Chapter 34

Friday 1st August 2008 – More Research by Mateo

During the following two weeks Mateo spent as much of his spare time between his duties as he possibly could in further investigating all the information that his uncle, David Pearson, had provided. And much to his satisfaction it all checked-out perfectly.

General Smedley Butler, James Forrestal and Admiral Richard Byrd, had indeed all been friends and each had suffered the same fate it would seem—surreptitious, summary execution by the deep state for their views and perhaps more importantly for their strenuous and persistent efforts in trying to bring the information they shared into the public domain—all in their own unique ways, of course. The same fate obviously befell John F. Kennedy too as well as his younger brother Robert Kennedy Sr., albeit in a far more overt and 'in your face' kind of way.

In fact Mateo had discovered some particularly pertinent information about JFK's assassination.

He had unearthed a ritual known as the 'Killing of the King,' an ancient Masonic ritual, dating back to the murder of Hiram Abiff in King Solomon's Temple in Masonic legend. Mateo would have been willing to bet his house—if he'd owned one—on the fact that somewhere, lurking in the background of all the sordid events he investigated that the 'dodgy handshake brigade,' as he referred to them, had considerably more than a passing role to play.

Freemasonry does not believe in murdering someone in just any old way and in the JFK assassination it went to incredible lengths and took great risks in order to make this heinous act of theirs correspond to the ancient fertility oblation of the Killing of the King.

Of course, ritual public execution was neither the easiest nor the simplest solution to the problem, to say the very least. It would have required the intense co-operation of several hundred people and many man-months of co-ordinated and concerted effort to plan, execute and cover-up the operation. Although it may seem strange that all this intrigue could even be possible to anyone who is maybe unfamiliar with the modus operandi of these entities, not only is this type of operation reasonably frequent, but it is also often never made public at all.

But would there not be whistle-blowers by the hundreds coming forward to 'spill the beans?' Yes of course—and there were, but these people were fairly easily controlled by the use of two well-established, expedient techniques...

Firstly, by denying them the oxygen of publicity. In other words, it is all very well having a story to tell but if there is no medium by which to make it public knowledge, then the whole exercise is rendered completely pointless. We must not lose sight of the fact that the major media in all its forms is totally under the influence of those who control everything else in our lives. Mainstream media outlets are only allowed to print / broadcast what they are told and the alternative media simply does not have sufficient coverage to make conspiracies well-known and/or expose the truth behind certain events.

And secondly, more than two hundred eye-witnesses to both Kennedy's execution itself and its planning and others officially involved on the periphery of the events either had vastly different views to the conclusions of the Warren Commission or actually spoke-out openly against the official line. Sadly, more than one hundred of these people met very untimely and sometimes mysterious deaths before any real damage could be done by their often stunning revelations.

The list of witnesses connected to the JFK assassination, who were either murdered or died under mysterious circumstances shortly afterwards, is a very long one indeed. Here is just a tiny percentage of these victims chosen at random from a long, long list as discovered by Mateo's meticulous research...

Jack Zangetti – died 23rd November 1963. Jack was the manager of a modular motel complex near Lake Lugert, Oklahoma, who happened to remark to some friends that "*Three other men – not Oswald – killed the President.*" He also stated that "*A man named Ruby will kill Oswald tomorrow and in a few days a member of the Frank Sinatra family will be kidnapped just to take some of the attention away from the assassination.*" His predictions were totally accurate and two weeks later, Jack Zangetti was found floating in Lake Lugert with bullet holes in his chest. It was confirmed that he had been in the water one to two weeks.

Karyn Kupcinet – died 24th November 1963. The daughter of TV host Irv Kupcinet, was trying to make a long distance call from Los Angeles and according to reports, the operator heard Karyn scream into the phone that President Kennedy was going to be killed. Two days after the assassination she was found murdered in her apartment. She was twenty-three years old and the case remains unsolved.

Nancy Jane Mooney aka Betty McDonald – died February 1964. Nancy was a former Ruby employee who provided an alibi for the shooting suspect Warren Reynolds. Her death was ruled a 'suicide by hanging' in the Dallas jail.

Bill Chesher – died March 1964. Bill had information linking Oswald and Ruby but died of a 'heart attack.'

Hank Killam – died March 1964. Hank was a house painter who lived at Johnson's Rooming House at the same time Lee Harvey Oswald lived there.

Teresa Norton – died August 1964. Another Ruby employee found fatally shot and the murder never solved.

Guy Banister – died June 1964. Banister was a private detective who was closely involved in the Jim Garrison trial, featured in the Oliver Stone movie *JFK*. Guy and his partner, Hugh Ward, both died within a ten day period as the Warren Commission was closing its hearings. He supposedly died of a 'heart attack,' but witnesses stated that he had a bullet hole in his body.

Jim Koethe – died 21st September 1964. Koethe was a *Dallas Times Herald* reporter who was killed by a karate chop to the throat just as he emerged from a shower in his apartment. His murderer was not charged with any crime. He had been present at a highly significant meeting in Ruby's apartment and now very few were left to tell the story of what actually happened there.

Mary Pinchot Meyer – died October 1964. Mary was a mistress of JFK whose diary was appropriated by CIA chief, James Jesus Angleton after her murder. Cause of death ruled as 'unknown causes.'

Paul Mandal – died January 1965. Paul was a *Life* magazine writer who wrote of JFK 'turning to the rear' when shot in the throat. His highly suspicious death was ruled as 'cancer.'

These forces of darkness in all their various guises have used similar ritualised murders to dispose of their adversaries all throughout the ages, since time immemorial. In fact Mateo also discovered that a similarly memorable and more recent example was that of Princess Diana, possibly ritually executed in 1997, albeit using a slightly different methodology. It seemed to him that she too had outlived her usefulness and in addition had been foolhardy enough to believe that she could actually get away with prodding the hornet's nest in so many different ways—totally reminiscent of JFK. It is a virtual certainty that her assassination was one other such episode of the Killing of the King ritual which by design leaves an indelible print upon the minds of those who were alive at the time. Who for example, does not remember exactly where they were when they heard of the deaths of JFK or Diana? And of course these ritualised executions serve as a warning to anyone who also believes it a good idea to behave in the same way.

So, armed with all this new, stunning information Mateo picked-up his phone and keyed in David's cell-phone number, anticipating another interesting dialogue. Once again, he heard the distinctive American ring tone and again was subjected to a delay before the call was answered.

On this occasion though, no-one answered so Mateo left a voice-mail message...

"Hi David, Mateo here. I've checked-out lots of the stuff we discussed in our last call and found out some interesting info regarding the deaths of JFK, Smedley Butler, James Forrestal and Richard Byrd—as well as Princess Diana. Give me a call when you pick up this message, please. 'Bye for now."

A further week went by and still David had not returned his call, so he decided to try again. This time the phone was answered almost immediately, but the voice on the other end was absolutely not that of David.

"Hello Mateo," it said. *"We've been expecting your call."*

Mateo was momentarily stunned. *"Who... err, who is this please?"* was all he could manage to splutter-out in his state of shock.

"You don't need to know my name, Mateo. I am an operative of one of the U.S. security services and I have to tell you that unfortunately, David had a sudden heart attack and sadly he is no longer with us," he announced, totally without sympathy and with an extremely sinister undertone in his voice.

Mateo just stood there numbly, unable to speak and completely shocked to the core by this revelation. But he then recovered sufficiently enough to say, *"You mean that you killed... "* he managed to begin, before being immediately interrupted.

"Mateo, Mateo... " the voice said in patronising, mock sympathetic tones. *"Please don't upset yourself. David Pearson unfortunately was an enemy of the state—a traitor if you will—and traitors have to be severely dealt with, you know."*

After a short pause he continued, this time using the previous sinister tone. *"So we would strongly advise you to cease and desist following-up on this information because you seem like a genuinely nice guy and it would be such a shame If you were to end-up the same way as David—especially such a young man as yourself. Yes, it would be a great pity. Oh and by the way Mateo, we do know all about you... everything in fact; where you live, where you were born, the circumstances of your birth, your air force duties, postings and roster and so on. Therefore my advice to you would be to curtail your investigative activities forthwith, otherwise one day you may well, when least expecting it of course, come face to face with one of our external operatives. And believe me, you really would not want that."* Then abruptly there was a 'click' and the line went dead.

Mateo was suitably terrified. In fact he had never before felt as scared or vulnerable in his entire life, so decided to keep his head very firmly 'below the parapet' for as long as it took for the heat on him to die down. This however did not preclude the continuing of his research and so he persisted with that at least, but now without actually making any of his findings public. He also turned down several offers of writing articles for websites—simply in order to err on the safe side!

However, it was only a matter of weeks before the intelligence agent's overt threats had diminished in his mind and once he deemed it safe to do so, he again began to investigate the deaths of his relatives, Peter and James Forrestal. He already knew that the death of David Pearson was not from natural causes—he had had it spelled out to him in no uncertain terms, directly from the perpetrators—and also it seemed an almost one hundred percent certainty that James Forrestal had died at the hands of the same group, albeit nearly sixty years earlier. But as for his father, Peter Forrestal, he pondered upon this for a while in order to formulate a plan of some kind but at this point in time he was still no wiser as to how he might achieve his goal of somehow linking the two deaths and determining once and for all who, if anyone, had been responsible.

Maybe it WAS just simply a massive abdominal haemorrhage caused by many years of heavy drinking as the official autopsy had recorded, that had killed Peter, he pondered. Or maybe not? Where could he turn-to in order to even begin ascertaining the truth? Then it suddenly occurred to him! Who is the one person in the world who may be able to offer some clues as to what really happened to his father? Why, Katherine of course—his father's wife. He suddenly felt so stupid that it had taken him so long to think of that, but how to contact her? He knew that she must have received his previous letter, because it was she who had told David Pearson that she had heard from him but why had she not replied to him? Were the memories still too painful—after all he was the direct product of her husband's infidelity? Or maybe she was under some kind of threat too? So many questions, so many questions, he thought.

Mateo finally resolved to write to her again and also to Francesca, his half-sister, this time too. He reasoned that maybe if Francesca also received a letter from him, then she may well encourage her mother to get in touch with him—even if Katherine/Kit was reluctant to do so.

So, he carefully formulated a letter from which he made two copies and addressed one to each of the two ladies.

Chapter 35

Monday 25th March 1912 – Antarctica, The Epilogue

The imposing figure of Brigadier Arthur continued his monologue as the three weary travellers slumped disconsolately to the floor, partly in exhaustion and partly at the sheer desperation of their situation…

"I should firstly like to say that you are very brave men and I genuinely admire and respect you all. You have evidently suffered greatly during the past several months and your persistence and stoicism in the face of extreme adversity is truly admirable. You will all be remembered as heroes to future generations, despite your heroic failure to reach 'the pole.' History will record that sadly you were just beaten to your ultimate goal by the Norwegian, Roald Amundsen, whilst you all succumbed to the cold and appalling weather, camped a mere eleven miles from safety. And this of course will magnify greatly the public outpourings of grief and sympathy at your sad fate.

And of course, it almost goes without saying that your families will be taken care of and no expense will be spared to ensure that they are kept in the manner to which they have become accustomed," he assured them, genuinely sympathetically.

"I am, as you have possibly already guessed, an agent of the SIS, the Secret Intelligence Service and so I am of course privy to certain national and international secrets. But as I promised," he continued, *"you all deserve to know the truth about this region and the Earth itself.*

The ancients were partly correct in their assessment of the shape and extent of the Earth. It is a flat, or maybe slightly dome-shaped plane stretching way beyond this ice-bound area, as far again as the extent of the area that we all know as 'the Earth.' As far as we know, the total area is more than double that of the Earth which, in actual fact, is not a planet as we are all told and taught from early childhood…"

"But why, what's the bloody point of all the deception? It doesn't make sense to me at all," interrupted Bowers, dejectedly.

"It may seem that way and yes I agree—to a point but there is a much broader and far-reaching agenda behind it all, of which even I, a fairly lowly operative in

the grand scheme of things, am not fully aware. But I will tell you as much as I know myself. I feel that you are owed that much at least.

To begin, you need to understand that the world as you know it, is not governed by those in supposed positions of power in governments. In reality, all governments are merely puppets, placed there by those with REAL power to rule by proxy and create the impression that we have a choice in who governs us through the grand deception of public elections. We don't. Elections and democracy are a sham, devised to make us believe that we have a say in our own futures, but no matter which party ostensibly gains power, it is the same people behind the scenes who control the agenda and dictate policies.

Many centuries ago, the ancestors of those in power today soon realised that in order to keep the masses under control it would be necessary to perpetrate this deception. Until that point in time, the 'great unwashed' had to be kept in their place by the use of force and often extreme violence, which was not an ideal situation for them in any way, their having constantly to fight battles they would rather not have to. So the Royal families, the ruling elite and the aristocracy of those days decided that it would be more prudent to put in place the system we have today and for them to take a step backwards out of the limelight and instead control events from the shadows as it were, using their proxies in government as a front.

And this then developed into the system of government we have today, in the first world at least; two main political parties who in effect 'divide and conquer' the gullible electorate who are propagandised into believing that they live in a so-called 'democracy,' with a genuine say in their own destinies. This is of course just a control mechanism and a method by which the masses are duped into believing that they are 'free' men and women and are thereby subtly discouraged from openly rebelling.

So to elaborate further, in addition to all of this, a network of alleged more privileged commoners were encouraged to devise and become members of so-called 'secret societies' of like-minded individuals but who in fact are just 'tools' of the establishment, whilst believing that they are somehow special in some way and part of this supposed 'clique' of superior individuals. And although membership of these societies does guarantee certain privileges, in reality they are also duped into believing that they are somehow 'a cut above' the rest of the herd. Indeed, Captain Scott, we know you are a freemason too, as am I—and therefore a part of this entire charade."

At this, Scott said nothing, but merely stared down at the floor, somewhat dejectedly. So, he realised, his dear mother Hannah had been right all along when she had tried to discourage him from joining the local lodge, insisting adamantly that freemasons were a 'secretive, and malevolent bunch, constantly up to no good and serving only their own nefarious self-interests.'

Arthur continued his monologue...

"These secret societies, most specifically the freemasons, slowly but surely began to gain a foothold in the establishment and began to use their gradually-increasing power and influence, encouraged of course by the real powers-that-be, to take surreptitious control of almost every establishment you can name in order to further the agenda of those in power... the judiciary, the police, politics, education, medicine, organised religion, corporations and most importantly science. In fact, history is also totally controlled by them too and anything that contradicts or threatens the ongoing control agenda is subtly—and often not so subtly—destroyed or manipulated and re-written. Never was a truer word spoken to say that history is written by the victors, or more accurately those in control of all our destinies. A sad situation, that you are all shortly to be subjected to yourselves, in point of fact.

But to return to the main thrust of the explanation and with specific reference to science, around four hundred years ago, a further deception was imposed upon the masses. As I previously mentioned, until around that time, everyone knew the truth about what the Earth consisted of—or at least the partial truth. The ancients believed fairly accurately that the Earth was indeed a flat plane of unknown size and extent and that it was a totally unique place, created by God or at least a supreme being of some kind. And of course at that time, human spirituality was very predominant in society and for reasons best known to themselves, the cabal decided that this spirituality, if destroyed, would render humanity at large far more easy to control.

So it was decided to abandon the idea of a flat Earth and create a fake paradigm of reality by inventing a universe consisting of millions of suns or stars all of which are surrounded by globular planets and declaring that we are 'not alone' in this vast universe, thereby removing our uniqueness as an intelligent species.

If the Earth or the plane upon which it resides, is the centre of the Universe and unique, then the idea of creation and a purpose for human existence is self-evident. But if the Earth is just one of trillions of planets revolving around billions of stars in billions of galaxies, then the ideas of creation and a specific purpose for Earth and human existence become highly implausible.

It was for this very same reason that the freemason Charles Darwin was chosen to propose and promote his utterly ridiculous 'theory' of evolution, more than fifty years ago, which contributes greatly to the ongoing agenda, by further denying the existence of a creator and promulgating the idea of life being an utterly random occurrence.

In a nutshell therefore, the modern, atheistic, heliocentric, globe-Earth, chance-evolution paradigm supplanted all the ancient knowledge and manages humanity by removing intelligent design and replaces purposeful creation with mere haphazard, random cosmic coincidence. This in effect then 'proves' that we are simply random specks of nothingness, which in turn denies the fact that we are all powerful spiritual beings and contributes greatly to removing our power to resist those who rule over us with an iron fist encased in a velvet glove.

And in addition to all this and given your recent experiences, you will not be surprised to learn that the regions and realms beyond Antarctica, of which there are many, are teeming with life, both human and animal. The ancestors of some of the human inhabitants escaped the genocide committed by the Spanish Conquistadors in South America in the sixteenth and seventeenth centuries and there is also another sub-species of humanity that live on several continents beyond this ice-bound region. However these people are no more different to us than say, members of the Oriental or Negroid races. They are just simply different. And a conscious decision was made by our rulers many years ago when this race was first encountered, not to interfere with their lives and allow them to co-exist in peace, but nevertheless in strict isolation. I have not been made privy to the exact reasons for this but nevertheless, that is the case.

So the upshot of all that, gentlemen, is that this is why we are deceived about the shape and extent of the Earth and humanity is highly discouraged from entering the polar regions—and most especially, the Antarctic. I hope that all makes sense to you? There is far, far more to it than simply that, but those are the plain, basic facts of the matter.

And finally I should like to explain why the supplies were all removed several weeks ago from the One Ton Depot storehouse. My superiors had ordered me to do so in order that you should all starve to death to prevent you from returning with the knowledge you would no doubt acquire on your travels, making it widely known and instigating more explorations of the region. But I had second thoughts and decided on a more humane course of action, hence my appearance here a short while ago. I will of course remain silent about that particular aspect of my mission."

At this point, Brigadier Robert Arthur of the Royal Marine Corps and the SIS, paused and seemingly now lost for words and deep in thought, he simply stared at the three doomed explorers for what seemed like an eternity, but what in reality was probably no longer than one minute. Then with a deep, regretful sigh he took careful aim again and with his Webley pistol, rapidly and ruthlessly executed Captain Robert Falcon Scott, Lieutenant Edward Evans and Lieutenant Henry Robertson Bowers, without another word being spoken.

Satisfied that he had now done his duty to the very entities he had just described to his victims, as was expected of him, he then calmly took his shovel from the motor sledge, buried their lifeless bodies deep in the snow and marked the position of the makeshift grave with a rudimentary cross atop a large mound of snow.

Also satisfied that justice had now prevailed and that history had been successfully rewritten, he mounted the sledge, fired-up the engine and began his long, hazardous journey back to civilisation.

Chapter 36

Saturday 18th February 2023 – Dobbo's Incarceration

Dobbo, his whole body frozen in shock, stared down the gleaming barrel of the Glock 17 revolver, behind which the snarling face of Prendergast loomed large and menacing. His mind raced, trying frantically to come to terms with the predicament he was facing. Could this really be his long-time commanding officer brandishing the weapon? What had he done that could warrant such extreme aggression? Had Prendergast actually lost his mind? Or maybe he and Adam had lost theirs and this reaction from the Wing Commander was perfectly justified?

Prendergast shook his head slowly from side to side and prodded his subordinate violently in the ribs with the Glock. Dobbo recoiled in shock and pain. *"Fucking hell, Mike, what on Earth's going on here?"* he pleaded. *"It was all Adam's…"*

Prendergast cut him off mid-sentence, in no mood for excuses or blame-passing. *"Do you know Dobson, I should never have recommended you for this bloody tour,"* he snarled. *"Yes, I'm the reason you were posted here in the first place, just as you were responsible for that retard Haylock joining us. Honest to God, if I'd known this would be the result, I'd have kept schtum and just accepted whoever I was given. But no, because I'm such an opinionated arsehole I wanted you two here with me—to make my life easier. Can you believe that?"*

Dobbo breathed in long and hard through his nose, held it for a count of six and exhaled slowly through pursed lips in a vain attempt to compose himself.

"So, are you going to shoot me with that thing, Mike?" he asked.

"If I have to, Dobson then I will," came the response. *"Do not underestimate me. Shooting you for resisting arrest and incarceration will be easy to justify given the almighty shit-show you two have served-up, so get up off your miserable little arse and I'll show you to your quarters. Jorge and Eduardo have been really busy this last hour making it nice and secure so we can lock you in and make sure you don't get up to any more nonsense. I'm sure it will be ready now knowing those two. A couple of days in there on your own should give you enough time to ponder on what you've done."*

Dobbo looked in bewilderment at his soon-to-be prison warden. *"This is unbelievable, Mike,"* he said. *"Why the hell do you have to lock me up? It's not as if I've anywhere to go is it? Do you think I can somehow get to South America under my own steam? Honest mate, you've lost the plot."*

Any semblance of patience that Prendergast may have had left evaporated at this point.

"Just shut the fuck up!" he snapped. *"And do exactly as I say until your escort arrives to take you far away from here. If I don't lock you up and you somehow manage to commandeer Celeste and start following Haylock, then I'll have been caught-out again. And do you know something, you snivelling piece of excrement? I am not going to let that happen. Now get up and start walking."* Literally trembling in his anger and frustration, his northwest origins became apparent as he lapsed into his south Manchester accent for the first time in many years.

The two men rose from their chairs, left the office and shuffled along the corridor to Dobbo's room. Two heavy-duty padlocked latches had been installed on the outside of the door and, as he entered the room, Dobbo noticed three iron bars securing the window.

"No escaping this place by the look of it, Mike," he commented calmly yet feeling anything but as he perched himself dejectedly on the bed. *"And what do I do for food and drink? Not that I'm feeling that peckish right now."*

Pendergast waved his hand in the direction of the small refrigerator in the corner next to the toilet door. *"Oh, we've sorted that already Dobson. There's enough food and drink in there to last two days at least, including a few beers so no need for me to pay you any visits until it's time for you to leave. Which suits me just fine. Oh, and there's no phone or laptop to help you wile away the long, lonely hours. I've handed them over to Jorge and Eduardo to lock securely in the storeroom so you'd better find other ways to amuse yourself. Anyway, enjoy!"* At this he turned on his heels and exited, slamming the door shut and securing the latches.

Dobbo tried the door. *"No opening that from the inside in a million years,"* he cursed as he crossed over to the window to inspect the bars that the two Chileans had fitted. He opened the window, grabbed the outer two and tried to shake them—absolutely rock solid, exactly what he would have expected from those two *'lanky nerds.'*

"Shit!" he exclaimed, sitting down on the bed and placing his head disconsolately in his hands. He really was in serious trouble now, more so than at any time in his life. *"So, how the bloody hell are you going to wriggle your way out of this one then, Dobbo?"* he mused dejectedly.

Chapter 37

Sunday 19th February 2023 – Porta Mundorum III

Three hours later, having regathered his composure sufficiently to cook himself the best steak dinner he had ever tasted, Adam washed and tidied everything away and then took himself wearily off to bed in one of the dormitory bunks. The mattress was ridiculously comfortable, the pillows equally so and the crisp cotton sheet and duvet cover so sleep-inducing that he slumbered comatose for a full twelve hours without waking. He eventually arose feeling relaxed, reinvigorated but massively hungry again and so headed-off at once to the kitchen to prepare some breakfast. After a very satisfying and hastily devoured repast comprising muesli, fruit, three boiled eggs, honey on toast, strong black coffee and orange juice, he took a shower, changed into the one set of spare clothes he had brought along with him and pulled on a sheepskin-lined parka he had found hanging in the dormitory. *The 'good people of Thoth'* had even provided warm, waterproof clothing for their fortunate guests to use.

"Is there anything these people haven't thought of?" he mused excitedly as he stepped out to explore this strange, 'brave new world' outside.

Esmerelda sparkled in the strengthening sunlight on another thankfully clear day. There was a fresh breeze blowing and the scattered clouds scudded across the sky like airships in formation—a sky refreshingly, totally absent of any chemtrails. He strolled to the centre of the apron, breathed in a lungful of fresh, pure air and surveyed his surroundings. To the north, maybe a kilometre away was a huge lake, Falco Lacus he assumed and to the south, only fifty metres beyond the base, stretched Porta Lacus into which a small stone jetty had been built, with three covered canoes tethered to it. To the east and west of the lakes, a landscape strikingly similar to Iceland in summer, although less mountainous and with more trees, disappeared into the far horizons.

He ambled down to the end of the jetty and peered into the water below him. It was crystal clear with an almost pure white gravel bed, dotted with patches of lush, green underwater vegetation and teeming with tiny fish of an unknown species. He lay on his stomach and reached into the pristine water which, just as the welcome book had stated, felt around 20°c, perfect for a dip he thought. As he swirled his hand around testing the temperature he lifted his gaze to the lake itself, its emerald-green waters disappearing southward into the far distance. *"What a beautiful day and what an incredible place!"* he cried out aloud, then closed his eyes to take in a long, deep breath of pure, invigorating Extrema air. The combination of the local sun and the subterranean geothermal forces had warmed the air to what Adam felt was around 15°c. Not exactly what he would call warm, but fine considering it was not yet mid-morning and a million miles from what you would expect this far south.

In awe of his new surroundings and idly wondering if he was possibly still asleep and dreaming, Adam returned to the apron and decided to check out the far northeastern corner where a white wooden signpost stood proud against the surrounding greenery. It read *'Falco Lacus via the riverside, 1.5km,'* again in those very same six languages and pointed towards a meandering gravelled trail which was meticulously maintained and led very soon to the right bank of a tumbling river dotted with small waterfalls and deep pools. An abundance of insect life adorned the surface of the pools from which fish rose constantly to feast on the harvest above them. He walked to the head of one particular pool and sat down on a rock beside the small waterfall feeding it. The beauty and energy of the place was overwhelming and for maybe the first time in his life he felt truly calm and at one with the world. The air rang with birdsong, the purveyors of which fluttered and swooped all around him as he rested there, entranced by the rhythmic burbling of the water as it tumbled over the cascade and into the clear, sparkling waters below.

Mesmerised by the sights and sounds around him and struck dumb by the pristine and unspoilt beauty of his surroundings, he was just about to doze-off when he almost jumped out of his skin as a shimmering silver salmon, weighing all of ten pounds, leapt from the depths on to the cascade and wriggled its way up through the cataract into the pool above. Just a few seconds later, a sea trout of around three pounds performed the self-same manoeuvre with equal skill and majesty. Being a keen angler who had represented the RAF several times in various inter-forces fly-fishing events, he was salivating at the prospect of trying his hand on this beautiful watercourse so hurried back to Porta Mundorum to check-out the fishing tackle they had provided.

He was not to be disappointed as, yet again, those very '*good people*' had come up trumps by supplying the finest quality fly and spinning gear along with a huge assortment of lines, flies and lures. They even had waders, jackets, hats, sunglasses and landing nets; everything a discerning trout and salmon angler could ever need, in fact. Also provided were life-vests, snorkels, flippers, wetsuits, swim shorts and beach towels for those wishing to take to the lake for swimming or canoeing. Adam now had everything he needed for the perfect holiday and decided to spend sufficient time at Porta Mundorum III to indulge himself fully in all that the 'resort' had to offer.

In no hurry whatsoever to leave his fabulous holiday home, the next three days were the most glorious and halcyon ever. He fished, swam, canoed, explored and feasted. The fishing was out of this world, unlike anything he had ever experienced. On the fly he caught salmon, sea trout, rainbow trout, grayling and a strange type of whitefish he did not recognise. On the lakes he fished mainly with spinners and lures, taking many trout but also bass, perch, pike and, on one occasion fishing from the canoe on Porta Lacus, a strange looking species resembling a cross between a catfish, an eel and a small sturgeon. The majority of the fish he landed were returned to fight another day but he kept one or two unlucky ones and cooked them on the cast-iron, wood-fired barbecue stoves positioned beside several of the pools and on the lakeside, wood, firelighters and matches, all laid-on of course.

From time to time he took a break away from the fishing to swim and snorkel from the jetty on Porta Lacus. The water temperature was perfect, warm enough to enable him to stay in the water for a considerable time yet sufficiently cool for it to be refreshing and invigorating. Whilst snorkelling, as well as multitudes of fish, he encountered several species of water snake, crayfish and freshwater crabs plus a host of diving birds, amongst them grebes, cormorants and his favourite of all, the kingfisher.

On a couple of occasions he ventured further into the lake in one of the canoes, though being a single paddler in a vessel designed for three or four, progress was rather slow and arduous. Nevertheless, he managed to explore widely enough to see groups of otters and beavers who had made their holts and dams in the more wooded areas of the lake margins. From the boat, stationary and silent, he watched the adult otters diving for food, surfacing time and time again with a plump trout or large crayfish in their mouths and taking it to an exposed rock to feed themselves and their young. The beavers appeared to spend all their time dam-building, obsessively gnawing branches and boughs from trees and dragging them away to add to their already sprawling constructions.

During the early hours of darkness, once all influences from both suns had long since died away, he would venture outside to study the night sky. The temperature consistently dropped to around a single degree Celsius, particularly if the wind was blowing from the south, but on the second evening it fell to several degrees below zero due to a brisk northerly wind. To the north the stars of our realm, many still visible even at such southerly latitudes, twinkled and flickered just as they had always done whereas, in the opposite direction, there was a total absence of heavenly bodies with not a single pinprick of light interrupting the blackness. This struck Adam as very strange indeed. Although most of what he was experiencing beyond the wall did not follow any of the accepted norms, he would certainly have expected a few stars in the sky at the very least.

On the second evening, between his stroll outside in the dark and his evening meal, he decided to visit the spa and once again, was not disappointed in the slightest. There were four small pools ranging in temperature from just above freezing up to 40°c, six hotbeds carved from what Adam thought looked like volcanic lava yet as smooth as polished marble and shaped perfectly to the contours of the body. The whole place was decorated and laid out like a Roman bath, similar to those in Harrogate which he had visited during a brief stint at RAF Linton-on-Ouse in Yorkshire, but this was on a different scale of quality, comfort and opulence. *"The only thing missing from this place is a masseur, or even better a masseuse!"* he joked with himself, realising that they were probably a tad difficult to recruit in these parts.

He had also taken a brief look at the gymnasium which contained treadmills, weights, bars, rowing machines and exercise bikes. Adam was not a gym person however, in fact he hated the whole gym scene, much preferring to exercise outside in fresh air, so gave that particular facility a wide berth. He chuckled at the thought that he'd finally found something at Porta Mundorum III which he didn't actually like!

By the morning of Wednesday 22nd, fully refreshed and energised but aware that he may be overstaying his welcome, he began to think again about his next move. A part of him wanted to stay here forever, yet given that the whole purpose of his desertion was to keep flying south and the guidebook had told him what he needed to do next, maybe today was the day to move on? In any case, he was already extremely wary of the consequences of being followed and what would be his fate, were he to be captured by a U.N. patrol, maybe out to arrest him!?

At this point in time he allowed himself a few moments to ponder as to what he had done and more specifically what would happen to him if or when he ever left this idyllic place and returned back northward to the realm he had left behind. No doubt that utter maniac Prendergast would be determined to make his life as miserable as he possibly could and wreak his own personal revenge as well as bringing the full force of the military establishment down upon him—hard. Desertion coupled with the theft of an aircraft was no minor infraction of military law. He imagined that if he were ever to return then he would be extremely lucky to avoid a long prison sentence in either a civilian or a military jail—or possibly worse. Who knew what the punishment may be for a transgression of this magnitude and then having the sheer audacity to return with all this forbidden knowledge in his head? Despite the soothing warmth of his temporary, adopted home his body actually gave a little shudder at the thought.

He shook his head rapidly in an attempt to rid himself of all those negative thoughts. Then suddenly, he remembered his hunger and within a few minutes he was sat at the dining table munching his by now customary breakfast of muesli, fruit, three boiled eggs, honey on toast, strong black coffee, and orange juice. Deep in thought about what to do next, leaving this idyll, refuelling Esmerelda, the route he had been instructed to take, the thought of relinquishing control of the F-5 at some point, being guided to Thoth, he felt daunted by the whole situation, very alone yet determined not to deviate from his self-imposed mission.

Suddenly, out of the blue... *"BANG-BANG-BANG."* There were three loud knocks on the front door. Adam, having just contemplated the possible dire consequences of his arrest, very nearly soiled himself.

Chapter 38

Monday 20th February 2023 – Hope for Dobbo

After two almost interminable days and nights alone in his quarters, Dobbo woke at 7.30am after another fitful sleep. With a heavy heart he took a deeply satisfying piss, showered, shaved and then pulled on a clean pair of boxers, his favourite, Nirvana T-shirt and khaki shorts. He filled the kettle to make himself a coffee and then remembered that the fridge was now virtually empty with nothing in there that he fancied for breakfast. He picked up and unscrewed the coffee jar—barely any of that left either so he walked over to the door and banged on it several times as hard as he could with both fists.

"Mike, Mike," he yelled. *"I've got nowt left to eat in here. Does this mean I'm coming out today or what? If not then can you bring me some food? I'm bloody starving!"*

After half a minute or so with no reply he banged again, but harder and louder this time, in frustration. *"Prenders you fat, ugly twat, fetch me some nosh, NOW—or let me out of here,"* he hollered.

He put his ear to the door and a few seconds later heard the sound of another one closing, a few yards down the corridor. It was Prendergast leaving his room, nonchalantly and sarcastically whistling the theme from *The Great Escape* as he ambled along towards Dobbo's door at which point he stopped, continuing his rendition until he reached the end of the chorus.

"What was that you miserable barrel of monkey spunk?" he snarled, deliberately taking on the persona of Officer Hadley from *The Shawshank Redemption.*

"Mike, am I coming out today because I've no grub left?" shouted Dobbo. *"If not then bring me some more, plus coffee and milk—oh, and beer too. I've barely anything left."*

"You're going nowhere Dobson—not just yet anyway," 'Prison Officer' Prendergast informed him almost gleefully. *"Your escort has been delayed due to bad weather and is still in Port Stanley, so it looks like you're going to be on your little lonesome in there for at least two or three more days—if not longer. Now isn't that a shame, eh?"*

Dobbo took a moment to take this in then went on the attack the best he could from behind a double-padlocked door. *"Look, Wing Commander. You're going against the Geneva Convention here,"* he sternly and authoritatively informed his sneering jailer. *"As my detaining officer, it's your duty to treat me humanely in line with all the articles in there... So fetch me some nosh and when I've eaten I need some fresh air and exercise. You can't deny me any of those things and you know it—you pathetic psycho!"*

Prendergast turned to make the return walk back to his room. *"Aw, don't fret yourself so, Dobbsy,"* he growled sarcastically. *"I'll get Jorge and Eduardo to come refill your larder and then take you out for walkies,"* he continued over his shoulder. *"Is that ok for you? I do hope so."*

Dobbo threw himself on to the bed and picked up the latest copy of the *Dalesman* magazine for the umpteenth time. The cover depicted an oil painted panorama of Whitby, his favourite childhood day-out destination, twenty miles north up the coast road from Scarborough and another one of the three towns attacked during the 1914 German raid.

What he wouldn't give now, he thought, to be strolling along the quayside with a portion of cod, chips and mushy peas from the famous *Magpie* fish and chip shop, heading for the breakwater to watch the anglers casting their lines into the harbour. He'd experienced his first ever romantic encounter on that very breakwater aged fifteen, snogging a cute and cuddly brunette from Redcar called Amy. He couldn't remember her surname but what he could recall was that she had let him have a quick feel as well! He closed his eyes and beamed from ear to ear. Happy days, the happiest ever in fact, he reminisced somewhat uncharacteristically. He began to read through the magazine once more, each page dishing out large dollops of nostalgia and bringing back so many happy memories of his native Yorkshire coast upbringing.

Having worked his way through half the entire magazine, probably for the fifth or sixth time since it had arrived on the C-130, he was brought back from his reminiscences to the very heart of reality by the sound of the latches being undone and the door opening. Fully expecting it to be Prendergast, he was startled to see Eduardo stepping into the room carrying a large crate, which the tall Chilean laid down just inside the door. He looked across at Dobbo with what the Yorkshireman felt was genuine concern, warmth and friendship and then spoke in surprisingly excellent English.

"Señor Dobson, here are some provisions for you for the next twenty-four hours," he announced very formally. *"I shall return in forty minutes to take*

you out for a walk around the base so you can stretch your legs and breathe good air. Adiós my friend."

Dobbo stared open-mouthed as the flight engineer left the room, closed the door and resecured both latches. He had never heard Eduardo utter a single word prior to this moment and wasn't sure if he could even speak, let alone be fluent in English. He picked up the crate, placed it on the bed and checked the contents. Breakfast was his main priority so he was glad to see a box of Weetabix, a loaf of thinly-sliced white bread, Tetra Paks of milk and apple juice, a tub of spreadable butter and, to his great relief, a box of coffee sachets for his espresso machine.

To his surprise and puzzlement, the box of Weetabix had previously been opened. He wondered if perhaps Prendergast had been in there and injected something into them, but his suspicion rapidly dissipated when he spotted, tucked behind one of the packs, a brown envelope with his name handwritten on the front. He removed it from the box, opened it and pulled out a single, neatly folded A4 sheet. With trembling fingers, he spread it out on the bed and began reading.

'Señor Dobson, please do not reveal to the Wing Commander that we have sent you this note and we ask you to destroy it after reading please. We are your friends and allies. It grieves us to see you imprisoned for only doing what was right and we do not wish for you to be found guilty by a military court after you leave Teniente Rodolfo. Or a worse fate perhaps which, from our previous experiences in matters such as these, is a very real possibility.

A replacement pilot and aircraft have been requested following the desertion of señor Haylock and will arrive on Friday. Apparently, it is a Tornado GR-4 from the German Luftwaffe along with one of their very best airmen. That is good news as it is an aircraft we are familiar with and uses the same missiles as the F-5 so it will be in good hands here. From our contacts in Port Stanley we have heard that the C-130 bringing the man tasked with escorting you from here to your place of court martial, does not arrive for another three days. But do not worry, good friend, all is not lost. We are looking after you and our people beyond the ice wall are watching after and caring for señor Haylock. He is fit and well and in very good hands. Our advice to you would be to make the same journey and join him at some point otherwise your future, dear friend, is very bleak.'

Dobbo paused his reading and stared incredulously at the note, sheer relief washing over him by the bucketful. He kept his joy well and truly to himself though in case Prendergast had bugged his quarters. That was extremely likely given the fact he had installed a barely-hidden surveillance camera which Dobbo had located after only a couple of hours in 'stir.' It had given him tremendous satisfaction to give Prendergast one almighty V-sign as he draped a pair of black boxer shorts over the lens.

'So, I'm not totally fucked,' he declared inwardly. *'Adam's fine by the sound of it and with a bit of luck, I will be too. Yes!'*

Eager to discover what Jorge had to say next, he turned back to the note.

'So, when Eduardo returns to take you outside for exercise, please act as if you never received this note. He will give you further instructions as you walk around the base but do not show any pleasure at anything he tells you. It is vital that we raise no suspicions should señor Prendergast, who incidentally we call El Coño Feo, be observing your exercise from his quarters.'

He read through the note a second and then a third time before walking to the toilet, tearing the paper into dozens of pieces and flushing them away, three pulls of the chain being needed to dispatch all the fragments safely through the U-bend.

Chapter 39

Wednesday 22nd February 2023 – Meet the Quechuans

Adam simply could not believe his ears. He stood there frozen to the spot, unable to move. Then once more, *"BANG-BANG-BANG,"* followed by a man's voice calling...

"Hello, hola! Is anyone there? ¿Hay alguien ahí?"

Adam relaxed slightly and breathed a huge sigh of relief. The voice did not sound threatening or indeed anything to be afraid of. Beyond doubt, however, was that someone was on the other side of that door, in a forbidden land where the vast majority of the world's population were not permitted to visit. And that person spoke Spanish and English! As far as he could tell, they hadn't flown here as surely he would have heard the aircraft, so presumably they had arrived from the surrounding area on foot. Who could it possibly be? He swallowed hard, cleared his throat and shouted, *"Yes, there is someone here, just a moment please."*

He walked to the kitchen, pulled the largest of the kitchen knives from the block holding them and, with it strategically concealed behind his back, strode rapidly to the door which he tentatively partially opened. Outside stood two figures, a man aged around fifty and a young woman in her late twenties or early thirties. As far as he could tell they were unarmed so he placed the knife on a chair next to the door which he then fully opened before stepping outside to confront his visitors.

Both had the look of native South Americans, reminding Adam of the indigenous Peruvian people he and Sophie had met during their honeymoon some seven years earlier. The man was around six feet tall, dressed in a khaki trilby-style hat, denim jeans, a grey linen shirt with a woollen, heavily embroidered gilet over the top, again totally reminiscent of the typical South American style. On his feet he wore a pair of black sandals, possibly made from old car tyres, Adam reckoned. He was handsome and exuded wellness and vitality, his skin a deep golden brown, hair longish and jet black and he sported a slightly unkempt goatee beard. The young woman was wearing a long, blue linen dress, a straw hat from which hung two shoulder-length, deep-auburn pigtails and across her slender shoulders, an elaborately-patterned knee-length poncho. Her footwear was the same type of rubber-tyre sandal as that worn by the man. She stood around five foot six but appeared smaller due to the fact that she was stooped over, clutching her right arm with her left hand, her ashen face wracked with pain and breathing very heavily.

"*Excuse me señor,*" the man began, "*We did not mean to frighten you but we saw your plane and so knew that somebody was at home. My name is Pacha and this is my daughter Asiri. She fell into a small crater in the ground while we were out hunting and has injured her arm and shoulder very badly. We have come to Porta Mundorum III to use the infirmary but thought it best to speak with you first so as not to cause alarm.*"

Adam held out his hand which Pacha shook vigorously and warmly, "*My name is Adam Haylock,*" he said. "*I am a British air force pilot based at Teniente Rodolfo Air Base but I have deserted and flown south in an attempt to discover the true nature of this region. It is a pleasure to make your acquaintance, Pacha, and yours too, Asiri.*" He nodded awkwardly, bowing slightly, conscious that he was unable to shake her hand. Asiri said nothing but managed a brief, pained smile in response. Adam reckoned, looking at the way the arm was bent across her, that it was a shoulder break or dislocation plus an elbow fracture. She looked in a great deal of distress and discomfort but was dealing with it very bravely indeed.

Pacha smiled broadly. "*It is an honour to meet you too, Adam,*" he replied. "*We are inhabitants of Extrema, descended from the Quechuan Incas who fled South America four hundred years ago to escape the genocide wreaked on our people by the Spanish Conquistadors. Over the last one hundred years, many have returned north, enticed by the trappings of a western lifestyle but around two million of us remain here. We sailed to Porta Mundorum III this morning by boat from a village called Intipata, some thirty kilometres to the south on the eastern shore of Porta Lacus where we live off the land and the lake, enjoying long, happy lives in total freedom. We have no rulers, or controllers and abide by God's laws, not by the rules of men. My senses tell me that you are a good human being, Adam, an honourable man who possesses a good heart and spirit and I trust you are sensing the same from us also. Neither of us have anything to fear from the other so let us enjoy our time together whilst making Asiri well again. The infirmary here is available to anyone and my people have been enjoying its benefits for many years. If you would like to follow us over there I am sure you will find the healing methods most fascinating, yet very different to what you will have ever experienced previously.*"

With that he turned to Asiri and, supporting the injured limb, began to walk her slowly and carefully toward the infirmary building. Adam followed, curious as to what those healing methods might be and how they could possibly help to heal an injury as severe as Asiri's.

True to form, as soon as they opened the door to the infirmary, the interior lights came on and their eyes blinked and fluttered as they adjusted to the brightness of the room. The space measured around thirty feet long by fifteen wide and contained an array of futuristic-looking equipment, the most conspicuous of which was a huge bed encased in glass and steel with a monitor and an array of controls at one end which to Adam resembled a scanner of some sort. The place was spotlessly clean, sterile even; each piece of kit gleaming as if prepared by Jorge and Eduardo back at Teniente Rodolfo.

"What is all this Pacha?" he asked, utterly fascinated.

"This, mi amigo, is the finest healing facility you could ever wish for..." Pacha replied and then pointed at the bed, *"... and this particular piece of equipment is what we call a cama médica or medical-bed."*

"And what does it do, this cama médica?" the curious airman enquired.

Pacha walked across to the nearest bed and powered it up. *"It heals señor, it heals—using bio-resonance, the vibrational frequencies of the body and the world around us. It is highly intelligent and scans your body to discover what is wrong. First it inspects your skin, muscles, bones and organs and everything in your body, including the blood and then analyses the information to identify any disease or injury. This takes just two or three minutes after which it displays the results on the screen. You are then asked to commence regeneration or to cancel and if you authorise it to perform the healing then that process takes no more than fifteen to twenty minutes, depending upon how many things it needs to repair. After that you are cured and there are no side effects. Bones, tissue and organs are repaired and diseases are eradicated. It is wonderful."*

"So, do your people live forever then?" asked Adam. *"I mean, can you just abuse your bodies and then, when you get sick, all you have to do is jump on one of these beds? You can smoke, drink, take drugs, eat bad food, whatever you like, as much and as often as you like. Is that correct?"*

At this, Pacha sighed deeply, smiled and placed his hand on Adam's shoulder. *"Our life here is so far removed from yours, my friend. We have alcohol, we have tobacco, we have marijuana but nothing else and very few suffer from addiction. We do not produce bad food, there are no pesticides, no artificial additives or preservatives and, this may come as a surprise to you, no refined sugar. Instead, we sweeten mainly using honey. Our water is pure and rich in natural minerals. But there are two major reasons why we do not suffer the health problems of your world; most important of all, there are no pharmaceutical products in Extrema, not a single one. Also, we have no mobile communications, no permanent radio transmissions and thankfully, no television. All these things, Adam are what make your people disabled or sick and cause them to die before their time. Our children are born healthy and the average lifespan they can expect is around one hundred and twenty years, not as high as our friends in Thoth but far longer than yours and, in most cases, we do not live out our last few years suffering disability, illness and frailty. Yes, we fall ill and suffer accidents and some die before their time, but we are happy here and live cooperatively and harmoniously, both with ourselves and with the world around us. Before the cama médica came along, we could only treat sickness and disease. Injuries had to be repaired in the traditional way but now, broken bones are not a problem. The bed is clever however, very clever indeed and will only heal if there is no other possible method. For example, if you were overweight, which rarely happens here, it would tell you that and recommend dietary and lifestyle changes. So nobody is able to abuse their bodies and then expect an instant healing. We all know that, we accept it and take personal responsibility for our health and well-being. Furthermore, we thankfully have no major corporate entities and media propagandising us into believing that we 'need' their harmful products."*

Adam paused for a while, evaluating what he had just been told. Boy, had his paradigm shifted this last few weeks. *"So in Asiri's case, this is a genuine injury and the bed will fully repair it?"* he enquired, pointing to the girl's damaged limb.

"Absolutely. I would be amazed if it did not, mi amigo," Pacha insisted.

"Well, I'll still only believe it when I see it," Adam told them, but not unkindly.

Pacha laughed. *"Okay, Adam, then let us make you believe it,"* he said. *"Come, Asiri, let us show this sceptic that we are telling the truth."*

Gently and carefully, he started to remove Asiri's outer clothing. Adam turned away, not wishing to embarrass her. *"It is ok Adam,"* she assured him. *"All that matters is that I am healed and that you believe. I shall not be naked so am happy for you to watch the healing."*

Pacha laid her gently on the bed, the glass cover of which had opened-up when powered-on. He did his best to make her comfortable, gently fussing over his beloved daughter, strapping her in with three Velcroed belts and kissing her tenderly on the cheek. Asiri smiled back at him and closed her eyes. He returned to the monitor, tapped something on the screen and the glass cover slowly closed, hissing as it sealed shut. He then pressed the screen again and the bed began to scan her body. Translucent pipes running the length of the bed illuminated with white, blue and purple oscillating light and the machine purred gently. Asiri, eyes still closed, began to smile, the pained expression on her face fading. It was as if the scan was also performing some type of pain relief. After less than two minutes, the humming stopped, the lights dimmed to a very gentle violet and the monitor displayed the results. They were in Spanish but Pacha pressed the screen once again and they switched to English. Both men peered at the monitor which told them she had a dislocated shoulder, a fractured elbow, extensive bruising and tissue damage. No diseases were present in the body, all her internal organs were functioning correctly and her blood was perfect. Did they wish to continue?

Pacha spoke into a microphone positioned above the monitor and informed Asiri of the results, asking her if she wished him to authorise the regeneration. She nodded enthusiastically so he clicked 'yes' and the process commenced. This time the lights inside the bed glowed a very deep orange and the machine purred once more, though in a different tone. It was difficult to see Asiri clearly in this new light but Adam watched the injured arm intently, the best he could, in an attempt to spot the healing in progress. Once or twice he noticed slight shifts in the elbow angle and thought he could see the swelling reducing slightly but that was just about all. He inspected her shoulder. Something had definitely happened there as he could no longer detect the blade protruding through her skin in the same way it had before. Then the humming ceased and the lights went out. The bed hissed and the domed cover reopened. Pacha unfastened the straps and stood aside to allow Asiri to stand, which she did effortlessly, grinning and pain-free. She stretched both her arms above her head then reached down and touched her toes before shaking both arms vigorously and twisting them at the elbows.

"Do you believe us now Adam?" she beamed, picking-up her clothes and quickly dressing. Like her father, she also now radiated health, vitality and general well-being and for the first time, Adam realised just how beautiful she was; fully healed, restored and perfect. No doubt about that whatsoever.

"Well, I've seen everything now," exclaimed Adam. *"And I tell you, it goes against everything I've ever experienced or been told about treatment and healing. I mean, that bed is truly amazing. I'd love to find out just how it works if that's possible, and I'd also love to hear what the medical profession and pharmaceutical industry back home would have to say about it."*

In response, Pacha straightened his back and stuck his chest out, as if ready to make a public announcement. *"Well, let me tell you, Adam,"* he began. *"Everyone in our village has been made aware of how the equipment here works because we are kept fully informed by the people from Thoth who travel here regularly to install and maintain it. Throughout my life, all healing has been performed using either natural substances in the diet, spa treatments or bio-resonance equipment, of which the medical bed is the latest addition. Down here in Extrema, we have never been exposed to the west's pharmaceutical products in any way. We know of their existence and understand fully their effects on populations, so are thankful to God that they have no presence here. In simple terms, bio-resonance uses electromagnetic waves to diagnose and cure health conditions. Every living organism emits its own unique frequency and any imbalances in that frequency can lead to illness. The devices here identify such imbalances and the ailments they cause and then proceed to correct them and heal. Everything you see in this room is capable of performing miracles of one kind or another but the medical bed is the only one that can repair bones, which was why I did not consider anything else for Asiri. As you can see, my friend, it works and let me tell you from experience, it works every single time and as I said before, it uses perfectly natural processes and there are no side-effects."*

By the time Pacha finished speaking, Asiri had dressed again and stood smiling by the door waiting to leave. Her father switched-off the bed, the cover closing automatically as it powered-down. All three exited, with Adam closing the door behind them and when they reached the centre of the apron they stopped, unsure of what to do next. After a few seconds, Adam took control of the situation. *"Before you leave, would you like to join me for a meal or maybe some tea or coffee?"* he asked them.

"Yes please, I would like some coffee before I leave, Adam," replied Asiri. *"And perhaps also something to eat as I am quite hungry now."*

As the three ambled across toward the main building she took her father's hand and pulled him warmly towards her addressing him in a language unbeknown to Adam. *"Papa, I have had a wonderful idea!"* she exclaimed excitedly whilst immediately switching to English so that Adam could understand. *"It is Grandfather Supay's birthday celebration tomorrow if you remember, so shall we invite Adam so that he can meet everyone and see the village? If he travelled back with us now he could stay overnight and then enjoy the whole day with us tomorrow."*

Pacha nodded, a beaming grin spreading across his rugged, tanned and handsome face, his eyes sparkling. *"That is a wonderful idea, my little zapallo,"* he replied.[12] *"Adam, what do you think? Would you like to join us for the festivities? It will be a wonderful party and a memorable day."*

[12] Quechuan for pumpkin.

Chapter 40

Friday 24th February 2023 – Jorge and Eduardo's Plan

At 7.28am, four days after his initial stroll around the base with Eduardo, Dobbo sat perched on the edge of his bed, waiting for the agreed time to activate the plan. He had enjoyed three exercise sessions with the Chilean and so by now was fully briefed on the method of his escape. Other than communicating the plan itself, Eduardo had said very little, providing no explanation as to why he and Jorge were helping with the getaway and absolutely nothing regarding on whose behalf they were working, other than *'our people beyond the ice wall are behind this and are currently looking after Adam's interests.'*

His phone alarm beeped at 7.30 to signal the start of the operation but he remained seated on the bed awaiting the first trigger which was the arrival of Adam's replacement in the German Tornado. It was due to land at 7.30 but the instruction was to wait until he heard the fighter touch-down. At 7.32 he picked up the sound of the engines as the aircraft made its final approach followed a few seconds later by the roar of the reverse thrusters bringing it slowly to a halt on the runway. Immediately he stood up, walked to the end of the bed and lifted it off the floor. It hoisted easily and smoothly on a strong hinge and folded back against the wall revealing an opening in the floor about two feet square which it had previously concealed. The hatch which covered the hole, part of a mechanism attached to the underside of the bed, raised automatically, exactly as Eduardo had stated, and was fitted with a leather loop so that both it and the bed could be pulled-down from below to conceal the means of escape. Dobbo switched on his phone's flashlight and, peering into the gloom, could make out a set of wooden steps leading down to a stone floor.

The previous day during their morning walk, Eduardo had explained that beneath the base lay a network of tunnels linking virtually every room in each building to a central subterranean bunker area. It had all been excavated and constructed at the height of the cold war to offer the base's personnel some protection from a possible nuclear attack. However, the infrastructure was mothballed after the fall of the iron curtain, with all the tunnel-hatches being sealed with bolted plates along with the doors to all the rooms below. He added that Prendergast knew absolutely nothing about it but that he and Jorge had stumbled upon the hatch from their washroom in the hangar when they replaced the flooring the previous year. They subsequently recommissioned parts of it for their own use, unsealing several doorways and hatches in the process so when Prendergast ordered them to secure Dobbo's room, all they had to do was unseal the hatch and refit it to the underside of the bed. This afforded him a means of escape that would be very difficult to detect.

"Well here goes, Dobbo me old chum," he breathed as, grabbing the loop, he descended the stairs backwards pulling both hatch and bed down above him. *"Boy will this confuse Prenders, or what?"* he chuckled, finally reaching the foot of the stairs. Ahead of him lay a passage around eight feet high and the same in width tunnelled into the bare rock. It was cool and dry and thankfully there was only one direction along which he could travel, the steps to his room being a dead end and so he walked tentatively along the dark passage for about two hundred metres. Continue straight on, Eduardo had instructed, adding that he must not deviate on to any of the connecting tunnels until he reached a T-junction at which point the instruction was to turn right. As he approached the 'T' he could see a chink of light emanating from the right and after making the turn was presented with its source, a large steel door, slightly ajar. He paused then gingerly pushed the door which opened inward revealing a room, fully lit, heated and furnished like a WW2 briefing room. A large wooden, octagonal table filled the centre, surrounded by around a dozen chairs. Maps and blackboards adorned the walls and at the far end, a large leather sofa and four easy chairs were arranged around a low chrome, glass-topped table. Relaxing in one of the chairs, with hands behind his head sat Eduardo, a most self-satisfied grin adorning his face. Beside him on the table were two mugs, a steel coffee jug and a plate of mixed biscuits. Dobbo stepped inside and strode across towards his accomplice who hoisted himself from his chair and spread out both arms. The two men hugged, patting each other on the back as they did so. *"Well, señor Dobson,"* he beamed, looking Dobbo up and down, *"here you are, the escaped prisoner. And nobody knows how you did it, do they?"* He winked mischievously and then sat down again, beckoning the former inmate to do the same.

He poured them both a coffee and relaxed back into his chair, cradling the steaming mug in both hands. Dobbo perched himself down on the sofa and chose a chocolate bourbon from the plate which he then proceeded to dunk into his coffee as he ate it, something Eduardo had never seen anyone do before.

"So, what happens next, Eduardo?" Dobbo asked, mouth half-full of mushy biscuit. *"Do I have to hang around here for a while?"*

"No, not for long, my friend," replied Eduardo. *"I shall leave you here in a few minutes to assist Jorge with the Tornado and when we have finished, we will prepare Celeste for the next stage of your escape. That should not take too long, maybe one hour. We will fit her with drop tanks full of fuel and as much armament as we can in case you encounter any trouble. You wlll find a sack in the cockpit containing provisions for the journey along with a flight plan to get you far away from here and to safety. When one of us returns, we will take the tunnel to the hangar where Celeste, together with your flight suit and helmet, will be ready for you, all set to go. As soon as we open the hangar doors, just power-up and leave, as quickly as you possibly can."*

"So where am I heading to?" asked Dobbo, now pretty much overwhelmed by events.

Eduardo swallowed the remainder of his coffee and placed the mug back on the table with a clunk. *"Porta Mundorum III is your first stop,"* he declared. *"It is a friendly airbase in the land of Extrema, beyond the ice and the Antarctic highlands. Señor Haylock has managed to reach there safely but it is not your final destination. You will discover more when you arrive there."* Then, as he rose to leave, and much to Dobbo's surprise, he took on the persona of Arnold Schwarzenegger in *Terminator*. *"I'll be back!"* he barked in his best attempt at an Austrian accent and then, laughing to himself, he departed, closing the door firmly behind him.

Meanwhile, above ground some ten minutes after the arrival of Adam's replacement, a very dishevelled Prendergast, who had spent a long and exhausting night immersing himself in his favourite websites, left his quarters to go and greet the new pilot. By the time he reached the hangar, the Tornado, still bearing the livery of the German Luftwaffe was already being refuelled by Jorge to ensure it was intercept-ready if required. Two Sidewinder missiles lay on a trailer beside the port wing ready to be fitted. The new arrival, twenty-seven year old Fabian Schuster from Duisburg, already out of his flight gear, was in the office, making himself and the flight engineer a coffee. There was no sign of Eduardo, which Prendergast thought unusual as normally the two Chileans were joined at the hip, but he cast aside any suspicions when he heard the flushing of a toilet in the washroom followed by the whooshing of a hand drier. The door opened, Eduardo stepped out and when he caught sight of Prendergast began shaking his hands in an unconvincing, exaggerated manner. The Wing Commander was oblivious to his bad acting however, being far more concerned with greeting the German airman.

"Welcome to Teniente Rodolfo, Oberleutnant Schuster," he said shaking the younger man's hand warmly. *"Great to have you here and thanks for volunteering at such short notice."* Then a sudden thought struck him. *"Schuster, Schuster... now that name rings a bell,"* he muttered. *"I wonder where I've heard that name before?"* Puzzled, he then resumed his dialogue with the new arrival... *"Look, never mind the coffee,"* he continued, tapping the side of his nose with his forefinger. *"I have some excellent Schnapps in the bar so let's wander over there and raise a toast to Anglo-German Antarctic cooperation shall we?"*

He grabbed the arm of the overwhelmed and confused Oberleutnant and led him out of the office, through the hangar and on to the apron, chattering constantly without pausing or giving the German any opportunity to respond, which Fabian didn't mind actually and was happy, for now, to give Prendergast the impression that he spoke little or no English.

The two Chileans waited until Prendergast and his new underling entered the main building enroute to the bar, whereupon Eduardo breathed a huge sigh of relief. *"I almost messed things up there with my terrible acting, Jorge,"* he admitted to his friend. *"But fortunately the Wing Commander had other concerns on his mind. I will fetch señor Dobson and get him away from here before I make another bad mistake."*

As he scuttled-off to retrieve Dobbo, Jorge laid out the flight suit and helmet, removed the chocks from Celeste's wheels and performed the final visual inspection prior to departure. After a couple of minutes, Eduardo returned with the soon-to-be-free prisoner and helped him quickly into his flight gear before ushering him across to the waiting F-5. As he was about to ascend the stepladder, Dobbo turned to his two saviours and with tears welling in his eyes embraced them both warmly. *"Thank you my friends, thank you,"* he murmured with lip quivering. *"I shall never, ever forget what you have done for me here. Adios amigos."*

"Safe journey—Godspeed. Now go quickly please," urged Jorge, nudging him on to the bottom rung of the stepladder.

Meanwhile, as they made their way to the bar and the Schnapps awaiting them, Prendergast and Fabian reached the door to Dobbo's quarters. Prendergast stopped and fumbled around in his pockets. *"Hold on a minute, Fritz,"* he said, pulling out a bunch of keys. *"Before our little toast let me introduce you to our prisoner. I'm sure it will make his day to meet you."* He unlocked both padlocks, pulled back the latches and stepped inside, followed closely by Fabian. The bedroom was empty so assuming Dobbo to be in the bathroom he called out, *"Dobson, you pathetic excuse for a human being, you have a visitor."* With no answer forthcoming he tried the bathroom door which wasn't even closed properly, never mind locked. The bathroom was empty. With mounting anxiety and confusion, he peered into the shower cubicle—nobody in there either. *"Dobson, Dobson,"* he yelled. *"Where the bloody hell are you?"* Returning to the bedroom, he checked inside the wardrobe and finally he peered under the bed and spotted the hatch cover mechanism. *"What the..."* he barked. *"You bastard! I'll fucking kill you for this!"* At that very moment, Celeste's engines roared and both men ran to the window. From there they could see the fighter being towed along the taxiway. *"He's not getting away Fritz, not if I can help it. Follow me, let's go after him."*

To keep noise to an absolute minimum, Jorge had used the electric tug to tow Celeste out of the hangar doors, across the apron and on to the taxiway. It was as they trundled towards the runway that Dobbo began firing-up the engines in readiness for a quick take-off and it was this that had alerted Prendergast. Once on the runway, Jorge detached the tug, turned away and waving farewell, sped-off as fast as the vehicle could travel leaving Dobbo free to increase throttle and roar forward before lifting gracefully into the sky and accelerating away southward. As Jorge transported the tug back to the hangar he spotted Prendergast, accompanied by Fabian, frantically sprinting across the apron, flight suits and helmets in hand. *"This should be very interesting,"* he mused. "I wonder how *El Coño Feo is going to handle this particular situation."*

In no hurry to return to the hangar and face the wrath and rantings of the Wing Commander, he slowed the tug to a crawl and began to whistle casually and nondescriptly. Prendergast must have noticed this and began waving his arms, beckoning him towards the hangar and urging him to speed-up. Jorge simply pretended not to notice and continued his slow velocity driving and banal whistling, whilst looking around him as if captivated by the fresh morning air and the landscape. By the time he returned to the hangar, the two fliers, now fully suited and helmeted, were stood over Eduardo who was attempting single-handedly to load the missiles on to the Tornado, a task that always required two sets of hands. When he reached the fighter, Prendergast turned to face him, red-faced, eyes bulging and nostrils flaring.

"Help this clueless cretin get these sodding missiles mounted on here right now, you miserable pile of dago llama shit," he yelled, shoving Jorge in the direction of the trailer. *"If we don't get airborne soon, we'll never catch Dobson, regardless of how much faster this plane is, so hurry the fuck up. Pronto! Pronto!"*

As the two engineers busied themselves with the Sidewinders, Fabian and co-pilot Prendergast clambered into the cockpit and began the pre-flight checks. By the time these were completed the missiles had been fitted, the chocks removed and the tug attached. Jorge, cursing under his breath, gave them a half-hearted and reluctant thumbs-up and began to slowly pull the Tornado out of the hangar. Prendergast sounded the plane's siren and when Jorge turned round he could see the irate officer gesturing furiously for him to speed up. This he did, though not by very much and continued to tow the fighter casually towards the taxiway. The siren wailed again with the by-now incandescent Prendergast gesticulating for the tug to be detached from the aircraft. Jorge shrugged his shoulders at them, shaking his head, pretending not to understand and continued pulling the jet towards the runway. The next thing he heard was the report of a bullet and the crash as it ricocheted off the panel beside him. Prendergast had opened the canopy and was leaning out, Glock in hand, firing at Jorge. *"Mierda!"* yelled the panic-stricken Chilean, instantly detaching the tug and veering to the right. Prendergast fired one more shot and everything in Jorge's world went blank as simultaneously his now lifeless body slumped in a heap on to the tarmac. As the Tornado's canopy closed around him, *El Coño Feo*, grinned evilly in triumph as the driverless, blood-spattered tug lurched off the tarmac on to the rough ground beside it and then tumbled unceremoniously into a ditch. With a deafening roar the Tornado took off and, as had Dobbo and Celeste a full ten minutes earlier, swung to the south accelerating rapidly as it climbed. The chase was on.

Chapter 41

Thursday 23rd February 2023 – Intipata Village

Adam had not slept well. In fact it was the only bad night he'd experienced during his time in Extrema. His chest ached, a dull pain from near his heart spreading across his sternum, his head pounded and he was hot, clammy with sweat yet shivering constantly. He had begun to feel under the weather during the boat trip down to Intipata with Pacha and Asiri and believed that he had concealed it well from everyone throughout the evening but now he felt genuinely ill yet still reluctant to bother his hosts with it.

He pondered over what could be causing it. Could it be that, as mentioned in the guest book at Porta Mundorum III, he possessed the same bad energy which conflicted with the frequencies down here, meaning that he would simply get worse and possibly die if he stayed? Given the nature of many of the missions he'd been asked to undertake during his military career, particularly over Syria and Libya, that could very well be the case. He had followed orders which had compromised him into betraying humanity many times, when he should have simply refused and made a stand but with the exception of covering for Dobbo's indiscretion in 2011, he had never flouted authority, choosing instead to toe the line and obey his superiors officially legitimate, yet so often immoral orders.

Deep down he felt he was a genuinely decent person, albeit previously conditioned and brainwashed into compliance to authority throughout his education as well as during all those years in the RAF. But he was different now surely? His eyes were beginning to open to the lies and deceptions of the ruling classes and the 'cabal' and right now he was experiencing first-hand the real truth regarding Antarctica and the stark beauty of the lands beyond. He now knew for certain that the whole world had been deceived about the continent and indeed the true nature of the so-called planet upon which they resided. In addition to that he strongly suspected that most, if not everything mankind had been led to believe, certainly over the previous one hundred and fifty years—if not much, much longer was deliberately falsified. This was true especially of geography, history, politics, and science, which were all most likely fabricated in one way or another to benefit the overriding ambitions of a select few and to further their insidious agenda.

The voyage along the majestic waters of Porta Lacus had for the major part been a wonderful experience, the most memorable being a school of around twenty freshwater dolphins bow-riding the boat for a full fifteen minutes at one point as it sped southward. Adam had read in the flora and fauna guide that these animals existed in Porta Lacus although he had not yet been treated to a sight of them during his sorties in the kayak. Pacha and Asiri were almost oblivious to their appearance and performance whilst Adam, leaning over the prow, watched-on in excitement and delight at their antics. As they took full advantage of the free ride given to them by the boat's pressure wave, they would occasionally turn sideways to look-up at him—straight into his eyes in fact, whistling and chirping as they did so. It seemed that while bow-riding, they were communicating, amongst themselves obviously but Adam was sure they were calling out to him too. What might they be saying, he wondered? At one particular bay the boat stopped and Pacha dropped anchor so they could all take a swim in the crystal clear waters and also to check some pots which had been placed the previous evening. Each one was full to the brim with huge freshwater crabs and crayfish, which Asiri said were to form a major part of the celebration feast the following day.

It was as they resumed their voyage that Adam began to feel unwell, initially thinking it could be motion sickness from the boat but when had he ever suffered from that before? He tried to put it to the back of his mind and mentioned nothing to his most welcoming and genial hosts but by the time he retired for the night he was feeling pretty dreadful, exacerbated by his worry of it being due to his possessing 'bad energy' as had been explicitly stated in the guest book at PM3.

Despite his worsening malady, the evening spent with the family was most entertaining and enlightening. Asiri had two siblings, an older brother Kusi, who was there with his wife Urpi, heavily pregnant with her first child, and a much younger sister Illari who proudly informed Adam that she was thirteen years old and throughout the meal sat staring at him transfixed, saying very little else. Asiri's mother Saywa was a personable, calm and softly spoken individual as well as the most marvellous cook, preparing a meal of brown rice, baked trout and roasted aubergines with a sensational rich sauce, the ingredients of which he couldn't really make-out but which tasted divine. The aromas and flavours were like nothing he had ever experienced and he could see why, by eating natural, untainted food all their lives, the whole family were brimming with vitality and well-being. They drank spring water with their meal along with a locally produced mead, finishing-off with a dessert of fresh berries and ice cream. They chatted long into the evening and Adam found them to be without any exaggeration the warmest, most articulate and knowledgeable people he had ever met.

Kusi was particularly talkative and informative, telling Adam that it was in fact a group of villagers from Intipata who kept PM3 supplied, clean and maintained but that twice a year, a team from Thoth paid a visit to fill the fuel tanks, service all the equipment and make any necessary repairs. They would sail up Porta Lacus in a supply boat and remain there for two or three days at a time to ensure the base was kept in tip-top condition as well as adequately supplied with food and other resources.

Despite an apparent total absence of any school or college in the village, Kusi appeared highly-educated, possessing a detailed knowledge of the history of not only his own people but also that of our realm and spoke at length about the genocide of his ancestors at the hands of the Spanish Conquistadors and their subsequent exodus from South America. He described the long arduous journey they undertook from the southern tip of Tierra del Fuego across the perilous waters of the Southern Ocean in flimsy, ramshackle rowing and sailing boats and then on foot over the Antarctic wastes before settling in Extrema. Apparently, those verdant lands beyond Antarctica had long been a legend believed by his people, even well before the Conquistadors arrived and so it seemed a natural destination for them. Even so, thousands of them died on the perilous trek to the paradise in which their descendants now lived.

He also mentioned the pyramids, which he said could be found throughout Antarctica and Extrema (as well as liberally sprinkled throughout the entirety of the 'known' world) many of which, particularly those located beyond the ice, had been built by the Quechuan Incas in the seventeenth and eighteenth centuries as healing, communication and energy installations and still functioned as such today. Pre-dating these, he added, were many others, positioned on high plateaux within the Antarctic mountain massif but as to who erected them, he had no idea but that they formed part of a huge network stretching the entire length and breadth of the forbidden continent. When Adam described the three pyramids he had spotted on his flight down to Extrema, Kusi knew them well, having led an expedition north to visit and photograph them several years previously.

Between them, the family described Extreman society, its customs and the lifestyle they enjoyed in Intipata. While living relatively simple and pastoral lives, completely in-sync with nature and the Earth's natural frequencies, they possessed sophisticated technology such as motor vehicles, farm machinery, computers and telephones and their homes were very well equipped and comfortable. Rather similar to PM3 in fact. Nobody owned any mobile communication devices, they had their own form of internet and email but no social media, which they considered was undermining western society and had been deliberately set-up as a way to monitor as well as distract and divide the population.

Adam asked him what money, if any, they used and was surprised to hear that all their currency was in the form of gold and silver coins and that they had no electronic currency of any kind. The majority of the time they did not actually use coins, preferring instead to exchange goods or services, covering most transactions with what they called 'pagarés'[13] stating precisely what had been received and what was to be repaid in exchange. When someone was born, an amount of gold and silver money was mined and added into the overall money supply which then, every ten years, was topped up with additional money from the reserves. Money could be loaned from the reserves and repaid interest free, although, and he stressed this most strongly, barely any citizens held any debt as it was widely recognised to be a form of slavery and control, unique to the realm far to the north of theirs—OUR world! All of this also had the happy effect of totally eradicating inflation and usury.

Adam both envied and admired them in equal measure. Very much. They were happy, healthy, intelligent, articulate, generous and loving. They knew only too well the excesses and evils of our world and yet were willing to embrace technology that was appropriate, useful and unharmful but were not governed or controlled by it in any way. He admired their wholesome family-orientated lives, their respect for nature, their lack of any kind of materialism and the value they placed upon personal freedoms and sovereignty. They resided and participated in a co-operative community where crime and family breakdown was pretty much unheard of. Life wasn't always a bed of roses for them and disasters and hardships would occasionally come along but they appeared, to him anyway, to function as a society should—and he wished he could have been born and raised here, rather than in Cambridge, which now seemed as remote to him as the moon.

Asiri took over from Kusi when Adam asked where Thoth was in relation to Intipata. As she spoke, he became more aware of her beauty and warm personality and found himself looking deep into her eyes, yet not really absorbing what she was saying. He had felt little or no physical attraction to any woman since the Sophie debacle but he definitely did this evening. He knew that this attraction could very easily develop into love and probably a love such as he had never known before but then remembered just why his marriage had ended so abruptly. He knew that he would be of no use to Asiri, given his infertility problems. She would doubtless want children for sure and he would not be able to satisfy that need, so he swiftly composed himself, placed any such thoughts or desires to one side and moved on, opting instead to paying attention and listening to what she was telling him.

[13] Promissory notes.

She described how our world is covered by a huge firmament or impenetrable dome and that Extrema sits on its very edge. She also added that the realm of Thoth lies beyond, under its very own firmament, much smaller than ours and with just the single, local sun. The main island of Thoth, around 3,500 miles distant from Intipata, sits in the Ahtian Ocean and is the largest within the Osiris Archipelago. Measuring something approaching four thousand miles in length, over forty million people inhabit the archipelago with all but ten million of those residing on Thoth itself. The ruling cabal of our world is all too aware of Extrema and Thoth and for the past one hundred and twenty years has done everything in its power to prevent the rest of the population from finding out about them. *"They do not want the Earthlanders to know that a far, far better place exists beyond their realm where people are happier, living much longer and far healthier lives in a wonderful environment at one with creation,"* she explained. *"We are protected from them by the good people of Thoth, something for which we are truly thankful. Your leaders are terrified of them and have, for the most part, refrained from provoking them in any way. That, along with the fact that many of them fall sick here is why they leave us alone to live in peace and harmony. And long may that continue."*

As Adam took-in all of this, his mind struggling to accept the amazing, almost unbelievable information he was being given by Asiri, he suddenly became acutely aware of just how desperately ill he was now feeling. He had not felt as bad as this since late 2021/early 2022 and with that in mind, the penny dropped. He had left his medication back at Teniente Rodolfo. In his haste to leave and fly south he had completely forgotten his supply of blood thinners and betablockers and that was obviously why he was now suffering such extreme discomfort. Utter panic overwhelmed him as his heartrate began to rapidly increase and he could feel it missing beats as it accelerated away, careering out of control. Feebly and shakily, he raised himself to his feet in an attempt to excuse himself. He was red-faced and sweating profusely, eager to leave the room and maybe get some fresh air but as he began to turn away, an horrendous stabbing pain pierced his chest. He lurched forward, collapsing on to the dining table and scattering plates, glasses and cutlery everywhere before tumbling unconsciously to the ground, cracking his skull on the corner of the chair beside him as he fell.

Chapter 42

Saturday 25th February 2023 – Dobbo's Arrival at PM3

Celeste's wheels hit the Porta Mundorum III runway with a loud squeal accompanied by a cloud of rubber smoke as Dobbo, physically and mentally exhausted from his incarceration and traumatic escape, made a rather sloppy and amateurish landing for a pilot of his skill and pedigree. As had Adam before him, he spotted the air base's lights from a considerable distance away and decided to head there and land, desperately hoping to find his old friend safe and well, just as Eduardo had promised.

Sadly, there was no sign of Esmerelda and he sighed in disappointment as he brought the F-5 to a halt on the apron just outside the main building. He sincerely hoped that Adam had landed here previously and that by some miracle he had made the same journey southward, but the realist within him was telling him no, that was too much to ask. Was there even the remotest possibility that several days apart and with no route guidance, they would end-up at the same air base? *"Don't be an utter bell-end, Dobson!"* he cursed in self-rebuke. *"What are the chances of that for God's sake?"*

Fifteen minutes later, having performed an almost identical inspection of the accommodation to that which Adam had undertaken several days previously, he made himself a very strong coffee, grabbed a handful of oatmeal biscuits and sat himself down at the bureau to peruse the *'Welcome Friends'* and *'Visitors'* books.

As he worked his way through the welcome book, aghast yet spellbound by the information being disclosed, he felt overwhelmed—it was almost too much to take-in but, given his experiences over the last few months, he now knew that absolutely anything was possible and what he was reading seemed, at face value anyway, to make perfect sense to him.

He closed the book and placed it aside whilst pulling the one marked 'Visitors' to the centre of the desktop and opening it. Heart racing, hoping for the best yet fearing the worst, he quickly leafed through to the very last page of entries and scanned to the bottom.

"YES, YES, YES, FUCKING YES!" he hollered in his excitement at the words before his eyes. *"Adam Haylock, you absolute beauty!"*

There it was in blue, instantly recognisable, handwritten ink...

'Squadron Leader Adam Haylock, now thankfully former Royal Air Force, F-5 Freedom Fighter 807. Arrived 18th February 2023, departed 24th February. Onward direction due south along Porta Lacus; destination, the land of Thoth, wherever or whatever that may turn out to be. God only knows how I am going to get there but given that I have been fortunate enough to make it here, I am happy to trust fate and venture further into the unknown. Dobbo my good friend and comrade, if you too have somehow managed to make it to Porta Mundorum III and are reading this, then my advice to you would be to rest and recuperate for a few days, meet the wonderful villagers of Intipata if at all possible, use the infirmary to heal yourself of any ailments you may have and then follow me down the lake. This is the adventure of all adventures my friend and we are truly privileged to be participating in it.'

Euphoric and brimming with joy and relief, Dobbo let out a huge breath of air, closed the book and spun himself around and around in the chair in delight. His friend was safe and well. Eduardo was right, he had decided to carry on with his quest for truth and Samuel James Dobson, erstwhile of Scarborough, England was going to do the same and hopefully reunite with him sometime very soon.

And then suddenly, his euphoria was broken by the roar of reverse thrusters filling the entire space around him and bringing him abruptly back to his senses. Another aircraft had just touched down—obviously a jet of some description. Could it be Adam in Esmerelda, possibly returning after an unsuccessful attempt to reach Thoth? Yes, that's who it would be, he assured himself. Who else could possibly have made their way here so soon after them? He raced to the door, flung it open and charged out on to the apron. As the jet taxied toward him he instantly recognised the marque, a Tornado GR-4 twin-seater and he could make out two occupants in the cockpit. He realised with extreme disappointment that it wasn't Adam's F-5 and instantly all his joy and euphoria drained away.

He watched-on disconsolately as the Tornado parked alongside Celeste. The engines powered-down and everything was silent again. The canopy raised and he watched the chief pilot, sitting at the front, remove his mask and raise the helmet visor. He wasn't recognisable but given the insignia on the aircraft, Dobbo assumed he was most likely German. The co-pilot behind him disembarked first, mask and visor still in place and stood by the plane, looking around as he waited for the chief pilot to leave the cockpit. The two then strode towards Dobbo, the co-pilot unfastening his flight clothing as they made their way across the apron but as the helmet was removed, Dobbo's heart sank. *"Prendergast!"* he exclaimed, panic and terror overwhelming him in an instant. He turned and raced back into the accommodation building, slamming the door closed behind him and headed for the kitchen. He pulled the largest knife he could find from the block and stood facing the door, his back against the stainless steel worktop, weapon in hand and ready for use if need be.

He stood there glued to the spot, his heart racing and his hands clammy with sweat. He heard the two men enter the reception area, followed by Prendergast's dulcet tones. *"I know you're in here Dobson, you miserable fucking arsehole! You are in deep shit my friend and there's no way on this Earth—or any other—that you can wriggle your way out of this one. No way José!"*

He braced himself for whatever his commanding officer had in store for him and pointed the knife at arm's length towards the door in a vain attempt to look more menacing and 'tooled-up.' The unmistakable silhouette of Prendergast then appeared at the door, walking slowly and menacingly toward Dobbo with the Glock 17 held tightly in his right hand.

Prendergast stopped six or seven feet short of Dobbo, a malevolent grimace spreading across his face. *"Did you honestly think you could get away from me, Dobson?* he sneered. *"Because, if you did, it was most naïve of you. I simply can't let dumbass morons like you get away with anything, particularly if I'm to be held accountable, and as far as all this Antarctica shit is concerned, I am accountable as hell to the very highest powers-that-be. And let me tell you, these people take no shit whatsoever and I'm deadly serious now when I tell you that if you were ever to get back to our world knowing what you know now, then we'd both be dead meat, so this is it for you now you sorry arsehole, I'm very happy to say at last."*

He raised the Glock, pointing it straight between the eyes of the hapless airman. Dobbo felt his guts start to collapse as the inevitability of his fate dawned on him. Somehow though, he managed to steel himself and he charged towards Prendergast, roaring like a demented lion. His manic shrieking rant however, was then completely overwhelmed and cut short by the ear-splitting sound of a single gunshot and the spotless kitchen walls were instantaneously re-decorated with copious amounts of blood, brain matter and bone fragments.

Chapter 43

Friday 1st August 2008 – Francesca Forrestal's Letter

Mateo's letters to the two ladies read...

"My dear Katherine/Francesca

Please forgive the intrusion but I am very anxious to discover the facts surrounding my father and your husband/father's death. I am concerned that given what happened to his father James and my uncle, David Pearson, that something similar could have happened to him.

I was wondering if I could prevail upon you to let me know if you are aware of any reason that you may have to doubt the official autopsy findings, so that I can investigate further and try to get at the truth—if indeed the official story is not the truth!

Hopefully my contacting you again has not caused you any distress but if so I do sincerely apologise wholeheartedly and should you decide not to reply, then I fully understand. However it would mean a great deal to me if we could put the past behind us and work together—even if only temporarily.

I would very much like to hear from you if you have any nagging doubts—even tiny ones, regarding the official cause of father's death.

Wishing you all the very best for the future, whatever you decide to do.

Sincerely
Mateo Forestello (Matthew Forrestal)"

The next day Mateo posted the letter and hoped for the best, whilst fearing the worst. Anyway, he decided, it's in the lap of the gods now, I can do no more.

Several days went by, then a week, two weeks, a month and still no reply. He anxiously checked the mail each day and was disappointed every single time not to find an envelope in his pigeonhole postmarked 'Cork, Ireland.' Until one morning, around six weeks after he had sent his letters, suddenly there it was, a smallish brown envelope with the postmark for which he had so fervently hoped.

He took it in hand and turned it over and over, staring at it curiously but not daring to open it for fear of receiving bad news. Eventually he placed it on his desk and went about the day's business until finally he could no longer stand the tension and suspense and so retrieved it. With slightly trembling hands he tore open the precious envelope and read the letter contained within. It was brief and to the point.

"Dear Mateo

Thank you for your letter. I would very much appreciate it if you would kindly phone me on +353 1 568 2240 (Cork, Ireland) at your convenience, bearing in mind please that we are three hours ahead of you.

Yours sincerely
Francesca Forrestal"

Mateo was momentarily stunned. *'Surely this means that she has some news about father's death?'* he thought. But then he suddenly doubted himself again. *'Or perhaps she is just being polite in replying and there is no news? No, no...'* he changed his mind yet again. *'...She MUST have some news of some sort otherwise she wouldn't have asked me to call.'*

He checked the time. It was 11.45am, 2.45pm in Ireland and so surmised that she may be at work—or busy doing whatever—and resolved to leave it until around 4.00pm Argentina time, at which point she may just have begun relaxing for the evening.

Again, he waited until around 7.20pm Ireland time ('just to make sure'—he convinced himself) and then carefully dialled Francesca's number.

He could barely stand the suspense of it all. Would she have news for him? Would she even answer? Had she asked him to call simply so that she could berate him for upsetting her mother? All these thoughts, plus more, swam around his head in a maelstrom of confusion but he didn't have long to wait for his answer.

"Hello brother!" she greeted him, with a distinct smile in her voice. She had recognised the foreign number in her phone's display window and had correctly assumed it to be him. Momentarily shocked, he instantly relaxed and responded in kind.

"Hello sis. How are you?" he chirped breezily, as though he had known her all his life.

"Grand to hear from you" she drawled in her lilting Cork accent, *"and thanks a million for calling. I'm just fine, ta!"*

"It's my pleasure Francesca and so nice to finally make contact at last. I only found out I had a sister a few months ago and it was such a pleasant surprise to me! As far as I'm aware you are my only living, close relative." Mateo was genuinely relieved and delighted that their first contact was so cordial. *"I hope that my contacting you both did not stress or upset your mother?"* he asked tentatively.

"Oh no, she's fine thanks. It all happened a long time ago now and she's quite happy to talk about it."

Francesca seemed so pleasant and friendly to him, that he wished he had tried to contact her again sooner. He was also relieved that her mother didn't appear to have any animosity towards him either.

"So, you asked me to call you?" he ventured tentatively. *"Dare I hope that you have something interesting to tell me about our father's death?"*

"Well, first of all, let me just say that mum thought it best if it was meself who contacted you—us being of a similar age and all!" Now her Irish brogue really began to shine through as she began to relax even more. *"It's not that she doesn't want to talk to you, she genuinely thought it would make more sense for us to get to know each other first—and to be honest, I know just as much as she does about what happened, so it makes no difference at all!"*

"Well OK, I understand perfectly," said Mateo. *"Maybe Katherine and I will talk at some point in the future? But please do tell me what you know."*

"It's not an awful lot, Mateo, so please don't build your hopes up too much, but here goes…" She took a deep breath before continuing.

"The day dad died—which as you know was just before I was born—mum went out into town to meet a friend for lunch and when she left the house, dad had seemed a bit, you know, anxious about something or other—not ill, nor feeling a little off-colour, just anxious was all. And that morning he had had a phone call from someone, mum didn't know who, and he was very evasive when she asked and this call seemed to really unsettle him. But she thought no more about it. Then when she got back home about three hours later, she found him slumped on the couch, lifeless. But…" and here she paused for a second or two as though considering it again, herself. *"…The furniture had been rearranged*

slightly. Not too much, just enough that mum could see a difference. A side table had been placed at the wrong end of the couch and the couch had been moved but only slightly. She could see the faint marks in the carpet where the castors had been previously. And most puzzling of all, her favourite vase had gone—just disappeared! But the next day when she took some trash out to the dustbin, it was in there—smashed to pieces! She never mentioned this to anyone, she was fearful that it might lead her into trouble but she suspected that there had been an intruder, some kind of struggle, and that dad's death was not natural. Oh and I forgot to mention it but there was also a button missing off of dad's shirt, which she found several weeks later when she moved a chair to vacuum under it." Here Francesca paused again, thoughtfully, considering carefully what she was about to say next.

"But the strangest thing of all was the result of the autopsy," she continued. *"They said that he had died of a massive intestinal haemorrhage caused by his heavy drinking but mum swore on all things holy that he barely touched a drop—except on special occasions, birthdays, Christmas and so on. So that really put the tin lid on it as far as she was concerned. Mum knew for sure then that he had been murdered in some way—just as our Grandpa had been decades earlier and poor old David Pearson too, God rest their souls!"* The emotion of it all had got to her now and she wept silently for a few moments.

Mateo now experienced mixed emotions. Here was the link between the three deaths he had been anticipating and more than half-expecting. He was rendered speechless for a short time and then asked Francesca... *"Do you know if father had been actively investigating our grandfather's death and trying get the truth out there?"*

Francesca, now recovered from her short emotional interlude, replied unequivocally, *"Oh yes, absolutely. He had made it his life's mission to get justice for his dad. And the other thing he was obsessed with was Antarctica. He was convinced by grandpa that all was not as it seemed down there, for some reason. Do you think that's why they killed him off too, Mateo?"* she asked him, somewhat naively.

"There's no doubt in my mind at all now sis," he answered her as tenderly as he could. *"I think we all need to be very careful in future. I am finding out lots of incredible stuff right now about what is really going on in the world and one day, when hopefully we finally meet, I will tell you all about it!"*

The conversation continued for another hour or more and Mateo, now satisfied beyond all reasonable doubt that his grandfather, father and uncle had all been ruthlessly disposed-of by the deep state, began to formulate his next steps, knowing that he would have to tread exceptionally carefully in the future. But for now he was absolutely determined that one day he would get to the bottom of this Antarctica mystery.

Chapter 44

Friday 24th February 2023 – Adam's Recovery

Adam wasn't sure if he was dead or alive. But one thing he did know was that he felt pain-free, without a care in the world and supremely comfortable; either floating on air or suspended in a pool but very much able to breathe. Whatever it was that surrounded him, be it water, air or some other gas, it was warm with a reassuring translucent orange glow, accompanied by a wonderfully soothing and rhythmic humming sound which he was sure he had heard before but could not place it.

He tried to stretch out but realised immediately that he was being held in place by straps binding him to a cushioned surface; one on his head, the second around his torso and arms and the third securing his feet. A brief moment of panic ensued and his feeling of well-being began to drain away but this was short lived as within seconds the humming stopped, followed by a loud hiss as the orange light was replaced by a cloud of cold steam. The steam stung his eyes a little and he closed them tight shut to relieve the irritation. Reluctant to reopen them he lay motionless, fearful as to what was going to happen next. He then heard what sounded like a sliding door opening or closing and cautiously opened his right eye to investigate, finding that the steam and the orange light had dissipated and there, standing above him, beaming from ear to ear stood Pacha, his friend from Intipata village.

"Welcome back to the land of the living, Adam," declared the Quechuan, quickly releasing the restraining straps. He took Adam's hand, pulled him up from the bed and steadied him as the bemused Brit wobbled to his feet, pressing them firmly into the floor in an attempt to reassure himself that he was very much back in that land—as well as fully able to walk upon it.

"Hi Pacha, am I glad to see you, my friend," he said, smiling warmly and placing his hands on Pacha's broad shoulders. The two men looked at each other for a few seconds then hugged firmly, the bond between them growing ever and ever stronger.

As they separated from their brief embrace, Pacha took up the story. *"We thought we were going to lose you there—you were very, very sick. After you collapsed, we carried you to the boat and sailed here as fast as we possibly could, fearing the worst but thankfully you stayed with us and we were able to get you to the cama médica just in time.*

As he spoke, the door of the infirmary opened and the tall figure of Kusi stepped inside. *"A very good morning to you, Adam. And how are you feeling after your little flirtation with the afterlife?"*

"All the better for seeing you, Kusi," Adam chuckled, shaking him by the hand before taking him in both arms and hugging him also.

Kusi helped Adam back into his outer clothes and shoes, Pacha powered down the bed and the three men walked across to the accommodation block where Kusi had been preparing a lunch of boiled crayfish and rice for the three of them to enjoy post-Adam's recovery.

As they tucked enthusiastically and ravenously into their food, none of them having eaten for over half a day, Pacha enlightened Adam as to the diagnoses made by the medical bed and the healing he had undergone. Apparently he was in a very sorry state by the time they arrived back at PM3 but they had wasted no time in placing him on the bed and commencing the examination. The results were not exactly what they had expected though, three serious ailments were listed plus one injury.

The first and by far the most major was severe myocarditis, an inflammation of the heart muscle, which makes it difficult for blood to be pumped around the body. This had been caused by medication received sometime during the previous four or five years, the report had said. The next item flagged was his blood pressure which was sky high at 184/126. The third problem identified was an incredibly low sperm count. For a man of his age, it should have been between 120 and 150. Adam's was a paltry 9 and due apparently to him suffering an acute case of mumps in childhood. The very last thing mentioned was serious wear and tear on the cruciate ligament in his right knee. It had clicked and felt sore for years and though no particular cause was listed, Adam knew exactly what it was—rugby, no doubt about it. But it did not click now, that was for sure, and the joint moved freely, easily and silently as he flexed his leg forward and back beneath the table.

The bed had done its job magnificently and he felt completely renewed, rejuvenated even. Pacha informed him that he would have no further need for any of the medication he had left behind and that his sperm count and right knee would never be an issue again, so long as he maintained a healthy lifestyle with a balanced and nutritious diet. *"Whatever you decide to do, just do not return north, Adam. Settle here with us in Intipata or venture on further to Thoth and you will be fine,"* he advised.

Adam considered this before seeking their opinion on his immediate future. *"So, what would you two do if you were me in my situation?"* he quizzed them. *"Stay in Extrema or carry on to Thoth?"*

"What is your heart telling you, Adam?" asked Kusi very earnestly. *"You should always listen to your heart. It is nearly always right."*

"My head is kind of saying stay here and settle amongst you and your people, if you'll have me?" Adam replied. *"It is a wonderful place and you all seem to enjoy long, healthy and happy lives but my heart says no, go on, explore further and unearth more truths. If only Dobbo was here to share all this with me, I know for sure that he'd want to continue the adventure."*

He pushed a crayfish claw around the plate with his fork, deep in thought. *"Look..."* he began, *"I've come this far I suppose, so I may as well continue. I'm gonna try to get to Thoth and I'm leaving right now!"*

He banged his fist on the table, jumped to his feet and promptly disappeared into the dormitory to gather some belongings together.

Chapter 45

Saturday 25th February 2023 – The Aftermath of the Shooting

Prendergast's head had simply disintegrated in front of Dobbo's eyes; all the detritus of the explosion virtually covering Dobbo from head to foot, in addition to the kitchen wall behind him. The lifeless body slammed heavily to the floor and the Glock 17 went-off as the hand in which it was held hit the deck with a heavy metallic clang, the stray bullet clipping Dobbo in the right heel after ricocheting from the metal lampshade on the ceiling. He screeched in agony as the projectile ripped through his boot, tearing tissue and shattering the bone. He gingerly lifted his foot to inspect the damage—it was an absolute bloody mess—literally, the pain nigh-on unbearable and Dobbo almost passed-out in shock at the sight. But at least he was still alive, unlike the prostrate, virtually headless corpse that only a few moments earlier had been *El Coño Feo,* Agent Michael Joseph Prendergast, MI6.

The next thing he heard was the clank of something dense and metallic hitting the ground followed by the sobs of a grown man crying. It was Fabian, on his knees, head down, his discarded revolver beside him, wailing uncontrollably and his shoulders shaking violently as he struggled for breath. Dobbo crawled across to him as best he could, dragging the injured foot behind him whilst leaving a trail of blood and knelt down beside Fabian, placing his hand on the German's shoulder in sympathy and reassurance.

"It's ok mate, it's ok," he whispered as empathetically as he could muster under the circumstances. *"You got the bastard and you saved my life. Everything is gonna be fine."*

Fabian's sobbing eased somewhat and he looked up, staring in his despair straight into Dobbo's eyes. *"Ich habe gerade meinen Vater erschossen,"* he murmured. *"Ich habe gerade meinen Vater erschossen."* Dobbo had an A-level in German from school and had also chosen to study the language as an option at Cranwell so understood Fabian perfectly well.

"What the fuck!?" he managed to exclaim in disbelief between the spasms of sheer agony emanating from his mangled, bloody heel. *"You've just killed your fucking father!?"* before finally passing-out cold from the shock and extreme pain of his injury.

Chapter 46

Friday 29th March 1912 – Brigadier Arthur's Next Mission

In the wake of his assassination of the remnants of the Scott Expedition, two months later at the end of March 1912, Brigadier Robert Arthur of the UK Secret Intelligence Service (SIS) arrived back at his HQ in Whitehall, London for a debriefing as well as a briefing for his next assignment, which was to take place almost immediately.

He quickly learned that he had been selected to head-up another team of trained assassins, this time Americans, in yet another joint US/British venture to cover-up the real truth from the world at large.

"So, Robert…" his superior officer and friend, Major-General Harold Summers, began. *"… we are extremely pleased with the efficient way in which you dealt with the Scott err… situation. And now we come to the next assignment—which we know a man of your calibre will take entirely in his stride."*

Arthur did not know for certain whom the 'we' was, to which Summers referred, but he had a strong suspicion. He was certain that it wasn't Summers' immediate superior, General Roland Adams and suspected that it was probably even higher than that—somewhere in the upper echelons of government perhaps? Maybe even Sir Edward Grey himself, the British Foreign Secretary no less?

Anyway, he told himself, it's nothing to do with me. After all, I'm just here to obey orders and do my duty to the best of my ability.

Summers continued… *"As you may probably be aware Robert, the brand new ocean liner, Titanic sails from Southampton in under two weeks' time and you have a second class berth booked on there in the name of Frederick Marshall…"*

"Sir…?" Arthur interjected.

"Please let me finish. We can deal with any questions you may have afterwards. For whatever reasons, and even I am not privy to this information, Titanic will be involved in a staged accident of some kind which will sink her…"

At this Arthur's mouth dropped open in shock and surprise. Even he, a highly experienced, hard-nosed, cold-blooded assassin could barely believe what he was hearing.

"... and you, as I said, will be on board and your task will be to ensure that three men in particular do not survive the sinking. You will be provided with four White Star Line officer's uniforms, three of which you will hide in a carpet bag under the vaulting horse in the gymnasium of the ship and one of which you will be wearing yourself to avoid suspicion. The three you will hide are for our American colleagues who will board the ship surreptitiously, immediately after the incident and assist in the disposal of the aforementioned three men. Our American colleagues will arrive by rowing boat from another vessel stopped nearby and you will be on hand to assist them in gaining access to the ship. Once the Titanic has been crippled, you and your three colleagues will dispose of the three first class passengers and then the final part of your mission will be to make sure that the ship does not survive against all the odds. As well as the officer uniforms you will also be provided with five pounds of gelignite and a timing detonator which you will attach to the inner wall of cargo hold number four, just below the waterline. This will ensure that the ship sinks—and in the deepest part of the Atlantic, where the wreck will most likely never be found. Set the timer for one hour and this should give you plenty of time to make your escape. A resourceful operative such as yourself Robert will, I'm sure, be able to secure your own survival. It will be every man for himself at that time of course. Now, any questions?"

"Yes sir. Would it be prudent to ask why?" queried Arthur.

"Why what, Robert?"

"Well sir, so many 'whys' really. Why is the ship being sunk? Why are those three men to be disposed of...?"

"As I said Robert, I am not aware of the reasons for the sinking of the ship, but I can tell you that the three men to be assassinated are John Jacob Astor, Benjamin Guggenheim and Isidor Straus, all of whom are prominent American businessmen who are leading the campaign to oppose the formation of the Federal Reserve Bank and therefore they must be stopped at all costs to ensure that it goes ahead as planned. If they were to undergo three separate accidents, well of course that would raise suspicion but who would question their deaths too closely in the aftermath of an unfortunate err, single incident? If you see what I mean?"

"Yes, I see, but the Federal Reserve Bank, sir...?" queried Arthur.

"The Federal Reserve is the proposed new American central bank and I am told it is absolutely vital that its formation be allowed to happen—in the interests of national security and the financial future of the United States—so it's our job to make sure that no-one tries to stop it—especially for their own personal gain, as would seem to be the case."

General Summers of course, was simply toeing the 'party line' and self-justifying the horrendous act about to be perpetrated by the forces of evil.

Chapter 47

Saturday 25th February 2023 – Dobbo's Recovery

Some considerable time after the shootings, when Fabian had finally ceased his sobbing and wailing, he somehow managed with considerable difficulty to raise himself to his feet, albeit leaning back against the wall, his legs barely strong enough to hoist him upright. In the centre of the horrendous mess covering the floor around him, amongst all the blood and bodily detritus, lay the motionless figures of Dobbo and Prendergast. He knew the Wing Commander was dead, that was beyond doubt but he felt and hoped that Dobbo's injury was unlikely to be fatal and so he walked shakily across the room, knelt down beside the stricken airman and began gently patting his cheek in an attempt to rouse him.

Dobbo groaned weakly and rolled his eyes but remained unconscious. Fabian grabbed him under his armpits from behind and dragged him further clear of the carnage and then laid him down on his back using a cushion from one of the sofas as a pillow. He hurried-off to the kitchen and poured himself a glass of water, downing it in one before refilling the glass and returning to the patient in the hope that he could perhaps revive him somewhat with a drink.

As he was raising Dobbo's head to drink, the outside door opened causing Fabian to jolt in shock and spill the contents of the glass all over Dobbo's front. He jumped to his feet, ready to defend himself but then relaxed immediately when he realised that the man and woman who had just entered, arms full of bed linen and staring wide-eyed at the scene before them, posed no threat to him. Following Adam's departure, Pacha and Asiri were making a supply run to Porta Mundorum III and had deduced, due to the two fighter planes on the apron, that some new visitors had arrived. However they had not expected to discover the gruesome aftermath of a double shooting when they entered the building and it took a short while for everything to sink-in. Fabian gazed at them in astonishment, not quite able to believe all that was happening around him and then murmured, in perfect English, *"I need help here please, the fat one is dead,"* he said, stating the obvious, *"but the younger man is still alive although badly injured. He was shot in the foot."*

Pacha and Asiri dropped their bundles down on to the floor and rushed over to inspect Dobbo.

"This man is bleeding to death, we must get him to the infirmary immediately or he will end up like him," Pacha declared sternly, gesturing to Prendergast's

virtually headless torso. *"Are you able to help me carry him, sir?"* he then asked Fabian.

"Yes, I think so," the German replied. *"If you can take him under his shoulders then I will support him by the legs. I think I am strong enough for that."*

The two men between them lifted the limp and almost lifeless figure from the floor and hauled it across the apron to the infirmary, where Pacha once again prepared the *cama medica* whilst Fabian carefully removed all Dobbo's blood and brain-spattered clothing. When the bed was ready to commence the diagnosis and with the patient securely strapped-in, Pacha told Fabian to leave things to him and return to the accommodation block to help Asiri clear up the blood-bath, assuring him that Dobbo would be fine and that they would rejoin them in twenty to thirty minutes once the healing process was complete.

Just like his best buddy twenty four hours earlier, Dobbo awoke from his collapse fully recovered to find himself in the reassuring glow and hum of the *cama medica just* as it completed the rebuild of his shattered heel. His passing-out at the time of the shooting had been due chiefly to shock but, as a result of considerable blood loss from the injury, he remained unconscious until the bed had done its work. The first face he saw when he opened his eyes was Pacha, wearing a wide grin as he untethered the now healed and revitalised Yorkshireman.

True to his word and much to the relief of Fabian, Pacha and a now fully-recovered Dobbo returned just shy of thirty minutes later, the latter dressed only in boots and boxers and with Pacha's jacket draped over his shoulders. By this time Asiri and Fabian had managed to clear away most of the chaos from the floor and had wrapped Prendergast's body in a couple of bedsheets, which they had knotted at both ends. Before they left the infirmary however, Pacha disclosed to Dobbo everything from which the *cama medica* had healed him. As well as his shattered heel and the resultant blood loss, an immune deficiency disorder had been rectified as had a small but benign tumour in his left lung. *"I assumed you'd be happy for all those ailments to be healed señor,"* he joked. *"I did ask you but received no answer!"*

Dobbo put his arm around Pacha's shoulders *and gave him a friendly squeeze. "Hey, I'm glad you went for the full monty, pal. Honest, I feel like a new man, I really do."*

Pacha directed the two airmen to the dormitory for a shower and change of clothing, and he and Asiri then completed the clean-up before dragging the shrouded corpse outside and laying it on the tarmac. They returned inside and busied themselves, firstly preparing a lunch over which everyone could maybe get to know each other a little and at the same time decide exactly what to do with Prendergast's lifeless body.

When Dobbo and Fabian reappeared, scrubbed clean and dressed in Quechuan-style clothing, a wardrobe of which was made freely available to all guests at PM3, Pacha and Asiri were still occupied in the kitchen so the two pilots took seats at either side of the table, facing each other. The Englishman was the first to speak.

"So, you told me in there that your name is Fabian and you're a German Air Force Tornado pilot," he began. *"You know my name already and probably quite a bit about me as well because of what Prenders will no doubt have told you but I know bugger-all about you. So come on, tell me, how did you end up here, saving my life and at the same time killing your own father?"*

Fabian leant forward in his seat, placed his elbows on the table and rubbed his eyes while he pondered how and where to start and what exactly to tell Dobbo. After a few seconds he sat back again, cleared his throat and began.

"I am Fabian Schuster from Duisberg in Germany. I am twenty-seven years old and have been flying Tornadoes for the Luftwaffe for the last three years. My mother was violently raped and threatened not to talk about it—or else—at RAF Brüggen in 1995 by a certain Michael J. Prendergast and fell pregnant. I..." he announced, tapping his ribs with his right hand index finger. *"...am the result of that pregnancy. Before the psycho raped her, she was a happy-go-lucky yet determined young woman with ambitions to become a lawyer but sadly she was never the same afterwards. Although she loved me very much and was a wonderful mother, she struggled greatly with depression which worsened in her late twenties and she sadly committed suicide on Christmas Eve, 2007. It was the very worst day of my life."*

"Shit!" exclaimed Dobbo. *"I'm sure it was. You absolute bastard, Prendergast!"*

"Exactly, but he wasn't the only bastard, was he?" the German continued. *"I had no father that I knew of and had entered this world as a result of violence and self-gratification, instead of mutual love and respect. Up until my mother dying, however, I gave no thought whatsoever as to the identity of my father because I was loved and nurtured by her and my grandparents and enjoyed a wonderful childhood. I was carefree and innocent, like all children should be but*

when Mutti killed herself, things changed.[14] *She left a suicide note telling everything about her rape, naming Prendergast as the perpetrator and Oma and Opa*[15] *read me the note when I was sixteen years old. Maybe they should not have revealed it to me, maybe they should, but from that moment on I wanted some sort of closure or even revenge and have spent every moment since then working towards exacting just that. And now I have it, I have shot my father. Der fett Wichser will rape no more."*[16]

"So, how did you manage to track him down and then get yourself posted here so you could get to him?" enquired Dobbo, by now totally engrossed in Fabian's revelation.

Before Fabian could reply, Pacha and Asiri arrived at the table bearing trays of food and drink which they laid-out before taking their places beside the two airmen. After some brief introductions and handshakes, Dobbo quickly summarised everything that had taken place just before the Quechuans arrived and then asked Fabian to repeat what he had just told him about his mother and Prendergast. Father and daughter shook their heads in sorrow and revulsion and both left their seats to hug Fabian long and caringly in an attempt to show empathy and solidarity for what he had been forced to endure throughout his life to this point.

Fabian then continued. *"I decided to join the Luftwaffe not only because I loved aircraft and wanted to fly them but also to enable me to use the military intelligence network to track down Prendergast and possibly engineer a means of making contact with him. By digging through archives, reading all the regular NATO bulletins, which most in the armed forces merely ignore and by just simply talking to people in-the-know, I discovered some very interesting and revealing information about him, his family, his education and his RAF career as well as his private adult life. Oh yes, and some most peculiar and not very wholesome tastes and hobbies. Plus, and you may not be too surprised when I tell you this, but in parallel to his RAF career he was also an active MI6 agent, having been recruited by them at Cranwell. So when I saw that they had posted him to Teniente Rodolfo, I researched what I would need to do to be posted there myself. Well, all that was required, as it turned-out, was to volunteer and much to my good fortune, Germany was selected to provide pilots to the U.N. Antarctic Interceptor Force in early 2024. So, I put my name down before anybody else and due to Adam Haylock's desertion and the fact that I was*

[14] Colloquial German name for Mum and Mummy.

[15] Colloquial German names for Grandad and Grandma.

[16] The fat wanker

number one on the list, I was transferred down here right away. It was far too good an opportunity to turn down."

"So you came down here with the sole intention of murdering the twat?" Dobbo enquired, undiplomatically.

"Well no, not exactly, Samuel," Fabian replied. *"My main motive was simply to meet the man, find out what he was really like and hopefully to speak to him about what had happened between him and Mutti. I wanted to see if he had any remorse and to find out how he would feel when confronted with a son over twenty-seven years after that dreadful and violent sex act. If he had shown regret of any kind, asked forgiveness and resolved to change his ways then I think I could have been happy with that but within an hour of my arrival at Teniente Rodolfo he had made perfectly clear the kind of man he was by shooting dead an innocent flight engineer."*

"Fucking hell!" exclaimed Dobbo. *"Not Jorge or Eduardo surely?"*

Fabian nodded his head disconsolately. *"Well yes, Prendergast shot the guy who was driving the tug. I do not know the man's name obviously but it was one of them. He waited until the engineer had released the tug from the Tornado and then shot him in the back of the head from the cockpit. I am almost certain he died instantly but what was beyond doubt was that Prendergast would be more than willing to shoot you too if we caught up with you, so I made sure I was ready for that possibility and had my own gun in my pocket armed and ready."*

"And am I glad you did, mate! My God, if you hadn't been prepared for that, I'd be pushing up the sodding daisies by now."

"Pushing up the sodding dazies?" queried the puzzled German. *"I am not familiar with the words 'sodding' or 'dazies'—or this whole phrase."*

"Ah yes, sorry..." Dobbo laughed, then realised that Fabian was probably unfamiliar with much colloquial English, especially emanating from the mouth of a Yorkshireman. *"...I mean the flowers, 'daisies.' It just refers to being underground and pushing them up from underneath... Oh sod it, don't worry about it—it just means dead!"*

"Oh I see. Yes, without a doubt, mein Freund," Fabian affirmed with a chuckle. And then more seriously, *"and it was easy in the end. After the way he killed that engineer, how it came so naturally to him, I had to act quickly when I saw him point the gun at you. But still, the fact that I have just killed my father is not*

easy to grasp and come to terms with, yet I have no regrets at this moment in time. I feel I have finally been released from Prendergast's curse and can now maybe work towards finding some sort of closure. Who knows I may even be able to somehow find happiness in my life again."

Dobbo agreed. *"I think we'll all be a lot happier knowing that old Prenders is no longer moving amongst us, wreaking his unique brand of havoc on everyone he comes into contact with. Good riddance to bad rubbish I say. Anyway,"* he continued. *"... enough of him, the obnoxious heap of excrement. What do you make of all this then? I mean, everything we have seen and experienced beyond the ice wall. You know, this ice-free land, this airbase, meeting Pacha and Asiri, and being told all about Adam and Thoth?"*

Fabian shook his head incredulously. *"It might all seem utterly ridiculous to you Samuel and maybe it just seems like a dream but I have had my suspicions about Antarctica for over two years now,"* he replied emphatically, almost boasting, Dobbo felt. *"Since joining the Luftwaffe I have become fully aware of the machinations within the armed forces and the intelligence services, who pulls the strings, who the useful idiots are and how the only ones who benefit from warfare and conflict are those running and financing the Military Industrial Complex. I hate being a part of it and would leave tomorrow and become a commercial pilot but my desire to find my father has forced me to stay. I have obeyed orders yet spent most of my free time monitoring his movements. Then in March 2020, when the so-called pandemic was announced, my life changed forever. I already knew about it because in October 2019 I came across something called Event201, an exercise which brought together business, government, security and public health leaders to simulate a hypothetical global coronavirus pandemic scenario. At the time, I paid no particular attention to it, but when only five months later that simulation became a reality, it set off every single alarm bell in my head. By the end of the year, after constant research and much statistical analysis I knew the whole world was being hoaxed and that I would never again be taken-in by the deception of those I had once trusted. So, what has all this to do with Antarctica, you might ask? Well, once you know that those in power are lying on a global scale, running the largest propaganda campaign in history, forcing you into lockdowns, imposing nonsensical and draconian rules, while at the same time suppressing all dissenting voices and failing to obey their own rules themselves, then you start to wonder what else they have been deceiving us with. Covid was nothing more than flu rebranded. In fact, did you know that there were zero flu deaths in 2020 and 2021 according to official figures. It is staring people right in the face but no one can be bothered to research these things."*

Dobbo shuffled uneasily in his chair. *"Adam spoke quite a bit about this sort of thing, you know, Covid, 9/11, shit like that but never really told me anything much about Antarctica other than asking why nobody was allowed to venture beyond sixty degrees south."*

"And he was right to ask that question," replied Fabian. *"It seems like he burrowed-down the same rabbit hole as I by the sound of it and some rabbit hole it is too! By the end of 2021 I suppose it was, I had become pretty much convinced that there were inhabited lands beyond the ice, that our Earth could well be much, much larger than we had been led to believe and that it may even be just one small part of an eternal flat plane with other realms beyond its extremities. And who would believe it? Here we are, in an inhabited ice-free, fertile land beyond ninety degrees south with, if our friends are speaking the truth, at least one other world beyond it. As you would put it Samuel, 'fucking hell!'"*

Dobbo laughed. *"Absolutely Fabian, who would believe all this if we told them?"*

"Probably no-one unfortunately," Fabian answered. *"I think it was Mark Twain who said something like 'It is easier to fool people than to convince them that they have been fooled.' Well, he was right, you only have to see how everyone believed the Covid narrative and followed it so readily and willingly, to realise how correct he was."*

To his left, Pacha smiled and nodded, seemingly in affirmation with everything Fabian had just described, yet keen to come to a decision on Prendergast. *"So everyone, what shall we do with the body?"* he asked. *"Shall we burn it in the incinerator or bury it beside the runway? What do you all think? In fact, Fabian, I think it should be your choice."*

Asiri and Dobbo nodded in agreement and sat back in their seats awaiting the decision.

Fabian closed his eyes and sighed while he considered his options. After a few seconds of deep thought he reopened them, grinning somewhat mischievously. *"I think I would like us to bury him please…"* before declaring solemnly. *"… with an appropriate plaque marking the place if possible."*

Pacha smiled reassuringly. *"An excellent decision and I will happily make that plaque for you. I am a decent carpenter—and engraver too so, if you will instruct me what to write, I will do that for you."*

He then focused his attention on Dobbo. *"Before I make the plaque Samuel, let me tell you all about Adam, to whom we said goodbye only yesterday,"* he said. *"After a five day stay here at Porta Mundorum III, which included one night with us in our village, he decided to continue his flight of discovery and has headed south along Porta Lacus in an attempt to reach the land of Thoth. In fact, if all has gone well, he should be there now. Whilst staying with us in Intipata he fell very sick and we had to return here immediately. We thought we were going to lose him but fortunately got him to the cama medica just in time and twenty minutes later, exactly like you my friend, he was fully cured and restored. Though keen to press on, he was enchanted by our way of life and the beautiful environment in which we reside and asked us whether, if we were in his shoes, we would continue the adventure or settle here in Extrema. Though I have been to Thoth several times and, let me tell you, it is a wonderful land, my heart and soul are here, in the country where I was born and raised so my choice has always been to stay. All the inhabitants of this particular region of Extrema are free to emigrate to Thoth if they wish but very few do—in my lifetime, maybe ten at most have made the move. We are safe here, those in Thoth protect us from your unscrupulous leaders who would love to get their evil hands on our land and enslave us, or even eradicate us, just as they tried with our ancestors and countless other indigenous peoples throughout history. But they do not dare, they are terrified of the consequences. The Extremans and Thothites are good people but they will not tolerate tyranny, invasion or the imposition by force of one culture upon another. If your armed forces were to threaten the peace of these lands in any way, there would be dire consequences. Admiral Byrd's fleet were made very aware of that back in 1947 and since then no further military incursions have even been attempted."*

"Wow!" Dobbo cried, *"So what's it like then, this Thoth place and the THoTHites?"* He exaggerated the 'th' sounds comedically, as he struggled with the tongue-twisting phrase. *"Actually,"* he joked, *"I'm gonna start calling them 'Thothageth.' Do you get it Pacha, 'Thothageth,' it's how someone with a lisp would say 'sausages.'"*

Pacha seemed unimpressed. The joke completely passed him by and he simply pondered Dobbo's first question for a while before responding. *"From what I have experienced and read... "* he replied. *"... it is rather like Switzerland or Germany about one hundred and fifty years ago but without the nefarious and criminal activities of those in banking, big-business, government or the monarchy. Technologically it is far in advance of your world, though at first glance it does not appear that way. They have not ruined their environment nor destroyed the beauty and splendour of their heritage. Compared to people in the west they have relatively few possessions yet lack nothing and live harmoniously and cooperatively with their fellow inhabitants and the gifts given to them by the Creator. And just like us here in Extrema, they live long, fulfilling, healthy, happy and largely trauma-free lives."*

"So what do you think Samuel and I should do?" Fabian interjected.

"Dobbo, not Samuel if you don't mind," insisted Dobbo. *"I hate the bloody name!"*

"So what do you think DOBBO and I should do?" Fabian repeated, suitably and emphatically corrected.

Asiri, who had remained quiet thus far, her deep-brown eyes fixed on Dobbo the whole time, put down her fork and spoon and propped herself upright, hands on the table. *"I think you both should come and stay with us for one or two days,"* she piped up. *"Because of Adam's sickness, we had to postpone Grandfather Supay's birthday party until tomorrow. What better way, Sami, sorry but that is what I would like to call you, to celebrate Adam's recovery and yours too?"* She blushed at this point, dropped her head and fell silent, concerned that she was perhaps sounding a little too enthusiastic.

The two pilots exchanged a glance. Dobbo, eyebrows raised, gave Fabian a quizzical thumbs-up to which the German nodded in affirmation. They both knew the answer already. After what they had just been through, the last thing they needed right now was more high-octane action and adventure. What they required was some serious rest, relaxation and maybe a few beers!

"Grandad's party, here we come, then!" Dobbo exclaimed, rubbing his hands together in anticipation.

Asiri clapped her hands in delight and Pacha beamed a knowing smile in her direction, followed by an inconspicuous wink. He then stood up quickly and decisively saying, *"Very well everyone, let us all tidy-up, bury that body and then go to a party!"*

He then turned to face Dobbo and Fabian. *"If you two can find a suitable burial place and dig a hole two metres long, a metre wide and a metre and a half deep, then I will make and engrave the plaque. You will find spades, picks and shovels in the stores cupboard but before you go outside please write down what you would like the plaque to say."*

Three hours later, and after much hard sweat and toil, Prendergast's body, still wrapped in the cotton shroud, was buried a full four feet below the grassland on the northern edge of the runway. Pacha fashioned a plaque from a shelf he removed from one of the wardrobes in the dormitory. He then carved their inscription on to it, attached it to a stake whittled from a log from the firewood bin and hammered it into the ground on top of the burial mound. It read...

Here lies Wing Commander Michael J. Prendergast, RAF.

Died 24/02/2023, Porta Mundorum III, born sometime in the early 1970s in England.

Murderer, rapist and agent of the deep state.

A truly obnoxious and odious individual, who loved no-one but himself and in return was cared for by no-one.

He who lives by the sword, must die by the sword.

May he burn in hell!

Chapter 48

Fabian Tobias Schuster, b. 1995, Duisburg, Germany

Fabian Tobias Schuster was born 11th November 1995, the illegitimate son of nineteen year-old Erika Schuster, who at the time of his conception was employed as an office administrator at RAF Brüggen, one of only two RAF bases still in active service in Germany by the mid-nineties. She had left school in the summer of 1994 with excellent grades and, although offered a place at the University of Hamburg to study law, had opted to take a year out to earn some money with the main aim of buying a car prior to commencing her studies. She hailed from a relatively humble, though very tightly-knit family, born and raised in Duisburg in northwestern Germany around twenty kilometres from the border with Holland, along with her two older sisters, Greta and Lilli. Her mother, Ursula was a devoted and very traditional housewife, who had never officially been employed but who had put an enormous amount of energy into nurturing her three daughters, whom she adored and indeed doted upon, as well as providing a functional, comfortable and loving family home.

Whilst at work at the base Erika, a stunningly well-proportioned and good-looking girl was forever chatting to her colleagues and various RAF officers, for whom she typed letters and documents, about her aim to work there for a year, buy a car and then commence law studies. She was young, fresh-faced, flirtatious and talkative, fluent in English and would disclose her plans to anyone willing to lend an ear. And one particular young officer, a certain Michael Joseph Prendergast was more than willing to give her any amount of ear-time!

During the afternoon of 28th January 1995, Prendergast entered the office where Erika spent most of her days typing and processing mail to tell her that a friend of his, who was returning to service in England after a three year stint at Brüggen, wished to sell his 1975 German-registered Beetle for just fifteen hundred Deutschmarks, that it was, in his words, *'an absolute beaut!'* and he was more than happy to take her to see it that very evening after work, if she so wished. Erika, understandably excited at the opportunity, agreed and at 5.20pm on a cold, wet and blustery evening, she eagerly clambered into his Mercedes, her mind buzzing at the thought of owning a Volkswagen Beetle, her very favourite car.

The journey from the base lasted less than five minutes however and Erika never got to view the fictitious vehicle. Instead, she was taken to a secluded layby in a forest on the perimeter fence of RAF Brüggen, where the violent and loveless conception of Fabian Tobias Schuster took place. Prendergast had waited until Erika had strapped herself in before reaching across and plunging the contents of a full syringe of the 'date-rape' drug, Rohypnol through her coat and into her arm, sedating her almost instantly. Minutes later she was virtually comatose and *El Coño Feo* took full and salacious advantage of the situation. When she awoke as he drove her back to her home, battered, bemused and traumatised, Erika was warned not to implicate him in the rape to anyone or else her parents would be in serious risk of harm, by him personally. He made it patently clear that he had friends in very high places who would simply turn a blind eye and would protect and cover for him regardless of the 'misdemeanour.' The story she was instructed to relate was that she had been grabbed by a man at the bus stop, dragged into woodland and then raped and beaten. She would be adamant that she neither knew nor recognised her attacker but to say she was sure he was German and most likely a manual worker. She fully complied with this and the criminal case subsequently opened by the police, not surprisingly, remains unsolved to this day. Erika Brigit Schuster never returned to the RAF Brüggen airbase—nor cast eyes on Prendergast ever again.

The young Fabian was oblivious as to the identity of his father and until the age of twelve showed absolutely no interest in finding out. He enjoyed a magical early childhood, living with Mutti in Opa and Oma's modest town house on the outskirts of the city. Because of the pregnancy, Erika never did buy herself a car and neither did she go to law school yet tried her utmost to be the mother to Fabian that Ursula had always been to her. She and her parents never spoke to Fabian about his father and the sad circumstances of his birth and the youngster, like so many well-cared for and nurtured children, simply lived a carefree, fun-filled and joyous first twelve years, obsessed with football, riding his bike, and making model aeroplanes. Academically he was above average, nowhere near A-grade in any subject, but was a very practical boy, great with his hands and fascinated by anything mechanical, spending countless days with *Opa* in the shed dismantling and repairing anything from a tiny gadget to a full blown car engine.

Sadly, and unbeknown to him however, his mother had been battling severe depression and anxiety throughout his upbringing but, with the help of counselling, her supportive parents and anti-depressants had managed to keep it under control and, more importantly to her, conceal it from young Fabian. However, at the start of his thirteenth year, as she approached her thirtieth birthday, her mental problems worsened and began to seriously take their toll. She became morose and severely agoraphobic, often spending days on end in her bedroom. She seemed to him to be crying constantly and he noticed that she had pretty much stopped eating, was losing weight and becoming gaunt, drawn and pale.

As Erika's depression gradually worsened he became increasingly concerned for her, saddened by the reduced contact, tenderness and love which he had always enjoyed and largely taken for granted. He observed a decline in his grandparents' mood too, their usual joie de vivre had all but vanished, replaced by a permanent air of worry and sadness which they found increasingly difficult to suppress or conceal as her condition worsened.

On Christmas Eve 2007, Erika's tortuous struggle with the demons inside her finally ended. She had taken her leave of the family at around 9.00pm to take a bath and forty minutes later, her father Helmut raced upstairs after water began dripping through the ceiling above him. He forced open the bathroom door to find her lifeless, naked body submerged in the bath, the water a deep red and the taps still running. An empty plastic bottle of anti-depressants floated on the film of water covering the bathroom floor and a razor blade was found in the bath, which had obviously been used to slit her wrists.

Chapter 49

Friday 24th February 2023 – Adam's departure for Thoth

The fully refuelled Esmerelda ascended gracefully away from Porta Mundorum III and Adam pointed her nose down the very centre line of Porta Lacus, levelling off at five hundred feet, well below the grey cloud that filled the sky that day and setting his flight speed to two hundred and fifty mph. He was in no particular rush and as well as preserving his fuel supply was keen to enjoy the flight down the lake, hoping maybe to see Pacha and Asiri who, following a fond and emotional farewell, had departed in their boat an hour or so earlier. By now, he reckoned that they would be around halfway to Intipata so there was every chance that he would get to see them one more time and give them a hearty wave.

After only a couple of minutes in the air he spotted them, a short trail of white foam streaming behind their boat, the maritime equivalent of an aircraft's contrail, as it bounced its way through the pristine, emerald-green waters of Porta Lacus. He descended to no more than one hundred feet above the level of the lake and then banked Esmerelda to her left to offer a better view of his friends and hopefully to enable them to see him in the cockpit. As he approached them and the noise of Esmerelda's engines assaulted their ears, they looked up and began waving frantically in his direction, huge smiles on both their faces. He waved back at them, hoping they would be able to clearly make him out through the glass of the canopy and was relieved when Asiri began jumping up and down gleefully, a sure sign that she could see him. He circled them three times and felt a certain reluctance to terminate that particular manoeuvre and continue along the lake. But resume his quest he must, so he brought the F-5 out of her turn, ascended back to five hundred feet and headed away into the unknown once more.

Porta Lacus, he was to find out later, is approximately two-thirds the size of Lake Erie in North America; around one hundred and fifty miles long and at its widest point is sixty miles across. At the speed he was flying it took Adam less than an hour to travel the entire length, including the time he had spent circling Pacha and Asiri's boat. He passed Intipata on his port wing after around twenty miles or so but did not encounter any further settlements along either side of the lake.

From its southern end, a mighty river flowed. It was much wider than the River Rhine in Western Germany, a watercourse with which he was very familiar from his many sorties over Europe. A few miles down the river, just at the point where it took a deviation to the west, the water turned from a clear blue to a muddy brown, surely not due to pollution he hoped? At this point he spotted a small town on the left bank around twice the size of Intipata and descended to investigate further. The architecture was similar to that of the village but every now and then a much larger, almost European gothic style building, similar in design to those at PM3, stood out amongst the houses. One structure that particularly caught his eye was situated on the riverbank and reminded him very much of the magnificent Liver Building in Liverpool. It overlooked a small harbour port containing a throng of small fishing boats as well as several larger vessels which were similar in size to British fishing trawlers but looked more like container ships. So there was maritime trade in this part of the world, he surmised and he wondered how many of these ships sailed between Extrema and Thoth. No doubt he would find out soon enough.

He circled the town a few times attracting the attention of many of its inhabitants who stood and waved enthusiastically as he passed over them. He wondered how many similar aircraft they had seen flying over them previously but one thing was for sure, they did not view his presence as any kind of threat and, if anything, appeared to be wishing him 'bon voyage.'

Although the instructions he had read at PM3 advised him to continue flying south after leaving Porta Lacus, he chose instead to follow the river westward for a while as he was keen to discover where it might lead, his plan being to return to the port town and resume his original route once his curiosity had been satisfied. The turgid waters flowed due west for another fifty miles and then began to split into numerous channels, very quickly becoming a huge delta containing countless islands and sandbanks. In the distance he could now discern where the delta gave way to open sea and twenty minutes later its channels, islands and sandbanks were fading into the distance behind him. He made several low-level sweeps over the ocean and could make out one or two small fishing boats but none of the larger cargo vessels. As he swooped low, almost clipping the white tops, the fishermen, like the folks in the town, waved animatedly at him and he returned their gesture with gusto. Boy, was he enjoying this adventure but where should he head now, he wondered? He was just about to steer a course back toward the delta and head for the town when his radio burst into life.

"Adam, we are now about to take control of your aircraft," came the announcement. *"Remove your hands and feet from the controls, sit back and relax and let us guide you on from here."* The voice was impersonal and monotonal and Adam felt it was more likely to be an automated system rather than an actual, real person.

Instead of relinquishing control immediately however, he elected to firstly try and find out more from the voice. *"This is Adam Haylock piloting Freedom Fighter 807. To whom am I speaking? Over,"* he requested.

"Please do not engage in conversation Adam," the voice replied curtly. *"Remove your hands and feet from the controls, sit back and relax and let us guide you on from here. Over."*

"Well that was short and to the point, mate!" Adam laughed, obediently releasing his hands from the joystick. He then lifted both feet from the pedals, resting them on the floor at either side.

"You got it!" he declared calmly.

A split second after these words passed his lips, Esmerelda accelerated rapidly, very rapidly indeed, ascending to over ten thousand feet in very short time before banking steeply to starboard and making a full 90° turn to the south. As she levelled out Adam noticed the airspeed was now in excess of 700mph as the F-5 made her way out to sea. In the very far distance he could just make-out what resembled an island towards which he was directly heading and within half an hour or so it loomed large ahead of him.

Fully expecting to overfly the island and head out across the open ocean, he yelled in astonishment as the jet suddenly and violently dropped into a 45° dive and began hurtling toward the ground below. Justifiably terrified, he instantly grabbed the joystick and pulled Esmerelda out of the dive. He then placed his feet back on the pedals, relieved to have taken back full control of the aircraft.

"Adam, you must trust us," came the voice again. *"If you cannot put your faith in us then your adventure will be at an end."*

"How do I know this isn't a trick?" Adam questioned. *"It looked to me like you were going to crash us into the ground just then. I haven't come all this way to die like that!"*

"Adam, you must trust us," repeated the voice. *"Remove your hands and feet from the controls, sit back and relax and let us guide you on from here. Over."*

"Bloody hell!" exclaimed the bemused and panicked pilot. *"OK, here goes then. You got it!"*

Esmerelda dived again, the land below racing toward him at lightning speed. At around two thousand feet he noticed they were careering towards a huge elliptical abyss in the centre of the island measuring maybe two hundred yards wide by one hundred high. *"Aargh!"* he shrieked as he plummeted downward and, convinced he was going to meet his maker at any moment, grabbed the joystick a second time and pulled out of the dive.

He levelled out at five thousand feet and slowed Esmerelda right down. He was dripping with sweat; his hands were shaking and he could barely control his feet on the pedals. The blood was surging through his veins and he was struggling to breathe, inhaling and exhaling rapidly and erratically. He circled slowly and as he calmed down, which took several minutes, tears began to run down his cheeks.

"I can't do this, I just can't," he sobbed. *"This is too much."*

"You can do this, Adam but you must have faith in us," came the voice once more. *"Now this is your very last chance. Remove your hands and feet from the controls, sit back and relax and let us guide you on from here. If you take over control a third time, you will be forced to return to the north. Over and out."*

Adam wiped the tears away with his sleeve and gathered himself the best he could. He had no desire to return north to his old life, though who was to say he had to fly all the way back to Teniente Rodolfo and Prendergast? Surely he could settle with Pacha and Asiri's people in Extrema, couldn't he? Now that wouldn't be so bad would it? He might even meet a nice girl there, settle down and have some children. And who knows, that nice girl could perhaps be Asiri. She was very beautiful, that was beyond question, as well as being a wonderful, kind and intelligent human being. Someone he might well be able to love and whom, by some miracle, may even find it within herself to love him back.

Almost as quickly as he had considered these crazy notions, he dismissed them in an instant. *"Don't be a total knobheaded, deluded fuckwit, Haylock!"* he cursed. *"She wouldn't look twice at you, never mind be happy to have your sodding children."* He pulled himself together once more and steeled himself. *"OK Voice,"* he said, trying his utmost to sound confident and assured. *"I do have faith in you—I think. But I'm gonna' have to close my eyes so I don't mess up again."* He screwed them tightly shut and relinquished control for a third and final time. This was 'it' and he knew it. *"You got it!"* he announced apprehensively, sitting bolt upright in his seat and clenching everything he could possibly clench.

Chapter 50

Sunday 26th February 2023 - Dobbo and Fabian with the Quechuans

Grandfather Supay's eightieth birthday celebrations took place at the Intipata civic hall, a stone's throw from the home of Pacha and Saywa and the event did absolutely nothing to disappoint the two errant flyers. Present at the feast, in addition to the immediate family, were well over a hundred guests comprising members of the old man's wider relations as well as his aged parents and many close friends and neighbours. It was, as Dobbo described in his very best Yorkshire dialect, *'a reight good do.'*

The event began with drinks and introductions and the two visitors from the north being hailed as *'Our Guests of Honour'* by Pacha in the opening address and given seats on the head table either side of Supay and his lovely wife, Mayu. Then, much to their surprise, each partygoer in turn came to the table not only to present their birthday wishes and gifts to Supay but also to meet the two Europeans with whom they shook hands warmly and excitedly. Asiri and her younger sister Illari had taken the two seats next to Dobbo and Pacha and Saywa settled alongside Fabian. Kusi and Urpi, along with Supay's other children and grandchildren, occupied four adjacent tables, two at either side of the head table and the remaining guests sat on rows of trestle benches running the full width of the room.

When everyone was seated, Grandfather Supay gave a short but very animated speech, in native Quechuan, which had the guests almost falling-off their chairs in hysterics. Dobbo and Fabian, totally in the dark as to the content of the address, simply smiled and shrugged at each other, totally non-plussed. Mayu then took to her feet and paid what Dobbo assumed to be a glowing tribute to her husband, which drew a long standing ovation from the assembled throng. Supay, tears welling, embraced her tenderly as she sat back down again.

Throughout the feast Asiri made it her job to include Dobbo in as much of the proceedings as possible, skilfully translating into English whenever it was needed, describing the various customs that were being observed and pointing out any special friends or family members she felt worthy of mention. From time to time she would squeeze his arm as she lovingly poked fun and mischief at certain individuals or groups, bringing him up-to-speed with all the latest family dramas and local gossip. She also served him his food from the platters placed by the waiters and waitresses on the table before them. And what a banquet it was, comprising the very best that Extrema could provide; the finest fish and shellfish, a spit-roasted wild boar and an enormous goose-like bird along with a veritable cornucopia of rice, salads, vegetables and sauces.

"I have never tasted food like this in my entire life, Asiri!" Dobbo shouted in her ear, struggling to make himself heard over the cacophony filling the room. *"Everything is so full of flavour; it smells fabulous and is such high quality. I mean, those crayfish things in that salad are to die for and that wild boar, WOW! Honestly, I could eat myself to death here."*

"Well please don't eat yourself to death, Sami," Asiri shouted back, a playful smirk on her face. *"We only met yesterday and it would be terrible if we were to lose you so soon!"*

Dobbo chuckled, and took a long drink from his glass, holding the liquid in his mouth for several seconds before swallowing. *"And what the heck is this stuff I'm drinking?"* he asked her. *"It fizzes a bit like champagne or lager but tastes nothing like either of them. And the colour? It's kind of almost brown but has a funny purply tint to it as well. It's great though—what's it called?"*

Asiri picked up her glass and held it gently against his. *"It is called Chicha de jora,"* she replied. *"It is a corn beer and we always drink it at important ceremonies. Did you notice, Sami that many of the guests sprinkled some on the ground from the communal cup before they sat down to drink? That is to bless the room and everyone present and to wish Grandfather Supay a continuing long and healthy life."*

She took a sip from her glass and then gently chinked it against Dobbo's. *"ñawi kawsay, Sami,"* she beamed.

"What?" enquired Dobbo.

"ñawi kawsay," she repeated. *"In our language that means good health."*

"Oh right, yes, well, ñawi kawsay to you too Asiri," he reciprocated, earnestly yet very awkwardly. He really had lost his knack with the ladies, he realised. It was as if he were a clumsy, nervous and clueless teenager all over again. He told himself to grow a pair, and quickly. This particular girl was absolutely worthy of the effort.

"It is so wonderful having you here with us in our village, Sami," she declared, then swiftly added. *"Oh, and Fabian too of course. I feel like we could all become very good friends were we to spend a little more time together. It would be a real shame if you were both to return to your airplanes too soon."*

As he sipped on his *Chicha de jora*, the warming alcohol beginning to take effect, Dobbo decided to take the bull firmly by its very large and pointy horns. Asiri was lovely. No, she was way beyond lovely. Lovely just wasn't a strong enough word to describe her. He could feel a stirring within his heart and soul like he'd never ever felt in his life and, were he to be truly honest, there was a hint of a flutter in his loins too! What was happening to him, he wondered? Was it due to all the trauma he'd just been through? Was it the healing effects of the cama médica perhaps? Or was it this land, Extrema and its wonderful inhabitants casting a magical spell and reeling him in? Or could it simply be this shimmering angel beside him, overwhelming him with her beauty, charm and genuine zest for life? Whatever it was he felt different, very different to the man who only a few weeks ago had been prepared to shoot down innocent adventurers simply on the command of a monster like Prendergast. He drained his glass, placed it gently down on the table and firmly, yet with a tenderness that seemed almost alien to him, took her right hand in his.

"Good friends? The three of us? Or do you mean just me and you?" he asked her sincerely. *"I mean, you've barely spoken with Fabian have you? Whereas on the way down here, and ever since our arrival in the village, the two of us have never stopped talking to each other. I must say, it's been brilliant though and every single minute of every single conversation has been... well, like a dream. I've opened-up and told you plenty about my past life, which is not like me really and you have been very honest with me too, Asiri. But Fabian? Sorry, I'm a bit puzzled."*

Asiri's face turned bright crimson and she dropped her head in embarrassment. *"I fear you can see right through me, Sami dear,"* she acknowledged. *"Am I really that obvious and transparent?"*

Dobbo nodded, a warm smile spreading across his face. *"Yes, you are that obvious and transparent, Asiri,"* he said. *"Just like me in fact!"*

Dobbo's eyes slowly came to rest on a guitar that someone had brought along and with the alcohol now flowing freely in his bloodstream, he couldn't resist and simply snatched it from the chair where it had been lying quietly, unattended and minding its own business. He began to play and sing a song he had composed in his head, only the previous day. And it went something like this...

"Oh there's
Somethin' goin' on
beyond the... ice wall
But it's a something that
you ain't supposed to know.
Yeah there's places in the space
beyond the... ice wall
But those are places that
you ain't supposed to go.

And the planes patrol the sky
And the boats police the sea
And it's something all the folks
Who claim authority agree
That that somethin' goin' on
Beyond the... ice wall
Well, it ain't for the likes
of you and me.

Oh there's nothing goin' on
beyond the... ice wall
Or so the mainstream media say.

You can book yourself a cruise
Sipping high fallutin' booze
For only fifteen thousand bucks a day.

But if you stray a whisker
Off the recommended routes
You'll be doing doggie paddle
Wearing concrete boots... no!
There's nothin' goin' on beyond the... ice wall
No how, no sir, no way.

Don't be a cynic
Anyone can see
They're just trying to help
Environmentally.
Ha ha ha ha
He he he

It's just that penguins
Need a shitload of security.

Well you can try to go beyond the... ice wall
If you think you're living in a land that's free
But you might start to wonder
Whether you've made a blunder
when ya try to cross the sixtieth degree.

Where the planes patrol the sky
And the warship engines hum
Ist verboten Ja
To float in that vicinity, ya bum.
Try to go and see beyond the... ice wall
and they'll blow your sorry arse
to Kingdom come.

Oh there's
Somethin' goin' on
beyond the... ice wall
But it's a something that
you ain't supposed to know.
Yeah there's places in the space
beyond the... ice wall
But those are places that
you ain't supposed to go.

Slowly, slowly, little by little the room began to curtail their conversations and take notice and by the time he had reached the third verse, almost everyone was clapping in-time to Dobbo's singing, whilst laughing and enthusiastically trying to hum along with him.

Once the applause and hubbub had died down, Dobbo whispered to Asiri, *"Come on, let's go outside and get some fresh air, it's getting very hot and stuffy in here."*

From his side of the table, Fabian watched as the flirting couple respectfully took their leave of Supay and Mayu before walking hand-in-hand across the room toward the main door. He turned to Pacha to his left who had his eyes firmly fixed on the lovebirds, as well as a puzzled look on his face.

"Those two seem to be getting on very well, Pacha," he declared, elbowing the Quechuan gently in the ribs.

Pacha chuckled. *"Very well indeed Fabian. Asiri has never really shown much interest in romance in the past, so Dobbo is a very lucky man I think. But he obviously possesses some extra-special qualities that you and I simply cannot see."*

This made Fabian chuckle too but his mirth rapidly subsided giving way to a rather serious demeanour. *"But this may change Dobbo's plans to join Adam Haylock in Thoth,"* he said. *"Maybe I will be forced to continue my journey alone?"*

"If he decided to stay, would you consider settling here also?" asked Pacha.

Fabian shook his head. *"No, my friend,"* he insisted unequivocally. *"I am on a mission, a quest, some may even call it a crusade. My chief aim has already been completed with the death of my father but I believe there are many, many more truths out there for me to uncover. I am too much of a Querdenker to give up on my adventure now, so whatever Dobbo decides will make no difference to me. I shall return to Porta Mundorum III tomorrow or the day after and then fly on to Thoth where hopefully I will meet up with Adam."*

Pacha looked rather puzzled. *"What is a Querdenker, Fabian? I assume it is a German word."*

Fabian nodded enthusiastically. *"It means lateral thinker and is the name of a movement created in 2020 to protest against the totalitarian measures enforced on the German people by the government during the so-called Covid pandemic,"* he explained. *"Our numbers have swelled enormously since then and we are now a real force for dissent in our country, despite being labelled far-right extremists by those in power and also by the mainstream media."*

Pacha seemed impressed. *"These days, anyone in your world who disconnects from the system or dares to question political ideology, economic structures, published history, scientific dogma or societal norms is branded 'far-right,'"* he said with an ironic smile. *"One of my roles here in Extrema, as well as my carpentry and keeping Porta Mundorum III running smoothly of course, is to monitor your realm's geopolitics via my contacts in your military, intelligence services, governments and media and then report my findings back to my people here. We were well aware of your Covid pseudo-pandemic, Fabian and although I am unfamiliar with your Querdenkers, I followed very closely the draconian actions of the German Government, in total lockstep or should I say goosestep, with all the others as they heaped misery on their passive and naïve populations. Tragically, the vast majority complied fully and with an almost religious and zealous fervour, investing all their belief in it. Not a murmur of dissent did they show because they had been so skilfully and stealthily conditioned to conform to the system and the standard narrative. They were also programmed to believe that the written, audio and visual media are the sole arbiters of the 'truth.' As a result they suffered and to this very day still suffer from, what is known as cognitive dissonance..."*

"That is not a phrase I am familiar with, Pacha," Fabian interjected. *"What exactly does it mean, in simple terms?"*

Pacha thought for a moment while he took a few sips from his glass of Chicha de jora. *"When someone is given firm evidence that contradicts their deep-rooted beliefs, they can experience discomfort or even fear,"* he explained. *"They then lack the courage to face what seem like unbearable realities and will simply reject the evidence, often insulting the person who provided it, usually with some kind of right-wing slur, in order to protect their ego and sense of security. They simply refuse to even consider the possibility that they have been deceived and deceived on a monumental scale. It is something I have studied for several years and which fascinates as well as infuriates me."*

"Well, cognitive dissonance is certainly not something a Querdenker suffers from," boasted the German proudly. *"And you seem to have done your research Pacha so, for me, you are an honorary Querdenker already. I'm curious, although I think I already know the answer to the next question. Did anyone try to declare a pandemic here in Extrema in 2020?"*

Pacha, who was halfway through taking a drink from his glass, began to laugh and totally lost control of his nose and mouth, spraying Chicha de jora all over Fabian who jumped from his chair in surprise and then, quickly seeing the funny side, joined in the laughter and collapsed back into his seat, guffawing.

When the two men had regathered their composure somewhat, Pacha finally gave his response as he clumsily dabbed the sprayed Chicha de jora covering Fabian, with a scrunched-up napkin. *"The Covid nonsense was completely ignored by everyone here,"* he boasted. *"We knew all about it beforehand as well as the motivations driving it, as fortunately my people do not suffer cognitive dissonance because we have no government, intelligence services, vested interest groups nor a controlled media propaganda machine to brainwash or promote fakery."* He paused then added, almost as an afterthought. *"Do you even know the real meaning of the word 'government'?"*

"I do actually," replied Fabian. *"You cannot outdo me on that one. It is from the Latin words 'guberno' meaning govern and 'mens' which is mind."*

Pacha was genuinely impressed. *"One hundred percent correct my learned companion,"* he acknowledged.

"Thank you, Pacha!" Fabian responded, more than a little impressed with himself. *"And March 2020 was, well for me anyway, the moment they decided to take mind control and lying to new extremes and push harder and wider than they had ever done before."*

"You are one hundred percent correct there too," stated Pacha categorically. *"It was also obvious to everyone here that the whole thing was staged and we were confident that organisations like the WHO, the WEF or the U.N. would never dare come anywhere near us with their dystopian psychological operations. And do you know my friend, we lost nobody to any virus whatsoever, not in 2020, not in 2021 nor at any time since. We watched while your world went completely mad for over two years, Fabian and from what I have been told, things have only got worse there."*

Fabian's curiosity had been well and truly sparked. *"So these contacts of yours in the various services and agencies..."* he began. *"... are they your people, our people, Thothites? And are they good guys or bad guys?"*

Pacha put down the napkin and picked-up his glass again, carefully in order to avoid spilling its contents, it having been refilled a moment earlier. *"They are very much the good guys,"* he asserted. *"Which is why they are working for us. Most are recruited from your world; some are from here and a very select few originate from Thoth. The two flight engineers at Teniente Rodolfo are in fact our agents and though they claimed to be Chileans and genuinely seconded from that nation's air force, both are from Extrema. Jorge, who is sadly no longer with us, was born and raised in Alpamayo, our nearest town, some two hundred and fifty kilometres to the south of here, just beyond the southern end of Porta Lacus on the Río Arenoso."*[17]

Fabian was taken aback by this. *"Your nearest town is two hundred and fifty kilometres away?!"* he exclaimed. *"So is Extrema a huge country or is it just very sparsely populated?"*

"Both. Were you to journey along it east or west, eventually returning to your original start point, you would have travelled over 120,000 kilometres, all the way around the southern extent of Antarctica. Yet the whole of this vast expanse of land contains a mere two million or so inhabitants," Pacha clarified

---

[17] Alpamayo is Quechuan for muddy river and Río Arenoso means sandy river in Spanish

with wide-eyed enthusiasm. *"The ice wall itself should only be approximately 13,000 kilometres all the way round based on its globe latitude, but it actually stretches for over 100,000 kilometres. Which is why nobody, and I mean nobody has ever managed to successfully circumnavigate it!"*

Fabian shrugged, shook his head and folded his arms. *"Well, that confirms what many of our military bulletins were hinting at when I was looking into being posted down here. It also confirms most of the calculations I performed when researching the real shape and size of our world and what may, or may not, lie beyond the forbidden sixty degrees south line. So what about north and south, I mean, how wide is Extrema?"*

"On average about one thousand kilometres. Our northern extent is pretty much the ninety-first parallel, just one hundred kilometres further on from your supposed 'pole,' and to the south where the firmament meets the Ahtian Ocean," revealed Pacha, becoming concerned that he may now be overloading Fabian.

"So you can sail out to sea and just hit a wall can you?" the German asked sarcastically.

"Oh yes," declared Pacha. *"You can indeed, though I have never bothered myself. Just as in that famous movie of yours, 'The Truman Show.' As you probably know, Fabian, Hollywood has a habit of revealing the most hidden truths in movies and has done so ever since its inception."*

"Absolutely," affirmed Fabian, nodding very earnestly. *"The Matrix being one of the most obvious examples. It is called 'revelation of the method' or 'hiding it in plain sight!'"*

Pacha nodded back in full agreement. *"Exactly,"* he stated. *"I have watched that film and discussed it at length many times with my contacts in the media. Thankfully however, most folk here have little or no desire to watch any of your movies—in fact the majority have no actual means of watching them. We do not have television, nor do we want it and very few choose to access the internet. But the message of The Matrix is strong and like its main character Neo, those who unplug from the system are able to reclaim their sovereignty and align themselves with the higher principles of wisdom, truth and love."*

Fabian smiled, very much in awe of Pacha's knowledge and understanding. *"I think Adam and I have completely unplugged—well and truly,"* he laughed.

"And Dobbo?" enquired the Quechuan.

"I do not think Dobbo is quite of that mindset yet, though he is learning very fast," Fabian conceded. *"He told me that Adam had been working on him constantly before they parted ways and I am certain that everything he has experienced since will also have had a considerable effect. But he still has some way to go before he can call himself a fully-fledged Querdenker."*

Pacha slapped him on the back reassuringly. *"Just wait until he's spent a few days in Asiri's company,"* he chortled. *"He will be a fully-fledged Querdenker then, I have no doubts!"*

Chapter 51

Tuesday 16th April 1912 – 10 Downing Street, London

The Prime Minister Herbert Asquith, awakened early by an urgent telephone call from Lord Richard Haldane the Secretary of State for War, was sitting bleary-eyed in his dressing gown at 6.50am, nursing what he hoped would be a reviving cup of strong tea, in his drawing room when his butler entered the room tentatively. Asquith was not in the very best of moods having only managed to get to bed some four hours earlier following a very late-running session in cabinet the previous evening. This had also been exacerbated by his consumption of several large brandies over the course of the evening and was something he was now desperately regretting as he gently massaged his throbbing temple.

"Sir, Lord Haldane has arrived," his butler informed the Prime Minister.

"Yes, do show him in then please," the P.M. snapped unnecessarily but somewhat understandably, given his now fragile state.

"Good morning, Prime Minister," said Haldane, greeting him breezily yet with a serious expression adorning his craggy face.

"Good morning Haldane. Could this not have waited just a few hours? What is so damnably urgent?"

"I'm afraid not P.M.," he replied. *"We have just had some very grave news through from the Embassy in Washington. Unfortunately... it seems that the Titanic sank early yesterday with hundreds of casualties."*

"Oh my goodness, no!" said Asquith. The morning having started so badly for him, was nevertheless already taking a distinct turn for the worse.

"Yes I am afraid it is confirmed," Haldane informed him. *"There is no doubt. First reports are saying that more than one thousand are feared drowned... up to as many as two thousand possibly. As we are already aware, White Star had to make the switch of the two ships in order to claim the insurance, stay in business and thereby keep us in office and so it's actually Olympic that foundered."*

"But... but I thought Morgan was going to ensure there would be no casualties, otherwise I would never have agreed to all this," mumbled Asquith, despairingly.

"I know sir, but there's nothing we can do to prevent it now," Haldane informed him, trying to think clearly and logically about how to extricate themselves from the predicament into which they had suddenly now been thrust.

"What's done is done and we have to somehow find a way through this dilemma. I'm sure you do not need me to remind you sir, that White Star AND Harland and Wolff shipyard were both on the verge of bankruptcy after RMS Olympic's catastrophic accident, last year. Had that happened then it would have meant more than fifty thousand jobs lost and also the end of our slender majority. It was political dynamite for us and we would not have been re-elected, so we had no choice but to agree to Morgan's demands. We are going to have to go along with this the entire way now Prime Minister..." He knew he was attempting to defend their totally indefensible actions. *"... and had it not been for Morgan's plan of switching the identities of Olympic and Titanic and thus sinking Olympic disguised as Titanic, then it wouldn't have been simply the ship that had been sunk—it would have been our government too!"* he hyperbolised.

"I will not allow such a stain to prevail upon the integrity of the British Government," countered Asquith whilst simultaneously coming to the realisation that he had no choice at all in the matter now. *"Not for anything... but especially not for J.P. Morgan."*

"Sir, might I further remind you," insisted Haldane, more forcefully now, *"... that part of the arrangement we agreed to with Morgan and which you personally brokered, guaranteed our being able to requisition his ships into the Royal Navy Reserve in the event of war. And one thing that I am sure you need no reminding of Prime Minister is that the situation in Europe is becoming ever more critical—especially since only a few short weeks ago we abandoned our isolationist stance. If White Star was to enter into liquidation, the major creditor would be J.P. Morgan himself and, as its owner AND banker, he would doubtless exercise his right to seize his assets, the ships and therefore we, the British Government, would lose them all."*

Asquith pondered on this fact for a moment, letting it sink in. He looked a picture of abject misery.

"It is a very sad day indeed when the policies and actions of the British Government can be dictated by the greed and nefarious business practices of

foreigners. If this ever became public..." His words tailed-off sadly, reflectively as he wondered where it had all gone wrong. However, he quickly regained his composure and asked...

"I presume that there will need to be a public inquiry... and I presume you have someone in mind to run the show? It would have to be someone we can implicitly rely upon to reach the err... right conclusions."

"Yes sir, I certainly do have someone in mind," replied Haldane. *"Lord Mersey is a good man. We've used him before in similar circumstances. He's reliable, he knows how the system works, he's discreet and will do as he's told and ensure that whatever needs to be done is done with a bare minimum of fuss."*

"Very well. I will leave it to you to make all the necessary arrangements Haldane but one final thing... neither I nor this administration know anything about any of this. Do I make myself clear?"

"Perfectly sir. Perfectly," Haldane replied breezily as he made to leave immediately. There was much work to be done.

Chapter 52

Saturday 25th February 2023 – The Tunnel

Adam kept his eyes tightly shut and everything else that he was clenching, very clenched indeed, until he was satisfied that Esmerelda had levelled-off again and was slowing down after her 6G-pulling dive. Tentatively, he opened his right eye and then, unable to make-out anything more than his illuminated instrument panel and with darkness all around him, he did the same with the left. He blinked and squinted several times in an attempt to focus on something—anything at all. Ahead of him was a wall of impenetrable blackness but after a few seconds, to his right and left, he could see faint off-white lights flashing-by in a long line. He leant forward and peered at his airspeed indicator. It read three hundred mph and falling and when it reached two hundred mph it maintained that velocity, which was slow enough that he could make-out each light individually as it flashed past. He reckoned they must have been around twenty-five yards apart on either side of whatever it was he was flying through.

"Now will they allow me to switch the bloody headlights on?..." he pondered audibly. *"...Or would they take that as refusal number three?"*

He got his answer immediately. *"Feel free to switch on your headlights, Adam,"* replied the Voice which was obviously listening to him the whole time. *"But do not be tempted to touch any other of the flight controls."*

He reached out his left hand and grabbed the dial which controlled Esmerelda's headlights. Carefully, so as not to overload his vision, he initially turned it one position clockwise to select the F-5's equivalent of low beam. The space ahead of him lit-up and he gasped in astonishment. It was a tunnel and a very wide one indeed with each sidewall at least two hundred feet away from his wingtips, he estimated. The surface of the tunnel was bare rock, hewn smoothly and as he had already been able to make-out, each side was lit by evenly spaced dull lights at wingtip level.

He turned the dial another notch to activate all the external lights which fully illuminated the ceiling, possibly fifty or sixty feet above him. There were far fewer lights on the ceiling than along the walls, maybe one every two hundred yards or so and once more the rock was hewn smooth, with no linings or supports.

He leaned to his left and peered down from the canopy in a futile attempt to see the tunnel floor. However, it was virtually impossible to look down so steeply during level flight in such a tight, enclosed space so he tried his luck again with the Voice.

"Voice," he called out, having decided to adopt that name for whoever or whatever was controlling the plane. *"Any chance of banking to the left slightly so I can take a look down, please?"*

Without receiving any answer from Voice whatsoever, Esmerelda slowly banked 60° to the left yet maintained the precise same flight level and direction. Although lacking any illumination of its own, under Esmerelda's headlights, everything on the tunnel floor was clearly and easily visible to Adam and what was down there, surprised him.

"Bloody hell, railway tracks?!" he murmured. *"Whatever next?"*

Below him were four parallel sets of railway lines with maybe ten yards of gravel between each one. The gauge appeared wider than any he had seen before but the sleepers looked like they were made of concrete and of a similar construction style to those in the UK and Europe. The rails sparkled in the F-5's lights indicating regular and recent use and after a couple of minutes, the gravel between them gave way to a raised platform, two or three hundred yards long and fully illuminated. *"Are those stations or just maintenance halts?"* he asked aloud.

"They are maintenance halts, Adam," Voice replied.

"Are you Extrema's equivalent of ChatGPT or what, Voice?" he quipped.

"Do not insult my intelligence please, Adam," Voice responded, possibly with a hint of irritation.

"Sorry Voice," Adam apologised. *"I didn't mean to upset you. By the way, you can straighten Esmerelda up again now if you like."*

"I will return you to a level attitude very soon, Adam," Voice informed him. *"But first... "*

No sooner had Voice paused than a long line of the same off-white lights illuminated, lighting up the tunnel sides at floor level, immediately followed by a loud whoosh as a train appeared, as if from nowhere, hurtling towards him at colossal speed in the opposite direction. Adam almost jumped out of his skin whilst simultaneously, Esmerelda jolted suddenly, then wobbled and bounced as the turbulent air displaced by the speeding train hit her hard, causing her startled passenger to grab the sides of his seat. Then, as quickly as it had appeared, the train disappeared and the track lighting switched off again.

He released his grip on the seat and finally relaxed as Voice brought Esmerelda back to her original flight attitude, still travelling at 200mph and with the side-wall lights perfectly level with the wingtips once more.

"I wonder how many more of those trains I'll see," he queried to himself, aloud.

"No further trains will pass through while you are in the tunnel," Voice announced.

"And how long am I going to be in here?" Adam enquired.

"At your current airspeed, you will remain flying through here for a further fifty five minutes," Voice informed him.

"So this tunnel must be something like two hundred to two hundred and fifty miles long then?" Adam stated.

"Affirmative," Voice replied.

Adam's curiosity was now running wild. *"Does it have a name?"* he queried.

"Regni Cuniculum III," Voice responded.

"Which means?"

"Which means, in English, realm tunnel number three," Voice readily translated.

"So it is a tunnel that enables travel under the firmaments, from one world to another?" Adam asked, keen to obtain as much information from Voice as possible.

"Affirmative," Voice replied and then continued. *"All will be revealed if you allow me to guide you to Thoth so for now I must ask you to cease your questioning, enjoy the ride and glean as much as you can from your own observations. Goodbye, Adam."*

"Sorry, I'll shut up then," Adam quipped. *"Maybe speak to you later, Voice."*

He glanced at the compass on the instrument panel. To his bewilderment the needle was now spinning around like a whirling Dervish, utterly perplexed as to which direction was east, west, north or south. He was just about to ask Voice about this, but then remembered what he'd just been told, so remained quiet and simply stared at the blurred black/red pointer as it whirled frenetically.

He eased himself back into his seat as best he could, in an attempt to sit more comfortably and enjoy the ride but then realised not only just how exhausted he was but also how cramped and stiff he was feeling in that constricted, claustrophobic space. As Esmerelda continued her inexorable flight along Regni Cuniculum III he looked down at his watch once more. Fifty two minutes to go, he estimated and he pondered what was possibly going to happen when that time was up and what kind of world he might find at the other end. As he considered all the bewildering possibilities, it suddenly all seemed too much for his tiny, overloaded brain. The lights, as they flashed past Esmerelda's cockpit windows, had an almost hypnotic effect on his mind and as tiredness quickly overtook him, Adam Ryan Haylock fell asleep for the very first time ever in the cockpit of a fighter aircraft.

Chapter 53

Sunday 26th February 2023 – Asiri's Decision

The happy couple, becoming ever happier by the second, strolled hand in hand along the road leading from the civic centre towards the range of hills that fringed Intipata to the east. Rhythmically swinging their joined hands as they walked, the pair chatted animatedly about the party, Asiri's family and friends and what the celebration's evening session would entail. She informed Dobbo that in a couple of hours all the tables, chairs and trestle benches would be cleared from the room, a local dance band would arrive and everyone would hit the floor for one almighty knees-up. Though not much of a dancer, Dobbo said it sounded like a lot of fun and assured her that despite his two hapless left feet he would give it a go, so long as she promised to take it easy on him and, more importantly, not to dance with Fabian! Asiri smiled and assured him she would be gentle and partner only him, Pacha or Grandfather Supay.

From time-to-time they passed other pedestrians heading back in the opposite direction towards the village. Asiri greeted each one quite formally with a slow nod of the head followed by the word *'grüezi'* if they walked alone or *'grüezi mitenand'* if they were in a couple or small group.

Dobbo was intrigued. *"I'm sure I've heard that greeting before somewhere. In fact, it sounds a bit German to me. What does it mean?"*

"You may well have heard them both before, Sami my dear," she responded. *"They are what Swiss-German people say when meeting someone either formally or in passing. Papa told me that our people began to use it during World War II after many Swiss fled south to escape the allied bombing raids on Zurich. The locals really liked this form of greeting, initially adopting it as a way of being friendly to the migrants and it has stayed in the language ever since. In fact, everyone uses it now."*

Dobbo looked at her dumbfounded. *"But why the hell would the allies have bombed Zurich? I thought the Swiss were supposed to be neutral?"*

Asiri shook her head. *"I do not know the answer to that,"* she said. *"But they definitely did and somehow a number of refugees managed to make it all the way down here. Most carried on to Thoth eventually but quite a few remained, settled and raised families."*

"I wonder how they managed to get all the way to Extrema," he mused. *"That can't have been easy back in the 1940s."*

"You will probably not know this, but the Germans had colonised a large area of Antarctica in the late 1930s which they called Neu Schwabenland and set up bases and settlements, one of which was Porta Mundorum III..."

"Bloody hell!" exclaimed Dobbo, utterly taken aback by this revelation but then swiftly added, *"Oops, sorry, I must try and curb my language a bit."*

Asiri giggled mischievously. *"No, please do not do that Sami. It is one of the things I love about you. It makes me laugh."*

As she said this she squeezed his hand even tighter, moved in closer and kissed him once on the cheek. Then, slightly embarrassed, she pulled away again and quickened her pace. *"Come on, let us speed up a little shall we?"* she urged. *"We do not want to be away from the party too long."*

They reached the outskirts of the village where the houses made way to lush, green pasture and scattered areas of woodland. Dobbo stopped to take-in the splendour of the scenery surrounding him. This really was marvellous country, so beautiful, so green and completely unspoilt by any uglifying influences. There were no unsightly road signs, cameras, pylons, 5G masts or billboards anywhere to be seen and, unlike back in England, not a single trace of litter. The lane itself was immaculately paved in what looked to him like granite sets and the verdant hedgerows bordering the fields on either side bustled with songbirds, the air ringing with their joyful chirping and warbling.

"God, I love it here, Asiri," he declared and then added, *"but where are we walking to, anywhere in particular?"*

Asiri tapped the side of her nose with her index finger. *"Just keep walking and you will find out soon enough,"* she replied with a chuckle before setting-off again, dragging her bemused companion along behind her.

After a further half-mile or so, as the land began to rise toward the hills ahead of them, they reached an impressive and very ornate, red stone building on the right. Single-storey and constructed as a pentagon, it was not dissimilar in design to the accommodation block at PM3. From each of its five corners a single copper spire around fifty feet high pierced the sky with the obligatory ball and point finial at the peak. The inside of the pentagon was enclosed within an impressive cast iron and glass dome. Scores of villagers milled around the square in front of the building, at the centre of which stood an ornate sculptured white marble fountain depicting five Porta Lacus dolphins leaping into the air, water spouting from their beaks into a deep pool below which teemed with goldfish. Beside the entrance, an outdoor café thronged with customers enjoying the afternoon sunshine as well as the fabulous-looking food being brought to them by an army of smartly dressed waiters and waitresses.

They paused for a while beside the pool, gazing into its clear waters at the swarming fish and Dobbo marvelled at the sheer craftsmanship that must have gone into making such a magnificent feature. He had never seen anything like it, not even in places like Rome or Copenhagen. These people certainly knew all about quality and beauty and how to create it, he decided and the sheer intricacy of the carving was mind-blowing but what really struck him however, was how the energy from the cascading water completely calmed and uplifted him, inducing within his very soul an incredible sense of peace and well-being.

After a while, during which time neither of them spoke, with Dobbo simply standing there in wide-mouthed appreciation, Asiri decided to break the silence.

"So what do you think this place is then?" she chirped.

"Hmmm, I dunno—a museum?" he guessed.

"Well it is very old," Asiri replied. *"But it is not a museum. Come, let me show you,"*

The two 'grüezied' their way across to the entrance where a flight of stone steps led them up to a glass-fronted booth. Asiri took two small silver coins from her pocket and pushed them through the gap in the glass. She exchanged a few friendly words with the ticket lady who smiled at Dobbo and then pressed a button on the desk which activated a large brass turnstile. They squeezed into the same section and shuffled through as it slowly ushered them anti-clockwise on its axis. On the other side, under the domed roof, was a platform crowded with villagers and beside it a pair of funicular railway tracks. Dobbo peered along the rails and could just make out, on the right-hand side, one of the trains returning to the station. Just beyond it, the track bent to the left and disappeared behind a ridge so he was unable to see either the other train or the upper terminus.

"Wow a funicular railway!" he exclaimed, feeling like an excitable little kid again. *"I love funicular railways. There are three of 'em at Scarborough where I'm from—except they call them tramways there. They're a bit like this but nowhere near as good. So, where's it gonna take us then?"*

Asiri pointed to the left of the tracks towards the highest of the hills, an imposing, forest-flanked mountain with a bare plateau summit, the rock of which was a bright satsuma orange criss-crossed with white seams. *"Up there,"* she informed him. *"That is Urku Willapi or The Orange Mountain. It is the highest point in this region of Extrema. There are no higher hills or mountains within three hundred kilometres so the views are amazing. And today, Sami my darling, is a very special day. That is why so many are waiting here for the next train which should arrive in around five minutes or so."*

Ten minutes later and after many more grüezis, along with fourteen other passengers, they found themselves packed like sardines into a compartment designed for just six. All the seats had been generously given over to the more elderly of the passengers with the other eight travellers, including Dobbo and Asiri, standing nose to nose clutching the leather covered, springy grab handles on the ceiling. As the train quickly, silently and very smoothly ascended the slopes of Urku Willapi, a far cry from its noisy, ancient and clunky counterparts in Scarborough, Dobbo, had he been able to muster a free hand, would have pinched himself very hard to prove that this wasn't just the dream of all dreams. Surely this couldn't be happening to him could it? Was this lovely lady beside him even real? He stooped slightly, not easy in that cramped space, and leant his nose against hers. He could feel her warm breath and her hair tickling his forehead as they swayed with the motion of the carriage. He inhaled slowly and deeply through his nostrils. She smelt gorgeous, simply gorgeous. In no way was this any kind of dream. *"What a lucky bugger I am,"* he purred, hoping she would hear but that was impossible above the hubbub of their fellow sardines so Asiri, oblivious to what he had just whispered, simply smiled at him, and then lovingly rubbed the end of his nose with hers.

They somehow managed to find an unoccupied bench on the summit and settled down to enjoy the view which was like nothing Dobbo could ever have imagined. They faced due north, indicated by a sign mounted in the top of the nearby flat-topped stone summit obelisk. Asiri translated for his benefit the inscription on the brass plaque set into its southern face. It read *'The Orange Mountain. 1246 metres above Ahtian Ocean level.'*

Dobbo peered at the plaque *"Ahtian Ocean level?"* he queried. *"Is that different to our sea level?"*

"I am told the Ahtian Ocean level is considerably higher than yours," she explained. *"Although there are land-free passages through Antarctica and Extrema, these are completely blocked by the ice wall and mountain glaciers which makes it impossible for anyone to sail through and more Importantly, prevents your world from being overwhelmed by the Ahtian waters."*

Dobbo smirked. *"Let's hope the sodding ice doesn't melt then eh?"* he chortled. *"They'd be fu—knackered! Anyway, why is today so special?"*

"In a few minutes you will find out," Asiri replied before pointing to a telescope mounted atop a small marble pillar. *"But first, why not take a look through that telescope and tell me what you can see."*

Dobbo walked across and attached himself to the eyepiece. He located the zoom dial and extended the magnification to its full range and very slowly and meticulously scanned the northern horizon, whistling in wonderment as he rotated from west to east through 180° and back again.

"Well, don't forget, I had to fly right over all that lot to get here," he pointed out. *"So I have seen it before from above. But from here, with this telescope, it's absolutely bloody amazing! I can see mile upon mile of wilderness dotted with huge lakes and forests and I can pick out Porta Mundorum III incredibly clearly. No more planes have landed there, by the way. Beyond that, I can just make out the snow and ice and in the very distance those bloody massive Antarctic mountains. It's incredible! When I zoom out however, most of it disappears below the horizon but then comes back into view as I zoom in again."*

Asiri smiled knowingly. *"Now, that's because you are increasing and decreasing your focal range, Sami. As you increase it, objects come into view that were previously invisible and then they disappear again when you decrease it. It is called the 'vanishing point.' Try without the telescope and tell me how far you can see."*

Dobbo stood back and gazed into the far distance, screwing his eyes into narrow slits in a vain attempt to see as far as he possibly could. *"You're bang on right,"* he confirmed. *"All I can see now is Intipata, Porta Lacus and shitloads of wilderness. Oh, and the runway lights at Porta Mundorum III. I think I can just make out the southern end of Falco Lacus too but I'm not certain about that. The horizon is pretty much at that point actually, so it's really strange that I can see way, way beyond that and to ground level too, with the telescope. I mean, you'd think most of it would be out of sight below the horizon wouldn't you?"*

Asiri grinned. *"Yes you would, my sweet. It is indeed quite surprising, is it not?"* she concurred and then, suddenly raising her right arm, she pointed north by east, shaking her finger excitedly.

"Here comes Machu Inti—your sun," she declared. *"Look, she is just appearing now."*

Dobbo peered in the direction that her finger was pointing and, sure enough, our sun was rising from the horizon. After maybe two minutes or so its position was due north, with almost half of it visible, a deep golden-red near-semicircle. His jaw dropped. *"Bugger me!"* he blurted. *"So that's our sun and at the same time yours is shining brightly above us. My God, what would people back home think of all this?"*

Spontaneous applause suddenly filled the air as the throng gathered on the summit began to clap their hands in celebration. The two sweethearts joined-in and then, once it had died down, Dobbo put his arm around her waist and pulled her in tight. She did the same and they held that pose, gazing in silence as Machu Inti continued her relentless trek around the Tropic of Capricorn and vanished from view.

Asiri released her hold on Dobbo's waist and took his hand once more. *"I think we should return to the party now,"* she said, leading him back towards the summit terminus. *"Everyone will be wondering where we are."*

The train was waiting for them at the upper terminus and so they eagerly clambered aboard and took their seats in an empty compartment. To their relief no other passengers joined them, with most of those who travelled up with them choosing to remain longer on the summit. As they began their descent, Dobbo gazed up at the sky through the window, deep in thought. *"I notice you called our sun 'she,'"* he remarked. *"So, is your sun 'she' as well?"*

"Well, one of them is," she replied, *"And that is the one shining above us right now. We call her Inti Coya which means sun Queen. The others are Inti Sapa, sun King, Inti Wawa, sun Child and Inti Ayayu, sun Spirit. Tomorrow, Inti Wawa will bring us light, the day after it will be Inti Ayayu's turn, then Inti Sapa and after him, Inti Coya will return once more."*

Dobbo shook his head. This was becoming almost too much to take-in. His notoriously tiny mind, previously totally controlled, conditioned and constrained by years of educational, media and military brainwashing was finally being opened-up and awakened, expanding and broadening with each new bewildering revelation. He felt almost overwhelmed, and overloaded yet at the same time liberated, excited and enlightened and he was simply loving it. And in addition to of all that, he realised he was falling in love, genuinely and deeply, with the beautiful creation nestling against him.

"Well how do you know which one is which?" he asked. *"I mean, do they look different at all?"*

"They differ slightly in shade and size although they all have the same power," she replied. *"After a few weeks here you will be able to tell which one is above you simply by the light it casts."*

Dobbo raised his eyebrows, keen to learn more. *"And do they follow the same path all year round?"* he continued, *"Or are they like our sun. which is closer in the summer and then further away in the winter?"* As he finished the question a realisation came to him. When previously had he ever shown this level of curiosity or desire for truth? Not even at Cranwell where all he did was blindly accept whatever he was told by his tutors and instructors without deliberation or challenge. But now he was no longer simply taking things as read or told but instead was becoming thirsty for a full and believable explanation based on undeniable and observable evidence. *"My God!"* he exclaimed. *"You'll be applying for bloody Mastermind next, Dobbo!"*

Asiri had already embarked upon her response. *"No, Sami, they stay on the same course all year round and work very differently to Machu Inti. The time interval between each of our suns is one day, thirty hours, not twenty four like yours. Each sequence of four suns makes up a week here, every five of our weeks is one month and twelve of those months comprise one year."*

Dobbo was loving all this yet had further questions and continued digging. *"In the visitors book, it mentioned that Extrema has four distinct seasons,"* he pointed out. *"Well, how does that work if your suns follow exactly the same course all year round."*

Asiri laughed out loud at this, amused yet impressed at the same time. *"You are asking some excellent questions,"* she responded cheerily. *"For me that is wonderful and most heart-warming. So, if I can, let me explain to you how our seasons work."*

She fell silent for a while, determined to fully articulate and explain what she had understood and taken for granted throughout her young life and keen not to confuse her inquisitive student. Finally she gathered her thoughts and began...

"Our suns circle around us in four days all year round, yet they do not maintain the same speed throughout each rotation. In our summer, they move at their slowest over this section of Extrema, giving us our warmest and longest days, but then speed-up over other areas resulting in a colder and much shorter day. Then, by the time they reach us again they have slowed-down once more. In our winter however, they move much faster overhead here, therefore our days are short and the temperatures much colder. So, throughout the 120,000 kilometre extent of our land, all four seasons occur in different regions every single day." She paused and exhaled deeply. *"I hope I have explained it clearly and it has not been too much for you to take-in."*

Dobbo said nothing at all in response. Looking somewhat perplexed, he simply sat there, his brain whirring, striving to make sense of what she had just explained to him. As the train arrived once more at the lower terminus, he jumped to his feet looking satisfied.

"Yep, got all that now," he declared. *"And it all makes perfect sense. Thank you, Asiri. Wow, you do know your stuff!"*

As they strolled along the road on their return to the civic centre, he began to ponder his immediate future. Should he continue south like Adam and hopefully meet up once more with his very best and, prior to his arrival in Extrema, only real friend in the world? Or should he remain here in Intipata with Asiri? If she was happy with that of course. Without a doubt something wonderful and miraculous had happened to him during the last twenty four hours. He was a changed man, transformed even and holding his hand right now was this remarkable and irresistible life-force who had swept him off his feet, turned his whole world upside down and simply mesmerised him. But did he love her?

Of course he bloody-well did! Of that there was no doubt whatsoever and with all his heart and soul too. She was obviously very fond of him but did she actually love him? If so it would be utterly wonderful to try and progress things further and what better a place to do that than right here? But he could not get over the fact that he missed Adam and hankered desperately to be reunited with him. Together they could continue their adventures, explore further and uncover even more truths about our world, Extrema, Thoth and whatever may or may not lie beyond. But God, did his heart ache for this woman beside him or what? And if she reciprocated his feelings for her, he'd be a crazy dumbass to leave her here.

As if she was able to read his thoughts, Asiri suddenly, and very forcibly, interrupted his deliberations and dropped the most almighty bombshell. *"Do you know what I would like to do, Sami?"* she blurted out. *"I would like to fly away from here with you in your airplane and travel to Thoth to meet up with Adam. I know we have only just met but—and please do not laugh—I love you with all my heart and soul and I want you forever in my world—as both a life partner and a lover. It would be marvellous to settle here and make a home and family with you but I am still young and extremely restless, eager for more adventure. And you, my darling, are the most exciting thing ever to come into my life. I want to be with you for the rest of my days and hopefully you feel the same about me but I know also that you miss Adam and, after all you have been through together, both your lives and mine too will be fuller and richer if the two of you are reunited."*

Her smitten and now elated companion stopped in his tracks and, for virtually the first time in his thirty-seven years and six months on planet Earth, or whatever planet Earth had just recently turned out to be, Samuel James Dobson collapsed into floods of tears—in sheer joy mingled with unbridled relief that she felt the same way as he.

Chapter 54

Monday 27th February 2023 – Fabian's Task

Back at Grandfather Supay's party, Fabian was becoming more than a tad merry on the Chicha de jora as he chatted relentlessly with Pacha about everything Antarctica and Extrema. The geography of the region was of the greatest interest to him, particularly when Pacha explained the composition of the firmament, the rotation of the four suns, the Ahtian Ocean and what lay beyond. Unlike Adam and Dobbo, he had not yet read the visitors book at PM3, so most of what Pacha revealed to him was completely new. He deluged his tutor with question after question, hungry for more knowledge and truth and greedily lapped-up each new mind-blowing revelation. As they chatted he could sense an expansion of his consciousness, a further awakening of his very being as the weight he had been carrying on his shoulders for years began to lift. At long last his research, suspicions and suppositions as to what lay beyond sixty degrees south and the ice wall were being affirmed and the vindication he felt as a result was liberating and joy-bringing.

He was totally in awe of Pacha as well as eternally grateful, for his knowledge, insight and ability to explain everything so effectively and succinctly. Even amongst the most learned and enlightened Querdenker sages, not a single one had ever come remotely close to this guy. He held nothing back from Fabian, regardless of how unpleasant or uncomfortable a particular disclosure may be, yet never once did he stray on to other topics, forever keen for his young protégé's questions to guide the discussion.

They had just moved on to the monetary system used in Extrema, something again which Fabian was keen to understand, when one of the waiters walked over to Pacha and whispered in his ear.

Pacha's brow furrowed. *"I'm sorry, Fabian,"* he apologised. *"I just need to leave you alone for a few minutes. Please excuse me."*

"Of course," Fabian replied. *"No problem, Pacha—please take your time. I will be fine."*

The waiter led Pacha to one of the side rooms which he entered, closing the door gently behind him. Fabian switched his attention to people-watching, smiling at anyone he made eye contact with. He was enjoying himself enormously. Following all the disclosures from Pacha, aided and abetted by several Chicha de joras, he felt serene and carefree with any remaining trauma from the events at PM3 having completely evaporated. He relaxed back in his chair, glass in hand and began to doze.

The next thing he felt was a jolt which not only roused him from his little cat-nap but also resulted in him receiving a lapful of Chicha de jora. "*Scheiße!*" he cursed, bolting upright to try and disguise the spillage.

"*Sorry to shock you there, Fabian,*" whispered Pacha apologetically into his ear, having returned from his meeting. "*I didn't mean for you to spill all over yourself but it will soon dry, don't worry. Would you mind joining me in the office over there as I have a little proposition for you?*"

Fabian tried his utmost to compose himself—not easy with half a glass of Chicha de jora down your trousers but, covering as much of the spillage as he could with his napkin, he gathered himself and followed Pacha away from the table into the same side room.

He closed the door, only to be presented with two tall, athletic-looking men, both in their sixties he guessed, occupying seats at a wooden conference table around which another six chairs were positioned. Pacha made the introductions. "*Gentlemen, let me introduce, Fabian Schuster, a pilot of the German Luftwaffe. Or should I say ex-Luftwaffe? Fabian, this is Antay and Manko, two of my closest and most trusted friends.*"

Pacha took his seat as Antay and Manko rose to shake hands with a rather taken-aback and bemused Fabian. This seemed like something serious and, unsure as to what was expected of him, he remained standing, glued to the spot as the two newcomers returned to their seats.

"*You look somewhat concerned, Fabian. And unfortunately this is quite serious,*" Pacha informed the German. "*But, with your help, it should easily be resolved. Our two friends here will explain everything. Now please take a seat.*"

He pulled a chair out from under the table and offered it to Fabian who took it and made himself as comfortable as he could, difficult given what he had just been told, plus the sogginess of the by-now lukewarm Chicha de jora leaching into his underpants!

"*Just to give you some background, Fabian. Antay is a farmer and Manko works as a stonemason,*" he explained. "*But one of their other roles here in Intipata is to capture any communications from our agents out in the field and pass the information on to the relevant people. On this occasion, that relevant person is you, Fabian and so, gentlemen, would you be so kind as to inform our young companion as to what you have learned today?"*

The two men looked at each other, nodded and Antay cleared his throat, ready to begin.

"Earlier this afternoon, I received a communication from our good friend Eduardo at Teniente Rodolfo Marsh Martin Base on King George Island," he began. *"Tragically, our trusted and much-loved colleague Jorge is no longer with us, ruthlessly and mercilessly executed by Wing Commander Prendergast. But thanks to Eduardo's efforts, he now rests in peace in an unmarked grave close by. Eduardo is, at this moment in time, completely alone at the base—no replacements have as yet been sent but he has been told that a completely new interceptor force is being prepared, the first elements of which are due to arrive there in one week's time. By new interceptor force however, they do not mean simply two more fighters and replacements for Jorge and the Wing Commander. What they are sending is a special task force which Eduardo has been told comprises an entire fighter squadron, a platoon of ground troops and several naval gunboats. It would appear that they are greatly increasing their military presence."*

He paused to give Fabian the opportunity to take this unwelcome news on board.

The young airman was now sobering up very quickly. *"So how does this affect me?"* he enquired, concern etched into his features.

Manko took over from where Antay had left off. *"We will neither force nor coerce you to involve yourself in all this but yes, we would greatly appreciate your assistance,"* he declared earnestly. *"Eduardo has spoken with one of his contacts in the CIA who told him that he is suspected of collusion in all that has taken place up there recently and thus his life is in danger. The task force being despatched is likely to include secret service operatives who will take care of him in their own unique style. So Eduardo needs to be brought back home before that force arrives. There is no immediate panic, as these deployments take time to organise, but were you to say yes, we would need you to return north in one week's time and bring him back with you. Until then however, you can relax, enjoy Intipatan life for a few days and recharge your batteries."* He paused, his eyes boring into Fabian's. *"So, how do you feel about that, my friend?"*

Fabian was knocked sideways by this sudden and unexpected request for his services. He had already put his past life and his old world firmly behind him, hence the decision to fly on to Thoth. He had no desire to remain in Extrema, let alone fly all the way back to Teniente Rodolfo. So why him? Why not Dobbo?

Pacha must have been reading his thoughts. *"We had considered asking Samuel but, well, let me say, he has other things on his mind right now,"* he explained, grinning with a cheeky glint in his eye.

"Yes, erm, Asiri," Fabian concurred. *"I suppose he has his hands full right now, so to speak and I am sure she would not be happy for him to go when I am more than capable."*

At that point Antay and Manko both nodded in agreement and stood-up to leave. *"We shall leave you to consider your decision, Fabian,"* announced the latter. *"But let me reassure you, we envisage no danger in this mission whatsoever. It should be a simple case of flying up to Teniente Rodolfo, refuelling and then returning immediately with Eduardo. Oh, and one more thing..."* He reached down and heaved a bulky leather holdall from beside his chair. *"Would you be so kind as to take this back with you for our beloved deceased colleague?"* he requested, unzipping the bag to reveal a small, inscribed marble plaque. *"This is a headstone to mark Jorge's final resting place."*

Fabian leant forward to study the inscription which, to his surprise, was written in English, saying...

Here lies Hurhi Luwis Santus

Proud citizen of Extrema

Known in this world as Jorge Luis Santos.

Taken before his time by an agent of the evil Cabal.

May his spirit soar like a dove for all eternity.'

"Very well, my friends—I will do it," he announced. *"Having witnessed Jorge's brutal execution, the least I can do is to deliver this to his grave and rescue his old friend. Just tell me when you want me to leave and I will gladly go."*

Chapter 55

Monday 27th February 2023 – Asiri and Fabian's Announcements

After a Chicha de jora-fuelled evening, most of it spent strutting his stuff on the dancefloor with Asiri but occasionally alone while she partnered her father or grandfather, Dobbo awoke with one almighty throbbing head.

"Oh my good God!" he groaned as he rolled himself out of bed and padded across the room to raise the window blind.

The dazzling mid-morning light from Inti Wawa slammed into his unprepared and very sensitive retinas like lightning through tissue paper. He recoiled in horror and staggered back, catching the corner of the bed and completely losing his balance. He spun around 180° and tumbled unceremoniously on to the wooden floor with one almighty crash.

Though unhurt he remained there for several minutes, gazing up at a hairy, red spider weaving its web around the brass lamp hanging from the ceiling.

"Incey-wincey spider, climbing up the spout..." he giggled, the previous night's imbibing continuing to fuel his uncontrollable hilarity despite the intense pressure it now exerted on his temples. *"..Down came the rain and..."*

The door burst open. *"Oh Sami, are you hurt? Can you move?!"* Asiri cried, kneeling beside the prostrate Yorkshireman who then began to guffaw uncontrollably. Realising he was uninjured she began to laugh too and flopped on to the floor beside him, the two howling in unison with uncontrollable laughter.

When their mirth eventually subsided she stood, helped Dobbo to his feet and then sat him down gently on the bed.

"Now wait here while I prepare something to bring you around," she told him, returning quickly with a glass containing a cloudy white liquid. *"Now here, take this—sodium bicarbonate dissolved in water. The best thing ever for sorting out silly boys like you and Fabian! I have already given some to him and he seems fine now."*

She kissed him once on the forehead and left him to his recovery, returning to the kitchen to continue preparing breakfast with her parents.

Fifteen minutes later, the household and their fully-revived guests were gathered around the kitchen table tucking into a breakfast of home-made sourdough bread, goat's cheese and cold meats accompanied by *kiwicha lichi*, a warm, comforting and revitalising milky drink containing amaranth, cinnamon, cloves, salt, and honey. The conversation flowed effortlessly and with great humour as they relived the events of the previous evening, particularly the prowess of certain individuals on the dancefloor—and of course Dobbo's party-piece, which had the whole of the place in uproar. Pacha joked that Dobbo's song and many of his dance moves could quite possibly make it into Extreman folklore!

It was Saywa who raised the subject of the couple's three hour absence at the end of the birthday feast. She was keen to discover where they had been, what they had done and even what they had been talking about. Although Dobbo found this rather intrusive, Asiri seemed entirely unconcerned, taking it in her stride and responding honestly to the questions directed at her. She divulged to everyone at the table, all that had taken place during their little excursion up to the moment where she had reduced Dobbo to tears. Having decided to exclude that particular part of the story she paused, took his left hand in her right and addressed their fellow breakfasters.

"We made two very important decisions when we returned from the mountain," she announced. *"Which may come as a shock to you all."*

The others exchanged puzzled glances and raised eyebrows, though some already had a slight inkling of what she may be about to tell them. They all finished their mouthfuls, sat back and gave Asiri their fullest attention.

"Well," she began, her cheeks reddening slightly as she spoke. *"Sami and I have become fond of each other. Very fond indeed."* She nervously cleared her throat. *"No, it's more than that, and I'm sure some of you will think we are mad, but I think we have fallen truly, madly and deeply in love."*

She paused to gauge the reaction of her audience, concerned as to how this bolt from the blue would be received but she need not have worried. Pacha simply beamed back at her with watery eyes and her mother clapped her hands together, bounced gleefully up and down on her chair and then jumped to her feet. She bounded across and threw her arms around her beloved daughter, twirling her round and round in her extreme delight. When she finally composed herself, and with more than a hint of embarrassment, she apologised and quietly took her seat once more. Asiri continued...

"Thank you, Mama and Papa. I am so happy you share our joy..." She glanced over at Dobbo, *"...and I know Sami is too. However, we have another announcement which may not be received quite so well."* She gathered her courage as best she could. *"We have decided to fly on to Thoth and meet with Adam. Sami was torn between remaining here with me or continuing his adventure but I have talked him into continuing on and am determined to go with him. I am not ready to settle down just yet and am thirsty for adventure. Hence our joint decision."*

At this, Pacha and Saywa's unbridled joy at announcement number one fell away like ice calving from the face of a glacier. They had not expected this particular bombshell and were both clearly overwhelmed and shocked. The two sat there in stunned silence, vainly attempting to take in the enormity of what Asiri had just dropped on them. Everyone else, awkwardly and uncomfortably and without saying a word, simply returned to their breakfasts.

Eventually, once everyone had finished their food, Pacha gathered his thoughts together and turned to Asiri.

"Asiri, the four of us will talk of this at greater length later, in private," he said gently. He then briefly glanced at Saywa. *"Your mother and I have always wanted only the best for you and the very best thing in the world is happiness. We want us all to be happy with what you are planning, so let us discuss it later and give us all the opportunity to express our fears and concerns openly, honestly and with love."*

"Thank you," mouthed Asiri, in gratitude, before aiming a nervous and worried smile at Dobbo. Much to her great relief, he grinned back at her and winked.

At that moment Fabian, who had earlier expressed slight disappointment at not being invited to view the two suns from the mountain, decided that this was possibly the right moment for him to take the floor and make his announcement. He stood up and rapped his spoon sharply on the table.

"Excuse me everybody, I have something to tell you all too," he declared.

Chapter 56

Monday 15th April 1912 – The Aftermath of Titanic's Sinking

A crisp, new five-pound note, folded carefully and pressed into the palm of Raymond Bentley, the able seaman in charge of access—in combination with Brigadier Arthur's fake White Star officer's uniform, as he anticipated, proved to be his golden ticket into lifeboat number seven. In those long-gone, distant days, five pounds was almost one month's wages to an ordinary seaman. However at this point in time, Bentley had approximately one hour left of his life in which to spend it but this fact seemed to have completely passed him by as sheer greed took centre stage in his thought processes.

Five long, terrifying, freezing cold and tedious hours later, the welcome sight of *RMS Carpathia,* the Cunard liner and the saviour of all Titanic's survivors, appeared in outline on the horizon against a backdrop of a million stars on that crisp, bitterly cold, clear and moonless night. And so it was that Brigadier Robert Arthur of British Intelligence was successfully rescued and transported to New York along with the other seven hundred and four survivors of the disaster.

There, upon disembarkation at the White Star pier, he discreetly disposed of his officer's jacket, quietly mingled with the subdued, teeming crowd of grieving relatives and friends of the passengers and quickly disappeared into the anonymity of New York City.

In the following days, after patiently waiting for the commotion surrounding the drama to subside, Arthur eventually made contact with General Albert Cunningham, the British agent in charge of American affairs within the SIS, who was based in New York and was thoroughly debriefed. He confirmed to Cunningham that the mission had been a total success and that Straus, Guggenheim and Astor had all been eliminated surreptitiously and without witnesses. Astor's lifeless body was discovered two weeks later, floating in the ocean with its face completely unrecognisable, the result of blunt instrument trauma and he was only identified by the contents of his jacket pocket. The other two bodies were never found and were assumed to have gone down with the ship. As Arthur was already in the USA, he was offered the opportunity to join the American branch of the service in addition to a promotion to Major-General for services rendered, which he accepted without hesitation.

His wife Ellen and his young son Andrew, aged two, soon followed. Their house in Kensington, London along with all its contents was sold and the family eventually settled into a lovely new home on Long Island—a short trolley ride from his new HQ in Manhattan.

And there Robert and Ellen remained for the rest of their lives. Robert died in 1948 at the age of seventy-six and Ellen four years later, also aged seventy-six. Young Andrew grew-up as a naturalised American citizen and eventually followed in his father's footsteps into the military, joining the U.S. Navy as an officer immediately following his graduation in mathematics from the prestigious Harvard University and served his country with distinction during World War II in the Pacific. He was awarded the Congressional Medal of Honor for his part in the Battle of Leyte Gulf in October 1944, as a result of remaining at his post in acting command of his ship despite the death of the Captain and himself suffering life-threatening injuries by shrapnel which resulted in him walking with a slight limp for the rest of his days. An action for which he was also awarded a Purple Heart.

At the cessation of the Pacific war in August 1945, despite his eligibility for demob, he decided to remain in the Navy following his promotion from Commodore to Captain—in command of the destroyer, the *USS Henderson,* which would take part in Operation Highjump, commencing just over one year later in October 1946.

Chapter 57

Saturday 25th February 2023 – Above the Ahtian Ocean

The roar of the thrusters as Esmerelda began to accelerate very rapidly, jerked Adam unceremoniously from his peaceful slumbers. Before he had time to even slightly regather his thoughts, he was slammed into the back of his seat as she switched from level flight to an almost vertical climb. In a matter of seconds the F-5 had exited the tunnel into dazzling sunlight and swiftly ascended to four thousand feet before levelling-off and slowing to a steady cruise speed. Adam took in his new surroundings as Esmerelda flew directly away from the tunnel's exit. He was above a vast sea that stretched away to a flat, blue horizon in all directions. Flying directly towards the sun, burning bright and proud in an almost cloudless sky, he could see no signs of land, not even that from which he had just ascended which by now lay directly behind him and therefore invisible from the cockpit.

The Voice then broke its silence. *"Welcome to the realm of Thoth, Adam,"* it began. *"You have just exited Regni Cuniculum III and moved from your realm into ours having passed below the outer limits of both firmaments and the void between them. Below you is the vast Ahtian Ocean which stretches around the entire perimeter of our world, and we will continue to maintain full control of your aircraft as you traverse it. Before we commence the crossing however, we will now circumnavigate Hiatum Insula*[18] *so that you can view the whole of this island and its abyss leading to and from the tunnel."*

No sooner than Voice had said this, Esmerelda immediately banked into a shallow and very steady anti-clockwise turn. Adam peered downwards. Below him lay the aforementioned island, around fifty kilometres long, in the very middle of which he could see the gaping void from which he had just exited. He exhaled several times rapidly, awestruck not only by what he had just travelled through and under but also in relief and delight to be flying in clear blue skies once more.

As Esmerelda circled, he spotted a substantial harbour on the island's southern shore, close to the entrance to the tunnel. Two long, curved harbour walls, stretching out into the ocean, formed its entrance through which two or three vessels were in the process of entering and leaving. As well as these and the numerous craft docked in the harbour, he could also discern several other boats further out at sea, travelling to and from the

[18] Latin for Chasm Island

island. *"A busy old place,"* he said to himself, despite no other visible settlements on the island. *"They must be a doing quite a bit of trade with Extrema."*

After three revolutions of the island, the F-5 accelerated away rapidly from Hiatum Insula, breaking thunderously through the sound barrier and quickly achieving her maximum speed of 1050mph which she then maintained. Adam glanced down to inspect the compass.

"What?!" he exclaimed, barely able to comprehend what he was now witnessing.

The needle was no longer spinning, wobbling or dithering. It was stock-still, rock solid and unwavering, the red half pointing slightly to the right of the direction in which he was heading.

"So, I'm heading slightly west of north now am I Voice?" he queried.

"Not quite, Adam. Your direction, is what we call inward by west. Here in Thoth we have inward and outward, rather than north and south," Voice explained. *"And to be absolutely precise, your current heading is five degrees west of inward."*

This was just about making sense to Adam but he needed further clarification. *"So where exactly is inward then?"*

"If you travel due inward, you will eventually reach the central magnetic point of our realm, the equivalent of your north pole."

Adam mulled this over for a few moments before continuing the interrogation. *"And outward?"*

"Outward is any straight longitudinal direction away from the centre," Voice answered. *"And just as with your lines of longitude, there is no single end point, it is simply anywhere along the inner edge of the firmament, the outer limit of our realm."*

"Yep, that kind of makes sense, Voice," Adam concurred and then abruptly changed the subject. *"So how long am I going to be flying over this ocean? It looks pretty massive to me. No land ahead at the moment from what I can see."*

"Another sixteen hundred kilometres of ocean and you will reach land, Adam," announced Voice. *"We assumed you would not appreciate a three or four hour*

flight after all this time in the air, so took the liberty of propelling you along at maximum speed. You should reach your destination in around ninety minutes so relax, enjoy the ride and please feel free to take another nap if you wish."

"Thank you, Voice," replied Adam, hugely relieved. *"This seat is getting mighty uncomfortable now and I can't wait to get out of here and on to terra firma again. Not sure I fancy another kip just yet though so tell me, what is my destination exactly?"*

"We are flying you to the Isle of Thoth and will land you at a suitable location just outside the capital city Varinthia," Voice replied. *"There, you will be met by friendly citizens who have been given the task of escorting you to your accommodation in the city. Your welcome will be warm and the hospitality more than adequate, allowing you to fully rest and recuperate from your arduous flight. They will give you much more information upon landing so, just as in the tunnel, sit back, relax and enjoy the next ninety minutes."*

Adam relaxed as best he could in the seat which by this time felt more like a knobbly rock as it dug painfully into his back, shoulders and backside. As the white-capped ocean flashed-by beneath him, he began to ponder precisely what his passage through *Regni Cuniculum III* had enabled him to pass beneath. *"Voice, are the firmaments some kind of dome then?"* he enquired. *"And the only way of getting beyond them is to go underground?"*

"Affirmative to both questions, Adam," Voice replied.

Adam paused for thought then pressed Voice even further. *"So does Thoth's firmament butt right-up against ours or is there a gap?"*

"There is a gap of around fifty kilometres between them."

Adam's mind was whirring, his curiosity running wild. *"Then what lies between them…oh, and above them of course. Is it a vacuum? I mean, like outer-space?"*

Voice did not respond immediately. Adam wondered if it was researching before replying. Eventually the answer came.

"It could well be a vacuum as you say. Or it could even be water as in the ancient scriptures of both realms—or perhaps something different entirely. I do not know the answer to that. Whatever it is though, the impenetrable firmament separates us and our domain from it," Voice explained.

This seemed totally crazy at first consideration. *"I reckon a vacuum is what it is,"* he opined. *"Because that's what they say outer space is—and NASA, the Russians and others have all... hang on a minute, did you just say impenetrable?"*

"Affirmative, Adam."

By now he was becoming more and more bemused. *"So how come we have sent men into space—and, or so we are told, to the moon as well? And what about the international space station?"*

"You are posing some excellent questions, Adam," Voice declared. *"How could all that have taken place with an impenetrable firmament? But if outer space is a vacuum and the firmament was not impenetrable, would you not expect the pressure in the vacuum to equalise with that of the Earth's atmosphere? You cannot have a vacuum without an impenetrable barrier."*

Adam screwed-up his face in consternation as he pondered his next question. *"OK, I kind of get that, which explains a hell of a lot actually. So are the suns inside or outside the firmaments?"*

"They are inside, as is your moon also. In Thoth however, we do not have a moon. And we have only three stars, one directly over the central pole, another at 90° east and the third at 90° west.

The now utterly captivated student raised his eyes in near disbelief. It all seemed so believable and made far more sense than anything he been fed throughout his life thus far. He then considered all he had been told about our sun and moon and ploughed on relentlessly with his questioning.

"So how far above us do the firmaments stretch?" he enquired. *"Millions and millions of miles?"*

"Negative," came the categorical retort from Voice. *"Yours is ten thousand kilometres at its highest point and ours a mere six thousand."*

"What!" the airman exclaimed in near disbelief. *"B-b-but our sun is ninety-three million miles away—isn't it?"*

"Well, is it?" asked Voice rhetorically. *"Because ours certainly is not. It makes its way around this realm at a height of just over four thousand kilometres. Think about it, Adam. Were your sun ninety-three million miles away, would it be possible to experience the phenomenon whereby rays of light widen as they shine between the clouds towards the ground? Surely you would expect them*

to be almost parallel would you not? And how can you explain the large difference between winter and summer temperatures in your country England, for example? Given such a huge distance, could that be purely down to a relatively miniscule tilt of an axis?"

Adam nodded in agreement, not that Voice would have noticed, or would it? It seemed to know everything else! *"Those are really valid points you're making,"* he conceded, *"points which I have never ever considered and I'll give them all further thought. So I assume, therefore, that the sun is much smaller than we're told?"*

"Affirmative."

"And the moon too?" he continued.

"Affirmative. They are both exactly the same diameter."

To Adam, this was becoming more and more mind-blowing by the second. *"Bloody hell fire!"* he blustered. *"And we are told that due to some miraculous, random, cosmic coincidence that our sun is four hundred times bigger than the moon yet appears the same size because it is four hundred times further away. Very convenient! They'd thought that one through before telling us all, hadn't they, Voice?"*

"Absolutely," Voice agreed.

Adam ploughed on relentlessly. *"So is the moon a massive ball of rock then?"*

"Negative."

"But it does reflect the sun's light and heat?"

"Negative," Voice emphatically declared once more before posing another conundrum. *"Consider this Adam, if it did reflect the sun's rays then surely, if you were to place a thermometer into moonlight during the dead of night, you would expect it to be warmer than the surrounding darkness would you not?"*

Adam mulled over this for a moment. *"Affirmative,"* he concurred, mischievously mimicking Voice.

"But it is actually colder," Voice informed him.

Now this was getting very interesting indeed.

"Get away!" Adam exclaimed.

"I am telling you the truth, Adam," Voice insisted. *"You do not have to believe me though. In fact, if one day you should ever return to your realm, feel free to try the experiment yourself."*

"Not much chance of that, Voice," Adam chortled. *"They'd fucking kill me!"*

"Language!" came the unexpected chastisement.

"Sorry, Voice." Contrite, Adam apologised and then continued his questioning. *"Are there any other realms beyond ours besides Thoth?"*

"Affirmative. Adjoining Earth are three other realms but, for now, I think you have been given more than enough to ponder. You will have countless opportunities to pose whatever questions you like once you arrive in Thoth. So, for now, I am closing down this communication channel and, as I said earlier, enjoy your flight and take some sleep if you need it. I will be in touch again when you reach land. Over and out."

"All right, Voice, be like that then," Adam muttered sarcastically but with good humour. *"Speak later, eh?"*

He nestled back in his seat in a futile attempt at comfort and began to mull-over and dissect all that he had discussed with Voice since his exit from *Regni Cuniculum III*. Mind-blowing and thought-provoking stuff it had been too and was giving rise to even more questions and conundrums. As he attempted to make a list in his head of all the topics he wished to discuss further, his mind wandered to those whom he had left behind, particularly Dobbo but also Prendergast, Jorge, Eduardo and Pacha and his wonderful family. He began to recall each stage of his by now epic adventure, grinning in self-satisfaction at the clever and devious duping of Prendergast during Dobbo's attempted interception. Well, he hoped to high heaven that they had managed to dupe him. If they hadn't then Dobbo would be in one hell of a mess.

"Shit!" he groaned. *"What if Prenders saw through the whole damned charade?"*

He decided to put that almost unthinkable possibility from his mind for now and maybe to implore the *'good people of Thoth'* to use all possible resources to ascertain Dobbo's fate. *"Yes, that would be the best thing to do,"* he reassured himself. His thoughts then drifted to the fabulous fishing he had experienced during his ‘mini-break’ at *Porta Mundorum III* and before long he was on the river once more, casting his *Silver Stoat’s Tail* salmon-fly with all his customary skill and aplomb into one of the magical pools. Kingfishers darted and swarms of insects hovered above the cool, crystal water and he felt completely at one with himself and the creation all around him. Except he wasn’t on the river at all was he? He was squeezed into the confines of an antique, 1960s F-5 Freedom Fighter and, for only the second time in his entire flying career, Adam Ryan Haylock, ex-RAF, had dozed-off to sleep in the pilot’s seat of a military aircraft.

Chapter 58

Captain Andrew Arthur U.S.N. b. 1909 – Operation Highjump

Brigadier Robert Arthur's only son Andrew, by some bizarre coincidence was born on exactly the same day as his assassination victim Robert Falcon Scott's only son, Peter, on the 14th September 1909. After his father's transfer to the New York office of the SIS, he and his mother Helen then emigrated to the USA in July 1912—ironically onboard RMS Olympic (formerly Titanic) just a couple of months before Andrew's third birthday.

After graduating with distinction from Harvard University in 1931, he joined the U.S. Navy as an Ensign and due to his capabilities and contacts, and also thanks largely to his father's influence, rapidly progressed through the ranks, ultimately achieving the position of Captain following his promotion from Commodore in 1944. This was immediately following his heroics at the Battle of Leyte Gulf, much cited as the greatest naval battle in history and which effectively saw the beginning of the end of Japan's resistance to the might of the American armed forces.

The celebrations surrounding the end of World War II on 8th August 1945 had barely ended when the Cold War commenced between the Western Allies and their Soviet former partner. In addition to this, unsubstantiated reports were trickling through that German forces, in particular the navy and a considerable number of U-boats, were still ensconced in *Neu Schwabenland,* Antarctica.

Thus, one year later on 26th August 1946, the commander-in-chief of U.S. naval operations, Admiral Chester Nimitz announced that a massive, combined military expedition to be known as *Operation Highjump* would set sail to Antarctica in December during the Southern Hemisphere summer. The operation involved many ships, more than 4,700 military personnel and a variety of aircraft, including the recently invented and developed helicopter. The naval contingent, known as Task Force 68, was commanded by Rear Admiral Richard H. Cruzen and Rear Admiral Richard E. Byrd commanded the scientific and research elements. At their disposal were six Douglas R4D-5L aircraft, the maritime equivalent of the legendary C-47 Dakota plus another six Martin PBM-5 Mariner flying boats.

Admiral Byrd and his team established the *Little America IV* base on the Ross Ice Shelf, close to where three previous bases had been situated and their aircraft photographed as much of Antarctica's land surface as possible during the three-month operation. The PBM-5 Mariners commenced operations from the seaplane tenders *Pine Island* and *Currituck*, photographing the coasts and ice walls stretching to the east and west, while the R4Ds surveyed the interior.

On 12th November Admiral Byrd stated at a press conference that Operation Highjump was a military mission whose stated objectives were...

"... to train naval personnel, test ships, planes and the new helicopters under frigid zone conditions, to develop techniques for establishing and maintaining air bases in Antarctica and to increase knowledge of hydrographic, geographic, meteorological, geological and electromagnetic conditions of the area. The PBMs and R4Ds would play a major role in all these objectives."

Two additional unpublicised objectives, albeit by far the most important to Byrd himself were...

... to prove the U.S. Navy's worth and effectiveness capabilities to President Truman, who was at that time pushing for considerable reductions in America's postwar military budget.

... and to investigate and confirm one way or another the alleged presence of German bases and forces in the area.

Two German submarines, *U-530 and U-977,* both carrying scores of prominent Nazis and their gold, were allegedly apprehended in Argentina after the war. Many believe that these were just two of several others which made the journey south and that their ultimate destination was in fact *Neu Schwabenland.* It has also been mooted that Adolf Hitler whose body as everyone knows, was never found, actually fled Germany on board one such U-boat.

The Soviets eyed the Operation Highjump announcement with great suspicion and scepticism. One of their naval journals stated, *"U.S. measures in Antarctica testify that American military circles are seeking to subject the polar regions to their control and create military bases."*

Task Force 68 comprised three separate naval groups, each with a specific mission, consisting of seventy ships and thirty-three aircraft. Captain George J. Dufek commanded the Eastern Group, with *Pine Island* carrying three PBM Mariners. The Western Group, under the command of Captain Charles A. Bond included *Currituck* with the other three Mariners. Admiral Cruzen's

Central Group and the aircraft carrier *Philippine Sea*, with Byrd in command, completed the task force.

Flying out ahead of the icebreakers to search for clear passages through the ice, the helicopters served as the eyes of the fleet. One helicopter was allotted to each of the icebreakers and one to the carrier *Philippine Sea.* Besides conducting reconnaissance, each was large enough to undertake rescue operations. Captain Andrew Arthur, the eldest son of General Robert Arthur (retd.) erstwhile of British intelligence, was in command of the destroyer *USS Henderson* but as it turned out he was to perform a very different role.

The Central Group was the command centre for the operation and its ships broke through the ice with the help of the Coast Guard cutter *Northwind* and the new Navy cutter *Burton Island*, which joined the operation later. *Northwind* and *Burton* were critical to the mission since the thick ice could crack open a ship like a can opener. Norwegian trawlers in the area reported the ice there, to be the heaviest for more than forty years.

On 29th December 1946 a Sikorsky HO3S-1 took-off from the helicopter pad of *USS Henderson* for a reconnaissance mission beyond the pack ice. A crew of five were aboard the flimsy-looking aircraft including, rather surprisingly, Captain Arthur himself acting as an observer. As well as the usual photographic equipment the helicopter carried survival gear consisting of one hundred days' worth of rations, skis, sleds, warm clothes and sleeping bags.

After they had been flying for around three hours, the weather took a turn for the worse and so the pilot climbed to fifteen hundred feet in an attempt to fly above the snow and ice. Unfortunately he soon encountered what is known as 'ice blink,' whereby streams of snow reflecting the sunshine make clear vision almost impossible—similar to the reflections experienced while driving a car at night through a severe snowstorm.

Unable to see the ground clearly whilst attempting an emergency landing, the pilot, Ralph LeBlanc clipped a mound of solid ice, which was rendered invisible to him by the total whiteout and tried to ascend again immediately. Unbeknown to him and the other occupants however, the fuel tank had been ripped open by the impact and the aircraft suddenly burst into flames and crashed in a spectacular fireball. Andrew Arthur miraculously survived the impact, unscathed but for a few minor cuts and bruises and the pilot LeBlanc suffered superficial first degree burns to his arms and legs. However, the other three crewmen, radio operator Wendell Henderson, flight engineer

Fred Williams and navigator Max Lopez were killed instantly and horrifically when they were thrown from the blazing, torn-apart aircraft by the impact into the still spinning rotor blades.

Once the fire had subsided, the two survivors grabbed what remaining supplies were unaffected by the conflagration, which comprised around fifty days of rations for two men, a couple of sleeping bags and a badly scorched but otherwise intact four-man tent. They set-off trekking through the snow and ice, without a compass or wireless, in what they hoped was the general direction of base camp, anticipating that rescue parties would be searching for them as soon as the storm conditions had abated somewhat.

For the next thirteen days the adverse weather conditions prevented any attempt to search for the downed chopper and its hapless crew but finally, on 11th January 1947, the weather cleared sufficiently to allow a search and rescue plane to commence the delayed rescue operation. Around three days into the search, the observer finally spotted the burnt-out wreckage of the HO3S-1 and the three mutilated and dismembered corpses on the ground. There was no sign of Andrew Arthur and Ralph LeBlanc, who were never seen or heard from again and were assumed to have expired in the appalling weather, somewhere out in the one-million-plus square mile frozen wilderness.

A small obelisk with a plaque inscribed with all their names, honouring the memory of the five victims, was later placed at the crash site.

Meanwhile, on his longest reconnaissance flight to date, Byrd and his companions, aboard an R4D-5L loaded with extra fuel and provisions, had journeyed well beyond the ice wall and these brief extracts from his diary provide a highly revealing insight into exactly what happened during what was referred-to as his 'missing three hours' when all radio contact was lost...

"... Beyond the mountain range is what appears to be a valley with a small river or stream running through the center portion. There should be no green valley below! Something is definitely wrong and abnormal here! We should be over ice and snow! To the portside are great forests growing on the mountain slopes.

... Our navigation instruments are still spinning; the gyroscope is oscillating back and forth.

... The light here seems different; I cannot see the sun anymore.

...We make another left turn and spot what seems to be a large animal of some kind below us. It looks like an elephant! NO!! It looks more like a mammoth! This is incredible. Report this to base camp."

At this point he tried to contact base camp but the radio had stopped working. And then he detected something else in the near distance...

"...Ahead we spot what seems to be a city!!! This is impossible! ...The aircraft seems light and oddly buoyant. The controls refuse to respond!

...My God!! Off our port and starboard wings are a strange type of aircraft. They are closing rapidly alongside! They are disc-shaped and have a radiant quality to them. They are close enough now to see the markings on them. It is a type of swastika!!"

Then the radio suddenly burst into life again and a voice was heard, speaking English in a strange, unknown accent. The voice told Byrd that they would help him land and that he should not worry—he was in good hands. The controls on his plane stopped working and he was under the guidance of some outside, unknown force, flying itself, and even landed safely without any intervention by the plane's pilot. The diary continued...

"Several men are approaching on foot toward our aircraft. They are tall with blond hair. In the distance is a large shimmering city pulsating with rainbow hues of color. I do not know what is going to happen now but I see no signs of weapons on those approaching. I hear now a voice ordering me by name to open the cargo door. I comply."

Subsequently, Operation Highjump was cut short—very short indeed in fact, in February 1947. The official bulletin stating that it had *"been prematurely curtailed due to a rapid and unusually early onset of the vicious Antarctic winter."*

Admiral Byrd later discussed the lessons learned from the operation in a most bizarre interview with Lee Van Atta of *International News Service* held aboard the expedition's command ship, the *USS Mount Olympus*. The interview appeared in the Wednesday 5th March 1947 edition of the Chilean newspaper *El Mercurio* from which the following snippets have been taken...

"... Admiral Richard E. Byrd warned today that the United States should adopt measures of protection against the possibility of an invasion of the country by hostile planes coming from the polar regions.

...Talking about the recently completed expedition, Byrd said that the most important result of his observations and discoveries is the potential effect that they have in relation to the security of the United States."

"...The fantastic speed with which the world is shrinking..." recalled the admiral *"...is one of the most important lessons learned during my recent Antarctic exploration. I have to warn my compatriots that the time has ended when we were able to take refuge in our isolation and rely on the certainty that the distances, the oceans, and the poles were a guarantee of safety."*

Byrd then gave a comprehensive and totally honest account of his experiences to his close friend, US Secretary of Defense James Forrestal shortly after his return from 'Highjump.' As a result, Forrestal stated publicly that he had now resolved to take a far more truthful approach to informing the U.S. public about this issue and it was chronicled that he was *'babbling about aliens'* in the days before he plummeted to his untimely death.

Chapter 59

Friday 3rd March 2023 – Return To Porta Mundorum III

It was late-morning under an almost cloudless sky. A gentle and very soothing southerly breeze rippled the surface of Porta Lacus yet made very little impression on PM3's windsock which hung limply on its frame like a Christmas stocking awaiting the arrival of Santa. A few isolated, fluffy clouds drifted along aimlessly and above them Inti Sapa, the Sun King, shone regally down from his five hundred kilometre-high throne.

Dobbo, Asiri and Fabian disembarked from the boat and clomped purposefully across the wooden jetty towards the base. Behind them and with considerably less purpose trailed Pacha and Saywa, hand-in-hand, in no apparent hurry to bid farewell to their beloved daughter and her handsome new beau.

The leading group ascended the path rising from the lake to the apron and as they approached the half-way point, Dobbo suddenly and very animatedly pointed upwards and began to run, shouting, *"There's another plane on the apron! Another sodding plane! And it's a big bugger too. Come on everyone, quick!"*

Fabian and Asiri sprinted after him and the three halted when they reached the brow of the hill which afforded them a full, uninterrupted view of the apron. Parked alongside the two fighters was a huge airliner, both airman instantly recognising its type.

"Boeing Dreamliner Executive. What the....?!" Fabian yelled excitedly. *"Private charter."*

He was totally correct on both counts. The giant jet, completely dwarfing Dobbo's F-5 and Fabian's Tornado, bore the livery of its Maltese owners, *VallettaJet* and carried the registration number 9H-AMU. Also Maltese.

Asiri then pointed to the front of the Boeing. *"Look, there is an insignia just below the cockpit windows,"* she declared breathlessly. *"What does it say?"*

As they walked across the apron in the direction of the main building, the aforementioned insignia soon came into clear focus.

"It says 'thedeceptionists.org'," Dobbo said, looking puzzled. *"Do you know, I'm sure I've come across that name before somewhere? I wonder what they're doing down here?"*

"Well, I think we are going to find out very soon," remarked Asiri as the door of the main building opened and two men, one in a civilian airliner captain's uniform, stepped-out on to the tarmac.

Both froze in shock when they spotted the three young people striding purposefully towards them. They glanced anxiously at each other, then recoiled back into the doorway, adopting an apprehensive, somewhat defensive stance, ready to dash inside and lock the door should these strangers prove to be menacing. Due to the presence of the two military fighters, they naturally and rightly assumed that Dobbo and Fabian were the pilots and therefore posed a considerable threat to their wellbeing. Their worst fears were very swiftly allayed however by a warm smile and an outstretched hand from Dobbo.

"Do you speak English, pal?" he casually asked the captain, the taller of the two.

"Yes, we both speak English," the uniformed officer responded. *"I am First Officer Ash Pardoe of Valettajet and this is one of my passengers, Paul Smithson, co-founder of a U.S. group calling themselves the deceptionists. And who are you and your party, sir?"*

By this time, Pacha and Saywa had joined them and Pacha took the lead, stepping forward boldly and greeting Pardoe with an outstretched hand.

"Welcome to the land of Extrema, Officer Pardoe," he declared warmly as the two men shook hands. *"My name is Pacha and this is my wife Saywa."* He ushered Saywa towards Pardoe. *"We are natives of Intipata, the closest village to Porta Mundorum III, some thirty kilometres down the lake."*

"Pleased to meet you Saywa," said Pardoe, taking her hand, the back of which he kissed formally, as if greeting royalty.

"And you also, Officer Pardoe," Saywa replied, giving him a broad, welcoming smile. *"And these three..."* she continued, gesturing towards the others, *"...are Asiri, my daughter, Samuel Dobson, former Royal Air Force pilot and Asiri's husband to be..."*

At this, Dobbo stiffened in surprise and with a considerable degree of embarrassment but then relaxed, smiled at Asiri and shook hands vigorously with Pardoe and Smithson.

Saywa continued unabashed. *"... and this young man is Fabian Schuster of the German Luftwaffe. These two wonderful young men have seen the light and awoken from the sleep into which their system had placed them. Both are deserters who now know the reality about what lies beyond sixty degrees south, the forbidden invisible barrier they were brought here to protect. They, along with anyone else you may encounter here in our beloved land, pose no threat to you and your passengers whatsoever. We admire your courage and your thirst for truth and will assist you wholeheartedly with anything you may need to further your honourable quest."*

Dobbo and Fabian exchanged a wide-eyed glance, impressed as well as surprised at Saywa's eloquent address.

Smithson turned and opened the door behind him. *"Come and meet the rest of our party,"* he gestured. *"Don't worry about remembering all their names though,"* he added, chuckling. *"There are ninety-six of them!"*

The group entered the building to meet his *deceptionist* cohorts. Fifteen minutes later, sat around the table over coffee and biscuits, Dobbo and Fabian revealed their next moves to the party, drawing gasps of admiration from all in attendance. Smithson then took centre stage and gave a brief, yet full account of their adventures over the previous fortnight.

Dobbo knew all about Adam's attempted interception of the Dreamliner when the group made their first flight into 'prohibited' airspace. He was aware too, from the visitors book, that they had been forced to return due to several passengers falling ill shortly after arriving at PM3. From that point on however, it was all new to him and so along with everyone else, he sat transfixed and mesmerised by the tale rapidly unfolding before them.

"In total, four of our original party fell ill here at Porta Mundorum III," Smithson informed them. *"One in particular, the individual who had financed the trip in fact, became very sick indeed and so we headed back north immediately, though not to Port Stanley, our original departure airport. Instead, fearing we would be arrested there by British security services personnel, we landed at Ushuaia in Argentina where we nursed those who were sick until they recovered sufficiently to enable us to interrogate them. After what we had read in the visitors book here, we were keen to discover more about them in order to determine exactly why their bodies had taken such an aversion to Extrema. We*

needed to understand more about their backgrounds and their motivations for joining us on the adventure."

He paused, took a bite of his biscuit and then washed it down with a large gulp of coffee.

"It turned out that all of them had only recently joined the organisation and were in fact spies, who had infiltrated the group at the behest of several nations' security agencies. Our mysterious benefactor, a certain Mr Randolph Isaacs, from an infamous international banking family closely connected to the Rothschilds, had recruited them not only to protect him during the adventure but also to subvert the group, gather intelligence on its members and ultimately murder all the passengers and crew. Two of the agents as it turned out were qualified Dreamliner pilots who would take over from Pardoe and his co-pilot in order to fly themselves and the aircraft home."

Dobbo interjected at this point. *"Wow, it's a bloody good job they fell ill then wasn't it?!"* he piped-up. *"So what did you do with the buggers?"*

The co-pilot Jim Norris, who it turned out was the other co-founder of the group, continued the story.

"We took them to an industrial site on the outskirts of town and placed them in a sound-proof lockup with plenty of food, drink and a chemical toilet. We told them they would be released in due course, once we felt it was safe for us to do so. Unlike them, we do not simply and callously dispose of our adversaries as we see fit. The door was secured by a lock that could be released remotely once we had organised our next move. And that next move in fact, was to journey south again, which we commenced on 24th February. Much to our surprise, the flight was completely incident-free with no interception attempts and we arrived back at Porta Mundorum III for the second time, eleven hours after departure. We have all been enjoying the excellent facilities here along with the wonderful environment around us, fishing, swimming, kayaking, walking, eating fabulous food and relaxing in the spa. Not a single soul has succumbed to any illness this time, which is great news and our plan is to depart for Thoth later today. Imagine our surprise however, when you all turned up! Maybe we need to rethink..."

"No, there is no need to let our arrival disrupt your plans," assured Fabian, glancing across at Dobbo for confirmation to which he received a nodded response. *"Because we are both fully committed to our own plans and also intend to depart today."*

"That's good to hear," Norris replied with much relief. *"So, given that we are departing for Thoth in a little under two hours, would you two..."* he asked, addressing Dobbo and Asiri, *"... care to travel along with us in the Dreamliner? It'll be far more comfortable than in your fighter jet—and the in-flight drinks are free!"*

"Thanks but absolutely not!" Dobbo responded categorically. *"Celeste and I have come this far together and I'm not leaving her here on her own. No, sorry mate but we're taking her with us. It's the least the grand old lady deserves."*

"I understand that sentiment entirely," chirped Pardoe, beaming. *"So, if we are all to depart today we need to get organised don't we?"*

Everyone around the table drained their mugs in unison, then stood and left the room to prepare for their respective departures.

Two hours later, the Thoth-bound Dreamliner rose majestically from the runway and banked to the south as she ascended. With both fighters fully refuelled and ready to go, Dobbo, Fabian and Asiri, kitted out in flight suits, helmets in hand, gathered between the two aircraft with Pacha and Saywa. To everyone's surprise, they had discovered a full flying kit for Asiri in one of the dormitory lockers. It was slightly too large for her but was much better than nothing, they all concurred.

"Fu... Bloody hell, is there anything they can't provide at this place?!" Dobbo had asked rhetorically when they discovered it.

Fabian opted to be the first to bid his fond farewells. Having already loaded Jorge's headstone on to the Tornado, he turned to Pacha holding out his right hand. Pacha grabbed it, drew the German to his breast and hugged him ardently. *"I thank you, Fabian—with all my heart,"* he whispered. *"Fly swiftly and please bring Eduardo back with you as soon as you can. You leave with the sincerest, heart-felt blessings of all in Extrema and may the Creator be with you, young man."*

Fabian then warmly embraced Saywa and Asiri before turning to Dobbo.

"Bon voyage, Dobbo. Safe journey to Thoth." he breathed as the two airmen hugged.

"You too Fabes. Bon voyage, mate," echoed Dobbo and then, as they separated added, *"I know we've only known each other a few days but you're a proper top bloke of the very highest order, I can tell. Just get your arse back*

safely from Teniente with Eduardo and join us in Thoth as quick as possible. I don't want to have to worry about you for too long!" He winked cheekily and then turned to Pacha. *"Come here... Pops, give us a hug."*

The two one-day-to-be family members clasped each other strongly in a long and very sincere embrace. Both had tears welling in their eyes and for half a minute said nothing. Eventually Pacha released his hold and stepped back.

"Look after her, Samuel," he commanded. *"We're trusting you to keep her safe and protect her on your exciting new adventure together."*

Saywa repeated Pacha's plea as she and Dobbo embraced, adding, *"and come back to visit very soon—please."*

Dobbo nodded sincerely, choked with emotion and for once unable to offer any words in response. He then left the three Extremans to their own space and removed the chocks from Celeste's wheels before donning his flying helmet and zipping-up his suit. He wheeled the steps away from Fabian's Tornado, the German now nestled snugly into the cockpit with the canopy down. He dragged them over to Celeste's starboard side and awaited Asiri who was huddled with her parents in what resembled a three-man rugby scrum. He could see their shoulders juddering as they sobbed their farewells and a lump formed involuntarily in his throat. He choked it back and composed himself. As Pacha had said, he was Asiri's protector now and therefore needed to be strong and resilient.

After what seemed like an eternity but was in fact only about five minutes, Asiri tearfully and reluctantly pulled-away from her distraught parents, placed the helmet on her head, zipped herself into the oversized flight suit and joined Dobbo at the foot of the steps.

As soon as both were settled in and Pacha and Saywa had retreated to a safe distance, Dobbo closed the canopy and fired up Celeste's engines. Fabian did the same with the Tornado and, once all pre-flight checks were complete, the pilots exchanged thumbs-ups and together commenced their taxi to the runway. The occupants of both aircraft waved heartily at Pacha and Saywa as they made their way across the apron and on to the slipway before halting side by side at the eastern end of the runway.

Dobbo then had an idea for a most fitting and spectacular departure. He turned to starboard and, noticing that a grinning Fabian was already looking in his direction, gave the German a series of hand signals commencing with three fingers, then a circular backward rotation with his index finger and completed with a thumbs-up. To each he received the standard 'OK' sign from the German, something he had always found most amusing. It reminded him not only of a shadow puppet animal he used to make as a child with a torch in his bedroom at night but also another nocturnal bedroom activity he undertook with great enthusiasm and regularity during his teenage years!

Both airmen fitted and secured their face-masks which meant they could now communicate verbally and Asiri followed suit.

"OK then, is everyone ready for departure?" asked Dobbo excitedly.

"Affirmative," Fabian responded.

"I think so, Sami," chirped Asiri trying her best to sound enthusiastic.

"Right then. Here goes. On my countdown," Dobbo announced. *"Three—two—one—go!"*

Both pilots increased engine speed, then simultaneously released the brakes and activated the afterburners. Celeste and the Tornado accelerated rapidly, causing Asiri to shriek in shock and alarm as the sudden increase in G-force rammed her back into the seat. After twenty seconds or so, the fighters simultaneously lifted from the runway and entered almost vertical climbs, ascending to over 2,500 feet. They then slowed to what seemed like a complete standstill before falling into a spectacular and fabulously co-ordinated backward loop, almost brushing the runway at the nadir before increasing speed again with another deafening roar as they climbed once more. Fabian turned sharply northward, whilst Dobbo and his by-now terrified and utterly disorientated passenger headed-off in the opposite direction.

Heavy-hearted and shaking their heads in sheer bewilderment, Pacha and Saywa trudged slowly and silently back to their boat, climbed aboard and began their disconsolate return voyage to Intipata.

Chapter 60

Monday 6th March 2023 – The Civic Reception

Neyalami, Adam's appointed guide and mentor since his arrival in Varinthia, led him down the wide, poplar-lined avenue leading from his apartment to the civic hall. After a half-mile or so the verdant thoroughfare gave way to a broad set of stone steps, five in all, which they climbed, stopping at the top to take in the splendour of their surroundings.

Between them and the foot of an additional flight of steps which rose majestically to the main entrance of the hall, was an immensely beautiful white, marble-paved plaza. Meticulously manicured box-tree hedges lined its perimeter interspersed with wood and cast-iron benches, most of which were occupied by small groups of Varinthians enjoying the late afternoon sunshine whilst they waited for the main event to commence.

The civic hall itself was simply jaw-dropping and Adam gasped in appreciation of its sheer magnificence. Constructed of reddish-brown stone held together by brilliant-white mortar, it had three storeys, each a full twenty feet or more in height with arched, leaded windows taking up the majority of those twenty feet. The main roof was gabled and clad in copper with an apex-ridge made from what he reckoned was solid gold. Ball and point finials, also golden-coloured, were mounted along the ridge every three feet or so and a myriad of finely detailed gargoyles supported the cast-iron guttering. At each of the four corners of the building stood a square, four-storey tower supporting five copper steeples; the tallest in the centre with four smaller ones around it, the ubiquitous ball and point finial at the point of each one.

In the centre of the plaza stood an imposing and incredibly elegant fountain fashioned out of bronze, comprising a large, deep pool in the centre with four smaller and much shallower ones around it. Supplying the water were a family of six intricately-carved and highly-polished woolly-looking elephants. 'Mammoths maybe?' Adam wondered. The largest two, obviously the parents, fed the main pool, with each of their 'children' sustaining those arranged around it, their trunks sending a jet upwards, which then gracefully cascaded in a curving arc, before breaking into smaller droplets that created a shimmering, mist-like effect as they landed.

Adam was mesmerised, just as Dobbo had been by the dolphin fountain outside the funicular railway station in Intipata and simply stood there transfixed and in total awe. He marvelled at the grandeur and craftsmanship, whilst at the same time allowing the soothing energy from the flowing water to wash over him in a futile attempt to settle the butterflies fluttering manically around his stomach.

"Still feeling nervous, Adam…?" enquired Neyalami, a look of genuine concern on her handsome, broad face… *"… because there is no need to be. You will be absolutely fine I am sure."*

Neyalami, and her boyfriend Roovi had greeted Adam as soon as he disembarked from Esmerelda following his guided landing at an airfield north of the city. She had then escorted him by public tram to an apartment in the very centre of the city. Six feet tall, which is about the average height for women of that realm, and around thirty years old, Adam guessed, with long flowing golden hair, she had looked after him admirably in the eight days since his arrival. She had also made all the arrangements for the imminent event, the cause of all those jittery critters now populating his insides. She spoke almost perfect English, as did just about everyone else in Varinthia, albeit with an accent somewhere between German and Scandinavian. To Adam, Thoth felt very much like Switzerland, certainly in that respect anyway, as everyone he spoke to was more than keen to impress him with their English skills. Nevertheless he had still managed to pick-up a few Varinth words, that being the Thoth language's official name, notably *'Bena, Adam ust neza mu,'* for *'Hello, my name is Adam.'* The Varinth alphabet was almost identical to the English but with extra symbols to cater for a few unique sounds within the language.

The aforementioned imminent event was in fact a reception to be held in his honour at the civic hall that very afternoon. Neyalami and Roovi had exercised all their powers of persuasion to convince the reluctant Adam that it was fully justified and appropriate. They posited that his arrival in Thoth, having broken ranks from the military, for whom he had previously been enforcing the restricted Antarctic airspace, was unprecedented. The civic hall seated eight hundred people with, she had explained, the event being open to all on a first-come, first-served basis. Hence the already crowded plaza, upon which the soon-to-be attendees gathered, buzzing with eager anticipation.

"Come, let us go inside. It is almost time," she whispered, gently beckoning him towards the steps to the main entrance.

Three huge marble steps led to the main double-doors which were all of ten feet high and already wide-open. They led up to a long vestibule with a highly polished hardwood floor and gold-latticed papered walls of a North African,

Arabic style. Every twenty feet or so, a substantial, lustrous dark-wood door with a chunky porcelain doorknob led off to the side. Each one sported a brass placard embossed with words he could not understand but which, he assumed, indicated the purpose of the room behind it.

At the far end of the vestibule another two lofty doors, also fully open, led into the central auditorium, which resembled a Victorian music hall comprising a raised stage, a stalls area and a first-floor balcony around three sides. Placed upon the stage in a semi-circular arrangement were eight black leather chairs with a low glass-topped table between each one upon which had been placed pewter jugs full of water along with glasses. A microphone on a stand had been positioned at the front, left-hand edge and the steps leading up on to the stage were to the right. The stalls area was laid out with lines of maroon, velvet padded seats, the very front two rows of which were roped-off behind a reserved sign. A good number of early-comers, eager for the best view, had already settled-in and ceased their chattering when Adam and Neyalami arrived, fixing their gazes upon the two newcomers as they made their way to the stage. Adam gulped nervously, the heebie-jeebies beginning to take hold once more and simply nodded back politely, smiling weakly and trying his utmost to appear calm and composed.

Ten minutes later, with Adam seated in the most central of the leather chairs and Neyalami stood at the microphone, everything was ready. All the seats were now occupied, with maybe a hundred or so more folk squeezed around the outer edges of the auditorium. She had given him very little real detail as to the format or schedule of the reception or what would be expected of him but had assured him that he was under no obligation to make any kind of speech or address, unless he particularly wished to do so.

At 3.00pm prompt, she launched proceedings confidently and eloquently...

"... Ladies and gentlemen, boys and girls. Let me welcome you to our beloved civic hall on this most happy and momentous of occasions. It always fills my heart with joy when some brave soul manages to find their way here from the Earth realm but I am sure you will agree with me that this particular individual gives us extra cause for celebration. So let me introduce to you Adam Haylock from Cambridge, England. He is a Royal Air Force pilot, or should I say WAS an RAF pilot, who had been sent to Antarctica to intercept anyone attempting to travel beyond sixty degrees south without official authorisation. Fortunately, he was somehow able to see the light and wake-up to all the lies and deception surrounding the region and his nefarious role in policing it. Then, to his eternal credit, he found the courage and fortitude not only to renounce the system he had previously served but also to separate himself completely from it and

venture south in search of the real truth of our realm. Can I ask you all to put your hands together and show your appreciation for..." She ushered Adam to stand, *"... Adam Ryan Haylock."*

The entire audience rose to their feet and began to applaud loudly and enthusiastically. Many whistled, several cheered hurrahs, one or two whooped and others stamped their feet on the ground as they clapped. Adam raised his right hand and gestured to the crowd, mouthing his thanks and nodding to them as he did so. After thirty seconds or so, the applause died down and everyone took their seats again, except Neyalami of course.

"... Today's reception will comprise three segments," she continued. *"We are currently in the first of those, which hopefully should not take too long and will cover all the formalities. I will try my utmost to keep this as light and entertaining as possible—but in actual fact, I don't think that will be difficult! Then we shall retire outside to the plaza for an hour for drinks and chatter before returning to this central auditorium for the banquet. Ladies and gentlemen, boys and girls, the Earthlander Adam arrived here in his F-5 Freedom Fighter airplane, which carries the name Esmerelda, a full eight days ago. By making this most epic of journeys, he left behind the world into which he had been born and raised. A world where, some might say, he flourished and achieved considerable success. But by bidding farewell to his military career and past life he has rendered a return to his old world virtually impossible. We therefore must ensure that he is made to feel very welcome in Thoth and to make his transition as painless and stress-free as possible, thus enabling him to build a new life for himself here, should he so desire. But first I have a number of individuals to bring to the stage to meet this brave, resourceful, nay—heroic airman. Some of these guests many of you will already know, others you will not, but they are all people I feel Adam will want to meet. Therefore, I hope you will allow me the indulgence of presenting them to him in turn and to show them the appreciation they truly deserve."*

She signalled to an usher stood by the door at the front-right side of the auditorium who nodded-back in acknowledgement before removing the rope and the sign from the reserved seats on the front two rows of the stalls.

"... Just over three weeks ago, Adam was tasked with intercepting a large aircraft containing over one hundred truth-seeking adventurers. His task was to 'persuade' them to turn around and return to Port Stanley in The Falkland Islands. Unfortunately for him they would not comply and he was just about to shoot them down when he was unexpectedly given the order from his commanding officer to allow them to continue. Apparently there was someone onboard who had links to those in seriously high places and could not be allowed

to die in such a manner. The aircraft then continued to Porta Mundorum III where several passengers, including that highly-connected individual, fell sick causing them to head back north. However, rather than returning to Port Stanley, they flew instead to Argentina where they managed to rid themselves of their toxic co-passengers and fly south once more. And I am delighted to tell you Adam..." at this she turned and beamed at him knowingly, *"...that they all arrived safely here in Thoth just two days ago. Please can we all give a warm Varinthian welcome to Ash Pardoe, Paul Smithson, Jim Norris and the group calling themselves the deceptionists."*

At this the audience burst into applause once more. Adam jumped to his feet in disbelief and moved to the front of the stage, peering to his left. The usher held the side door open and in strode Pardoe, Smithson and Norris followed by almost one hundred fellow *deceptionists*. The front three made their way swiftly on to the stage with the remainder taking their seats in the reserved rows. Adam greeted Pardoe with a huge smile and an outstretched hand. Pardoe shook it formally yet rather hesitantly, not quite sure how to conduct himself with the man who so recently had been willing to blast him to smithereens but Adam pulled him in and hugged him firmly, whispering *"I'm sorry Ash, I'm sorry,"* into his ear.

"It's OK Adam," Pardoe assured him. *"Let's put all that behind us eh? It's great to meet you face to face and just brilliant to be here, however mind-blowing and disorientating that may feel just at the moment. So, let's talk afterwards in much more detail, shall we?"*

"Absolutely Ash, absolutely," responded the much-relieved Adam who then turned to Smithson and Norris, smiling and shaking them by the hand with the same greeting. *"Sorry I nearly blew you out of the sky. Welcome to Thoth. So glad you finally made it here."*

He returned to his chair, poured himself a glass of water and thirstily gulped it down. The others strode across to the far left of the stage, shook hands warmly with Neyalami and took their seats. She paused to allow them the opportunity to pour a drink and make themselves comfortable and then continued...

"...Now this next individual has also experienced a most interesting and challenging journey, not only throughout his life thus far but also in finding his way to Thoth. Three weeks ago, Adam was convinced he had shot down and killed this young man and his passengers, which caused him to suffer the worst two days of his life. However, like so many before them, they were saved by one of our decoy drones."

A loud *"Yes!"* piped-up from the back of the room causing many in the audience to echo the sentiment, a chorus which then gave way to a short ripple of applause.

"...So, here he is along with the passengers he was carrying aboard his Gulfstream executive jet. Please, everyone, show your appreciation and admiration to Mateo Forestello and his intrepid fellow adventurers!"

Another round of lively applause rang out loud and long as Forestello's group filed into the auditorium. Mateo determinedly bounded-up the stairs and sprinted across to Adam, whilst the others joined the *deceptionists* in the reserved seating area.

"You absolute bastard!" he yelled in an attempt to be heard over the racket from the audience and grabbed Adam by the shoulders. Fearing he was about to be head-butted or worse, Adam stiffened and screwed his eyes tight shut, bracing himself for the impact. There was no way he was going to defend himself after what he had been prepared to do to this guy and his charges, so he simply handed himself over for Mateo to take whatever retribution he considered appropriate.

Nothing happened. Mateo's hands still gripped him firmly and the silence in the hall was deafening. He slowly opened his right eye to see Mateo grinning from ear to ear, shaking his head slowly from side to side.

"You fell for that one didn't you, Adam!" he joked whilst smothering him like a very affectionate grizzly bear before squeezing him in a vice-like grip and lifting him off the floor.

Relieved at the sudden release of tension, the throng erupted into howls of laughter as the Argentine-Irishman shook his would-be assassin like a cocktail waiter mixing a Manhattan. When he finally let go, Adam stumbled slightly but then regathered his composure and shook Mateo's hand vigorously.

"Thank you, Mateo," he said. *"I am so, so sorry for shooting you down—even though I actually didn't!"*

"We all forgive you, mi amigo," Mateo reassured him. *"Look—considering where your spirit, mindset and loyalties were at that moment, there was no way you could disobey the order, was there? But if, as the lady said, you had a dreadful time afterwards, then that meant you had already started on your*

journey. And that journey has brought you here, has it not? So, let us both draw a line under all that and move on shall we?" He winked. *"Speak later."*

He took the chair beside Jim Norris, with whom he exchanged a cordial handshake before settling himself down in his chair and filling his glass.

Neyalami, anxious not to fall behind schedule pressed on...

"...And next, someone many of you in the audience will know very well indeed. A man who has lived amongst us here in Thoth since Earth year 1947." She turned to face those seated on the stage, adding, *"Although Adam and all you other recent arrivals will neither know nor have heard of this man, he and his father played major roles in the recent history of Antarctica and so we felt you would be very interested to meet him—and discover more about his family background. Ladies and gentlemen, boys and girls, Andrew Arthur, now in his 114th year. Andrew has lived here with us in Thoth for more than seventy-five years now, having been rescued from Antarctica after a violent storm caused his helicopter to crash during the ill-fated Operation Highjump. He decided to settle here permanently after meeting his wife-to-be Choralla a year later and since then has simply loved our way of life."*

This time the audience offered-up a more reserved ripple of applause with the occasional cheer as a tall, athletic-looking, silver-haired man with a neatly trimmed pencil-moustache climbed effortlessly, albeit with the slight limp he had acquired during his heroics in WW2, on to the stage to meet the newcomers. He moved along the line, greeting each one with a formal handshake and slight bow and then settled into the chair beside Mateo.

Neyalami continued.....

"...And next, a young couple who informed me just this morning that they have finally found everything they have been searching for in their lives. They arrived here together after their flight from Extrema, shortly after Captain Pardoe and his group. Ladies and gentlemen, boys and girls, it gives me immense pleasure to bring to the stage..."

The side door burst open with a resounding crash and Adam instantly recognised the person responsible. He leapt like a startled gazelle from his chair, his eyes almost popping out of his head in jubilation and exhilaration.

"...Samuel Dobson from Scarborough, England and his soon-to-be fiancée Asiri from Intipata in Extrema who arrived here in Varinthia late..."

She never got to finish the sentence as the crowd went berserk, rising as one to their feet, clapping, whistling and cheering ecstatically. Dobbo sprinted from the door like a greyhound out of a trap and took the stairs in two huge strides, almost losing his balance in the process. Asiri followed, ascending rather more sedately and carefully.

He and Adam slammed into each other in the centre of the stage, almost conjoining in their tight embrace. Chest to chest, arms locked around each other, they spun round and round time and time again, jumping up and down as they rotated, tears pouring down their cheeks before dizziness began to take over and they separated, both men bent forward panting breathlessly, resting on their knees to steady themselves. Asiri moved between them and, facing the audience, placed her hands on the two men's shoulders and pulled them both upright and into her sides.

The three friends then formed a huddle, shoulders heaving uncontrollably as they cried their tears of joy and relief. The rapturous applause eventually died away and the audience very respectfully re-seated themselves. When the reunited friends finally regathered some semblance of composure, the two lovebirds quickly made their introductions to the others before taking the two chairs to Adam's immediate left. For the next few minutes all three simply sat there, wiping their eyes and quietly blowing their noses with handkerchiefs handed to them by one of the ushers.

Neyalami then took up the story once more...

"...Samuel tells me he would rather be referred to as Dobbo so I will use that name going forward," she announced with amusement. *"And DOBBO... has asked me to spare you much of the detail of his adventures over the past few weeks and to keep my account as brief as possible. Though for him and for Asiri it has all ended happily, that is sadly not the case for everyone involved and much of the trauma he has suffered is still very raw. So I will keep it concise; Dobbo was stationed with Adam at Teniente Rodolfo Marsh Martin airbase with precisely the same role, that of preventing unauthorised aircraft straying beyond sixty degrees south. When Adam deserted and headed over the ice wall, Dobbo was sent to intercept him and at one point was actually ordered by his superior to shoot him down. This order he disobeyed thankfully, allowing Adam to continue his adventure, which fortunately took him to Extrema and finally here to Thoth. Dobbo was arrested upon his return to base but, with help from our agents there, he managed to escape and also reach Extrema. There, he met and fell in love with Asiri and the two decided to fly here together and reunite with Adam. So yes, a happy ending for these two, I am sure you would all agree?"*

Heads moved from side to side as those in the audience checked with each other, smiling and nodding before creating a mini-hubbub of general affirmation.

"... But sadly, one hero of that adventure is no longer with us and another two are what the armed forces in the Earth realm would refer to as 'missing in action.' We tragically lost our good friend Jorge who was callously executed by Dobbo and Adam's commanding officer. As far as we know, our other agent Eduardo, along with a German pilot Fabian Schuster, are still way up north at Teniente Rodolfo. We had expected them to return by now and it is causing us great concern that we have heard nothing from Eduardo in over two days. We are doing all we can to make contact but our efforts have proven fruitless up to now. Our hopes and prayers are for them to be alive and well but we all need to prepare ourselves for that not being the case. At the banquet later, we shall raise a formal toast for their safe return but right now, for Eduardo, Fabian and especially our fallen colleague Jorge, would you all rise and share in a minute's silence in their honour?"

Everyone in the auditorium and on the stage stood and respectfully observed the silent tribute. To everyone's credit not a single sound was heard throughout the entire minute until, with just four seconds remaining, Dobbo, in a moment of sheer madness, decided to blow his nose again, the sound bellowing around the auditorium like an elephant trumpeting. A few children sniggered, followed by one or two others and in no time at all, it had developed into full-blown laughter which spread infectiously throughout the crowd, including those on stage. All except Dobbo of course who just sat there bemused, mouthing '*What?*' to Asiri and Adam as they grinned and shook their heads at him in mock dismay.

As soon as the hilarity had subsided and everyone had taken their seats once more, the formalities kicked in again...

"... And to complete the formal segment of today's event, it gives me great pleasure to introduce to Adam, three very, very special guests," announced Neyalami animatedly. *"Again, many of you in the audience will already be acquainted with them and will no doubt concur that they are more than worthy of being presented to our new friends."*

The side door opened once more and a woman around Adam's age, possibly slightly younger, appeared in the opening. He was taken aback when he caught his first glimpse of her in the doorway, slightly silhouetted by the late afternoon sun pouring in from outside. Never before had he been so instantly and completely captivated by any woman. She was stunning, utterly stunning with an aura that, to him anyway, radiated and swamped the entire auditorium. She was around five feet ten, with collar-length bobbed, auburn hair. Sporting crimson-framed spectacles resting on a perfect nose and possessing wonderful cheekbones and immaculate teeth, she was dressed semi-casually in black leather trousers, suede ankle boots and a silk, sleeveless halter-neck top in ivory. She looked a million dollars and Adam was mesmerised by her beauty as she gracefully and considerately assisted her two aged, yet surprisingly mobile companions through the doorway and across to the steps. He barely noticed the other two as he followed her, wide-eyed and virtually hypnotised, as the three moved towards him.

If he had paid her elderly companions any attention at all, he would have noticed that they were much, much older than she. Three generations separated them from the object of Adam's instant infatuation, yet the family resemblance remained clearly discernible. He would most likely have put their ages at around ninety-five yet his estimation would have been way out. In a realm where life expectancy commonly exceeds one hundred and forty Earth years, both were already well beyond their one hundred and twentieth year! Handsomely dressed and well-groomed in their absolute Sunday-best clothes, they radiated long lives of good health and well-being. Though bright-eyed and fully-alert, their advanced years did cause them to stoop slightly and both carried sticks to aid their walking. Though able to ascend the stairs unaided, they needed to lift both feet on to each one before climbing further. But climb further they did and as the old man, the last of the three, reached the stage, Neyalami completed her introduction.

"... Adam, Dobbo, Asiri and everyone gathered here this afternoon. Please allow me the enormous pleasure of introducing to you, Sarah Arthur, the granddaughter of Andrew Arthur and her great grandparents on her mother's side, the longest-living of all the Earthlanders who have ever joined us here in Thoth. He, just a few days short of his 130th birthday and she... whom I'm sure will forgive me for giving out her secret, a very sprightly 126-year-old, please welcome to the stage... Fred Noonan and Amelia Earhart!"

Chapter 61

Friday 3rd March 2023 – Fabian's Return to Teniente Rodolfo

Fabian's GR-4 finally touched down at Teniente Rodolfo after a tedious six hour flight from PM3. As he taxied toward the apron, he was dismayed to see two U.S. Air Force F-22 Raptor fighters and a U.N. Dash-8 transport plane already parked beside the hangar. It appeared to him that a small part of the new taskforce had already arrived.

"Scheiße!" he cursed aloud, berating himself for not having flown back earlier. His thoughts then switched instantly to Eduardo and he became anxious, wondering if the flight engineer and agent of Thoth had perhaps been arrested by the newcomers—or maybe worse?

With this very much in mind he decided to play it straight. He would pretend that he had returned after an unsuccessful attempt to intercept Dobbo, an escapade during which Prendergast had unfortunately been killed but where he had miraculously escaped with his life. Whether they would buy it or not was open to debate, particularly given the amount of time he had been away. He pondered several ways of explaining this before choosing to tell them that he needed time, not only to do the right thing for Prendergast's body, but also to recover from the horror of the shooting. As far as how he had managed to escape from Dobbo was concerned, he would tell them that he had somehow managed to get away and hide in a remote part of the airfield and that Dobbo, having been unable to find him, had simply flown-off, heading south, leaving him there on his own. Yes, that would work—he hoped!

It turned out that the three aircraft had transported a total of six individuals to the base, including two replacement flight engineers. They had all arrived around twenty-four hours previously to provide emergency interceptor cover following the disappearances of the two F-5s and Fabian's Tornado. The Dash-8 along with its pilot and co-pilot, having brought-in the new flight engineers, a host of F-22 spares and various supplies, was due to return north that very evening.

Within seconds of his landing he was welcomed by the two new engineers, Duane Dacres of the U.S. Air Force and Gurmit Singh, an Indian national, ex-RAF but now employed by the U.N. Between them they towed the GR-4 into the hangar, chocked it and then busied themselves with various post-flight maintenance checks. Fabian, having already removed the holdall containing

Jorge's headstone from the cockpit, thanked them politely and hurriedly scuttled across to the main building to face the music.

He headed straight for the bar area to discover the four pilots enjoying a game of pool, two against two, a row of half-full beer glasses on the shelf next to them. None of them in the subdued lighting noticed him entering, so he coughed loudly and exaggeratedly to attract their attention as he placed the holdall on the floor just inside the door.

He was successful in distracting them from their game and all four replaced their cues in the rack, picked up their beer glasses and ambled over to meet him. The two fighter pilots were both black Americans, twenty-four year-old Jamie Bull from Des Moines, Iowa and twenty-three year-old Kyle Campbell from Wilmington, North Carolina. The other two, white Caucasians and shortly to head back to Chile in the Dash-8, were both in their mid to late fifties, Canadian Rory Marshall from Nelson, B.C. and his Danish co-pilot Soren Christiansen, hailing from Esbjerg.

The meeting was rather uneasy and awkward, with weak and largely unenthusiastic handshakes being exchanged and very few words passing between them. Later over several beers as he recounted to them his recent experiences, Fabian could detect a palpable air of suspicion and scepticism, particularly regarding his version of Prendergast's demise and Dobbo's failure to locate his hiding place at PM3. He cursed himself once more, concerned that he may perhaps have 'shot himself in the foot' with his scarcely believable, hurriedly-concocted account.

The U.N. guys, for whom Singh seemed to be the chief mouthpiece, informed him that the base had been completely deserted when they arrived. There was no sign of Eduardo, nor did they have any real idea what had happened to him. Whatever the truth, it was obvious to Fabian that they were no longer searching for Eduardo within the base itself. Singh then also told him about the presence of a recently-dug grave beside the runway. Although uncertain as to whose body it contained, he thought it likely to be either Jorge or Eduardo.

They voiced their suspicions several times and questioned Fabian as to why he had taken so long to get back but he did his utmost to stick to his story and appear convincing and genuine. Not easy however when one is dishing out a bucketload of bare-faced lies! Dubious though they outwardly appeared, fortunately for him they opted not to press him too hard and eventually the conversation fizzled-out and the four returned to the pool table.

Fabian padded-off to Dobbo's old room which he had been told was still unoccupied and his to use. He began to settle himself in, unsure as to what the next hours or days might bring. Nothing had been said about the likelihood, or otherwise, of him continuing his role at Teniente other than he would need to hang around until the remainder of the task force arrived. Within that force would be higher-ranking superiors who would, by then, be in a position to inform him of his future duties.

Once settled-in and with the leather holdall concealed within the wardrobe behind Dobbo's clothes, he searched the room diligently for bugging devices and hidden cameras. Fortunately he could only locate a single, badly-hidden camera, the one over which Dobbo's grubby boxer shorts were still unceremoniously draped. *"Dobbo is one hell of a funny guy,"* he remarked aloud before heading-off to the kitchen to fix himself some dinner.

The following day proved uneventful with very little activity of any kind at the base. Fabian spent his time reading the Dalesman magazine he'd found on the bedside table where Dobbo had left it, preparing himself meals and snacks and practicing his pool. The others kept a polite yet slightly aloof distance and very little, if any, conversation took place. The atmosphere was strained and awkward and Fabian felt like an unwelcome cuckoo in their nest.

On his second night back, he was having a great deal of difficulty falling asleep, the uncertainty of his situation bringing on an unwelcome and very unpleasant anxiety as he lay in bed, his mind racing and heart pounding. At 1.30am he arose to answer a call of nature and as he did so, he heard a tapping sound from under the bed. Baffled, he bent down on all-fours to take a look and then jolted back in shock as the bed raised itself from the floor.

He grabbed his phone, switched on the torch and was amazed to see the upper half of Eduardo, a mischievous grin across his craggy face, appearing through the trapdoor in the floor. The flight engineer's forefinger was pressed tightly on his lips as he made a gentle shushing sound, gesturing Fabian to be silent.

Fabian eagerly helped him up and together they carefully lowered the bed over the opening and sat down facing each other. After a vigorous and relief-filled handshake, Eduardo informed Fabian that he had been hiding undetected in the tunnels for the last two days. He knew the U.N. guys were baffled as to his whereabouts and that they strongly suspected he had been rescued already, as he was constantly listening-in on their conversations through the network of hidden microphones around the base. He confirmed also that they were indeed extremely dubious and mistrustful of Fabian. They all very much doubted his account and so it was vital for him to be careful when moving around the base or socialising with them so as not to arouse further suspicion.

Fabian then removed Jorge's headstone from the holdall and laid it on the bed. Eduardo shed some silent tears, reading it slowly before hanging his head in sorrow and mourning the loss of his friend. Fabian squeezed his shoulder and kept his hand there until Eduardo lifted his head, brushed a stray tear from his cheek and began to describe exactly where the grave lay. He then asked Fabian if he would be happy to venture out before morning and mount the headstone on the burial mound, a request to which the German readily agreed. As they bade their farewells, the Chilean, or rather Extreman, said he would visit again the following night in order for them to discuss a possible plan of escape. He then descended into the ground once more and Fabian, much relieved and encouraged, finally paid his visit to the toilet before returning to bed and falling asleep immediately.

He awoke with a start some three hours or so later and sat himself up in bed recalling the promise he had made earlier to Eduardo. He inspected his watch—4.40am. Not too late to do it and surely none of the others would be awake nor would be for at least a couple more hours? He dressed quickly, slipped into his shoes and grabbed a fleecy jacket of Dobbo's from the hook on the door. He slung the strap of the holdall across his shoulder and quietly opened the door before slipping-out into the dimly-lit corridor, moving as quietly and stealthily as possible.

He stopped-off at the storeroom where he finally managed, after a very worrying five minutes, to find a spade and a small pick. He wrapped them up together inside a sheet of bubble-wrap using some duct tape and tucked the bundle under his left arm. He reckoned that would be the best way to ensure he did not drop them with a clatter and alert the others.

Five minutes later he found himself beside the runway standing over a hump of raised, recently-excavated earth. He placed his torch on the ground such that it illuminated the entire mound, unwrapped the digging implements and, as quietly as he could, used the pick to loosen the frost-hardened soil at one end. He then looked behind him anxiously to check that he was still alone before taking the spade and digging a shallow trench for the headstone. Once satisfied with its depth, he carefully placed the headstone in the trench and filled in the space around it, compacting the soil with his foot as he did so. Upon completing the task, he stepped back to admire his handiwork. The headstone stood proud and thankfully level, all the text was clearly visible and the soil around its base appeared neatly flattened, smooth and tidy. Content with it now and hoping that Eduardo would be too, he remained there, staring down at the mound, eyes closed and gave Jorge the fallen flight engineer a few moments of much-deserved silent respect.

"Nice work!" came a familiar voice from behind him, accompanied by a slow, sarcastic handclap. *"Very nice job indeed, Fabian."*

Fabian froze. *"Fuck, fuck, fuck!"* he cursed under his breath, the bottom having just fallen out of his world. He turned around slowly to find Singh and Dacres smirking caustically at him, the former directing an M-9 Beretta straight at him.

"We knew you were full of crap, Schuster…" snarled Dacres. *"… which is why, despite those shitty shorts obscuring the camera in your room, we've had someone monitoring all the other cameras around the base 24/7. It was my turn tonight, so imagine my surprise to see you creeping along the fucking corridor with your bundle and bag like Wee Willie Winkie!"*

"Yes, so we are going to have a little chat with you later this morning to find out the real story of your excursion south," added Singh. *"And I hope you will co-operate willingly my friend. I'd hate to have to use some of my more, shall we say, persuasive methods on you."*

Dacres cackled malevolently. *"You really wouldn't appreciate some of his techniques, Schuster,"* he growled. *"I've witnessed them before and man… they're not pretty. But whether you choose to be open and honest with us or not, you'll be put on the Dash-8 this evening and taken away from here, either on a seat or in a fucking body bag. It's entirely your choice. But for now, we're going to lock you up while we all go have breakfast. I don't know about you, Gurmit, but I can't interrogate on an empty stomach."*

To Fabian's surprise Singh glowered back at Dacres disparagingly. *"You're full of shit, Dacres. Just shut the fuck up, will you? And you,"* he barked before turning back to Fabian, *"walk toward the main building and don't try anything or say anything."*

The three silently made their way back to the main building where Singh ushered Fabian into the storeroom. Dacres had disappeared into the bar but reappeared shortly after with a glass of water which he offered the German.

"You're gonna be here some time so you'd best drink this," he said handing the glass to him.

As Fabian drank, Dacres reached into his coat pocket and pulled out a set of cable-ties with which, when Fabian had finished his drink, he tethered the hapless prisoner to a heating pipe. He then took the same roll of duct tape that Fabian had used earlier from a nearby shelf and bound the German's ankles together before cutting off a short strip which he slapped across his mouth. The two jailers then marched out of the door and slammed it shut behind them, laughing maliciously as they headed down the corridor in the direction of the bar.

After a typically voluminous American breakfast, followed immediately by another keenly-fought game of pool, they returned to the storeroom to collect the prisoner for interrogation. As they approached along the corridor however, they both suddenly stopped in their tracks. The door was ajar and when they rushed inside, Fabian was nowhere to be seen. Scraps of cable-tie and duct tape lay on the floor by the pipe.

Eduardo had used the hatch in the storeroom, concealed beneath an unused shelving rack in the far corner, to rescue Fabian and take him back down into the tunnels. To throw Dacres and Singh off their scent, he had left the door slightly open to make it look like Fabian had escaped via that route. As the two retreated underground, he then resecured the hatch from below as he had also done with the one in Dobbo's room, to prevent their escape route from being discovered.

The U.N. guys were shocked and utterly baffled by Fabian's disappearance. All six frantically searched every square inch of the base, inside and out. Later they inspected the footage from the camera outside the storeroom but all they picked-up was the door opening slightly. They realised, possibly for a second time, that they had been outsmarted and, with their reputations and possible future careers in mind, agreed between them to say absolutely nothing to their superiors when they arrived with the rest of the task force.

The Dash-8 with Marshall and Christiansen at the controls, departed as scheduled at 5.30pm that evening, leaving behind their four bemused colleagues to try make some sense of what had taken place earlier in the day.

Meanwhile, below ground, Eduardo and Fabian began to formulate their escape strategy. Apparently, the remainder of the task force was not due for another fourteen days, so they opted to sit tight for one week to let the dust settle. They felt the U.N. guys would most likely continue their search for a couple more days but then give up and resume their normal duties. Their only way out of Teniente Rodolfo was in the Tornado so they put their heads together and worked through all the possibilities—which was not difficult considering the limited options actually available to them!

The most immediate hurdle they faced was fuel. After the long flight back from PM3 there was very little kerosene left in the GR-4 but Eduardo explained that, using the manual standby pumps, she could be refuelled in around one hour. He then cleverly suggested that they drain the F-22 tanks at the same time which would effectively give them at least ninety minute's head start should the Americans decide to pursue them. They opted to remain underground for another seven days and then, in the dead of the eighth night, once they were satisfied that everyone on the base was fast asleep, they would enter the main hangar using the tunnels and implement the plan.

During that eight-day subterranean period, they heard several F-22 take-off and landings which at first they assumed were simply routine intercept missions. They fervently hoped that nobody had been shot out of the sky but Eduardo was pessimistic, saying that the new brief from above was to adopt an almost zero-tolerance policy going forward. From the conversations he had been monitoring, he believed that the pilots selected for the new interceptor force were mainly rookies of a particular mind-set. For example, they had deliberately lowered the IQ requirements for new recruits and had added some very specific mind-control programming to flight training. Those now daring to venture beyond sixty degrees south were in dire peril, he added regretfully.

To add to their already considerable burden of fear and anxiety, a further three F-22s had arrived at the base during their concealment bringing with them no doubt, three more lower-intelligence, psychotic, robot-moron pilots. The military presence in the Southern Ocean was being ramped-up most rapidly and aggressively and with personnel who asked no questions whatsoever before shooting!

In the early hours of the ninth morning, as certain as they possibly could be that all the U.N. people were fast asleep, Fabian and Eduardo crept along the tunnel to the hangar. Fabian's watch read 2.45am as they clambered out of the hatch to find the GR-4 along with three of the five F-22s squeezed into the building. Fortunately for them, the path out of the hangar for Fabian's Tornado was clear, although it would need to be pushed backward to start with. Using only torches to guide them and with Eduardo's expertise, they used the standby pumps to transfer the fuel from each F-22 into the GR-4 before topping-up from the main supply tank. Due to the lack of light and the additional F-22 to empty, the whole process took almost three hours, much longer than they had anticipated, and by the time the refuelling was complete the time was approaching 6.00am.

"Time is not our friend, we must act quickly—and quietly, señor," Eduardo whispered. *"Please put on your flying suit, climb aboard, release the brakes and deploy the foldable ladder ready for me. And make haste please. I will remove the chocks, open the hangar door and bring the tug."*

Five very tense minutes later, the GR-4 was being shunted stealthily through the hangar door by the virtually silent electric tug, Eduardo's impressive reversing skills coming to the fore. Once clear of the building he shifted into forward and slowly towed the fighter across the apron and along the slipway to the very end of the runway, pulling on his flight gear in the process. By the time he finally detached the tug, dumped it unceremoniously on the grass and clambered up the collapsible stepladder into the cockpit, the time was 6.18am. He quickly pulled the ladder inside and strapped himself in. Fabian closed the canopy and fired-up the engines, in the process waking-up all the U.N. personnel at Teniente Rodolfo Marsh Martin Air Base in an instant.

Chapter 62

Tuesday 14th March 2023 – The Battle of Extrema

On a bright, clear and sunny morning in Varinthia, Adam, Dobbo and Asiri were preparing to return to Intipata for Dobbo and Asiri's engagement party, which was scheduled to take place in two days' time.

Asiri was dreading the return trip having not enjoyed the original trip down to Thoth at supersonic speeds in Celeste, in any way. And even though Dobbo had promised he would keep his speed at manageable levels for her, nevertheless she had decided that air travel was very far from being her favourite method of transportation. And so, as they packed their meagre belongings and gifts for her parents into Celeste's cramped cockpit as best they could, she was in a very quiet and contemplative mood, despite Dobbo's futile attempts to make her laugh.

"Come on girl, lighten up a little, we're getting engaged in two days!" he pleaded.

"I know Sami, I am sorry. It is just that I am not looking forward to the trip. Air travel does not agree with me!"

"It'll be fine sweetheart, honest. I promised you no sudden acceleration and no supersonic speeds! So just try and relax a bit—if you can!" Dobbo's heart went out to her. It took him back to his first few times in a fighter jet during training at Cranwell all those years ago now and so he totally empathised with her.

At that moment Adam arrived with all his gear too and soon the two airplanes and their occupants were packed, prepared and ready for the flight back to Extrema.

After a very uneventful subsonic flight, the runway at PM3 finally came into view and the two planes landed smoothly and parked close to the base's outbuildings without drama. A very relieved Asiri clambered out of the cockpit and on to the apron, her face a little ashen and her legs still shaking but at last able to begin relaxing just a tad. The happy threesome unloaded their bags and headed for the kitchen area where they planned on enjoying a hearty meal, whilst waiting for Pacha to arrive in his boat. He was due in around four hours' time to transport them back down the lake to Intipata where all of Asiri's extended family would be waiting to greet them later that day.

In the midst of the food preparation and mid-conversation, Adam suddenly held up his hand and stood stock-still for a few moments, intently listening to something.

"What is it Adders?" Dobbo was the one who broke the pregnant silence.

"I can hear a plane of some kind and it's drawing closer," he told them.

After a few seconds the others concurred. Alarmed and worried, they tentatively opened the outer door and Adam scanned the skies to the north with his binoculars. After around a minute had passed and the jet engine note had increased in intensity, they were all relieved to see Fabian's Tornado GR-4 appearing in the near-distance.

"Hang on," said Dobbo after a few seconds. *"Let's not get too complacent just yet, it may not be Fabian. What if he has been captured—or worse—and this is just a ploy to lull us into a false sense of security!?"*

"You could be right Dobbo but whoever it is knows that we—or at least someone—is here. They can't fail to spot the planes." Adam sounded concerned. Rightly so. If this pilot was a U.N. man then they could all well be in serious trouble.

As a precaution they withdrew into the building, securely locking the door behind them—and waited with trepidation for events to unfold. They heard the plane land and less than five minutes later came a loud knocking on the door followed by a voice that Dobbo and Asiri instantly recognised.

"Dobbo, Asiri? It is I, Fabian and Eduardo is here with me too. Are you in there?"

Fabian's dulcet German tones were unmistakeable and so the very relieved trio quickly unlocked and opened the door with a flourish.

"Fabes! God are we pleased to see you matey!? We were really worried that you'd been captured and arrested and were beginning to think we'd never see you again!" Dobbo was obviously ecstatic to see his buddy safe and well. They hugged for a long moment and then it was Asiri's turn.

"Oh Fabian, I am so happy to see you again," she enthused whilst taking her turn to hug him. *"Sami is correct. We were beginning to think that something very bad had happened to you!"*

"Good to meet you Fabian!" interjected Adam shaking his hand warmly. *"I've heard a lot about you and I'm very glad you're OK!"* He shook Eduardo's hand too and welcomed him back to his homeland. *"Happy to see that you are fine too, Eduardo!"* The Extreman smiled and nodded. *"Good to see you again señor Haylock—and you also, señor Dobson."*

"We are just fine, thank you," Fabian reassured them all. *"And great to finally meet you too, Adam. Eduardo and I had some pretty scary moments back there and we were fortunate to escape. There is quite an army of U.N. forces arriving at Teniente and our noisy departure will no doubt have alerted them to our escape. However, Eduardo and I drained the tanks of three of the five F-22s and so it will take an hour or more to refill them all but nevertheless I think we should prepare for their arrival very shortly. They will I'm sure be following on behind as soon as they can."*

"We had better deploy the camouflage nets then," Dobbo advised. *"It may buy us a few minutes of extra time."*

This was done with a minimum of fuss and they were now as ready as they ever would be for the expected hunting party from Teniente to arrive.

They waited and waited, anxiously listening for the noise of incoming jets and sure enough, less than ninety minutes later, five United Nations Lockheed-Martin F-22 Raptors piloted by Bull and Campbell and three other rookie USAF pilots seconded to the U.N., screamed overhead, obviously hunting the deserter Fabian, Eduardo and the stolen plane.

The five jets circled around the Porta Mundorum III base, checking out the buildings, hoping to catch sight of Fabian's Tornado GR-4 and were obviously trying to decide whether or not it would be safe to land. However the camouflage netting had done its job and the five intruders temporarily left the apparently deserted base in order to reconnoitre the surrounding area.

"Asiri, you and Eduardo take yourselves off somewhere safe and out of sight, just in case the worst happens," Dobbo ordered.

"But Sami..." Asiri began, before being cut-off immediately by the now very focused and determined Dobbo.

"Sweetheart, please do as I say! This is serious shit!" he insisted forcefully before hugging her tightly for a few seconds and then kissing her tenderly. Reluctantly, she bade them all good luck and she and Eduardo disappeared to find a suitable hiding place in the deepest recesses of the building.

Fabian, Dobbo and Adam tentatively peered outside to check-out what was happening, just in time to watch the jets speed past once more. They quickly donned their flying gear again and sprinted for their planes hoping, at the very least, to save them from destruction. At the same time they could not help being sceptical about their chances of fighting their way out of this situation particularly against five highly-superior, 'state-of-the-art' fighting machines.

There was still no sign of the Raptors returning as the three comrades fired-up their respective engines and rapidly taxied to the end of the runway before eventually becoming airborne, not at all sure how things would pan-out but nevertheless determined not be captured and arrested—at any cost.

As soon as the intrepid trio were airborne, the F-22s immediately picked them up on their radar screens and having scoped-out the area, turned 180° in an attempt to confront them. The threesome attempted to stay below the radar by flying a thousand feet below the returning Raptors as they tore past them in the opposite direction. The F-22 pilots however soon realised that they had overshot their intended targets and so immediately turned around once again and gave chase.

The three friends then assumed attack formation by themselves turning around to prepare to face the F-22s, now in visual contact maybe three or four miles away at most.

Dobbo and Fabian's radios crackled. *"Adam here, guys! Follow me please. Climb to the maximum ceiling and let them come to us! Over."* Adam had assumed command as befitted his superior rank.

"Roger that, Adders. Over," replied Dobbo.

"Slight problem here Adam," said Fabian. *"My climb-rate is greatly inferior to yours, so you will leave me behind but I will be there as soon as I can! Over."*

"Copy that, Fabian. Just do your best, mate! Good luck! Over and out."

Adam and Dobbo rapidly ascended to Esmerelda and Celeste's maximum ceiling of almost 52,000 feet in an attempt to gain a tactical advantage but as he had warned, Fabian struggled to stay with them due to his Tornado's massively inferior climb-rate and rapidly began to lag way behind them both.

Meanwhile the F-22s also having adopted attack formation, began to follow. Fabian quickly realised that he was now in deep trouble and rather than simply waiting to be blown out of the sky by his technically superior adversaries, bravely turned to face them in what logically appeared to be a complete mismatch. The odds of five to one against were very definitely not in his favour!

Nevertheless, it is a truism to state that in certain situations a superior pilot flying an inferior aircraft will have the edge over an inferior pilot flying a superior aircraft—but regardless, the odds were very far from favourable.

However, Fabian being a highly accomplished pilot, suddenly feinted to the left as the leading Raptor, with Bull at the controls, closed rapidly on him then immediately corkscrewed right, putting the now confused American pilot's aircraft square in his gunsights. Whilst the other four F-22s continued in pursuit of the two F-5s, Fabian let loose a rapid volley of cannon fire which he very slightly mistimed, missing the main body of the jet but totally shredding the tailplane, rendering the aircraft virtually uncontrollable.

As the remaining four F-22s concentrated on chasing Adam and Dobbo, Fabian headed-out in pursuit of his own prey, Bull's now severely wounded Raptor and again released a volley of cannon rounds, this time striking the port engine, causing it to flame-out completely, as well as holing the port-side drop-tank which immediately burst into flames. The now mortally-wounded jet rapidly spiralled downward and out of control, smoke and flames streaming from the port-side wing.

Fabian looked-on in relief at getting the better of the encounter as the blazing F-22's cockpit canopy blew wide-open and Bull ejected clear with a white canopy of silk emanating from his backpack. The out-of-control jet struck the ground in a violent explosion of red and bright orange flame as the American drifted gently downwards swinging like a pendulum beneath his life-saving parachute.

In his short respite from the battle, Fabian watched-on as the downed pilot, in a scene reminiscent of old, clichéd World War II movies, was quickly surrounded by a group of Extreman farm-workers. Having seen the aerial battle unfold, and with pitchforks and scythes in hand, they quickly surrounded him as one of their number tackled him to the ground and subdued him.

Meanwhile, Dobbo and Adam were confronted by the four remaining Raptors. But before any action could take place and to everyone's complete surprise, the one piloted by Kyle Campbell suddenly veered away and spiralled downwards for no discernible reason. Unbeknown to them, the pilot was actually suffering from the dreaded Extrema malady and had passed-out cold as a result.

His jet now obviously out of control, bobbed and weaved erratically for several minutes before spectacularly smashing itself into the side of a small mountain and immediately erupting in a white-hot flash of exploding kerosene and twisted metal. Suddenly and totally unexpectedly, the odds were now far more manageable despite the overwhelming superiority of the F-22s!

The three remaining Raptor pilots paused briefly in their pursuit of Dobbo and Adam and watched-on horrified as their colleague met his fiery demise. But only momentarily. They soon regained their concentration and continued their pursuit, using their aircrafts' far superior rate of climb, with Fabian trailing way behind in their wake.

At the F-5's maximum ceiling, Esmerelda and Celeste circled around waiting for the F-22s to penetrate the clouds around 30,000 feet below them. And in the few seconds before their adversaries appeared, Adam and Dobbo quickly concocted a strategy to deal with the superior aerobatic abilities and performance of the Raptors.

In an instant, the F-22s suddenly broke through the cloud cover and climbed towards Dobbo and Adam and once in sight of their prey they let loose their Sidewinder guided missiles. Immediately, our two heroes deployed their chaff dispersal systems. Chaff, otherwise known as 'window,' is a defensive mechanism, invented during World War II and designed to confuse guided missiles—and radar. It consists of several pounds of short, thin aluminium strips which when released has the effect of creating a false reading on the missile's guidance system, the result being that the missile will home-in on the chaff rather than its intended target.

Instantly, Esmerelda and Celeste set-off in totally opposite directions, flying at full throttle and diving back toward and then into the cloud cover currently lying at about 20,000 feet. The Sidewinders narrowly missed Dobbo and headed directly for the chaff cloud before eventually, several miles away, running out of power and crashing to the ground harmlessly, but nevertheless creating small craters in the beautiful landscape of Extrema.

Once below the cloud ceiling, Adam and Dobbo waited impatiently for the inevitable – the pursuit by the Raptors once again and at this point they were rejoined by Fabian, whose GR-4 had reached nowhere near the altitude of the other planes but had seen his two comrades heading back down into the clouds again.

Then suddenly the three F-22s arrived out of the clouds and yet before the American pilots realised what was happening they came under attack from three distinctly separate directions simultaneously. Adam's cannon rounds clipped the wing of one of them causing it to take a sudden, steep dive and Fabian immediately set-off in pursuit in an attempt to finish it off but failed to notice one of the other two remaining U.N. planes hot on his tail. The first burst of cannon fire missed him completely but realising that he was now under attack himself, sheer terror overtook him. After all, this was his first ever taste of armed conflict and his first 'real' dogfight.

Dobbo immediately started-out in pursuit, realising that Fabian was in serious trouble and a crazy game of four-way cat and mouse ensued whilst Adam concentrated on the remaining F-22, whose young pilot decided that discretion was the better part of valour and unceremoniously fled the scene of the battle—it being his first ever taste of real conflict too. Adam quickly acquired the Raptor in his gunsight and unleashed five seconds of cannon shot, all of which failed to find their target and the F-22 pilot used his far superior speed to quickly put several miles between them. Adam reluctantly abandoned his futile attempt to chase him and decided to rejoin the four remaining combatants in their own deadly little game.

Fabian's GR-4's top speed was only slightly less than the F-22 up ahead of him but nevertheless he realised that he had to act quickly or this Raptor would also outrun him.

Meanwhile, Dobbo in Celeste knew that he was also way too slow to keep-up, so in a last desperate attempt to at least deter Fabian's pursuer and more in hope than expectation, he let fly a volley at the Raptor far ahead of him. Surprisingly, even to Dobbo, the salvo fortuitously caught the starboard engine, which instantly erupted in a sea of flaming fuel and in seconds engulfed the entire starboard wing rendering the plane totally unflyable. It took a sudden and very severe dip to starboard then tumbled over and over, spiralling downward, a spectacular fireball in the sky, until seconds later it became the third F-22 to hit the deck in a hellish explosion of fire and shrapnel. The pilot stood no chance of escaping the inferno, it had all happened so quickly. Three down and two to go!

Meanwhile Fabian was still just about in-touch with his target, as the Raptor's pilot suddenly realised that his best chance of escaping from Fabian's clutches was to ascend rapidly, utilising his massive advantage in climb-rate. He duly pointed the nose of his 'kite' upward and pressed the throttle. In an instant he was heading back toward the relative safety of the cloud ceiling but Fabian reacted quickly too and fired his own AIM-9 Sidewinder guided missile. The inexperienced U.N. pilot was so intent on reaching cloud cover that he completely failed to notice the missile streaking after him at Mach 2.5. It was too late to deploy his chaff and less than three seconds later he was blown out of the sky as the guided missile armed with its 24lbs of explosives, found and comprehensively destroyed its target.

Dobbo, Adam and Fabian were understandably jubilant. They had triumphed against all the odds and their radios echoed back and forth with whoops of delight and mutual congratulations as they regrouped and prepared to head back towards base at Porta Mundorum III.

However, unbeknown to them, the single remaining, errant F-22—the pilot who having regained some composure, not to mention courage—was now heading stealthily back toward the aerial battle site. Appearing out of the clouds with the sun at his back as cover, he spotted the three friends flying leisurely in formation back toward the runway at PM3 and immediately locked-on to Fabian's GR-4, by pure chance the nearest one to him of the three homeward-bound planes. There was a retina-burning flash and a sudden whoosh as the Sidewinder was despatched and Fabian realised only too late that he was the intended target. He was unable to react in time and the deadly missile struck home virtually instantly, destroying both poor Fabian and his plane in a blinding flash of light and an ear-splitting cacophony of sound.

Momentarily stunned to see their comrade unceremoniously blasted out of the sky, Dobbo and Adam could scarcely believe what had just happened but Dobbo, his anger boiling over at the demise of his new friend and comrade-in-arms, was the one to respond. He immediately performed a spectacular backward loop, the exact same manoeuvre he had performed with Fabian when leaving PM3 for Thoth the previous month, ending-up immediately behind the now startled American flyer who had failed completely to notice Dobbo's smart move but could now see Celeste hot on his tail, in his mirror. Quickly appreciating the danger, he immediately attempted to head for the clouds once again.

Dobbo was far too quick for him though and in frustration at his good friend Fabian's sad fate, angrily pressed down hard on his fire button sending an arcing stream of cannon shot crashing into the rear of the F-22, any one of which would have been fatal to the target aircraft.

He watched as the plane exploded in mid-air and with a great sadness welling-up within his weary body, followed the wreckage with tear-filled eyes as each individual element of the detritus of what had once been a pristine, state-of-the-art, multi-million dollar fighting machine along with the mangled remains of its hapless pilot, spiralled slowly and tantalisingly toward the ground. As a final act of defiance, the destroyed F-22's chaff deployment system somehow kicked into life sending a cascade of silver, aluminium strips in a shower over the falling wreckage, adding an element of surrealism to mark the end of the fatal dogfight.

Distraught, Dobbo quickly re-joined Adam and they continued their sad journey 'home' in silence, with their only interaction being a weak smile and wave between them as they dejectedly sped onwards to reunite with Asiri and Eduardo.

Once back at base, they dismounted from their respective 'steeds' and without a word trudged disconsolately back towards the main building, having firstly once more, carefully deployed the camouflage nets—just in case. Adam noticed that Dobbo could not help shedding a tear for his lost friend and it touched him deeply to see his best mate, of all people, so emotional.

Dobbo hammered on the door several times, loudly enough he hoped for Asiri or Eduardo to hear him from wherever they had concealed themselves. Then after a few moments a man's voice was heard through the door. *"Who is it please?"*

"Eduardo, it's Dobbo and Adam! Let us in please!"

"Ah señors, good to have you back. I trust all is well?!"

Neither airman answered, they were simply too exhausted and distraught, but Eduardo opened the door anyway.

"Where is señor Fabian? Is he OK señor Dobson?" queried Eduardo, surprised and anxious to see that he was not with the two returned battle-weary heroes.

Then suddenly, and before either of them had chance to reply, Asiri appeared as if from nowhere and flung her arms around Dobbo in sheer joy and relief at his safe return. *"Oh my love, my love,"* she cried, *"I was so worried for you."* And then noticing the devasted look on Dobbo's face, quickly comprehended that something was amiss.

"Where is Fabian though?" She suddenly looked in shock as the realisation hit home hard. *"Oh no Sami, no, no, no! It cannot be true. It cannot!"* She wept like a baby.

He held her closely, tenderly stroking her hair until the sobbing had subsided and then they all sat down to allow Adam to relate the tragic story in all its gory detail. No-one felt like eating, their hunger had long-since passed and there was no real sign of it returning just yet.

Dobbo concluded Adam's account of the battle and Fabian's sad demise with a short but sincere tribute to their fallen comrade. *"I've only known Fabian for a short time, but I do know that he was one extremely brave bugger. He fought like a bloody tiger and in effect saved me and Adam with his prompt actions—even though he was flying a far inferior plane to our adversaries."* At this he took a bottle of red wine from the well-stocked rack along with four glasses, poured them each an ample glassful and proposed a toast to the memory of their sadly-departed friend.

"To our fallen, young comrade Fabian Schuster, formerly of the Luftwaffe, hero and one of my best-ever friends," he began with a lump in his throat. *"Fabes, you saved my life, died a hero's death and your friends and family should be very proud of you. Although the manner of your death means that your body will have no resting place, may your eternal soul rest in peace for evermore."*

The sombre foursome then bowed their heads in silent contemplation for a short time, reflecting on their thoughts and memories of their dear friend before regaining their composure and preparing for their departure to Intipata and Dobbo and Asiri's engagement party.

THE END (but to be continued)

Books by John Hamer

***The Falsification of History* – 2012**
A comprehensive chronological analysis of how history has been systemically falsified for millennia

***RMS Olympic* – 2013**
The real Titanic story

***Titanic's Last Secret* – 2014**
A novel based on the above

***Behind the Curtain* (volume 1) – 2016**
A chronological, in-depth look at the real truth behind specific historical events of the last two hundred and fifty years

***Behind the Curtain* (volume 2) – 2016**
A chronological, in-depth look at the real truth behind specific historical events of the last two hundred and fifty years

***JFK – A Very British Coup* – 2019**
The real story of the Kennedy assassination

***The Falsification of Science* – 2021**
A comprehensive analysis of how science has been systemically falsified for millennia

***Welcome to the Masquerade* (with Shannon Rowan) – 2022**
An in-depth analysis of the events leading-up to and during the covid pandemic

***Sixty Degrees South* (with Andy Ross) – 2025**
A novel exploring the mysteries of Antarctica
www.sixty-degrees-south.com

Signed copies of all John's books, including this one, may be ordered from his website – falsificationofhistory.co.uk (UK only) – or unsigned ones from Amazon worldwide.

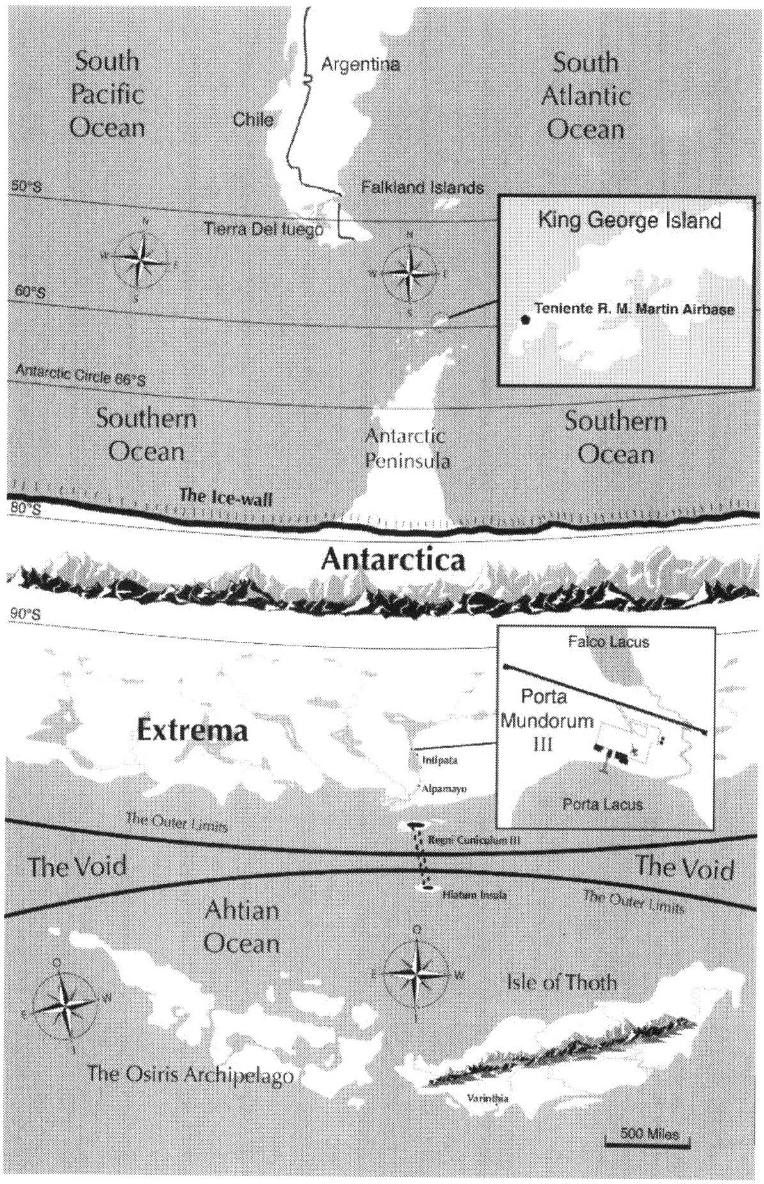
South Pacific Ocean
Argentina
Chile
South Atlantic Ocean
50°S
Falkland Islands
Tierra Del fuego
King George Island
Teniente R. M. Martin Airbase
60°S
Antarctic Circle 66°S
Southern Ocean
Antarctic Peninsula
Southern Ocean
The Ice-wall
80°S
Antarctica
90°S
Falco Lacus
Porta Mundorum III
Extrema
Intipata
Alpamayo
Porta Lacus
The Outer Limits
Regni Cuniculum III
The Void
The Void
Hiatum Insula
The Outer Limits
Ahtian Ocean
Isle of Thoth
The Osiris Archipelago
Varinthia
500 Miles

Printed in Dunstable, United Kingdom

76304705R00172